A Light Rain of Grace

A Novel

Jeannette Sears

A Light Rain of Grace
A Novel

Alien Music Books, a Division of Alien Music Publishing.
San Rafael, California USA
www.JeannetteSears.com

Publisher's Note: All characters and events in this book – even those based on real people – are entirely fictional. No part of the contents relate to any real person or persons, living or dead. The author and publisher both gratefully acknowledge the great Irving Berlin for his song "There's No Business Like Show Business," cited on page 114.

Cover Design by: Alexandra Fischer
Editing by: Deborah Grabien
A Light Rain of Grace
Sears, Jeannette, 1947 –

ISBN 10 1979774609
ISBN 13 978-1979774604

1. Fiction 2. Social Justice 3. History 4. Music
Second Edition
Printed in the United States of America

The Prophet: On Joy and Sorrow

"Your joy is your sorrow unmasked.
And the selfsame well from which your laughter rises was oftentimes filled with your tears.
And how else can it be?
The deeper that sorrow carves into your being, the more joy you can contain.
Is not the cup that holds your wine the very cup that was burned in the potter's oven?
And is not the lute that soothes your spirit, the very wood that was hollowed with knives? When you are joyous, look deep into your heart and you shall find it is only that which has given you sorrow that is giving you joy.
When you are sorrowful look again in your heart, and you shall see that in truth you are weeping for that which has been your delight.
Some of you say, "Joy is greater than sorrow," and others say, "Nay, sorrow is the greater."
But I say unto you, they are inseparable.
Together they come, and when one sits alone with you at your board, remember that the other is asleep upon your bed.
Verily you are suspended like scales between your sorrow and your joy.
Only when you are empty are you at standstill and balanced.
When the treasure-keeper lifts you to weigh his gold and his silver, needs must your joy or your sorrow rise or fall."

– Kahlil Gibran

My thanks to my husband Pete Sears who has filled my life with love and music, and inspired me always with his formidable talent. For his passion for social justice and commitment to preserving this beautiful planet, as well as making the world better through music and service to others, I dedicate this book to him.

My thanks also to my mother, Bonnie Dilger, who witnessed a massacre in Santiago, Atitlan, Guatemala, and lived to tell the tale in her memoir *Guatemala, Blood in the Cornfields.* I first went to Guatemala and El Salvador with her in 1975, exactly one day after the first big student massacre in San Salvador—so if the narrative in this story seems authentic, it's because I was there. Bonnie decided to stay on at Lake Atitlan and build a hotel with my brother, David…hence she was there when the death squads started killing the villagers. She was the first person Pete and I heard bear witness to the genocide that engulfed Central America in the 1980s, and to reveal our government's part in it. She continues to write books and work for the schools she started in Santiago. Her books are available on Amazon.

Contents

Jeannette Sears

Chapter One

1974—Meeting Juan

L.A. rippled in the summer. The hazy smog played tricks with your vision, created illusions in the toxic air.

For Emma, the woozy barrage of heat waves was a welcome respite from the infamous summer fog of San Francisco. Not that she had experienced much of the heat, nursing a hangover all morning behind hotel room black-out curtains — barely making it to Hollywood Studios by two p.m. Lyrics rose up from the overheated pavement, fragments of possibilities which Emma tossed about as she buzzed the studio door…

All the pain locked in your shimmering shadows,
Deflected by your dazzling style…
If you could measure heartache,
Would it be inch by inch, or mile by mile?

She needed more time to work on material, but at least she had enough to go on for the time being.

Inside the studio it was a different climate, an eternal air-conditioned spring, day and night. Musicians, engineers, and a scattering of friends milled around as usual, getting high, looking over each other's shoulders to see who was on the scene that day. A journalist from some entertainment magazine and a photographer awaited Emma, who had spaced out the interview.

The journalist was on his feet the minute Emma walked into the room. "Emma Allison, the original Foxy Lady in person! We've been waiting for you."

"Hope it hasn't been too painful. Sorry I'm late," Emma said, as her publicist ushered them into a private room. Flopping down on a leather sofa, Emma tapped a lavender-colored Sherman from her glitzy cigarette case. The journalist fell all over himself trying to light her cigarette, but she had her own lighter out faster.

He began pacing the room, jittery, but waving his arms enthusiastically. "Wow, look at how many of these gold records are yours, Emmy! Man, you've been on a long roll — five platinum albums in seven years! That's so cool. And you know, you're still as foxy as the first time I saw you at Devonshire Downs—in '69 that was."

"That's great, thanks. Yeah, hanging in there." Emma was smiling through her teeth, trying not to roll her eyes.

"You remember that show? You were wearing a long skirt. All I could see were your feet and ankles—it was a total turn-on. I have a question, Emmy; how does it feel to look out at the audience and know every guy out there wants you?"

Every instinct in her body screamed, "Ignore him. Just leave the room." She got as far as putting her hand on the doorknob, but she couldn't turn the handle. Instead, she turned back to the journalist, her eyes narrowed. "What a great question! Oh yeah, I remember that show. You were in the first row, weren't you? I kept coming through the whole set. It was fucking unbelievable, looking out there at you." She flashed an exaggerated sexy smile for the photographer, and then turned back to the reporter, scowling. "Okay genius, do you want to talk about the new record or not — and don't call me Emmy."

The reporter squirmed, but persisted with his line of questioning. "Okay … Emma then. But is it true that you were recently spotted at The Corral in Topanga giving a certain married actor head under the table?"

Emma nodded at a burly roadie who had been standing quietly by the door. He headed for the journalist.

The journalist attempted a smile. "Okay, okay, don't get so uptight, I'm just doing my job."

"That's it guys, wrap it up, got to work," Emma declared, abruptly ending the so-called interview, exiting the lounge with her best "who gives a shit" strut. Privately, she was kicking herself. *Why did I say that ... they'll print it as though I was serious. And that head incident ...I don't even remember if it happened ... is it ever going to go away!*

All day Emma tried to shake off the feeling of having blown it. She tried to tell herself it didn't matter — the guy was just another hack writer who was going to print shit about her no matter what. Her one consolation was that at least her producer, Bill, hadn't been in the room. *I'd never hear the end of it if Bill had heard that.*

By ten o'clock that night, she was ready to call it a day. Stretching, she pushed herself up out of the leather sound booth couch she'd been lounging on while listening to takes of a basic track. "We've been over the same shit so many times, I can't tell one track from the other," she said to Bill.

Bill yawned. "I hear you. At this point, we're beating it to death. Let's leave it till tomorrow when we'll have fresh ears."

"What, you're sick of the song already?" Emma teased, fighting a yawn herself. "I sure as hell am. Let's get out of here, go do something."

Gary, the assistant engineer, looked up. "There's a new Latino Rock group playing at the Whiskey. Word on the street, they're hot."

Emma felt her second wind kick in. "Let's check them out. Who's coming?"

A troupe of friends and musicians followed Emma out the door and piled into the limo with her, but Bill declined — said he wanted to go through the material and decide which song to concentrate on next.

Emma and her entourage were ushered into a rather cramped VIP area close to the stage, along with the movie stars and other entertainment business people. Low-key wasn't part of her vocabulary, but Emma tried to be respectful of the band and keep the noise down. It was a doomed effort from the start. Someone ordered champagne, and somebody else proposed a toast to her, and pretty soon, what with all of them shouting to be heard over the music, everybody in the club must have known she was there.
Emma glanced over her shoulder. People had ringed the roped-off area, and a number of them were arguing loudly with the bouncer about why they should be allowed in.

Trying to thrust bits of paper for her to sign past the harried doorman, the fans kept vying for her attention, even as the band broke into a soft ballad and the lead guitarist took a solo. Emma waved off their requests for autographs, gesturing pointedly toward the stage and cupping her hand over her ear, mouthing, *I'm trying to listen to the music*.

In the midst of the ruckus, Emma felt the lead guitar player's eyes narrow in on her. She didn't meet his gaze, but the impact shook her. *Jesus, what was that!* The guitar suddenly moaned loudly as its strings were bent to the breaking point, and she glanced up. In that instant, a note pierced her chest. A piece of her heart broke off, flew out of her body and lodged itself in the curve of the bent note. Her eyes locked with the guitar player's, but only for a second. The connection was too intense. *Did he hit that note on purpose?* The connection hovered in the lingering chord, but grew weaker as the party around her grew louder and she got more wasted.

It snapped when her actor friend, Hank, showed up and draped his arm around her as though she were his leading lady. He pulled her onto his lap and dumped a little pile of coke on the tabletop.

Suddenly impatient, Emma squirmed away. She managed to reclaim her own chair, and glanced back up at the guitar player, only to find he had turned his back to the audience. His body language was nonchalant, but she suspected he might be a better actor than Hank.

Hank pulled her over again, and handed her a rolled up hundred-dollar bill. Emma took a hit of the blow, and met the guitar player's eyes. A rush came on so strong that for an instant, she wondered if the coke was cut with something else.

She shrugged Hank's arm off her shoulder. The coke had counteracted the effects of the champagne enough that she felt more sober. "You've got to get that shit out of here," she told Hank. "I can't afford to get busted again."

Hank laughed. "When did you get so uptight, baby? Okay everybody, Emma says we have to get rid of the evidence."

The coke started disappearing fast and the conversations went up a decibel with each line — until the group of celebrities was practically drowning out the band. Emma glanced up at the guitar player, trying to catch his eye again, but he stared out into the audience past her. *Now he's deliberately ignoring me. Well, fuck him,* she thought, and turned back to the group at her table.

"Wait a minute, Hank. Maybe I need to help with the disposal of the contraband." She took another huge hit and turned her back to the stage. When somebody suggested they all leave and go to a party in the Hollywood Hills, she went without a backward glance.

As Emma edged her way into consciousness the next morning, her stomach clenched into a tight knot. There was too much light in the room, and her mouth was parched. As she reached for the phone to order room service, the previous evening's events stalked into her throbbing head. "Oh God," she moaned out loud, and began mentally grasping for excuses. *I'm not taking the rap for all of it ... I wasn't the only one making a scene ... things go down the way they go down ... you do what you can ... everybody gets too wasted sometimes...it wasn't my fault ... WHO was that guitar player?*

The excuses weren't working, not this time. No matter how she tried to justify it, she knew she'd been rude. She'd insulted the band by disrupting their set and then leaving in the middle of it. It was a matter of pride for her that no matter how out-there she might get, she always showed respect for other musicians. Now she'd crossed one of her only remaining lines of propriety … and with someone she would have liked to get to know.

As she sipped her coffee, the guitar player's image parked itself in her head and refused to leave. She tried to recall who had told her about the band, remembered it was Gary, and sorted through what she knew about them.

"From South America," Gary had said. But he couldn't remember the name of the band. His friend from Venice Beach had told him about them.

It's easy to cool things out, she decided. *I'll just have them come in and lay down some Latin rhythms on a track, and then, oh by the way, I'll ask the guy to stay and put down some guitar on a few more tracks.*

She asked Gary to arrange for the band, Las Sombras, to come in at six o'clock, and by the time she arrived at the studio, she had a plan for the day. However, she hadn't cleared it with Bill.

Can we just put off making a decision about the basic we did yesterday?" Emma asked Bill. "I've got a few songs that would be cool with some Latin rhythm instruments — a conga, maracas, maybe a Flamenco guitar line running through them."

Bill looked up from the soundboard and scowled. "I don't think it's wise to go changing direction midstream."

"No, it won't be—trust me. I like what we've been doing, Bill, I really do. But this other batch of songs, they're a whole, new direction. I'm going to fucking suffocate if I stay with the same old shit. Honestly, it's time for a change. You said so yourself—that we're not going to let the company pressure us into an over-produced, pop sound—that this record will have an impromptu quality …so, let's do it."

"I don't know, Emma. I really don't want to lose the momentum we've got going."

"It's got to be from the heart, Bill, you know that. In spite of what the record company thinks, my audience would be able to sense insincerity." Emma paused a beat, and grinned. "Or at least I like to think so."

Bill chuckled. "Yeah, okay, baby. We'll do it your way. Which songs do you want to concentrate on then?" He took notes on a clipboard as Emma talked and the musicians tuned their instruments.

The session musicians began laying down the basic tracks efficiently, preparing the songs for over-dubs, and Emma's mind was racing. *This is it ... exactly what I was looking for ... something different ... mixing up the cultures ... maybe make one song a bolero ... a sort of Latin acid-rock sound, like I did with bluegrass on 'Walk on the Water.'*

Her train of thought inevitably shifted, however, and took her straight to the guitar player. She went fishing for more information from Gary, who was working in the sound booth with Bill. "So Gary, did you stay for the second set? Meet the band, by any chance?"

Gary took off his earphones and gave her his attention. "Yeah, I stayed for both sets. They were hot. And yeah, I hung out with them after the show. They're looking to record — who isn't. Oh, I was wrong about them being from South America. They're all from some little country in Central America — El Salvador. And I can tell what you're trying to find out—his name is Juan."

"I'm impressed with your ability to glean details, Gary. You obviously have hidden talents."

Gary smiled. "Yeah, and I keep mine under a bushel — not like you, flashing in neon lights. First you turned the scene last night into the Allison Revue, then you split in the middle of their set."

"It wasn't my fault," Emma protested. "I left to keep those dumb-fuck movie stars from ruining their set."

"Dumb-fuck, are they?" Bill glanced up from the soundboard. "Your buddy, Hank, has a law degree from Harvard. An imbecile, obviously."

"Education isn't everything," Emma retorted.

Bill laughed. "You would know."

Emma tossed her hair back and smiled. "Fuck you too, Bill."

Las Sombras arrived half an hour late, huddling together in a group, and chatting in Spanish among themselves. A couple of joints and a bottle of tequila later, they were sharing road stories with Emma like old friends. But beneath the convivial group feeling, Emma was aware of a palpable tension between herself and Juan.

Remembering the shock wave from the night before, she avoided his eyes, but she couldn't help noticing their color — green; and she could feel them following her around whenever he thought she wasn't looking. She wondered if he sensed how often her eyes were on him, too.

"*Las Sombras*. Good name; what does it mean?" Emma directed the question to the group.

One of the sexy back-up singers made a show of handing a shot to Juan, leaning into him so her breasts were grazing his arm, and lightly pushing a lock of his hair back from his face as she spoke. "It means *The Shadows*. Juan came up with the name."

The Shadows. That man would come up with a name like that. Wonder what he's got hidden. Emma felt jealousy rear up at the way the singer had touched Juan's hair. His hair got her — long, and straight and shiny black, with a scattering of ultra-thin braids, the kind you either pay someone a fortune to put in, or someone spends hours on just for the pleasure of touching you. *Obviously, this man didn't have to pay for his braids. He's got a thing going with that back-up singer, but I don't see any ring on his finger, and anyway, what the fuck, this is California.*

The free love years were supposedly over, but no one would know it from hanging around the rock n' roll scene in the mid-seventies. Passionate relationships erupted between band members so often that Emma liked to say the emotional fall-out was about as intense as spilling a bag of popcorn. A love affair that seemed undying in a Cleveland hotel room was usually over by the time the band reached Atlanta — depending on where Atlanta was on the tour.

She had slept with almost every musician she'd had in any of her bands, and as she moved around the studio playing the hostess, telling jokes, deliberately spreading her attention out among all the band members of *Las Sombras*, she tried to keep her cool by telling herself that Juan would end up being just more spilled popcorn.

But something about this guy threw her game off. The way he held himself so contained got to her — as if there was an enormous reserve of bottled power in that wiry body of his. Juan Enrique Avelar — even his name took her breath away — had an edge that her body would not quit responding to, in spite of her best effort to deny it.

Juan looked calm, but she suspected that he, too, was staying hidden, watching and interacting from behind a carefully constructed exterior. Pot could make people paranoid, but she didn't think Juan was paranoid — far from it. He seemed in control of the situation, even though he said very little. The less he said, the further over the top Emma went, trying to appear unaffected by the chemistry between them.

"You guys were so hot last night." Emma realized she was gushing, but was unable to alter her course. "I'm sorry I had to leave, but you know how it goes. Those Hollywood people are so boisterous."

Juan's eyes met hers. "A woman like you does not have to apologize for anything," he said, with just a trace of an accent.

Emma wasn't sure how he meant that. Sarcastic? Flirtatious? She rattled on. "You guys have to come up to the Bay Area; it's such a different vibe. I'll show you around San Francisco."

"That would be so kind of you. We'll wear flowers in our hair," Juan said, with an enigmatic smile, his gaze moving rapidly up and down Emma's body.

Emma felt her pheromones flood the room. "Very funny," she managed, "but I'm serious. Maybe Bill Graham can book you as my opening act. I'll ask him if you want…God, I don't know, let's get started. We'll just lay down some rhythms and see where we go from there. We can put some guitar on later."

Juan sat in the control room with the engineer and Emma while the Latin rhythm section adapted their style to her music. The song came alive; the studio buzzed.

After they listened back to the track, everyone was silent for a moment, and then Bill spoke up. "Gotta hand it to you, Emma. You were right. It works."

"Damn right, it works. What do you think, Bill? Shall we do another track while we've got them here?"

"Okay, one more. Then I want to get Juan's overdubs before we call it a night."

Juan stood alone in the studio, his eyes closed as his fingers found the right fills. His face contorted as he screamed out a solo. Watching him from behind the glass of the control room, Emma scrutinized his face for some clue as to what constitutes perfection. Objectively speaking, he wasn't any better looking than Hank. She tried to calm herself with the comparison.

A solid round of congratulations followed Juan's overdubs, and then Emma announced that they had to celebrate the success of the session by going out to dinner at the Old World Café.

"You haven't experienced the best of L.A. until you've had the coffee milkshake at this place," Emma told Juan.

"Fantastic, we love the Old World. It's one of our favorite restaurants; isn't that right, Juan?" the sexy back-up singer said.

Her pointed comment wasn't lost on Emma, who chose to ignore it. Over dinner, between sips of her coffee milkshake, she inquired off-handedly, "Juan, are you free to come in tomorrow and do some more guitar over-dubs?"

Juan leaned back in his chair and cocked his head, "That," he said, "depends on how late you keep me up tonight."

Emma

Everything has changed in the past few days. Even my molecular structure has been altered. Christ, I only met Juan on Tuesday, but it feels like forever.

I can't remember the ride from the Old World to the Hyatt House, only ordering champagne from Room Service, and Juan making love to me before it arrived.
We got off together, the first time. Juan and I were in sync, and it was fucking amazing, although it could have gone either way in the beginning. Juan started out kissing me gently, while I tore at his clothes like a mad woman. He took his own sweet time, undressing me in a deliberate, methodical fashion, kissing every inch of my flesh, and I was into it, screaming like his guitar; and then suddenly, I wasn't. I had a flash of feeling penned in, held down; and it freaked me. My body was going through the motions, but I was floating away. It's not like it had never happened before, but guys don't usually notice. They're in the moment, and as long as the body is there, no problem. But Juan knew.

He knew the moment I left him. I was going down on him, which is usually a pretty solid diversion for a guy, but he felt it when I checked out. In the midst of my space walk, I felt his hands on my hair, and then cupping my face, as he pulled me up. He gathered me in close, and not just my body. We drifted together out into that space of pure sensation, my body opening and closing in waves, each one bringing me closer to the moment, and just when I was almost there, I opened my eyes. I never open my eyes when I'm fucking, but it was like Juan exerted this heavy pressure; he willed my eyes open, and there he was…those green eyes of his were the ocean, his body was the wave, and we came in together.

Every pore in my body was open, and there was no hiding anything. I was naked, exposed, like Eve just emerging from Adam's rib. That was the image, organic, full of soil, salty fluids, like being born. In close proximity to Juan, it was Eden; I had no choice in the matter. My body was leaking his semen, mingling with the musk of my own body, and I wanted him again, immediately, for always.

Room service got Juan out of bed. Our champagne had arrived, and that gave me time to process what was happening. Suddenly, I was pissed off. *This is bullshit—Eve out of Adam's rib—how about Adam out of Eve's vagina, which is the reality. Where did this male chauvinist shit come from!*

I felt like I had to step back from the whole scene, even as I watched him opening the champagne. He seemed so sure of me, so sure of himself, but Christ, just the way his hair hung over his sharp cheekbones turned me on. I was thinking *I bet he gets away with murder based on those eyes, and that little accent, and those long, slender fingers.* I wanted his hands on me again, those fingers between my legs, his tongue in my mouth, his breath on my face …which took me back to my Eden thoughts, and I got pissed off again. It was too intense, suffocating—I couldn't breathe…so I did what I do best. Grabbed the bottle of champagne, poured us each a glass, and slipped into my rock-star routine.

"That was fun, baby, it was really good," I said, as though it was just another party to me. "So, you want to fuck again?"

His eyes turned hard, emerald green. He didn't say a word. Just set his champagne down, pulled on his clothes, and left.

Blew my mind. Left me alone with my own bullshit. I hadn't meant it, of course. I didn't think he'd get up and leave. I was just trying to get the upper hand, not chase him away. I thought about calling some people, maybe going out or down to the bar, but I was too depressed. Obviously, I had really pissed him off, which was a total downer. But on the other hand, it said something that he got so uptight. Christ, I can be a jerk. And he was so goddamn beautiful.

As pissed and upset as I was, I respected him for leaving. He'd shown some balls. I regretted my stupid routine, wished I'd been real with him. It hit me suddenly that I didn't even know how to get in touch with him. Bill had his manager's phone number, but Juan and I hadn't even gotten as far as exchanging basic information before we'd ended up in bed. It occurred to me that this could be a game he played to get chicks to chase him. But I'd played my share of games, too, so who was I to criticize. I felt instinctively that if I could get him to come back tonight, I'd have him. We could start over. But I had no way to reach him.

'End of the line—forgot what it was like—everything on my time'...good first line. I found pen and paper and began the song, willing myself past desperation. Eventually, after finishing the bottle of champagne, I drifted into sleep.

I was awoken at some ungodly hour of the morning, by housekeeping pounding on my door. "Come back later," I growled. The hotel knew not to disturb me until I flipped the sign on the door. With a long day at the studio ahead of me, the last thing I needed was to be awoken a few hours after I'd finally fallen asleep.

The knocking persisted. "For God's sake, go away!"

"Open the door. I want to talk to you."

"Wait." I jumped out of bed, grabbed some mouthwash and gargled, then opened the door. I probably looked awful, but Juan looked worse. He was wearing the same clothes as last night. Obviously, he hadn't been to bed.

I opened my mouth to say something, and started crying.

I stepped toward him as he stepped toward me, and there was no power play going on this time. He put his arms around my waist. I reached up for his face. Relief surged through me, but I couldn't speak. "It's okay, Emma," he whispered. "Let's just lie down. We are both exhausted." He actually picked me up and carried me to the bed, like Clark Gable, for Christ sake. "I love you," he said, as he laid me down. I nodded, meaning that I loved him, too. He undressed and climbed into bed beside me. Holding onto each other like life rings, we fell asleep. Missed the two o'clock start time.

Bill came pounding at the door around three-thirty, then got housekeeping to let him in. He took one look at Juan and me all tangled up in each other, and went from worried to mad in no time flat. His mouth tightened, but he stayed cool. He hadn't gotten where he was in the music business for no reason. Yelled a little about keeping costs down so I might actually make some money on this album after expenses, then ordered room service and stayed for coffee with Juan and me. Bill and I had been lovers once, but that was years ago, and we had moved past it, into a good working relationship and a tight friendship. Still, I knew I could have him if I wanted him, so that was always there.

It was five o'clock by the time we got to the studio. The assistant engineers were clocked in, and had been playing ping-pong on my money since two. I wanted to get at one of my new songs, but since we were scheduled to do over-dubs, the studio musicians hadn't been called in. I decided to have Juan lay a simple guitar line down, make it acoustic.

Bill didn't like the idea. "You can't just throw an acoustic song in there willy-nilly. It won't flow with the concept of the album. There has to be continuity, Emma."

"Let's just try it, okay. If we don't like it, we don't have to use it. What's the big deal?"

Juan played an elegant intro, and then broke into a variation on my melody that took the song in an amazing, new direction. Made the music distinctly his own.

My words and his music. Our song.

Chapter Two

Talking 'bout the Early Years

Juan and Emma had been camped out in her Hyatt suite for almost a week, dividing their time between the studio and the suite's king-size bed, with an occasional meal out.

Juan was sitting in an easy chair scanning the L.A. Times. "Look Emma, our gig at the Whiskey got written up. *Sombras* finally made the pink section…just as I left them."

"What? Are you regretting your decision already?"

"Of course, I don't regret it. Although, you must admit that the timing is ironic." Juan beamed as he read aloud: "Juan Avelar took the band into the stratosphere with his soaring guitar lines…"

"Yeah, sounds great. Don't worry, baby; there'll be plenty more where that came from. Wait till our album is released." Emma stretched provocatively on the bed. "I wouldn't pay much attention to the critics anyway. If you believe the good, you're gonna believe the bad. It's a mind-fuck. I never pay attention to what people write about me."

"Really?" Juan raised an eyebrow. "Never? That, *mi corazon*, is because no one could ever write anything bad about you. You are perfect." He brought the newspaper over to Emma, handed it to her, then sat down beside her, and pulled her into his arms.

"That's right. It must be hard being around such perfection." Emma laughed, snuggling deeper into Juan's embrace. "My parents used to call me the embodiment of perfection…and don't you forget it. They believed that our generation was a direct result of atomic fall-out, and oh, by the way, I hold the secrets of the universe in my eyes."

"Your eyes are the color of the universe; on that we can agree. But did your parents really say such things? It seems impossible to me."

"You don't know the half of it. They fucked me up for life. Them and their beatnik friends. Imagine my confusion when I found out what atomic fall-out meant!"

"Your parents were beatniks?"

"Oh yeah, the originals. Jazz, art, poetry, astrology—the usual credentials. They were certifiably crazy. When I was about three, they used to tell their friends, 'A child will lead the way.' Seriously. And then everyone would look at me, and I had no fucking idea what I was supposed to lead the way to. So, I'd do some somersaults and maybe sing *Twinkle, Twinkle Little Star*, and that seemed to do the trick."

Juan laughed. "And thus your career was started. You must sing this song for me. It sounds enchanting."

"I'll trade a song for a back rub…back rub first."

Emma lay on her stomach as Juan poured almond oil over her back. She enjoyed the feel of his strong, guitar player's hands as he began to massage her.

"They say you hold trauma in your muscles." Juan was doing a version of acupressure. "These bunched up knots in your shoulder blades are caused by repressed, painful, memories. If I press here and hold it, does it bring something to mind?"

Abruptly, Emma sat up, and turned to face Juan. "Who told you that? Some hippie masseuse you used to fuck?"

"Do I detect jealousy, or did I just inadvertently tap into something significant? Relax, Emma. You're proving the point with your reaction. Lie down and enjoy the massage; either that, or you'll have to sing *Twinkling Star*."

Emma lay back down and closed her eyes. She didn't want to fight with Juan. He was probably right anyway. Although the massage hadn't necessarily brought up any issues, their conversation had reeled in a massive heap of old memories.

1963

On Emma's thirteenth birthday, her father's bass player, Rob, told her he would teach her to surf.

June had begun with dazzling blue skies in the Bay Area, so the lessons were to begin the next day. Emma's mother, Stephanie, was a little worried about sharks, but she trusted Rob, felt sure he'd look after Emma. Her father, Ray, yelled after Rob not to be drinking beer with his baby in the car, and waved as they took off for Sunset Beach. Although Rob was Emma's parent's age, he didn't seem it to her. Her girlfriends all thought he was dreamy.

It wasn't as easy to surf as she'd imagined. She didn't have the upper body strength to get out past the breakers, which kept crashing over her, causing her to choke on the salt water. "I'm no good at this, Rob," Emma called, treading water and trying not to go under.

Rob paddled over to her, effortlessly slicing through the waves on his board. "Come on, Emmy. Don't give up. It's normal to wipeout when you first start. You'll get the hang of it. Just copy what I do."

After numerous failed attempts, Emma was near tears. Rob finally put her on his board and paddled her out. Cradled between Rob's suntanned arms, Emma felt safe—protected by his experience and the strength of his body.

"Stay in the center," Rob told her. "Just stay low and hold on; I'm going to bring us in now."

The board lifted onto a wave, hovered precariously, then dropped into the curve and sped them toward the rocks. Rob pulled out just in time, and turned the board toward the sandy shore, where Emma, laughing, fell into his arms.

"That was super! I loved it! Let's do it again. I feel like jumping up and down."

"First you have to give me a kiss."

Emma gave him a peck on the cheek, and then hopping to her feet, she scooped up a handful of sand and deposited it over his head.

"You little tease; I'll get you for that," Rob laughed, chasing after her. Catching Emma as she ran toward the water, he began to stuff sand down her bikini top and bottom.

Emma felt her face turn red. She wrenched out of his grip and turned on him. "Knock it off, Rob. I'm not a little kid. It's not funny."

Rob threw his hands up in the air. "Whoa, sorry Emmy. I was just playing with you. Here, let me help wash the sand off." He began lightly sprinkling her body with handfuls of water, creating little shivers in the wake of his touch. "I know you're no kid. You're more woman than most women. Hey, what are you? Are you a real woman?" He began tickling her ribs.

"Stop it; that's too immature." Emma pushed him away again.

"Come on, don't be mad. Just give me one kiss. I'll show you how to do it like a woman." Rob pulled her into his embrace. "Come on Emmy, just one. You're driving me crazy."

Emma wracked her brain for what she should do. Scratch him? Bite him? Even as she tried to push him away, she knew it was futile. She'd just experienced his strength on the surfboard. Her mind raced. *Rob isn't like this. What's he doing? I can't kiss him like that—he's practically my uncle. I could bite him on the lip, but what if he hits me? He won't hit me...maybe he will. Is he crazy? He's not really making a pass at me... something's wrong. He's too strong, I can't get away from him.* She decided to try another tactic and quit struggling—just let her body go slack as she searched for another plan of action. Didn't work. Rob pulled her closer and forced his lips onto hers. She went rigid and submitted to the kiss, her cheeks blazing with embarrassment. It was a light, soft kiss, barely grazing, and for an instant, she thought she had misunderstood his intentions. But then his lips moved down to her neck, where he buried his head and groaned. "Oh man, I'm playing with jailbait. I think I better take you home before something happens."

On the ride home, Emma tried to act as if nothing unusual had happened, but she couldn't bring herself to meet Rob's eyes. He was his usual, joking self—telling her stories about the things he and her dad used to do when they were kids.

When she got home, she didn't say anything to her parents about what had happened. She was afraid Ray would be hurt because Rob was his best friend. And Stephanie would get really mad at Rob, and who knows what would happen then. Her thoughts went around in a circle. Maybe all guys are like that...it's just their way of joking. He said he was kidding around. Maybe he didn't mean it like I took it. But then why did he call me jailbait if he didn't mean it like that? He knew...but maybe I'm making a bigger deal of it than it was. She had been testing him, playing with her newfound power to see if it worked on older men.

She'd begun to notice lately that with just a certain look she could get boys to do anything. It felt like learning a trick, like some new gymnastics move. She and her girlfriends, Cynthia and Olivia, had been talking about it. They were going through the same discoveries, and they had begun practicing how to kiss with each other during pajama parties. As uncomfortable as she'd been when it happened Emma couldn't wait to tell Cynthia and Olivia that she had actually been kissed by a man.

After the surfing incident, whenever Rob came around, Emma felt an underlying tension that hadn't been there before. He made it a point to pay special attention to her, and as flattering as it was, it made her uneasy, despite how she bragged to her friends. He was as good-looking as Elvis Presley, but as old as her parents. He'd even been married, and had a little kid!

When he showed up while she was home alone one night in mid-July, she was immediately uneasy. He stood in the doorway with a cigarette hanging out of his mouth, looking cool. She cracked the door open a bit and muttered, "Ray and Stephanie aren't home."

"Well, can I come in?" Rob didn't wait for an answer, just pushed his way into the room as though he had a right to be there.

"Oh, okay, come in then." Her sarcasm was apparently lost on Rob. She shifted from foot to foot. "I guess I'll just call Mom and Dad. They're right up the street having dinner at the neighbors'."

Rob stepped close to her. "I came to see you, Emmy. I feel like you've been avoiding me. Are you mad at me?"

Emma stared at the rug, then out the window at the bay. "No, why would you think that?" She tried to sound casual, tugging at her short shorts, wishing they were longer.

"Well, can a guy get a cup of coffee around here?"

She was reaching up into the cupboard for the coffee filters when she felt Rob's arms encircle her waist. Her body went stiff. Burying his face in the back of her neck, he lifted her hair, and nibbled at her ear. "Come on, Emmy, quit playing hard to get. I know you like me."

"I do, I like you, but not like that." Emma knew she was beet-red.

"Not like what?" Rob turned her around and kissed her shoulders, then moved down to her breasts. "Not like that? Or that?" he teased, backing off.

Emma hunched her shoulders in an attempt to minimize her breasts. She ignored the knots in her back, and fumbled with the coffee, trying to keep her hands from shaking. *Please come home early, Mom and Dad...please.*

Rob took two cups down off the hooks. "Look, you're tormenting me; but you like that, don't you, my little Sausalito Lolita."

"Who's Lolita?"

"You are, in your little short shorts…and your sexy eyes."

Emma avoided his eyes. "I don't think so. I think you're being weird. I'm just trying to get this coffee done. Do you want cream and sugar, or honey?"

"Just honey, little honey. I might be weird, but that's why you like me. Come on Emmy, don't be so serious; I'm just joking with you. Let's go listen to some folk music in your room."

"No."

"You're not scared of me now, are you? I'd never hurt you. Ray's my main man; you know that. Come on, let's have our coffee and talk it over like adults," Rob said, heading toward Emma's bedroom. "You got any Joan Baez?"

Against every instinct in her body, Emma followed him into her bedroom. As she sorted through her records, she sensed Rob come up behind her, felt his warm, rapid breath on the back of her neck. Her own breath caught in her throat as Rob's saltwater scent engulfed her. She let him turn her around and kiss her. His taste was yucky, cigarettes and beer, but his lips were soft and his cheeks smooth.

She was still assessing the kiss when she felt his hand go down to her crotch, and quickly snake beneath her shorts, into her underpants. "No, don't do that!" Emma tried to wrench herself from his grasp, but he had pinned her against the wall. She could see the thousands of blond hairs on the arm that was pushed hard across her chest.

Rob smiled, but his eyes were cold and distant. "Just close your eyes and relax. That doesn't hurt, does it?"

Emma felt his fingers on the lips of her vagina. No, it didn't hurt, and part of her wanted to explore the sensation, see what it would feel like. But it was Rob doing it, and that made it icky. She made a half-hearted attempt to wiggle away, but his fingers were already secured under her clothes, and were now tapping her clitoris, gently and rhythmically. She felt herself getting wet and slippery, and that was more humiliation than she could handle. It was like she'd peed the bed or something.

"Stop it, Rob; stop it!" she screamed, but Rob paid no attention to her cries. His grip on her had turned to steel, and she knew in the pit of her stomach that her terrified pleas were not reaching him. So she tried for another avenue of escape, adopting a more reasonable tone, hoping that she would appear more grown-up. "Ray and Stephanie will get mad. Please stop. Please."

Rob was panting now, like a wild beast. "How will they know unless you tell them?" He threw her onto the bed. Holding her down with his left arm, he jerked her shorts and underwear off.

The sudden nakedness felt like a shock wave. She gasped for air, and broke into sobs. "No, Rob, no," she cried.

"Stop crying, Emmy. It will hurt at first—it always does, but then it's going to feel great. Trust me," he said as he forced her legs apart and pounded his way into her.

Emma felt her body tear open. Dark waves of pain crashed over her, choking her. She swallowed the vomit that was clogging her throat. Images of her mom's Thanksgiving turkey seared her mind—she was the turkey, split and stuffed with Rob's flesh. She'd been gobbled up, and spit out in pieces. Her sense of self lay drowned in the pool of blood staining her sheets.

"It will be better next time." Rob was grinning, his white teeth gleaming. He sounded like he was reassuring her about her surfing skills. "You wanted it as much as I did, my sexy little Emmy." He carried on talking, as he pulled on his Bermuda shorts, about how much he loved her and how good everything was going to be. Eventually, he left.

Emma made herself get up. She didn't want Ray and Stephanie to find their precious atomic-age daughter looking like somebody's leftover meal, even though she was pretty sure she looked different now, no matter what.

When Stephanie came home, Emma was trying to scrub blood out of her sheet. Stephanie smiled tenderly. "Oh honey, you started your period. How do you feel? Cramps? You're a little pale. Let me fix you some tea."

Emma stood at the sink, scrubbing the sheet with hot water—setting the stain. She was silent. She wanted to tell her mother what had happened, but it was too humiliating. If she had told her about the beach incident, this never would have happened. Rob had said it was as much her fault as his—that she had been leading him on. If she hadn't wanted him to do it, why had she followed him into the bedroom? Shame crept up from her bleeding vagina, flushing her neck and face.

"Sweetheart, it's nothing to be ashamed of. It's perfectly natural." Stephanie put her arm around Emma. "We should do a little female ritual to celebrate."

Emma shrugged off her mother's arm. "Don't tell Ray; please, Mom."

"That's silly, Emma. Ray will be happy his little girl is growing up. It's all within nature's grand plan, the yin and the yang, positive, negative. A woman's blood must flow to create new cycles of life. Sit down, drink your tea. It'll make you feel better. You need to hydrate."

Emma sipped the chamomile tea. *If I tell her, he'll go to jail. I'd be the one who put him in jail, when it was just as much my fault as his.* She tried to imagine Rob in jail, everyone knowing why—everyone feeling sorry for her. She thought about Cynthia and Olivia whispering to the others at school. *There goes poor Emma; she got raped by her father's best friend...look how pitiful she is. All the guys want to go out with her now because they know she puts out. What a slut. Emma Allison is nothing but a whore.* Emma took a deep breath. "Rob came by," she said, trying to sound nonchalant.

"How is he doing, honey? You know his mother has cancer?" Stephanie was puttering around the kitchen, putting things away for the night. "He's having a hard time right now. Elaine is suing him for more alimony—trying to cut back on his visitation rights. Did he stay long? What's the matter, Em? You look really pale. Did Rob say something…he didn't make a pass at you, did he?"

The question hung on Stephanie's breath for several beats, and the truth fluttered in Emma's throat. Emma gagged on it, then swallowed it, choked it down. A callus began forming around the silence.

Ray called out from the other room, "That's an absurd thing to put in her mind, Stephanie. Rob wouldn't do anything like that. He loves Emma like a daughter."

Rob had said, "I love you. You're my girl now. I'd give my life for you…but you can't tell anyone. It has to be our secret. Tell them I'm giving you more lessons—we'll go to my place next time." *Next time.*

Later that night, long after the house had quieted and the moon had dropped behind the Bay Bridge, Emma lay awake. A pervasive uneasiness had lodged itself deep in her chest and would not let her sleep.

Eventually, she got quietly out of bed and went to sit on the deck. The lights twinkled on the Golden Gate Bridge, and she wondered if she would have a baby now. Olivia had said that you could get pregnant the first time. She wished she'd paid more attention to her mother's explanations about sex and babies. Tip-toeing back into the house, Emma poured herself a glass of the wine that was in the fridge. Back out on the deck, she downed her first drink in one gulp, feeling it burn into her system.

With her knees pulled close to her body, she rocked herself, oblivious to the chilly night air. *Maybe it wasn't rape. Maybe that's just the way things happen, like Rob said. All the girls thought he was handsome… what if we're in love. How do you know?*

Exhausted from trying to come to terms with what had happened, Emma padded back to bed. *At least he loves me*, she thought, and dropped into a coma-like sleep.

When Olivia called about going to the movies, Emma said she was too busy practicing her songs for Wizard of Oz. She had the lead, so there was a lot of pressure. When Cynthia wanted to go to the beach, Emma said she was too tired.

Stephanie told Emma that her hormones were creating depression, and insisted that a coming of age ceremony would be just the thing to lift her spirits. "We'll invite all the female elders in your life, and your girlfriends, of course. I'll get Marilyn Little-Bird to lead us in a Sioux ritual. What do you think, honey?"

"I don't want a goddamn ceremony; don't you get that?" Emma snapped. "I want you to stay out of my life. I need privacy; I'm not a child anymore."

Emma heard Ray and Stephanie talking later that night as she tiptoed past their bedroom door, on her way to the kitchen to pour herself a nightcap. "It's just a stage," Ray was saying. "All teenagers go through it. We have to be patient, and keep our own egos out of it."

Emma paused a moment, debating whether she should burst into the room and tell Ray what his "greatest guy in the world" best friend had done to her. They both sounded so condescending as they discussed her "stage"—so sure of their superior understanding of everything—they always knew what was happening. Even when they didn't have a clue.

In the kitchen, Emma grabbed the gin, threw back a drink, and poured herself another. Turning on the tap gingerly, she replaced the gin with water. Her parents wouldn't notice—they never really noticed anything.

Emma began locking the door to her room, spending hours alone with her electric piano, writing songs and practicing standards. She supposed it was because they felt snubbed, but it still hurt when her oldest friends, Cynthia and Olivia, turned on her. She knew they were the ones who were spreading rumors in the theatre company about her supposed sexual exploits.

Rob was waiting for Emma one day after play practice, looking suntanned and handsome.

"What are you doing here?" Emma exclaimed. "Where's Stephanie? She's supposed to pick me up."

"She said you can go for another surf lesson. I have your bathing suit."

"I'm not getting in your car. I'll walk."

"Oh come on, you're not still mad at me, are you? Get in the car; I won't touch you. Let's go have a milkshake, and talk things over. This is silly, Emmy."

Emma picked up a rock and tossed it between her hands a few times, thinking hard about throwing it at Rob. *Look at him smiling all innocent and friendly—what a great guy. I could just whap him between the eyes.*

"What are you doing, Emma? Learning to juggle rocks?" It was Cynthia, who had walked up behind her. She and Olivia stood there posing, for Rob's benefit, obviously.

Rob leaned his head out the window. "What's shaking, ladies?" he called out, grinning, his teeth white in the sunshine.

"Hey Rob," Olivia cooed, approaching his car. "Want to take us to the beach? We're dying in this heat."

"Sorry, no can do," Rob said. "I'm teaching Emma to surf. Catch you another time."

"We could watch," Cynthia said. "I could call my mom. I know she won't care. And Emma wants us to go; don't you, Emma?"

"Maybe next week," Rob said. "Let's go, Emmy."

Emma was fuming as she got in the car. *After ignoring me for weeks, now Cynthia and Olivia start flirting with my boyfriend. I guess he's my boyfriend, whether I like it or not. Well, I don't have to do anything I don't want to do.*

She snuck a glance at Rob out of the corner of her eyes as they drove away. *He is handsome; everybody thinks so. Maybe I'm being immature. Maybe it was normal. I wonder if he really loves me.*

Grabbing fries and shakes to go from the local burger joint, Rob drove to a secluded stretch of Highway 1 and parked the car overlooking the ocean. It was always windy up on the headlands, but Rob knew of a perfect sheltered spot to sit. Emma balked when he grabbed a blanket from the trunk of his car.

"We have to have something to sit on. Son of a bitch, Emmy, what's up? You act like you're afraid of me. I'd never hurt you; you know that. I love you."

Standing at the edge of the blanket, ready to flee, Emma said, "You already hurt me."

"It always hurts the first time; I told you that. Come on, sit down. Let's have our fries. Friends, right?" Rob stretched out his hand to give the food to Emma. She took it, and sat down on the furthest corner of the blanket. "I've got plenty of girls who want me," Rob was saying, chewing on a fry. "Look how your friends act around me."

So-called friends, Emma thought. She didn't know what to say, since what he said was probably true. Off her balance, she tried for funny. "You're not supposed to talk with your mouth full. It's bad manners."

Rob didn't laugh. "I could have any of your friends, but I chose you, Emmy. We don't have to go all the way, but can't I at least hold you? You've been on my mind every night. You're all I think about." Rob reached for Emma's foot, massaged it briefly, and then ran his hand up her leg, ever so lightly. "I could show you some things that feel great, and we don't have to do it. Just being with you is enough. Drink your shake; I'm not going to hurt you."

Emma sipped at the shake, and broke out into goose bumps as Rob ran his hands over her.

"See, you do like it," Rob said. "Relax, and let me make you come. I'm an expert. You don't have to do anything…what about this…is this okay?"

Emma let him pull off her underwear, and to her surprise, he lowered his head and began to kiss her between her legs. She stayed very still, shocked that he would do such a thing, but more shocked by the sensation it produced. When her body finally settled down, Emma was too embarrassed to look at Rob.

"Please Emmy, just rub me. I'm hurting. You can't leave me like this."

"You said I didn't have to do anything." Emma raised her eyes to meet his. "I don't want to." She pulled her underwear back on.

"You bitch, little prick-teaser," Rob swore. "Don't walk away. I'll do anything."

"Take it back."

"Take what back?"

"The names you just called me."

"I didn't mean it. You know I didn't mean it. I'm hurting because I love you so goddamn much. Please don't be mad at me. You can't just leave me like this. You've got to help me. Just put your hand right here. I'll show you how to do it."

After that day, Emma came to accept that Rob was her boyfriend, even though they had to keep it secret. She was astonished at how easily she could make him moan and groan and beg for her favors. And she liked it that Cynthia and Olivia were so obviously jealous. She could tell they both had a crush on Rob, so she flaunted her power over him. He gave her cigarettes, beer, gin, anything she wanted, and although he was always trying to talk her into going all the way with him, he never tried to force her again.

"You're the boss, Emmy," he'd say. "I'm your slave."

At the end of August, she started her period. She tried to keep Rob from finding out, but it was hopeless. They were hanging out at his apartment one afternoon, and when he started rummaging through her purse for a cigarette, he saw the sanitary pads. To Emma's embarrassment, he held one up. "Emmy baby, what's this? You've been holding out on me."

Emma snatched it out of his hand. "Oh, please! You're an idiot. It's none of your business."

Rob put on his hurt face, with the bottom lip pout. “Emmy, don’t you see? We can have sex now like a real couple. We’re in love…and I’ll use rubbers. I’d never get you pregnant.”

“I don’t like sex.”

“Give it another shot. You like it when I go down on you—you’ll like balling even more. It only hurt because it was the first time. Come on, Emmy; let me show you ecstasy.” Rob lit a joint and passed it to her.

Emma inhaled deeply and slowly let the smoke out. “Get me a drink,” she ordered. “I want a Margarita.”

Rob mixed the drinks and brought them over to the couch where Emma was lounging. “You know, you can’t get pregnant when you’re having your period. A lot of women say it’s the best time to have sex.”

Emma fixed him with a cold stare. “That is so gross, I’m not even going to answer you.”

“Finish your drink. Here, have some more.” Rob poured more of the frozen liquid into her glass. "I can get you home late tonight because Ray and Stephanie are at a party. Let’s have our own party, what do you say?”

“In your dreams.”

“Don’t be like that, Emmy. A little bit of blood doesn’t turn me off. I like it. Besides, it’ll lubricate you and make the sex better. You shouldn’t be embarrassed about your period.”

“Christ, now you sound like my mother.”

Rob disappeared for a moment, and came back in the room holding a beach towel. “Here, lift your butt; let me get this spread out on the couch. This is going to be great.”

Sloppy drunk now, Emma let Rob slide the towel under her. “What the hell, right Rob?” Her words came out slowly; she couldn’t seem to form the sounds right. “It’s not like I have anything to lose, is it? I’m already a freak. Go ahead, who gives a shit, right?”

It was messy; her blood leaked onto the couch in spite of the towel. But Rob was right that it wouldn't hurt this time. It was over quickly, and he seemed really upset about that. He promised her that he'd make her come if she'd let him do it again. "No," she told him. "I want to go home."

Snuggled down deeply in her own bed that night, a water glass of gin and tonic tucked under the bed, and her teddy bear clutched to her breast, Emma mulled over the experience. *We must be in love... Rob says people in love like to ball...I don't know if I like it. It didn't hurt, but it feels weird now.* She heard her parents stirring in the kitchen, and for a moment she couldn't breathe. Reaching under the bed for her drink, she bolted it, then hid the glass back against the wall. *What would Ray and Stephanie do if they found out? Would they still love me? Would Ray believe me? He might think it was my own fault; well, it was. I should have said no. I'm not going to do it again.*

But she did. Even though each time they were together Emma told herself that it would be the last, Rob would always manage to get her to do it. He would cry, protest that he loved her too much to let her go, say that she'd ruined his life.

"Just one more time, Emmy. I need you," Rob would plead.

At first his desperate begging made Emma feel powerful, grown-up beyond her years. She could get this adult guy to do anything she wanted. But all of his attention, the rides and treats and compliments, couldn't cover up her growing conviction that she was more a freak than someone special. She had become *different.* Even the thrill of sex lost its potency. His proclamations of love became tedious. It was always about him—how he wanted her, how he loved her. It didn't seem to occur to him that maybe she didn't feel the same way. "No one will ever love you like I do," he'd say. Emma would roll her eyes and think, *Thank God*!

By September, she'd heard it all, and just wanted out. Rob had become pathetic. His whining disgusted her. When school started, her busy schedule made it easier to avoid him.

A guy who was in *Wizard of Oz* with her, a handsome high school senior, asked her to the Homecoming Dance at Tam High. A dance sounded like fun, but her stomach curdled at the thought of being around all those new people. She felt so *different*. So she told him it was too immature, and that she'd rather go hear folk music in Berkeley. She enjoyed the look of surprise on his face, and for a moment, she thought he might turn her down. But instead, he nodded his agreement.

At the folk club, he worked hard to impress her, but Emma knew more about music than he did, and as confident as he tried to appear, she could sense his nervousness. When he pulled into the local make-out spot at the end of the evening, she beat him to the punch. The guy was so surprised that he almost couldn't function. Rob's lessons had him eating out of the palm of her hand. In the heat of the moment, Emma's mind was clear. *If I'm going to have the reputation anyway, I might as well live up to it. And no one is ever going to take me the way Rob did again—ever.*

Word got around school that she was dating a guy from Tam High, and she started getting invited to all the dances and parties. But she didn't go. She felt older than the other junior high kids…*different*…as though they no longer had anything in common.

She shut herself off from her peers completely, preferring her music to socializing with the gossipy girls and the fawning boys. Cynthia and Olivia had quit speaking to her, even though they were in home room together and had most of the same classes. She told herself she didn't care—that they were just jealous. But she felt the loss of their friendship in her gut. They had been a threesome since kindergarten—done gymnastics and plays, and even gone to summer camp together.

Alone now, she wrote her poems and song lyrics late into the nights, but showed them to no one.

Rob went crazy when she told him it was over. He must have sensed that she meant it. He'd come to pick her up from school, but she suggested they take a walk on the bike path. When they reached the dog-run area, the place was almost deserted. Gathering her courage, Emma turned to Rob. "I want to break up." She ground her sandal toe into the dirt, and focused her attention on some dogs out in the field. "I mean it. It's over."

"What's going on here? Can't you even look at me?" Rob's eyes filled with tears. "Don't do this. We love each other."

Emma forced herself to meet his eyes. "I don't want to talk about it. I want you to leave me alone. You've done enough."

"*I've* done enough? Come on, Emmy, we're in this together. It's as much your fault as it is mine. You made me love you. You wanted it…I made you come, didn't I. It always felt good, didn't it? You know it did."

"I don't want to do it anymore," Emma said evenly. "You can't make me."

"You want to play it like that?" Rob's face turned an ugly red through his suntan. "What will your parents think of their precious little girl when they find out what she's been doing?"

Emma turned her back to him and started walking away. He yelled after her, "You can't just walk away from me. I'll kill myself…I'll kill you…I'll kill your parents."

Emma stopped in her tracks. Now she was angry. She turned to face him. "So that's what you're really like? You'd kill my dad, your best friend?"

"No I wouldn't. I didn't mean it. You're making me crazy. Don't do this. We love each other."

Emma met his eyes full on. "In fact, I don't love you anymore. I have a new boyfriend."

"I'll kill him."

"You're bluffing. You're not going to kill anyone." Emma had seen Rob grovel for sex too many times to take him seriously, or fear him. A buzz began in her ears and quickly filled her head with pressure, until she burst. She found herself right up in his face, jabbing at his chest, yelling.

"You ever hear of sex with a minor? Sex-Ed class, Rob. Guess what? Jail time. For you, not me. I'm the minor. I've got a few threats of my own. I don't ever want to see you at my house again, or I will tell Ray and Stephanie everything. I'll tell the police…and my school counselor. Don't come around anymore. Ever."

"Okay Emmy, if that's the way you want it. You're just a dirty little slut—always have been. You broke up my family, and now you think you can just walk away from it all. Fine. Adios, baby," he said, but then he fell down on his knees and cried at her feet.

"Oh, grow up," she said, then turned and walked away.

1974

Emma drifted in and out of sleep as Juan tried to massage the kinks out of her back and shoulders. There were a few knots that refused to ease up; they'd been there a long time and weren't about to give up that easily.

Juan finished the massage with a brisk towel rub to get the excess oil off her body. She stood up and stretched lazily. "Are you hungry, baby?" she asked Juan. "Should I order lunch, or do you want to go out?"

"We can go out later; I've got something else on my mind at the moment." Juan pulled her back into bed.

In the late afternoon, when the sun was less blistering, Juan and Emma walked down Sunset Blvd. heading east, toward the deli that made the best Ruben Sandwiches in town. "I want to know all about you…when you started singing, where you went to school, if you have siblings—everything," Juan told Emma.

Emma's arm was hooked in Juan's and she smiled up at him, snuggling closer as they walked. "What is this? An interrogation? What about you? Did you just hatch out of an egg and fly to L.A.? What about your childhood? I want to know about you."

"Without a doubt, my childhood was very different than yours. I think you could safely say that my parents are the opposite of beatniks. I don't like to talk about them. Tell me more about your family."

"Okay, fine. Ray, my father, is a jazz musician, but he works as a contractor to survive. My mother, Stephanie, is an artist. They're both crazy, but they're cool."

"Why do you say they're crazy?"

"Trust me, they are. But you'll love them; everybody does."

Emma thought about her childhood as they walked along. It was hard to explain what she meant by crazy. In a lot of ways, Ray and Stephanie were saner than straight parents, even though they dropped acid, smoked pot, and held beliefs that were more out there than hers. They loved her, and gave her the freedom to pursue her dreams.

"Do they live in San Francisco, too?" Juan asked.

"No, baby. They live in Sausalito, which is an arty little town just across the Golden Gate Bridge, in Marin County. They moved there when I was two because they wanted to raise me in a smaller town environment." Emma laughed to herself, then carried on. "An example of their craziness? They had found this little cottage that had a great view of the bay, and they really wanted it, but other people had put offers on it, too. On my second birthday, bang, their offer was accepted, and to this day they tell people that it was a sure-fire cosmic sign—that they knew it was meant to be because of the alignment of the stars or something on my birthday. Jesus!"

"You were lucky, Emma…to be raised by parents who obviously adored you."

"Yeah, I suppose so. Ray and Stephanie were always seeing signs in everything, but basically, they weren't that different than my friends' parents. When they weren't riding the cosmic waves, they worried and fussed over me, same as most parents—warned me about not talking to strangers, taught me how to cross the street carefully—all that kind of stuff. But then the craziness comes in again. They always insisted that I obey them and use proper manners, but at the same time, they were teaching me to always question authority."

Juan laughed. "I can see that would be confusing for a child."

"Not as much as you might think, though. I was still really young when I realized that while I couldn't always understand what my parents were saying, I usually knew what they meant."

"My experience was the opposite. I always understood what my parents were saying, but I had trouble discerning their meaning; and coming to terms with the motives behind their demands was impossible. But please, tell me more about growing up with your beatnik parents."

That was a tall order. Emma thought about the house she grew up in. It had seemed so big when she was young, but it was actually just a summer cabin, built before the bridge was constructed—when Marin was still rural. As she had grown, so had the house, with Ray adding rooms in the same hodgepodge manner as he approached his music. He had to follow architectural plans when he was on a job, but he could go hog-wild on his own home—make it a showcase for his and Stephanie's artistic sensibilities.

Situated in the hills overlooking the bay, the house nestled between the redwoods, secluded enough that Ray's jazz trio could jam to their heart's content. Stephanie had covered the walls with her own and their friends' paintings, and interspersed with the fine art were always Emma's current endeavors—colored pictures when she was young, then water colors, and eventually, posters from her gigs.

Throughout her childhood, Emma and her playmates would tear through the house, skipping and dancing, putting on plays, and playing hide-and-go-seek among the statues that seemed to be growing in the garden—she didn't feel *different* then. In those days, Rob was light years away.

"A penny for your thoughts, is that the right expression?" Juan was leaning down, trying to catch her eye. They had walked for blocks in silence without Emma noticing.

Emma blinked a few times and smiled up at him. His hair was blowing in the light wind that had arisen. "What? Oh yeah. My parents were only beatniks till the hippie thing happened. You might say they were the original hippies, but they hate that word. It's like trying to put a label on something that is elusive and defies description. Still, in order to have a conversation, you have to name and define things, right?"

"Yes, that's true. And some people hate definitions because it forces them to look at who they really are…as if you can compartmentalize elements of your life and keep them separate, and not ever have to look at the whole picture of who you have become."

"Wow, that's heavy," Emma said, and she meant it.

"It is not my intention to weigh you down. Tell me about your career…how you became a star."

Emma playfully whacked Juan on the chest. "Now you're making fun of me."

Juan drew her in close and kissed her passionately. "Come on, let's go into the restaurant before I change my mind and carry you off into the bushes."

Sitting across from each other in the cushy booths at the deli, they ordered their sandwiches and cream sodas, and then fell silent. Emma looked up and her eyes locked with Juan's. They sat in the comfortable silence and studied each other's faces. Eventually, it was Emma who broke the gaze, reaching for a cigarette. Juan lit it for her, and took one himself.

Juan spoke first. "I wasn't kidding, Emma. I would love to hear how you started out…who you played with, how old you were…everything."

Emma rolled her eyes. "Okay, you asked for it. I always liked to sing. I sang with Ray's jazz band once in a while when I was a kid—trying to imitate Billie Holiday, you know. But his band would get really out-there, very freeform, and I'd get bored. I got totally into musical theatre when I was a kid. I loved show tunes, and stayed with it all through school…even after I heard Chuck Berry and Elvis, who blew my mind. I went major crazy over rock n' roll…started singing rock and R&B constantly, with any little garage band that was playing parties…and *then* I heard Joan Baez and Bob Dylan, and singing folk songs became my life. I fell head over heels in love with the traditionals, and I learned to play guitar and piano so I could accompany myself. Wait a minute. I sound like I'm doing an interview. Heard enough?"

"No, I could never hear enough. When did you become a professional?"

"There's a guy involved…still want to know?"

"Of course there was a guy involved. I do not imagine that I am your first lover."

"You're more than a lover, baby. Don't you feel that? Why, is that all I am to you?"

"You are *mi reina*, my queen. You have captured my heart. But finish your story. Who was this guy and how did you get started?"

"I would go with Ray and Stephanie to these Beat coffeehouses in The City, just so I could sing to a real audience. I was always fidgeting through the long poetry recitations, but it was worth it when I got to sing—it was a rush, you know? By the time I was thirteen, I had amassed a pretty hefty repertoire of standards, and then at about fourteen, I was writing my own songs. They weren't very good, but it was good practice. Wow, and then acid happened, and I met Grant, and I joined *Altered States*. That's pretty much it."

Juan raised an eyebrow. He reached over and took her hands. "Who was Grant? One of the garage-band players? You were *fourteen* when you took acid and turned professional? I find this astonishing. What about school?"

Emma squeezed his hands, then freed hers to pick up her soda. "No, no, I didn't say I was fourteen. It was 1966…LSD was still legal, and Ray and Stephanie were taking it…and they let me start tripping the summer I turned sixteen. Our house was kind of a scene for people who wanted to get away from The City. We'd drop acid and then go hang out in the redwoods, or the beach. And there was this chick, Carol Hartwell, a friend of Ray and Stephanie's…way cool, the most beautiful woman alive…"

"No, not possible. *You* are the most beautiful woman alive. But please continue. Who was Grant?"

"Carol brought him over to hear me sing. She loved my singing. She was like that, always supportive, even when I was just fourteen and still green. Grant was the lead guitar player for this psychedelic band, *Altered States*, that was playing around the Haight. We all dropped acid and started jamming, and Grant liked my singing and invited me to audition for *Altered States*. The rest is history."

"So, you got the job. And Grant, he was your boyfriend? What about school? How did you manage that? Did you continue to live with your parents? Don't forget, my queen, I am a foreigner. I am not acquainted with *all* your history."

Emma laughed. "You're mocking me, you bastard."

"I assure you I'm not. I am fascinated by everything about you. I think you're leaving parts out because you don't want to make me jealous, but you needn't worry. I am not a jealous man, unless I should be. Your past is just that—only an interesting story. I know that you have had an astonishingly successful career, and that you are wildly talented, of course. But you have to fill in the blanks for me…please, continue."

"Okay, yeah. I dropped out of high school and moved to the Haight Ashbury district of San Francisco with Grant. We were a couple for a while…not long. The band worked out better than the relationship."

Emma thought about Grant. He had seemed so exciting to her at first. He was Carol's age, 21, and he epitomized the hip scene in the way he looked, the way he talked, and the way he played guitar. After the jam session, the whole group of people had wound up driving to Muir Woods, still peaking on acid. Meandering in the shade of the giant redwoods, the group splintered into couples, and Emma found herself on a secluded pathway, alone with Grant. She remembered being attracted to him, but also that in her stoned state, she had been a little scared of him, too. Nonetheless, when they stopped to rest among the lush vegetation and he started coming on to her, she responded by stripping off her blouse and pulling him down on top of her. He had age on her, but not experience…thanks to Rob. There was no way in hell she was going to tell Juan about Rob, not ever.

Juan was finishing up his meal, regarding her with a smile and one of his lifted eyebrows again. "Do you want some coffee? Perhaps a cappuccino?" He gave their coffee orders to the waiter who was clearing the table, and then turned his full attention back to Emma. "I remember the band, of course. I always liked the San Francisco sound. It must have been an exciting time to be there, right in the epicenter of the whole scene."

"Yeah, baby, it was. It was a trip. Hey, let's go to a movie at one of the big Hollywood Boulevard theatres—take advantage of our night off. What do you say?"

"Sounds great. I'll ask the waiter to call us a cab."

"The epicenter of the whole scene." Juan pinned it, of course. And he was right that San Francisco was exciting in the mid-sixties. People would later call 1967 the Summer of Love, but Emma thought of it more as the beginning of the end of the Haight Ashbury. She had spent the year of 1966 to 1967 singing with *Altered States*, developing a solid following within the community. The small clubs, and the Avalon and Fillmore ballrooms, were packed every show with hippies from all over the country who had come to the Haight to be part of the so-called "beautiful life." The problem was, a lot of these people brought their own individual bum trips with them, including speed.

But 1967 was great, even grand—while it lasted. That summer, *Altered States* played free concerts at spontaneous street events and at peace rallies in Golden Gate Park. They did benefits for the Haight-Ashbury Free Clinic and for any other good cause when their schedule permitted. Their popularity grew, and at the same time, the band dynamic grew weird.

For one thing, Emma had grown sick of Grant. He was always stoned, and it made him stupid and boring. All he ever wanted to do was smoke pot, eat, watch TV, and fuck—in the same way, every time. It seemed only natural to fall into a thing with the bass player, Jackson.

Jackson liked to do things. He and Emma hit the North Beach clubs together, hung out with other bands in the Haight, ate magic mushrooms, and explored Golden Gate Park into the wee hours of the morning. Grant seemed fairly oblivious to the obvious, rather like her parents, Emma thought.

When the split-up came, it nearly broke the band up, too. Grant went on a furious drinking binge, threatening to kill her and Jackson. She and Jackson hid out in West Marin, at a friend's cabin in Forest Knolls, until Grant collected himself and decided that the band was too important to wreck it over a chick. Reconciliation was reached at a band meeting and the guys all breathed a sigh of relief.

However, after spending a week and a half alone with Jackson in a cabin, Emma was sick of him, too. She called Carol and asked if she could stay with her until she found her own place. Even though Carol had introduced her to Grant, she always took Emma's side in the band squabbles.

Emma remembered vividly the first time she'd seen Carol. She'd been in her bedroom doing homework, but Ray and Stephanie coaxed her out to come parade her songs for their usual cluster of friends—and someone new who was there. Emma felt intimidated by the stranger's beauty, but drawn to her nonetheless. Obligingly, Emma sat in with the older musicians, played rhythm guitar and sang a few of her own songs. Her parents' friends always made a fuss over her voice and she took it in stride, but when Carol praised her, she felt a shiver of special pleasure. `"You're the real thing," Carol had said to Emma. She had taken a hit from the joint Ray passed her, and waving it around, she exhaled and announced to the room in general, "They're not going to be able to keep this girl hidden away much longer. I know talent when I see it."

Carol had invited Emma out for coffee after school one day shortly thereafter, and the two found common ground immediately. If the years between them made their life experiences slightly out of sync, their sense of humor and love of music closed the gap. When Emma moved to the Haight, she began hanging out at Carol's place whenever she could. And now, when she needed a place to go to get away from both Grant and Jackson, she turned to Carol, who took her in to her tiny flat without the slightest hesitation.

Emma soon found a flat of her own, but continued roaring around town with Carol. The summer of 1967 was being called the era of free love, and the two of them embodied the spirit of the times. Birth control pills could be easily obtained at the Free Clinic, and a shot of penicillin would cure the clap, so naturally they went with the conventional wisdom of the time: "If it feels good, do it."
The community's creed of personal freedom extended to fashion, too. Everyone wore what they wanted with absolutely no regard for what the rest of the world was wearing. People flaunted their fantasies in a colorful parade up and down Haight Street.

Emma was into thrift shops, and she had scoring the good stuff down to a science. She knew which day the new shipments would be put out at the Goodwill and Salvation Army, and she'd get there first thing to snatch up the bargains. Her biggest score was a snow-white, 1920s ermine jacket in perfect condition— she thought it made her look like a silver-screen star. She and her friend, Marianne, would grub through the bins of old clothing, find Granny Dresses in beautiful floral patterns, and buy them for a dime. Marianne would then dissect the old dresses and piece the disparate fabrics together into outrageous new outfits.

The guys were dressing up, too. Cowboy and Indian clothing was their style, and some of that influence made its way into Emma's wardrobe. Emma loved Mae West, and adopted some aspects of her floozy style, in spite of the fact that she was a reed who didn't have the stuff to strut that the bosomy actress did. But she made up for it by wearing layers of clothing, scarves, antique shawls, and ropes of Love Beads, and tying ostrich feathers into her blond, frizzed hair to give herself a bigger look.

People would stare at her in the Financial District when she flounced through town in lacy, see-through tops and flowing velvet skirts; but when she looked out into her audiences at the shows, she realized she didn't look all that different from her fans. On stage, she'd grip the microphone with bejeweled hands, rings on every finger, stomping her feet, letting the music move her, and she felt part of a happening—giving the audience her energy, and receiving theirs—in a continuous circle. Fans would tell her that her eyes were the same color as the huge sapphire she wore on her index finger, and just as stony, pun always intended. She loved her audiences, and felt accepted and loved by them. She didn't feel so *different* anymore.

She was free to do her own thing, and she did just that. When Jackson walked in on her getting it on with the rhythm guitar player in a backstage dressing room, she screamed at him to give her some space. By now the band was used to high drama, and they took the fight in stride. But the real drama was yet to come.

After the band played a huge hippie festival in Monterey in the middle of June, where they went over great, Herbie Goldberg, the big-time manager from New York, approached Emma. The band was really jazzed about his interest in them. What they didn't realize was that it wasn't *Altered States* he was after. They were all invited out to dinner with Herbie, but only Emma was invited for drinks afterwards.

Emma sat back comfortably in a lounge bar booth, watching Herbie approach her with a drink. He set an Irish Coffee down in front of her, squeezed himself into the booth, and then leaned across the table confidentially.

"Listen Emma, you've got to do your own thing. Look what happens with these bands. They just start to get somewhere, and then internal problems break them up."

Emma stared at him. It had been a long day. What was he trying to say? "We have our fights, but basically, we're cool."

"I don't think so. Rumor has it that you've already got infighting big time. Listen to me; the only way to make it in the business is to have control. You've got a lot of talent, and you're gorgeous to boot—I believe you can be a star, but only as a solo artist."

Emma was taken aback. "Well, yeah, I know what you mean about the infighting, but I'm used to singing with *Altered States*. They'd freak if I left them."

"Listen Emma, I can put together a back-up band for you in a matter of days. These studio musicians can play anything. Just consider it. I can get you a hefty advance. I'll get you a Porsche. Tell me what you want."

The next day, at the rehearsal warehouse, Emma paced the floor as the band members drifted in. Grant had some groupies with him, and a couple of dope dealers had accompanied Jackson. She'd been up half the night trying to decide what to do, and her nerves were jangled. Striding over to Grant, she snapped, "Listen to me, man, get all these people out of here. This is supposed to be a band meeting."

When the room had been cleared of all the hangers on, all eyes turned to Emma. "So what did he say?" Jackson asked. "Did he make us a good offer?"

"No, he didn't." Emma focused her eyes on the worn design of the funky Persian carpet. "I tried to stick up for the band," she said flatly. "I tried to convince Herbie that we're a package deal…but he wouldn't buy it. Basically, he just wants to sign me, and that's his final offer."

"So you accepted?" Jackson's disbelief was visible.

"For all your hip talk and your innocent eyes, you're just a bitch in disguise," Grant snarled.

Emma flashed a sarcastic smile. "Writing lyrics now, huh Grant?"

The guilty flutter in the pit of her stomach wasn't strong enough to get her to turn down Herbie Goldberg, but she *sort of* felt like she owed the guys something—they had been close to her, after all, like family. *But not really like family. More like Rob. They all got something in return from the relationship. And they'd do the same if Herbie wanted them to drop me. Thank God I'm leaving for New York next week.*

Stephanie threw a fit about Emma wanting to go to New York alone. "You're only seventeen—it's a dangerous city—anything could happen!"

"But I won't be alone," Emma argued. "Herbie will be there; he'll look after me. And I'll be in the recording studio all the time anyway. It'll be fine."

Stephanie wasn't convinced. "You have no idea what the rest of this country is like, Em. It's one thing for you to live in the Haight, but New York is different. You read about these things in the paper all the time—they have rapes, and people just walk right by—as if they don't see anything happening."

Emma wanted to say, *Sounds like some people I know,* but she bit her tongue instead. Laughing to herself, she draped her arm over Stephanie' shoulders and said cheerily, "Don't worry about me. I can take care of myself," adding under her breath, "I always have."

Stephanie looked stricken. Her eyes filled with tears. "What did you say? I don't believe you just said that. Honestly Em, you're too old to still be in the differentiation process with me… it feels like a stab wound when you make remarks like that. You might as well stab me. Do you really believe Ray and I didn't take good care of you—do you?"

"Jesus Stephanie, I was kidding, okay?"

Stephanie sniffled. "No, it's not okay. I don't know how we could have cared for you any better. You've been the center of our universe since you were born. I don't understand why you have to be so cruel sometimes."

"It was a *joke*. I'm just trying to get you to see that I can look after myself in New York—I don't need my *mommy* to chaperone me…Christ, I'd be a laughing stock."

"I don't want to tie you down like my parents did me, but I don't know, Em, I really don't."

"Come on Mom, don't you trust me."

"Ray will never give his permission, even if you browbeat me into consenting."

But Ray gave in, too. He always did.

…

Stephanie was right, as it turned out. Emma *didn't* have a clue about the rest of the country—New York could have been Mars—but it was exciting. Herbie sent a limo to fetch her from the airport and take her to the Chelsea Hotel, which was like something out of a film noir. Everybody looked a little shady and mysterious. Even the leaves of the October trees in Central Park were different than the evergreens of California.

Her first day at the studio, Emma met some musicians from North Carolina who were also staying at The Chelsea. Later that night the party began.

It seemed to Emma that the recording was coming along great. Everyone appeared to dig her songs, and the session musicians, well, they could make anything sound good. The piano player, Dan, was a gorgeous, native New Yorker who knew the ropes. He helped Emma get a false I.D. so she could hit the hot spots with the rest of the gang. And he put her to bed at night—crawled in with her, too. "You're jailbait, but baby, you're worth the risk," he liked to say.

Emma was intrigued with Dan, until Max, a B-3 player, was called in for one of the tracks. A chain-smoker, Max was the thinnest, most unhealthy looking guy she'd ever seen, but somehow his sickliness made him sexy. For over a week, Emma was sure she was in love with him. But then she met a painter who was in town for a big one-man show. He seemed sophisticated in an arty way, until she witnessed him kissing ass to sell his paintings, and referring to the gallery as "prestigious" fifty times. That affair drove her back to the bottomless pool of musicians—at least they were what they seemed.

The days grew shorter and colder toward the end of October, but the chill didn't penetrate the alcohol flush Emma had going. It wasn't so much a matter of wanting to get fucked-up every night, as no reason not to…at least until Herbie got wind of her sitting in with a band at a blues club. There he was, waiting for her in the studio the next day, looking like an angry gargoyle.

"Hi Herbie." Emma tried the upbeat approach. "Wow, I'm so glad you stopped by…there's some stuff I want your advice on."

"Yeah, well I'm glad you want my advice cause you're gonna get it. Let's be clear about a few things upfront, all right? I don't give a shit how stoned you get, or who you sleep with—it's your life—although I have to say, I did tell your mother I'd look out for you."

"Stephanie is cool about things," Emma interrupted. "She was just a little paranoid when she talked to you. Everything's cool, I promise."

"That's neither here nor there. The point is I didn't bring you here for you to blow your voice out at some two-bit club. I don't want you singing unless you're in the studio. You've got to save your voice for the record. I'm trying to build you a career, but you've got to cooperate."

"I'm sorry Herbie. I really am. I don't know who's been telling you stuff, but all I did was sit in with some friends for a few songs last night…that's all."

"You should hear what you sound like right now—you're hoarse, and you haven't even started vocals today. It's not professional. We're not paying the studio top dollar for you to fuck up. And you better remember that it all comes out of your royalties."

The bit about it not being professional got through to her. It was hard enough being the youngest singer on the scene, but to be scolded like a child by her manager hit a raw nerve. More than anything, she wanted to be regarded as a peer by other musicians—as a professional.

"Okay, got it—no more singing at clubs, Handsome Herbie. Whatever you say goes."

"Charm will get you everywhere," Herbie replied. "And you be careful."

Emma mulled things over all day. What she really needed was someone to hang out with. Guys could get to be a drag. Maybe Carol would come stay with her.

Emma put in a call to San Francisco, told Carol she'd send her a ticket and cover her expenses if she'd come. "I've got bread coming out of my ears," Emma told her. "We'll have fun—this place is a gas."

"Hey, you're telling me—I grew up there. It's kind of cosmic—I mean, you hit this right on. Eric and I just broke up. I think he's using again…and you know, I just can't be around it. It's fucking brutal."

"So you'll come. Out of sight! It'll be like a vacation."

"Yeah, I'll come, but don't call it a vacation. I fucking hate vacations. I'll buy the ticket and you can pay me back. I need to get out of here. See you tomorrow."

Carol showed up in New York wearing a Victorian lace blouse, tight leather mini-skirt, and hand-tooled boots from Texas with big gold stars in their centers.

"Fuck, you look like you own the city!" Emma grabbed Carol and hugged her excitedly. "Come on into the mixing room. I'm so glad you're here…a familiar face…you know."

Emma offered to pay the extra charge for a two-bedroom suite at the Chelsea, but Herbie refused the money. "Whatever it takes to keep you happy," he said.

"In line, you mean," Emma said, thinking, *Dream on buddy, you don't know Carol like I do.* Carol's low, cultivated tone of voice made her seem like someone who could be relied on, and she was reliable, but Emma also knew that she could get as crazy and wasted as anyone else…and more so at times. Even Carol's looks were reassuring. She rarely wore make-up, and let her long, chestnut-colored hair fall where it would, but her high-style hippie regalia draped her body with a model's sophistication and gave her a look of being carefully put together. She had Herbie in her confidence within five minutes of meeting him. Emma had no idea what Carol had told him—she just knew that whatever it was, it worked. Herbie fell all over himself to accommodate her.

Back at the hotel room, Carol rummaged through her suitcase, pulled out a small stack of records and plunked them down on the bed. "Look what I brought with me. I think I saw a record player in the living room, didn't I?"

"Wow, Big Mama Thornton, Robert Johnson, Billie Holiday—wow, you brought Billie! Out of sight! Let's put her on and have a toast to the great lady."

Emma felt bolstered by Carol, not tied down like she did with guys. And there was absolute honesty between them. She could bounce lyrics off Carol with the assurance that her feedback would be genuine—not coming from the competitive space of whose song would make it onto the album. Carol helped her keep it together, and in return Emma paid for everything out of her album advance. While Emma worked on songs, Carol did whatever was necessary to free her to concentrate on her music.

Always having someone to be with was like a social shield for both of them. They could use each other to fend off unwanted attention, and they could get totally plastered without worrying about some psycho following them and catching them alone in the hotel. They became a regular duo on the club scene, and got a lot of attention whether they wanted it or not. The whole San Francisco "Flower Child" thing was in vogue, and they epitomized "the look" with their distinct West Coast way of dressing. Once back at the hotel, they would crack up over each other's take on the evening's events. Often they brought guys back with them.

One night, toward the end of recording, they were lounging around the hotel room. Emma got up and stretched, then turned to Carol. "When the record's wrapped, we should go on vacation, maybe to Mexico—Acapulco—wouldn't that be cool!"

Carol's face darkened. "Emma, I told you I fucking *hate* vacations. I will *never* go on another *vacation* in my life…if you want me to go somewhere with you, just call it a *trip*…or a holiday, as the English say—a holiday would be cool, yeah."

"Chill out, Carol—what the fuck! It's just a word—it's the same whatever you call it. A rose by any other name—you know…so tell me what it is…something that happened with you and your old boyfriend, Ritchie?"

"No, nothing to do with Ritchie…just my fucked-up family. We were always going on fucking vacations, and they were always a nightmare."

"Yeah, I know what you mean."

"I don't see how you could. You've got the coolest parents in the world. You have no idea how the rest of us lived."

"Ray and Stephanie aren't perfect."

"Close to it though. Let's have a shot of tequila—if I can find some lime."

"There's stuff you don't know; nobody does."

"What, you're going to tell me Ray and Stephanie are secretly total assholes beneath their hip veneer? What? You have to tell me now—come on, spill it?"

"No, it's nothing. Whatever…it wasn't their fault." Emma paused, considered telling Carol about Rob—but couldn't do it. She didn't want to see Carol's eyes cloud with pity for the poor little rape victim. Just the word, "victim", caused her stomach to curdle. "Come on, Carol, you're changing the subject. Tell me what happened on your family vacations. You've never told me anything about your family."

Carol had found a lime, and was cutting it into neat slices. "My parents are totally straight. My little brother,

Evan, is okay though. In fact, he's cool. He has problems, but he has a lot of soul."

"So?"

Carol poured double shots, and downed hers before handing one to Emma. "Here, take it with the lime and a little salt. You don't want to hear about my family. It's pretty boring shit."

"Oh, but I do. Come on, let's pull the skeletons out of the closet and dance with them."

"Okay, here's a good one—let's call it family fun in the sun in the Caribbean." Carol poured herself another shot. "This was right before I went to England. Every year we'd go to St. John; my parents have a big house on the cliffs, and for years this maid, a youngish girl, kind of pretty, would come work for us for the month—my dad was screwing her, of course, and we'd all have to act like we didn't notice. But the last vacation, the one I'm talking about, Dad insisted on bringing our new au pair, who he was screwing, too—which just flipped the maid out…she sulked around, and Mom was pissed, as usual, so you've got two pissed off women sulking around, and I just wanted to get the fuck out, you know?"

"Jesus, Carol, so that's when you split and went to live with Ritchie?" Emma thrust her glass in front of Carol. "Hey, pour me another one, too."

Carol topped off both their shots. "Yeah, but things got worse first. One night I hooked up with a local—a reggae musician—spent the night with him, and came home in the morning to find my mother already piss-rotten drunk."

"Wait just a minute—we've all been there—what's a bit of spirits for the spirit, whatever the time of day!"

"No, it's not like that, Emma. My mother gets really nasty when she drinks, and she takes all these weird prescription drugs on top of it—she's not fun, believe me."

"Sorry, I'll shut up. So did you get grounded or something for staying out all night?"

"No, that wasn't exactly my father's style. My mom, well my mom had fresh bruises on her face, so I knew they must have had a bad fight. He almost never hit her in the face…because he didn't want people to know…"

"Jesus, Carol, I'm sorry—I don't know what to say."

"I guess the maid confronted my mom, and then my mom tried to kick the au pair out, and my dad just beat the holy shit out of her. I asked her where Evan was. The au pair was supposed to be taking care of him, but she had apparently split when the fight broke out. My mom hadn't even thought about Evan—didn't know where he was." Large teardrops welled up in Carol's eyes, and she bit her lower lip. Her usually confident voice was a whisper. "Sorry, Em, I'm okay…it was a long time ago."

Emma broke into tears, and went over and held her. "It's okay baby, you don't have to say anymore…was Evan all right?"

"Yeah…no, not really. He's never been all right…because they fucked him up so bad. I found him in a goddamn closet, his pajamas soaked with pee, shivering, in spite of the heat and all the humidity—it's really hot there, you know? And I had to pick him up and get him into the bathtub before my father saw him, because my fucking father would beat him for wetting himself." Carol wiped her eyes and composed herself. "My father came back, and he caught me in the bathroom—knocked me across the room with one blow—and poor Evan was screaming for him not to hurt me. I didn't shed a tear—just got up and got Evan out of the tub, while my dad's yelling at me the whole time, calling me a whore and a slut—and that was it. I got Evan squared away, told my dad I was sorry and I'd never do it again, and then when he went down to the beach club, I took money out of his travel bag, and hit Mom up for some cash. I told her I wanted to shop in St. Thomas, and she forked out some good guilt money…and I split. I would've taken Evan with me if I could've, but there was no way."

"Christ, you've really been through it." Emma went over to the wet-bar and came back with a bottle of Perrier.

"Here, drink this, just to help the tequila go down. So, how did you meet Ritchie Brown then?"

"Dumb luck, I suppose. After St. Thomas, I just kept going…I don't know what my mom told my dad—I doubt he cared anyway. So, I was hanging out in the islands with some hip people and they took me to a party on this private little island, and Ritchie was there. I was beyond flattered when the big rock star came on to me. I was so young, and everything moved so fast. Ritchie and I hooked up, and I went back to England with him. I haven't seen my father once in all these years since then."

"Wow, that's so heavy. I don't mean to focus on the trivial, but what was it like living with Ritchie? He's more famous than God. It must have been a trip!"

"Well, yeah, it was. But you know, he was strung out on smack, and I started using with him, and I got totally strung out, too. I can't really separate him from the drug. When I think of him, it makes me want to use."

"Even after all this time? Christ, it must be heavy."

"Yeah, it is…three years, and sometimes I still want to go out and score…but don't worry, I'm not going to. Never again—I'm through with that shit. And don't you ever go near it…it's a death sentence, Emma, it really is."

"Not gonna happen. Never appealed to me. I'll stick with psychedelics, thank you—it's all about expanding your awareness…*man*." Emma laughed, and reached for her bag. "And Valium, of course, that's good, too."

"That's my mother's drug of choice."

"How's your mom doing? Do you ever see her?"

"Not very often. She's still with The Bastard—still covering for him."

"Jesus, I'm not saying another word against Ray and Stephanie again—ever."

Emma lay in bed that night trying to process Carol's story. *It's always something with everyone.* All this time she'd imagined Carol's worldly, wealthy, New York parents who were so cool that they let her go live with a rock star all the way in England when she was barely sixteen…when Emma'd had to beg Stephanie and Ray just to get them to let her come to New York, and she was older than Carol had been…and then to find out that Carol's dad beat her and that she couldn't stand her parents…well, it changed everything. Still, Carol had a lot of soul and maybe that was all part of it.

Emma thought about Ray and Stephanie, who wouldn't dream of laying a hand on her, and how they played music or painted pictures when *they* got high. Still, for all their fussing over her, the whole thing with Rob had gone right by them. Maybe it was her own fault—she should have told them. But something sickening churned in her stomach at the thought of them knowing. It would change the way they felt about her. It changed the way she felt about herself.

…

Emma's first album, *Projections*, was recorded in six weeks flat, and released in time for Christmas. Emma was happy to be home in San Francisco, where the weather was milder and the scene more laid-back.

On a beautiful, clear afternoon in early December, Carol dropped by Emma's flat, clutching a stack of newspapers and magazines. "Open the door, Emma. You're a hit. The record is a hit!" Carol came in and flopped down on the sofa. "Look at these articles; and look at Billboard—you're number one."

"I know; Herbie called me this morning. Ain't life strange!"

"Getting stranger all the time. Listen to this: *Projections is a psychedelic trip into the workings of the human heart. Emma writes about her personal journey, and we all want to be there for the voyage.* Oh, here's another one; this is great. *In the midst of these tumultuous times, Allison's songs offer a glimpse of an inner sanctum of honesty and strength. She makes us all believe again."*

"Believe in what?" Emma rolled her eyes. "It's just rock n' roll; Jesus, these people are crazy."

When *Projections* soared up the charts Emma was honestly blown away. Never having given much thought to trying to reach a large audience, she had not intentionally written hit songs. She'd taken it for granted that the hippies in the Haight would buy her record, but she hadn't realized how many hippies were spread out all over the country.

Herbie booked a long college tour for her to promote the album. She would be on the road mid-January through April. He assured her it would be first class all the way—good hotels, room service, first class seating in planes, limos, the whole rock star trip.

Suddenly, people were fussing over her as if she needed all this stuff, expected it. Hell, the trip to New York had been her first time in a plane. It threw her off balance that people treated her so differently because of the hit record—almost like they were afraid of her…as if she were a visiting dignitary rather than an old pal.

Either that, or people she barely knew acted like they were suddenly her best friends. In the midst of all the hoopla, Emma began to feel isolated. Carol was really the only friend she felt completely herself with.

Celebrating the album's success over a bottle of Dom Perignon, the two women came up with a plan. Carol would be part of the tour, work as a publicist or assistant, or something. Carol said it was fine with her because she could travel and party. For Emma, the overnight big shot, it was crucial.

Chapter Three

Emma, 1974 — Working Things Out

A few days after we met, Juan left *Las Sombras* to play lead guitar with me full time.

The recording of the album went smoothly, in spite of Bill's initial misgivings. My relationship with Juan continued as it had begun, which is to say, definitely not smoothly. The first major bump in the bliss was that singer, Clara. She showed up in the studio and made a big scene, but you know, it didn't piss me off. I felt sorry for her, and it made me angry with Juan instead. I saw the power he had over her, and it made me aware of the power he had over me—that he could dump me in the same way if he wanted to—that I would be just as devastated. It made me furious. So of course, I did what I could to put some distance between us. And I was good at that. The day after Clara's big drama scene, I put on a show of my own.

We had been in the studio all day and Juan's guitar overdubs were sounding amazing, which for some reason made me uptight. On a dinner break at the Cock & Bull on West Sunset, we ran into some of my old English buddies from the heavy metal band, *King Snake*—started throwing down Margaritas with them, and soon we were singing pub songs and getting rowdy. Juan kept saying we should get back to the studio, and I started ribbing him that he was jealous cause he didn't know the songs.

Soon, the lead singer, Jack Riggs, was rubbing my shoulders, and I pressed up against him. "Let's dance," I said. "Sure baby," Jack said, and we started in grinding against each other in the middle of that stuffy restaurant, two drunken idiots.

The straight, old waiter got all twitchy and nervous. "No dancing is allowed," he said.

I laughed. "No dancing? How about fucking?" I could feel Juan glaring at me, trying to get my attention, but I ignored him.

"Look lady," the waiter said. "You're breaking fire regulations. I don't personally care if you dance or have relations, but you're going to get me fired if you don't sit down."

"Relations? Whoa, was that an invitation?" I taunted the waiter, throwing my arm around him, trying to get him to dance. "Are you coming on to me?"

I thought I was pretty funny, and the Brits in King Snake thought so too, but Juan was obviously not amused. Grabbing my arm, he tried to get me to leave, but my buried fury from the Clara episode had come roaring out, rendering me completely insensitive to his feelings and blotting out my feelings for him. My anger always took me by surprise. It would descend like a tornado and sweep up my entire being, and I'd feel like I was in there, somewhere, observing a psycho rage out of control—from a distance, as though the fury didn't really have much to do with me. Juan quickly gave up trying to reason with me and left the restaurant.

After throwing up in the ladies room, I snagged a ride back to the Hyatt House (or the Riot House, as it was known to the bands) with the Brits, who were staying there, too. We sat around smoking joints and playing music for a couple of hours, and eventually the pot sobered me up enough to wonder where Juan was.

I called our room. No answer. Called the studio next, found out he was still there, and hightailed it over there before he could find out I was coming. Bill and Juan were in the control booth listening to takes when I walked in trying my best to act casual. They both ignored me.

"Baby, I'm sorry," I leaned over and breathed into Juan's ear. "I'm so glad you're here, baby. I love you; you know I do."

Juan said, "Where else would I be? I'm working here. Doing a job." He stood up, walked to the door, and then paused and pinned me with a look of pure disgust. "Some of us here are professionals," he said calmly, and walked out.

It was as if he had somehow intuited my Achilles heel. How could he know that accusing me of being unprofessional would upset me more than any name he could call me! It was true, of course; I wasn't being professional. But then again, rock n' roll is tricky. You have to keep it together, but being outrageous is part of the job description…yeah, part of the job description—that seemed like a good way to put it to Juan. I didn't have time to fully formulate a defense though, because Bill started in on me before I could get a word out of my mouth.

"Where the hell have you been! It's not about you disappearing whenever you feel like it, Emma. There are people who depend on you for their bread and butter. You can't just blow off a whole day like that when you've booked their time. It's about consideration. You need to grow up."

"Oh, go fuck yourself; save it for someone who cares," I said, knowing Bill wouldn't take it personally.

Rock n' roll is a juggling act, and after all the years of doing it, I was still trying to get it right. I mean, you've got to have the passion, but you can't let the passion rule, because then you end up doing despicable things—like harassing elderly waiters and making an ass of yourself. Not to mention alienating someone you love.

Yeah, I went crawling after Juan. You bet I did. The storm had passed and it was obvious even to me that my own bullshit had created the tornado. So Juan had power over me…it's not like he was Rob or something. I cried, begged him to forgive me. When we got back to the hotel room, he held me like a child while I sobbed and promised that I'd never do anything like that again.

…

The next day at the studio we had record company men to contend with. They sat there listening to the songs as if they actually liked music.

"I love the new direction," the tall one said.

"Love the Latin influence," the other one said.

"It sounds great, but…" they more or less chimed in together. I knew what was coming next. "But, don't you have any songs more like 'Taking The Streets'?"

That was the single off my last record, of course. I explained for the hundredth time that I couldn't write like that—couldn't manufacture hit songs.

"We understand that, and that's fine," they said in tandem (or at least it sounded like that to me). "But perhaps you'd consider listening to some outside material in the same vein as 'Taking The Streets'?"

Jesus, now they wanted me to record somebody's imitation of my style instead of my own music. Typical.
The day actually turned out to be really productive after the execs left. Juan and I were practically on the floor, laughing over their transparent attempts to manipulate me. When we got back to work and I put vocals on "Restless Love," the song he'd been laying guitar on the previous day, the track was suddenly there. Bill was totally stoked about it; thought it could be one of the new singles. Even if it didn't sound like the last hit song.

That night and for most of the rest of the recording, Juan and I would go back to the hotel room and order room service, then stay up all night writing songs. It seemed like all I had to do was describe what I was feeling and the lyrics came out right. I kept an electric piano in the room for writing, but it was Juan who came up with most of the chord changes, and that was fine with me. His music had all the usual rock and blues influences, but he could also put a Latin slant on his guitar playing that would make a song sound like a psychedelic bolero.

Big changes for me on this record. The ultra-personal quality to the songs Juan and I were writing together made me feel vulnerable, and I was uncomfortable with the feeling. This time around, I was writing love songs that made me feel naked. Not that I'd ever been self-conscious about being naked before, but the whole thing with Juan just made me feel dangerously exposed…didn't fit my self-image of the road-hardened rocker. After seven lunatic years in rock n' roll…after surviving fuck-head Rob, I considered myself pretty jaded. But with Juan I was tender, as green as a spring meadow, my heart about as hard as the cloud of marijuana smoke that hovered over our hotel room—as constant, too. And I don't mean that facetiously. We were constantly stoned. Juan loved pot. I liked it okay, but my drug of choice was alcohol. Juan would become more reflective, quieter in the wee hours. I'd be drinking, and getting progressively more emotional as the night wore on. By about four a.m., we'd be burned out on song writing, have burned each other up with our lovemaking, and Juan would be ready to fall asleep. Not me; fuck no—I'd still be drinking, wanting to process our relationship. Luckily for Juan, I'd usually pass out some time around dawn.

Toward the end of the recording, we got the single, the title track, "Close To Your Heart." We'd had an intense day in the studio, and had gone to the Old World Café that night to celebrate our seven-week anniversary. Yeah, we had our bad moments, but the feeling between us was strong and our relationship was still a mutual wonder.

Living at the Hyatt House with Juan, cooped up in a one-bedroom suite with a balcony, high above Sunset, the boulevard of the stars, in the city of dream-spinners, I was happy.

We hadn't worked on songs that night…came back from the café and fell into lovemaking the minute we hit the room. Later, I watched Juan sleeping, admiring his face…the creamy tan of his skin, its color and texture, his dark eyelashes as they fluttered in his private dream world. I wondered what he was dreaming. It was only two a.m. and I couldn't sleep, so I got up and made myself a cup of Mu tea, then started scratching out words on hotel stationary.

Close To Your Heart
Feel my life overflowing,
Seems like this feeling, just can't be right
The streets of the city are flowing, with misery
And I'm feeling you through the night,
Make my life bright, make my life bright
When love comes calling, you get only one shot
Better grab it and hold it, or you'll lose all you've got
So close to your heart
We'll never part
You pulled me out, out of this world
Right into your heart
Now I can see
Where I want to be
So close to your heart
I can remember trying to hold on
When all my light was so far gone

Wrestling with darkness, always losing the fight
When morning seemed, like something I dreamed
The stars still gleamed, the moon still beamed
But I was alone, and its light was so cold
Feeling so afraid and no one to hold
So close to your heart...
(Repeat chorus)

I got so excited about the lyrics that I woke Juan up to help me write the music. He kept glancing up at me as he read the words, his eyes gleaming emerald.

"I got it," he said, grabbing his guitar. He came up with blues chords that fit the words perfectly—just like that. It was one of those songs that wrote itself. I found the right melody, and we had the song ready for the studio the next morning.

Bill's right eyebrow was raised in skeptical amusement when Juan and I launched into the song first thing, but his expression changed after the first couple of lines. When we finished, he smiled. "This song is what makes it all worthwhile—why I put up with all your bullshit, Emma."

"It's really goddamn big of you to say that, Bill." I replied. "But this one came from me and Juan. He should get credit for some of the shit, too, don't you think."

Bill shrugged. "Credit where credit is due, baby. The chord changes are pretty standard, but they work."

I glanced over at Juan who was lighting a joint. He didn't say anything, but he was bristling, so I turned back to Bill. "Yeah, of course Bill, it's all been done before, right? It's how you put it together that makes it unique. Juan's got a killer approach to blues."

Bill picked up the phone. "I'm sure he does. What do you say we get Nicky Tilden in to do keyboards on this one?"

"Right-on. He's the best!"

Gary, the second engineer, showed up with coffee. “I heard the tail end of a new song from the other room. “Sounds awesome, man,” he said to Juan.

Juan smiled. “Not too much like anything else, I hope?”

“No, not at all. Why?” He glanced from Juan to Bill, then dropped his gaze and began fiddling with the soundboard.

The session guys arrived, Nicky showed up that afternoon, and we worked a sixteen-hour day. When we got back to the Hyatt, Juan and I fell into bed in a stupor. Buzzed, we made it into the studio on time the next day. I put the vocals on, and we brought in some back-up singers who were flat-out pros. And then Bill did a rough mix so we could hear it.

Bill broke the silence that followed the song, “Let’s get those company assholes back in here and play them this one. Then see if they want a ‘Taking The Streets’ imitation.”

A few weeks later the recording was finished and we were working on mixes. We were listening to playbacks and suddenly the mutual resentments Bill and Juan had been harboring came screaming to the surface.

Juan stood up, threw his cigarette down on the carpet and turned to Bill, glaring. “The guitar is way too low.”

Bill returned Juan’s glare. “Excuse me?”

“I said…my guitar lines are buried in the mixes. Perhaps if you’d written the music, you’d have noticed that the guitar lines are necessary to flesh out the melody.”

Bill lost it and started yelling at Juan, “Who do you think you’re talking to! Buried your guitar? What do you know? How many albums have you made? You ever been in a real studio before? Just because you’re fucking Emma doesn’t mean you know shit about recording. You’re out of your league here, so just stay the fuck out of my mixes.”

"You stay the fuck out of my business," I chimed in, jumping into the fray. "You can't talk to Juan like that, you asshole."

"I can defend myself, Emma. Just stay out of it," Juan said.

"Fuck you both," I yelled, and stormed out of the room. Stalked over to the studio kitchen for a drink, where I ran into Nicky who'd just finished a session next door.

"Do you want to go get a drink?" he asked me.

"Yeah, sure, why not." I was thinking I'd only be gone an hour and it would give Juan and Bill a chance to settle down. Well, it turned out that Nicky liked to drink as much as I did, and that one hour stretched into a whole evening of hanging out in a bar on La Cienega, shooting pool, shooting the shit, and getting ripped.

I stumbled back into our hotel room at closing time, a little after two a.m. I figured Juan wouldn't be too pissed because it wasn't like I was out fucking somebody. You know, I didn't so much as kiss Nicky, not that he didn't want to. We just hung out.

Juan wasn't there.

I hated that about him—that instead of fighting, he'd withdraw. It left me feeling frantic and hopeless. Angry, too. I had all this energy and no way to vent it, so I went and knocked on the door of one of the Brits. A groupie opened the door, but when Alex heard my voice, he shouted for her to let me in. I smoked some dope with them and ended up passing out on their bed.

It was late afternoon by the time I awoke the next day. I threw myself off the bed and rushed back to our room. Juan still wasn't there. I called Bill over at the studio to see if he knew where Juan was and he said, "I think he went back to El Salvador."

A knot of panic arose from my stomach and began to choke me, until Bill started laughing. "He's here in the studio helping me mix, stupid. Some of us are professionals." I could take that from Bill.

Juan hadn't split. I was so relieved that I promised myself I would definitely start cooling it with the drinking. Feeling like I'd been given a second chance, okay, more like a twentieth chance, I resolved to make it up to Juan, to stop blowing him away with my crazy episodes. I'd get my act together—be more considerate, and let him know where I was and stuff. And I'd quit flirting with other guys. I'd show him how much I loved him. Just staying reasonably sober was half the battle. Juan went for it.

A few days later, he asked me to marry him.

"I want to protect you, take care of you, *corazoncito*," Juan said, as he kissed my face, my neck, my arms, my hands.

I was so taken aback that I froze, and just stared at him. Marriage was a novel concept…and I sure as hell could take care of myself. But it didn't take me long to arrive at an answer.

"Okay, I'll marry you." Suddenly I knew that it was exactly what I wanted, with no reservations.

Chapter Four

Juan & Emma – 1974

They set the wedding date for Thanksgiving Day weekend. Emma wanted to get married in Hawaii, on her favorite island, Maui. Juan said he'd never been there, but it sounded fine to him.

Coming up with a reasonably sized guest list for the wedding was proving challenging. They lay sprawled on their king-size bed in Emma's home in San Francisco, pouring over the names Stephanie had submitted, trying to narrow the list down.

Emma finally threw the list on the floor. "This is fucking impossible. We'd have to rent a really big place, and I mean *big*."

"So, we'll do it—whatever you want, *reina.*" Juan leaned over, picked the list up from the floor and laid it neatly on the nightstand. He smoothed back Emma's hair and began massaging her neck. "I definitely think we should invite everyone that Ray and Stephanie requested. They're such cool people…in a sense, they embody everything good about America."

"I'm glad you like them, but Christ, don't go overboard." Emma rolled over to her side of the bed, practically curling into fetal position. The bitterness of Rob washed over her, but she struggled to shake it off. Rallying, she turned back to Juan. "I'm looking forward to meeting your family, baby. Who do you look like, your mom or your dad?"

"You'll meet them after we're married—you can decide then."

"You're kidding, right? You're not going to invite your own parents to our wedding? Unreal."

Juan lit a cigarette, and passed it to Emma. "You think so because you don't know them. They are extremely negative people. I do *not* want to deal with them on our wedding day."

"Jesus Juan, that's heavy." Emma inhaled the cigarette smoke, watching Juan intently. "Obviously, you hate them. But why?"

"I didn't say I hate them; I don't hate them. It's more that I don't respect them…and I refuse to live the life they expect of me."

"So, it's because they try to control your life, and you don't respect them…but what specifically don't you respect? I'm missing something here."

Juan got up and began pacing back and forth. "Their values, Emma. It's difficult to explain concisely."

"I'm not going anywhere; why don't you try?"

"I don't like to talk about it, but my family is part of the oligarchy…"

"Wait a minute—the what?"

"Oligarchy is the term used for the elite few who own most of the land and wealth in El Salvador." Juan paused a moment; his face had gone colorless. He looked out the window and around the room, then dropped his eyes to the bedspread. "The injustice is staggering," he said in a low voice. "I didn't always see it, but it was always there. When I've tried to talk to my parents about our way of life, they say that I have been influenced by communists. It's impossible to talk to them."

"Well, they couldn't be that bad—they raised you."

Juan didn't smile. "They're not all bad, of course not. They have always treated me well—but I am not like them." Juan's voice dropped even lower, and began trailing off. "Their way of thinking is dangerously outdated…and I don't want to be part of the problem when it comes to a head."

Emma sat up in bed, fluffing the pillows around her. "Don't be so serious, baby—let's invite them anyway. Good or bad, they're still your flesh and blood. I'll help you entertain them. They'll have fun. It'll be cool."

"No, it would *not* be cool." Juan sounded alarmed. "Believe me, it would be a disaster. They would somehow manage to ruin our wedding day."

"Now wait a minute, nobody has that much power. You just think they do because they're your parents. Everybody has issues with their family."

"*Issues*—that's a rather euphemistic way to phrase it. My 'issue' with my parents is their absolutist mentality." Juan sat down on the bed and looked into Emma's eyes. "What I'm trying to say is that nothing we could do would please them. Everything we've done, everything we've created as a couple would be criticized. My father and mother are accustomed to absolute authority." He sighed deeply and crossed his arms over his chest. "All my life they've tried to control me—they control everyone in their sphere…" His voice trailed off and he fell silent. The silence sat between them for a few minutes, until suddenly he reached over and pulled Emma into his arms. "No matter how hard they try to bend me to their will, I slip away and follow my own destiny—and you, *amorcito*, are my destiny."

Emma jerked out of his arms. "I get it, now I get the picture…they wouldn't want you to marry me. That's what this is really about." Her voice went up a decibel. "Why don't you just come right out and admit that you're embarrassed by me—that you think I'm too fucking crazy for your proper, uptight family."

"I assure you that it is exactly the opposite. I'm embarrassed by my parents—you can't imagine what they're like, Emma—you have no idea."

"So why don't you tell me!"

"I don't like to think about them. When you focus on someone or something, you give it your energy."

"What kind of crap is that? We already have energy invested—plenty of energy. You can't just ignore it."

"What can I not ignore? We're arguing over something that has no reality."

"Your parents have no reality? Right-on, Juan—that's brilliant."

"My parents have their own reality, but the hypothetical situation we've been examining has no basis in reality."

"It has plenty of basis, and you can't fucking intellectualize it away. It's just like when we're in a fight—you think walking away solves everything—you think not talking about your family means they don't exist for you. And I thought I was the biggest bullshit artist!"

"I have upset you. I apologize; I'm so sorry. I have no desire to argue…I don't mean to be evasive. Of course they exist…it's only my own understanding of my parents that eludes me."

The sadness in Juan's voice softened Emma. "I'm sorry, too. I'm only trying to help. Regardless of what you might think, Ray and Stephanie aren't perfect either—but it doesn't mean I don't want them in my life. Your parents will come around when they see how happy we are."

Juan smiled. "Yes, of course they will. After we're married, they will accept you. They're Catholic. Marriage is sacred. And they will come to love you, once you are family."

"I'm not so sure about that. Honestly, I think they're going to be pissed off at me forever if they don't get invited to our wedding."

"You're the most hard-headed woman that ever lived! Don't you understand that they couldn't approve our marriage? It would challenge their authority in front of my siblings. Emma, you need to trust me. They will not bend on this. The social structure in my country is like steel. It's not penetrable or negotiable."

Emma wrapped her leg around Juan, climbed on top of him, and pinned his arms. "Penetrable? I know a thing or two about penetrable. But what else haven't you told me? Tell me; tell me everything about you—now, this minute. I want dirt. I'm not marrying some nefarious stranger with a hidden past—give me all the gory details—I demand it." She leaned over and breathed into his ear, "No holding back anything."

"But if I tell you everything about myself, you'll be bored within the hour—I promise."

"Never, you're never boring."

"But that is because I have spared you the details of my tortured childhood." Juan smiled wryly. "And I am your most willing prisoner here, so your powers of persuasion through force are severely limited. I suggest we switch to a more primal form of communication," he said, and pulled her down to him.

"Oh no you don't." Emma sat upright. "First, you talk to me. I want to know more about your past."

"Very well…I'll consent to a story if you'll light me a joint."

"Deal." Emma reached for the stash box and rolled a joint. She gave Juan a toke, then took one herself. "If I let you up, do you promise to cooperate? No retreating into the mysterious landscape of your unconscious, stoned or not. Promise, or I won't let you up."

"You drive a hard bargain, but I agree to your terms. I think I'll tell you about Cheryl." Juan took a few more tokes of the joint, then got up and paced around the room.

"Now wait a minute. I don't know if I can handle a Cheryl."

"You asked for it."

"I'm kidding—tell me about Cheryl. Believe me, with my history I'm in no position to object to anything."

Juan lit a cigarette, smoked one after the other as he told Emma about his freshman year at Brown University. "My big wake-up call came in World History class. We had just started the section on Central America, and the term "Banana Republic" was being bandied around the classroom. The discussion became very lively; at some point everyone in the class turned to me for an insider's perspective of the socio-political climate in El Salvador. I tried to explain that it was the responsibility of the families, the oligarchy, to keep law and order and prevent the communists from taking over. This gorgeous girl, Cheryl, laughed out-loud at my explanation. All those pretty, intellectual girls who had been flirting with me since I'd arrived on campus suddenly looked at me as if I were crazy."

"Wait a minute," Emma said. "How gorgeous was Gorgeous Cheryl? I don't like the direction of this story."

"Consider it finished then."

"No, I'm kidding—Jesus, Juan, you need to lighten up. What happened with Cheryl? I know—you fucked her brains out and she fell madly in love with you."

"Actually, you're not far off, but not precisely in that sequence. First, in front of the entire class she said that maybe I could peddle that 'fighting the communists' shit from my obvious place of privilege in El Salvador, but that I shouldn't try to sell it here—in the States, that is. And then I fucked her brains out that night."

"Of course you did…so, carry on."

"We got very stoned afterwards, and I started thinking about what she had said in class. It was extremely rude, and I became angry at her."

"After you fucked her, I notice."

"That's beside the point. Do you want to hear the rest of this story or not?"

"Of course I do, baby. So, what did she do when you turned psycho on her? I've never seen you turn psycho, by the way."

"I didn't say I turned psycho, Emma, although you may bring it out in me yet. Cheryl reacted calmly to my angry words and told me that I shouldn't take things so hard—that her position was just as hypocritical as mine because she was going to college on 'blood money'—money from her father who was part of the military-industrial complex that was, in her words 'fucking up the world.' She had very strong opinions."

Emma smiled, "Don't start making me jealous now."

"She didn't compare to you, not in any way."

"Yeah, right. So, what were her 'strong opinions'?"

"Not all that memorable, but she did turn me on to meditation. She told me about how the yogis teach that we should retreat from the world and work to change our inner selves, that we must go within to find peace."

"Sounds like someone I know," Emma said pointedly.

"Yes, now perhaps…but it was a new concept to me at the time. I felt that she was simplifying my predicament. It was fine for her to talk about retreating from the world—her family didn't have to live behind high, protective walls, so how could she understand. I told her that you Americans, with your large middle-class, couldn't possibly grasp the situation in developing nations. You have never seen real poverty."

"You had a good point. What did she say?"

"That she had traveled in India, and India is poor, too—that I should read Yogananda. She gave me the little blue copy of Metaphysical Meditations."

"I might have known that came from a girl."

"It's not because of Cheryl that I treasure it. Our relationship was over in a matter of months, but as you know, Paramahansa Yogananda found a place in my soul. I read Autobiography of a Yogi numerous times, and I tried to learn to meditate." Juan's eyes took on a far away look. "I concentrated on music, and gave up trying to defend my family or my country." His voice dropped to a whisper. "I tried instead to find peace within."

"And you think you succeeded?"

Juan met Emma's eyes. His tone was somber. "The only peace I've ever felt, personally, has been when I'm playing music. It's the ultimate form of meditation because you don't have to try to turn your thoughts off. It's as if the music has a consciousness of its own…and it doesn't have to explain itself to anyone. I know you understand."

"Yeah, right-on. Peace is not something you can find by seeking it. It might come to you, but if you go searching for it, it hides…or in my case, it heads for the hills…no, I'm kidding…I feel peaceful with you, baby, I do—like I'm where I'm supposed to be."

"You are wise, Emma."

"No one has ever accused me of that before."

…

The record company wanted Emma to go on tour in November to promote the record, and accused her of being irresponsible when she refused. They hashed it out, Emma arguing that she was burned out, needed a rest, the record guys arguing that she'd miss Christmas sales if she didn't do a fall college tour. When she finally broke down and told them she was getting married, they were mollified by images of the publicity her marriage would generate, and ended up offering to pay for the wedding in exchange for allowing important members of the press to attend.

"I don't need your goddamn money," Emma told them. "I can pay for my wedding myself. Jesus, we're not talking about a sideshow here. It's my *wedding*, for Christ sake."

"It would be a gift," the exec assured her. "All we ask is that you include a few members of the press on your guest list, and some of our people, naturally."

When Emma brought the argument to Juan, he cooled her out. "You think I don't know about business obligations and social obligations? In El Salvador, you can't separate them. Whatever we need to do, we'll do. We'll invite whomever we have to. It will be perfect. Then when it's over, when the guests leave, we'll marry each other in private. We will immerse ourselves in the tropical waters and whisper our vows with only Mother Nature as our witness."

Juan had a way of putting things.

Again, Emma and Juan went over the guest list. Since the record company was going to turn it into a spectacle anyway, they decided to go for broke and invite everyone on Stephanie's list, as well as all their own friends. There would be paid tickets to Hawaii for anyone who couldn't afford the trip, including the session musicians who had played on *Close To Your Heart*, the members of *Las Sombras*, and a bunch of their artist friends from Venice Beach and the Haight. Everyone was invited, except Juan's family—Emma couldn't talk him into it, no matter how hard she tried. It looked like half of California and a good portion of New York was going to descend on Maui for the wedding—or at least about four hundred freaks. Emma held the record company to their part of the deal—ordered expensive wines and champagne, lobster, oysters, and anything else she could think of for the reception—and put it all on their tab.

"They wanted a big bash, they'll get one," she told Juan.

She booked her favorite resort hotel in Kaanapali for the long wedding weekend, reserved all the rooms, and told them to charge it to the record company. The ceremony would be held under the stars on the hotel's lanai, surrounded by manicured gardens and overlooking a private beach.

Juan and Emma arrived in Maui a week before the wedding to take care of last minute details. During the plane ride Emma said to Juan, "It's paradise, it really is; just wait and see. Oahu is beautiful, but Maui is paradise. When you get off the plane, the first thing you'll notice is the fragrance. The trade winds carry the scent of plumeria. It's intoxicating, as if the scent is embracing you. You fall in love with the island immediately. And some of the best people in the world live there."

Emma watched Juan take his first breath in the small, outdoor airport in Maui, hoping that he would be as blown away as she always was. Far from any continents, the Hawaiian Islands were isolated—pristine, in spite of the airports and high-rise hotels. Emma felt the ocean in the air she breathed, in the sensual salt taste—heard the constant breaking of the waves through her bones.

Juan drew Emma in for a kiss. "You did not exaggerate, not even a little. It is as you described. Nothing at all like the tropics of my birthplace."

The next day, Emma took Juan to her favorite spot on earth, Hana. Located on the far side of the island, Hana could only be reached by driving forever on a twisty, shoreline road full of potholes. Around each bend on the left side of the road, the ocean changed moods, crashing giant waves on boulders one minute, lapping gently at white sand beaches in hidden coves the next. On the right, rainforest that sloped all the way down to the sea glistened brilliant shades of green, parting periodically to reveal waterfalls and deep, freshwater pools.

Emma knew which pool she wanted to stop at—one she had never shared with anyone before. They drove by it once before she realized they were there.

"Stop, pull over, this is it."

Juan backed the car into a small dirt space and turned off the motor. They heard the waterfall before they could see it. Following a narrow path lined with wide-leafed palms and wild orchids, they made their way down to the pool. Silently, they slipped out of their shorts and t-shirts, and dove into the clear, cool water. Afterward, they lay in the shade, drying off in the thick jungle heat.

"I feel like Adam, with Eve in the Garden of Eden," Juan said, reaching for Emma.

"Oh God, you'd never say that, baby, if you knew my associations with that image when I first met you."

"I don't understand."

"The first night we made love, and you got so pissed off at me—I guess I was sort of afraid of you, and it was tied in with the Adam and Eve myth."

Juan laughed. "You were afraid of me? That *amorcito*, is hilarious. You were the dangerous one. I feared it would be a disaster to fall in love with you, that you would break my heart into a million pieces…but I found the challenge irresistible."

"So, that's what I am to you—a challenge."

"No, there is no contest. I surrendered to you even as you spurned me. You are the conqueror."

"Fucking liar." Emma laughed and pushed him away. "You left me, after seducing me with your Latin charm—just took off into the night…where did you go that night anyway?"

"Nowhere. I just walked for hours—hung out in a coffee shop on Sunset trying to figure out what hit me. You made me feel like a fool, as if I had misinterpreted our lovemaking. I was feeling so much love for you, and you, my wicked queen, who acted as if you had no feelings, now try to tell me that *you* were scared of *me*. Very amusing."

"No, it's true. I chased you away because I was afraid. And when you showed up at my door that next morning, I knew I loved you. Anyway, *you're* the distant one. I'm easy to read—you always know where you are with me, good or bad."

Abruptly, Juan sat up and pulled his knees to his chest. "I wish that were true. Seriously, sometimes I upset you, and I have no idea what I've done. One minute you are witty and happy, and then suddenly you are angry, and drinking too much, and I can't reach you. I don't know what to do, so I do nothing. You must tell me what you need. How can I protect you if I don't know what is threatening you?"

"I sure as shit don't need to be protected. That's your macho thing again. You're not expecting me to turn into some little 1950's housewife because we're getting married, are you? And don't you dare clam up on me now, after saying what *you* wanted to say!"

"No, I don't want you to ever change. I want you to stay exactly as you are now, naked and beautiful, and imminently desirable."

"You're changing the subject again. Stop it, don't touch me." Emma laughed in spite of herself, brushing off Juan's caresses. When her laughter subsided, she leaned toward him and murmured, "Okay, change the subject, if you're going to be like that."

...

They arrived in Hana by moonlight. Emma was a well-known patron at the one resort hotel in town, and people came out of the woodwork to welcome her back.
Margie Kaula, the hotel manager, embraced Emma first. With tears in their eyes, the old friends congratulated each other on how well they looked, Emma exclaiming how good Margie's hair looked again, how full.

"Yeah, the cancer couldn't kill me, but the chemo made me wish it did. Look how skinny I am, like a *haole,* like you, all bones, hey. But you look good. How come you stayed away so long? We missed you." Margie turned her attention to Juan, grabbed him into her massive embrace. Margie was as tall as Juan, and even in her present, supposedly emaciated condition, she still easily outweighed him. "You treat Emma right, okay," she said, stepping back to allow the others a chance to check him out.

Bob, who ran the surf shop, was next to hug Emma and shake hands with Juan. Alana, who made the hotel's leis, stepped forward and threw ropes of the fragrant necklaces around Juan and Emma's necks. Then a jumble of people, hotel employees and other locals who must have heard over at the general store that Emma was on her way, welcomed them. Dinner hour was long over, but never mind. Sonny, the assistant chef who was also a musician, had put aside some food for them. The entire greeting party had been invited to the wedding, and everybody wanted to know if it was okay to bring a few guests.

Sonny said, "Remember you went to the waterfall on my Aunt Nell's place—the pool by the ocean that has the underwater cave and the island in the middle. When you were hiding out here a few years ago, remember? She remembers you and she's down for the drive to the other side. Gotta pick up some stuff in Lahina anyway. Oh yeah, and my cousin, Kapena, who took you to Red Sands Beach, he wants to come, too."

It looked like half of Maui was going to be at their wedding. Emma felt a special pleasure that Aunt Nell wanted to come. In an unexplainable way, that woman whom she barely knew had once helped her find her way back to the land of the living.

Juan and Emma dined in their cabin on the beach, listening to the Pacific waves break gentle that night, listening to old friends play Hawaiian music and sing Beatles songs. Later, just as Juan was drifting into sleep, Emma said, “I wish Carol could be there, too.”

“Be where?” Juan said drowsily. “Who’s Carol?”

Chapter Five

Emma, 1974, Road Stories

Who was Carol? Now that's a complicated question. I wonder which version I should give Juan. The funny, capable, totally hip, best friend I ever had version, or the stoned-out junkie one. Both are accurate descriptions, different sides of the same coin; I know that now. But I hate the word "junkie." It's just such a fucking abstraction. Like looking at one thing about a person and mistaking it for the whole picture. But on the other hand, calling a junkie a junkie is like calling a giraffe a giraffe. When you're strung out, the drug takes over. Heroin is dominant. It defines you, even if you swear it won't. No matter what else there is about you, the addiction always gets the upper hand.

Things were good for us, that first year on the road. Carol had become my publicist—no previous experience, just winging it, and she was mind-blowing. Who wouldn't want to talk to her! She had the same way with the press that she did with the band and everyone. She could always lighten things up—could have the most-full of themselves rock journalists cracking up, forgetting to be so critical, so unimpressed. Every other night we'd be in a new town, with new important people backstage we were supposed to be nice to so they'd give the show a good review. If some guy thought you ignored him, or didn't appreciate his importance, God help you. You'd read it in the paper the next day how shitty you sounded, how untalented you are, how your album is a disaster, how you've lost your magic for good. It could be brutal. So I learned to follow Carol's cues. She could remember everyone's names as if they were wearing nametags. It was fucking amazing.

She'd give me little hints. "You remember the really great radio interview you did by phone with Marvin yesterday? Well, this is Marvin. Marvin, meet Emma Allison. She loves your show."

I was lucky I could afford to do one night on, one night off tours right off the bat because of the success of *Projections.* It saved me from completely burning out my vocal cords, for one thing. With bands that shared vocals, a night between shows wasn't that important. Those singers took turns in concert, got to rest between songs. Not me. I was singing constantly at first. Didn't have a clue what I was doing to my throat. But by the end of the tour, I had learned to encourage the boys to take really long solos. In the middle of the set, Roger would play a killer ten-minute bass solo that would bring the audience to their feet, screaming. Meanwhile, I could slip backstage and go to the bathroom, have a drink and a cigarette. Toward the end of the set, before the encore, Jack would take an extended drum solo that would give me another break.

We were doing long sets back then, at least three hours, often longer. Sometimes I'd have run out of material by the third encore and would have to resort to cover tunes. It didn't matter. Those musicians could play anything at the drop of a hat. Herbie was right about that. They were better musicians than the guys in Altered States, and on top of that, it was my band—I was running the show. On the down side, the new guys were all from L.A. and New York, and they didn't have that San Francisco sensibility, that particular kind of craziness I was comfortable with.

Not that they weren't crazy in their own right. For one thing, they thought it was hip to smash up hotel furniture, and I just couldn't see how that was groovy. It was too violent, and besides, I had to pay for it. One night in Durham, Jack threw a TV off a fourteen-story balcony. He was just fucking lucky it didn't hit anyone.

For another thing, these guys liked different drugs than I was used to. None of them liked psychedelics. In *Altered States*, we used to all drop acid together, and even though we were competitive and fought and stuff, there was still that shared experience in a place outside our individual egos. There is no denying that LSD does expand your consciousness…either that, or make you fucking nuts—maybe both. But for most of us, it broke down our ego barriers, made us a little kinder.

No acid for the guys in my band on the first tour, though. They were into hard drugs: meth, cocaine, downers. We'd get wasted together, fuck around with each other, and fuck each other, too, but we never got close. That meth energy especially drove me crazy. Jack and Ron could rap for hours, going on and on about nothing, each one thinking he was Einstein or something. Carol and I got where we would just split as soon as they'd start in. We'd go hang out in the hotel bar, find some other guys to pass the time with—maybe the night with.

To round out that tour, there was Gene, the rhythm guitar player, who was into twelve-year-olds. The guys liked to say that those girls were twelve going on twenty, but I could see that in spite of their make-up and sexy clothes, they were just twelve—stupid, like I was at that age, and even younger than I'd been when all the shit happened with Rob. It's not like I thought of the girls as victims—I hate that victim mentality. It implies that girls are basically powerless, and the truth is that those girls went with Gene of their own free will, like I did with Rob—after the first time, that is. Whatever the reason, I couldn't handle Gene's trip.

Carol and I were fucking guys left, right, and center on that tour, and the guys in the band had a choice of gorgeous groupies at every show, so it wasn't like I had anything against anybody getting laid. But it was different with those young girls. Gene was openly contemptuous of them, as though it were their fault that he was attracted to them. Carol and I both wondered if he might be actually physically harming them—doing some weird sadist shit or something. We didn't know what to do though. There was always a "do your own thing" philosophy on the road, and even if you suspected something like we did, what were we supposed to do, call the cops? Yeah, right!

Things came to a head after a show in Boulder. A father came pounding on my road manager's door at around 3 a.m.

Ed gave us all a blow-by-blow account of the scene. This guy was shouting to the top of his lungs, calling us all degenerate bastards and insisting that his daughter was in the room. He told Ed that one of his daughter's friends had seen her and her friend leave with our guitar player, and that if Ed didn't open the door immediately, he'd get the police to break it down. Ed said the old guy was completely losing it, threatening to have all us longhaired, filthy hippies thrown in jail—pounding on the door and yelling, "She's thirteen, and Cindy is twelve! I know you've got them in there."

Fucking Gene! Of course they were twelve and thirteen. We should have let him go to jail.

Ed said he scrambled to open the door, and attempted to calm the guy down—and if anybody could, it would be Ed. He said he acted ultra respectful, calling the guy "sir", and everything—told him that as the road manager, it was his responsibility to get all the band members back to the hotel safely—that everyone left the concert in two limousines and he did a head count, so he could assure him that his daughter and her friend were not with one of the band members. Then he offered to help find the daughter—told him he'd make some calls to see if there might be some parties going on in the hotel that they could have been invited to—asked him to sit down and offered him a glass of water. Of course Ed knew where the girls must be, so he dialed Gene's room first—tipped him off that the dad was there—apologized for waking him, and asked if he might know if anybody had a party going in one of the rooms. Then he called all our rooms, asking the same questions, giving the girls a chance to sneak out of the hotel.

We were all pissed at Gene about that one, especially Ed, who threatened to quit if he had to do anything like that again. It didn't really change anything though. My one small comfort is that at least I never slept with Gene. Of course, at seventeen, I was probably too old for him anyway. And Carol never fucked Gene either. He was a great musician, but a creepy son of a bitch, and I had Herbie fire him at the end of that tour. But all these years later, I still feel bad that I didn't do anything to stop him at the time. There's not much I regret, because, you know, it's all about learning through your mistakes. But fuck, I regret not putting the bastard away where he couldn't hurt any more little girls.

"You're gonna live with regret—and it's gonna give you the blues—Maybe it ain't hit you yet—But some day you're gonna lose..." better jot this down. I can get Juan to write some chord changes tomorrow.

Funny how Carol and I were the straight ones on that first tour. All we did was smoke pot and drink—stayed away from powders and pills. The guys in the band were lunatics. Great professional musicians, but nuts. Still, except for Gene, we managed to more or less get along okay. Everybody just gave each other space, and things were cool for the most part. My lead guitar player, James Stanton, and my bass player, Roger Porter, were the best musicians in the band, and no matter how crazy they got, they were worth it. On stage they were maniacs. The audience loved them.

I couldn't believe my luck that the shows were selling out, that record sales kept rising, that we were treated like royalty wherever we went. We'd be seated in first class on a plane, weird looking freaks among businessmen, and the stewardesses would be catering to us—telling me how much they liked the record, asking Carol questions about the tour, flirting with the guys in the band. It really pissed a lot of those straight guys off, and Carol and I just cracked up about it. Well, they say that people have always loved musicians. I can't say we were all that popular at some of the hotels though—the ones where the boys trashed their rooms.

Toward the end of the tour, on April 4th, Martin Luther King, Jr. was killed. It's not like I was all that political, but it blew my mind, broke my heart, and made me furious. Growing up in the Bay Area with Ray and Stephanie, I had taken a lot of things for granted, like supporting civil rights, and being against the war in Viet Nam. There are pictures in the family album of me at a "ban the bomb" rally when I was only three. My parents were political enough that I didn't have to pay much attention to it. I found newspapers depressing, and I'd been raised to believe that it was all lies anyway. But, of course I was aware of Dr. King. He was one of the only public figures I admired. His death was like a personal loss, and it felt like the whole nation had been injured by his murder.

We were mainly playing college gyms and auditoriums, and you could feel the students' outrage at the assassination. I turned inward, wrote poetry and song lyrics. Retreated into the cocoon of my career.

The tour ended in Honolulu around the end of April. I was already back to focusing on my own trip by then, more than ready for a vacation. It was my first time in Hawaii and I was completely flashed out. Kawika showed up backstage after the show, like a godsend, and Carol and I both thought he was gorgeous, which he was.

"Why don't you come spend some time at my pad in Maui?" he asked us. "You can chill out, drink Piña Coladas all day, go snorkeling. Maybe I'll teach you to surf. What do you say, does that sound good?"

The "teach you to surf" line threw me for a loop, brought back the worst memories of my life, but I made a quick recovery. Anyway, I figured I could teach him more than he could teach me at this point in my life. Fuck it. Carol and I weren't sure which of us he was after, but we were game. Kawika Stewart's family had bought up half the island of Maui back in the Colonial days, but he was low-key hip. We spent a week at his house on a cliff overlooking the ocean, the three of us sleeping in his gigantic bed. The best thing that came out of that week, though, was meeting Dave Makai, the caretaker of Kawika's estate.

Sometimes you just click with people, and that's what happened with Dave. I was interested in the history of Hawaii and it was his favorite subject, so we spent hours exploring Maui together, him giving me the scoop about the old legends, kings and queens and spirits in the wind. Dave was about my parents' age, but he was already a grandfather. He never came on to me either. I met his wife and kids and grandkids, and just about everybody else in Maui, through him. Most of his family lived on the other side of the island, in Hana. Margie Kaula is his eldest daughter.

...

I was only home from that first trip to Hawaii a short time before I was back out on the road. The tour started on June 4th, one of the most horrible days I can remember.

Our first gig was in Minneapolis on the 5th, so we'd flown in the day before. I'd settled into a nice hotel room, ordered room service, and put on the TV. Carol dropped in with a bottle of champagne some time after midnight, and we were watching an old Jean Harlow movie at around 2:30 a.m. when an announcement interrupted the movie. Robert Kennedy had been shot at a hotel in L.A. and they didn't know if he was going to pull through. He died later that day, on June 5th. It was the end of any kind of hope I might have secretly harbored that things were going to get better through the political system.

I celebrated my eighteenth birthday, June 10th, in St. Louis. Herbie had booked us on a long, summer tour, June through the end of August. The only musicians I kept from the winter tour were James and Roger. James had suggested members of his old band from L.A. to fill in on drums, rhythm guitar, and piano. We held an audition of sorts at the end of May, and his friends sounded good to me. Herbie was pissed because he'd wanted to choose the band, but after assholes like Gene, I figured I could do better.

The band dynamic changed radically with the new guys, and continued to shift all summer. The first week out, I got into a thing with Eric, the drummer. You'd think I'd have known better even back then. Everybody but Eric and I could see disaster written all over the relationship from day one. We were crazy about each other for the first few weeks, and after that the whole thing was crazy. Without a doubt, Eric was the most jealous man I've ever met. But he was also the most experimental lover. He would get me into making love in totally unlikely places, wild sex, an unbelievable turn-on. I loved making it with him, but I soon realized that I didn't like being with him when we weren't doing it. When he wasn't being sexy, he was being a drag, nagging me about other guys all the time.

"I saw the way that guy in the front row was coming on to you, and you were playing right into it, weren't you," Eric would say. "He was thinking you'd fuck him. I know how guys think."

"Now I'm responsible for what people in the audience are *thinking*?" I'd say. "Come on baby, I'm the LEAD SINGER, for Christ sake. The guys are supposed to like me, remember?"

"Maybe, but you don't have to lead them on. You don't have to act like you want to fuck them. Or maybe you do. I could go find the guy and bring him back here. I could punch his lights out. I don't have to take your shit, Miss big-fucking shot!"

Yeah, we were a real gas to be around as a couple. We're lucky the band didn't throw us both out a hotel window. Jesus, it was just one of those road things and Eric acted like I was supposed to turn into the Virgin Mary when he wasn't around.

I broke it off around mid-tour by going back to my hotel room with an old friend of Carol's, a pot smuggler from Oklahoma who showed up at a gig in Ft. Lauderdale. Eric freaked out when I wouldn't answer my door that night. He raised a ruckus that got hotel security involved. Ed came and got him, but not before he had kicked in my door and taken a swing at my pot smuggler, blowing that romantic encounter.

From that night till the end of the tour, it was a battle of the wills between us. He seemed to think that if he were persistent enough, I'd go back with him. Every time I turned around, he was leaving me love letters and having flowers delivered to my room, telling anybody within earshot about how much he still loved me. Christ, talk about a ball and chain. Not to mention what a drag it was for the rest of the band. On stage, it was fine—he was back there on drums and I didn't have to interact with him. Off stage, we fought so much that nobody wanted to be around us. Eric vacillated between being lovesick and angry, and in both states, he was obnoxious.

Finally, Carol fucked him—just to get him off my back. We planned it so that I could walk in on them in bed together. After I "caught him" in bed with Carol, you wouldn't think he could keep raising hell about me breaking his heart, but it only slowed him down, didn't stop him. He was a bummer for the rest of the tour. To this day, he tells people that I broke his heart. Which is just utter bullshit.

But at least Eric toned it down when I took up with Al, the soundman, who was a roughneck from Oregon. Eric couldn't intimidate him, and he sure as hell couldn't have beaten him up either. That was the big attraction for me—that Al could keep Eric at a distance. Besides, Al was a lot older than me and had been through a lot of scenes on the road, so he didn't take it too seriously. I could do what I wanted again, and I went back to hanging out with Carol after the shows, drinking in the hotel bars. And snorting coke now, too.

We had three gigs in the New York area in August, and while it was a trip to be back there, you couldn't move during the day. It was too goddamn hot and muggy. Carol and I went to a movie one afternoon, and when we got back to the hotel, someone had left a message for Carol that really upset her. Usually she'd let me know what was up, but she didn't say a thing about the note. Just wadded it up, stuck it in her pocket, and announced that she had to split. I didn't get it. I knew she wasn't in love at the moment, so it couldn't be that. The only thing I could figure was that it must be some ex, or some jealous girlfriend of a guy she had fucked on the road.

I had a night on the town with some record execs and got back to my room late. There was Carol, asleep on my bed. She came to very slowly when I unlocked the door, like she was really stoned. I sat down beside her and she started crying.

"What is it, baby," I asked her. "It's okay whatever it is. We'll handle it, don't worry."

"It's my fucking brother. He's in trouble, big time."

"We can deal with it, don't worry. What is it? Tell me what happened."

"Evan got busted for dealing smack last week. He had to kick, cold turkey, in jail. He's only been out a few days and now he's already strung out again."

"So he needs money…what about your parents?"

"Our parents won't help him at all. He wants me to give him the bread for a lawyer. It's his second bust, so he could do some jail time over this, and I don't think he could handle it. He says he'll die in jail and I believe him." Carol dried her eyes, and began pacing the floor. "He never could take it. I told you what the scene was like in our house when I was growing up. Well, it was worse for Evan than me. It was like he always believed that my parents would get through it and then we'd be a happy family. Fuck. No matter how abusive our dad was to him, he'd always defend Dad—make up excuses for his behavior. Evan was sweet, you know? He really was."

"It's okay, Carol, I believe you. Tell me what he needs."

"It's not the money." Carol flopped down in a chair. "It's that I'm afraid he'll spend it on smack if I give him the money. I told him I'd give it to his lawyer direct, but he kept insisting that I had to give it to him. What does that sound like to you?"

"Oh shit, so you think he made up the bust to get money out of you?"

"No, he got busted all right. But I think he's so out of it that he thinks he can just shine it on, give the lawyer a retainer, and use the rest on his habit. He probably intends to start dealing again to get the money for the lawyer. I don't know what the fuck to do. He's my brother. I love him—no matter what."

I'd started pacing. "Okay, let's figure out what to do. We have the money to give him, so that's not the problem. We have to get him into rehab. That's the problem, right? That he doesn't want to stop?"

"I shouldn't have split on him. When I left home, my parents took everything I did out on him. And then when I moved to England with Ritchie, it was like Evan started to idolize me and what did I do? I shot up in front of him. He wouldn't be a junkie today if he didn't learn it from his goddamn big sister. It's my fault." Carol broke into sobs again.

"You don't know that, Carol." I handed her a tissue, and tried to soothe her. "You've got to give yourself a break here. We can't fix the past. Let's just concentrate on what we can do now, okay? Maybe we can bribe him into going into treatment, make the money dependent on him checking into one of those clinics. You don't think your parents would help him get clean?"

"They might pay for some rehab. I don't know. He's an embarrassment to them, so they might. But he sure as hell won't want to go."

"We'll take care of it. Let's call him."

Carol got Evan over, and we strong-armed him into going to a clinic that night. Ed took him to the place and made sure he was behind locked doors. We saved his ass all right—hired a lawyer who got him off the charges on a technicality. Carol said he was clean and sober at his hearing. Within six months, he was strung out again. Jesus. Fucking heroin. You'd think I'd have run from the drug after that experience.

Luckily, New York was one of the last dates on the tour, because Carol was pretty down after her brother's performance. I guess it's hard with families. I know I should be more understanding about Juan's trip with his parents, after seeing firsthand what Carol's fucked-up family did to her. Funny though, I always wanted a bigger family when I was little…wished I had a brother or sister.

…

Jeannette Sears

Seems like it's always something with families. There's always something fucked up. Juan is so secretive about his family, but whatever the problem is, we'll deal with it. We'll win them over. But I still think we should have invited them to the wedding.

Chapter Six

1974: The Wedding

After a few days in Hana, the sleepy little town on the rainy side of Maui, Juan told Emma he was beginning to understand why she loved the place so much. There was a general store, a snack bar at Hana Bay Beach, a small inn, and the pricey Hana Resort Hotel that offered private, individual bungalows. That was it. Not a single high-rise marred the shoreline of Hana. There were no clubs, and the only restaurant was the one in the hotel. However, dinner at the hotel was a big production number—a luau, complete with a roasted pig and live Hawaiian music.

After dinner, Margie and some of the other staff would put on a dance show. They would explain the origins of the various dances, and translate the graceful sign language of the hula for their guests. The Tahitian was the wildest dance, featuring all three hundred and fifty pounds of Margie shaking it up full tilt along with the younger, slimmer girls. Seeing people of all ages and sizes dancing together, vividly illustrated the original nature of the dance as a village activity. The show was for the tourists, the hotel guests, but Margie said it was also a means of preserving traditional Hawaiian culture.

The luaus were a time of sharing and Emma would usually join in, singing a couple of standards along with the band. One night she and Sonny did a version of "The Hawaiian Wedding Song." She had meant it to be campy, but when Juan's eyes met hers, it turned into a sincere rendition. Emma barely recognized herself with the last vestiges of her cynicism rubbing away. She and Juan were polishing each other smooth, like the pebbles washed in from the ocean.

The space between them, however, was almost visibly filled with electricity. Emma felt sure that she and Juan were shooting off sparks as they combed the beaches, hiked through tropical rainforests, and dove off rocks into the Seven Sacred Pools. They communicated without talking as they sunned themselves on gravelly beaches. Their time in Hana was a window of peace before the whirlwind of last minute preparations, the roar of four hundred-plus guests. Content just to silently share the joy of being together in such beauty, their honeymoon began before their wedding.

Back in Kaanapali, a gang of their friends had arrived a few days early to soak up the sunshine, so the party began before their wedding, too. The surge of electricity that greeted them left Juan and Emma a little shell-shocked after the relative solitude and laid back atmosphere of Hana. Emma was thankful she had hired her assistant publicist, Christina, to organize the wedding. Arriving in Kaanapali late by Hawaiian standards, around 1 a.m., Juan and Emma were greeted by one friend after another. They found themselves poolside with champagne before they even made it to their room. When Christina got word they were back, she came down and pulled Emma aside for a private chat.

"Listen Emma, a lot of these people showed up days before they were booked, and signed in on your tab. I don't think the label will cover for the extra days. What do you want me to do about it? I can't believe how greedy people are, after your generosity, to take advantage of it like that."

"Don't worry about it. Just put the extra days on a separate tab and I'll cover it. All these 'people' are our friends. Give them whatever they want."

"I don't think that's a good idea. They're already running up big bar and room service tabs, signing for everything. It's going to be expensive."

"Don't sweat it."

"You shouldn't have to pay for it. They're taking advantage of you, Emma."

"Jesus, Christina, it's my money. Give me a break. It's not your business."

Christina sat back and crossed her arms over her body in a rigid lock. "It's just not right."

"Look, a lot of these people haven't had a holiday in years. They're amazing artists, but they don't make any money. It's the same old story. A wedding is supposed to be a party for your friends, and the label is picking up what I would have spent anyway. So relax, have a Piña Colada, get laid for Christ sake. Whatever. End of discussion. What about my parents, have they arrived yet?"

"No, they're coming in tomorrow. A car will meet them at one. And we've got a few problems with the menu that I think you should look at. And a bunch of people who weren't on the list have been calling here saying you invited them."

"Juan and I will go pick up my parents. We'll drive; you can cancel the car. I trust you on the menu. If it looks good to you, go for it. You're the best. It'll be great. Just order a lot of extra everything. Everybody on this island will show up with their mothers and cousins and aunts and uncles and everybody they know. It'll be fun, you'll see. They're a gas."

Christina rolled her eyes toward the heavens. "Why me?"

...

Late that night, Juan and Emma lay in bed in the Honeymoon Suite looking out at the moon nestled between two palm trees. Emma snuggled closer to Juan and realized she was smiling. "Isn't it crazy how fast your life can change. Six months ago we didn't even know each other. I, for one, didn't think I'd ever get married. I didn't think I'd come even close to ever actually being happy, as in 'happy'. You know what I mean? Like, everything was going okay. It was good, yeah, but I wasn't like this. Happy, I mean. Come on baby, say something. Bail me out here."

"Mi querida preciosa, tu eres mi vida, mi corazon. Te adoro."

“That’s not fair. I don’t get to know what you’re saying…but I do like the way you say it.” Emma stroked Juan’s arm. She admired his beautiful forearms with the slender wrists, his hands with the long, sensitive fingers. “You have to teach me Spanish. God, your parents are going to think I’m stupid. I’ll take a course. I can learn, don’t you think. How long does it take to learn?”

“If I teach you Spanish, what will you teach me?”

Emma began lightly tracing the contours of his body with her fingernails. “How about this for starters?”

…

The next day, Juan and Emma picked Ray and Stephanie up at the airport and drove them to Lahina for lunch. After they ate, they cruised the art galleries, winding up at the one that handled Stephanie’s work. Images of beaches sold well in Hawaii, even if they were renditions of Northern Californian beaches. Jazzed to see Stephanie’s work hanging in such a good gallery, they headed into the bar of the Pioneer Inn to have a drink to celebrate her success. Juan limited himself to two drinks since he was driving, and it was a good thing he did because they got back to the car to find it had been broken into. Camera and recording things gone, and the real loss, Ray’s trumpet.

Juan called the police, who weren’t particularly sympathetic. “Too bad. You shouldn’t have left your things exposed like that.”

Ray was beside himself, but Emma told him not to worry. When they got to the hotel, she made a few calls to some local friends, and shortly after dinner the trumpet was back in Ray’s possession.

Another wave of friends had arrived at the hotel the day before Thanksgiving, three days before the wedding. Emma was relieved to see that her bridesmaid, Linda, had made it from Florida.

Emma spotted her dressmaker, who was to be her maid of honor, over at the bar. “Marianne, thank God you’re here,” You’ve got to help me get through this. It’s out of control already. How did the dress turn out?”

Faced with choosing a maid of honor, Marianne had been the only person Emma could think of. She had a lot of acquaintances, but few close friends.

It should be Carol. Fucking hell, it should be Carol. Should be, could be, there's no point in going down that path; let it go...Marianne is an old friend; we have history, it's cool.

But it wasn't. A suffocating sadness erupted in Emma, wrapping her in layers of regret. She went up to the suite with Marianne and examined the exquisite wedding dress, tried it on, made jokes, and laughed over old times. But it was all a sham. *You think you've dealt with something, and then suddenly it swoops down and grabs you again, like it just happened. It was a long time ago, and now here it is again, like it was yesterday, as powerful as ever, after all this time, with my wedding so close.* A fresh sense of loss engulfed Emma, who struggled to escape. "Hey Marianne," she said, "let's go down and join everybody for a drink."

Everybody was hanging out at the poolside bar, goofing off like kids—flirting, throwing each other into the pool, and throwing down drinks. Marianne and Bill hadn't seen each other in ages, and Emma watched as they settled right into a private conversation. *Foreplay,* Emma thought, with just a slight twinge of jealousy. *They'll be up in his room within the hour*.

Emma threw herself into the crowd, searching for Juan. Some of her friends had been invited to sit in with the local band. Ray was up there on trumpet, wailing away on an Audio-Valium version of "Stormy Monday." Emma scanned the crowd continually, drinking and looking for Juan. Surrounded by friends, Emma felt alone. She was on her sixth Rum and Coke when Roger and James rescued her.

They had been there. They'd known Carol.

Grabbing a bottle of champagne each, the old band mates stumbled out to the beach. Emma thought maybe Juan was down there, by the water. There was no sign of him.

She and Roger and James began to walk. By the time they reached the rocks at the far side of the beach, all the champagne was gone, and Emma was suddenly sick—had to throw up in the sand. Her head was reeling, but the guys wouldn't let her stretch out on the beach. They towed her back to the hotel, stumbling along with her arms around their necks, and there at the edge of the sand looking for her, was Juan.

"I'll take over now," Juan told James and Roger, scooping her up and carrying her over to one of the lounge chairs, laying her down carefully.

"I was looking for you everywhere; where were you, baby?" Emma slurred.

"It didn't look to me like you were looking so hard." Juan sat down on the edge of a deck chair. "In fact, it didn't look like you were looking at all. I was with Stephanie. She was showing me slides of her paintings, and then I came out to find you and was told you'd gone down the beach with some guys who used to be in your band. It occurred to me that I might not see you tonight."

"No, it wasn't like that. They're just friends."

"Yes, but you have a history of having sex with your friends, don't you Emma. Stay here. I'll go get you some coffee."

When Juan returned with the coffee, Emma was drinking champagne and smoking a joint with some old friends who had gathered around her lounge chair.

"Hey baby, come meet some people." Emma's words were slurred. "These are my old friends…right friends? Yeah, this is Juan—I fucking love him. Come on baby, come sit with me." Juan sighed deeply, and Emma said, "Jesus, you don't have to look like it's such a chore—it isn't, is it?"

She could see that Juan didn't want to do it, but he came and sat on the edge of her chair. "Why don't we go up now, Emma?" he said. "We have a big day tomorrow. No, I don't want any champagne right now, thank you. Come on, you need some rest."

"Can we just have a minute alone?" Emma said to her friends, and the little crowd reluctantly scattered. Turning to Juan, she looped her arms around his neck and pulled herself up. "What's the matter baby?"

"Just wondering how I'm going to get through the night." Juan accepted the joint Emma offered, and inhaled deeply.

"Are you pissed off at me baby? I don't want you to be mad. I'm sorry. What did I do?"

"Nothing, Emma, it's okay. Let's get another bottle of champagne."

When they finally got back to their room that night, they both passed out. Emma wanted to tell him about Carol, but she was too exhausted and too drunk. It wasn't the right time. They fell asleep clinging to each other, like life support.

...

On Thanksgiving evening, two days before their wedding, Juan and Emma almost split up. The hotel had become a huge party scene and Juan and Emma barely saw each other all day. They were both engaged in socializing with old friends, playing the host and hostess. At dinner that night, Stephanie was evidently proposing a toast to the happy couple, expressing her thanks for the joyous occasion that had brought them all together in this beautiful place on Thanksgiving, at just about the same time as the happy couple was up in their room having the argument of the century.
Juan was pacing around the room, agitated because they were late getting downstairs for dinner. "Come on Emma, you look fine; let's go. I'm hungry, and people are waiting for us."

"They can wait; don't pressure me; it makes me fumble."

"Everyone who knows you knows that you don't mind keeping people waiting, but I'm hungry. Let's go."

Emma slammed her brush down. "What's that supposed to mean? You're such a control freak. We're supposed to go when *you're* hungry; I can't even brush my hair. You can't wait two seconds."

"Come on Emma, let's not do this. Let's just go to dinner."

"You do this deliberately, don't you? Make it seem like I'm untogether—make a federal case out of nothing. It's your way of trying to control me."

Juan turned his back on Emma. His voice was flat. "Maybe you *need* someone to control you, since you don't seem to be able to do it yourself. You were so drunk last night you wouldn't even remember it if anything happened between you and those guys."

Emma picked up her brush and threw it at Juan. "Fuck you. Don't you turn your back on me. I've been on my own since I was sixteen, making my own money, controlling my own life. I'm not the one who lives off my parents, am I! Who are you to criticize me? Who makes the money anyway? I was famous before you met me. It's my music that makes it all happen. You can't tell me how to behave, with your narrow, little view of morality. Fuck you."

Juan turned around to face her. His jaw was clenched and he spoke through his teeth. "So that's how it really is. That's what you think of me. Now I know. I'm calling it off. Your conceit is astonishing, you uneducated, disgusting drunk. You little hippie whore. Enjoy your life; I'm leaving."

But he hesitated at the door, just long enough for Emma to see the pain beneath his anger. Emma felt that he must have seen the despair in her eyes, too. The poison they had spewed into the room lay in a dark puddle between them, but they simultaneously stepped into it, took a step toward each other—meeting in the middle, locking themselves into each other's arms.

Juan was trembling. "I'm sorry, *reina*. I didn't mean it. You are the most intelligent and most beautiful woman I've ever known. Forgive me, *amorcito*, forgive me."

"I'm sorry, too. You know I didn't mean it either," Emma sobbed.

"We have to vow to be more careful with each other, more tender," Juan murmured into her ear, his tears on her cheek. "We must never say things like that to each other again."

"I promise, never again. And I promise I'll cool it with the drinking. I'll really try, you'll see." Emma suddenly pulled back from Juan's embrace and wiped the tears from her eyes. "Wait a minute; you don't really think I fucked Roger and James, do you?

God, I've known them forever and we went through some heavy shit together, that's all. I'll tell you about it and then you'll understand. It's not a sexual connection, I promise."

"I believe you. It can be hard for me though."

Emma looked at him in disbelief. "I'm honored that you believe me—terrific, you don't think I'm a liar. But I have a question. What does it mean that you called me a whore? I don't understand that mentality. Is it some South of the Border chauvinistic shit? What does that really say about the way you think? Can a man be a whore, too?"

"I didn't mean it."

"But what does it mean?" Emma persisted.

"I guess it means what you called me. Telling me I'm living off my family, off your fame. It was a character assassination, that's all. I didn't mean it. I don't really think like that. Let's be fair, you started it."

A fresh round of arguing was cut short by a knock on the door. It was Bill, come to get them, telling them that everyone was waiting for them to start dinner. Relieved at the reprieve, Juan and Emma followed Bill down to the restaurant, happy to move on, to put the argument behind them. They sat at the head of one of the tables, beaming, having narrowly averted mortally wounding each other.

...

November 30th was another beautiful, sunny Hawaiian day. The hotel was bursting at the seams with the wedding guests. Flowers were everywhere, their scent pervasive in the tropical air. The wedding was scheduled to begin at sunset, but people were crowding around the lanai by late afternoon. Champagne fountains, set up at both sides of the lanai, were already flowing, and hors d'oeuvres were disappearing as soon as they were put out. Emma hated weddings where you had to stand around waiting for the ceremony to be over, hungry and wanting a drink—their guests could begin celebrating as soon as they arrived.

Emma and Juan had planned the ceremony, with the road manager, Ed, as the minister. Ed had one of those draft-dodger's Minister of the Universal Life Church licenses, perfectly legal. Emma chose Kahlil Gibran's poem on love for Ed to read in the ceremony. Juan chose a poem by Pablo Neruda to read to her. They had a string quartet lined up for the ceremony and dinner, and the stage set up for a rock n' roll jam afterwards. Everything was in place. There was nothing to be nervous about.

Emma was more nervous than she had ever been for any concert—had the jitters bad. It must have shown because Marianne, coming to help her dress, took one look at Emma and offered her a Valium.

"This will stop the shaking, baby," Marianne said.

"I think I need the whole bottle." Emma took the blue pill and swallowed it with a swig of tequila.

Marianne pursed her lips. "Well, that should do the trick. What do you need me to do? Are you hungry; have you eaten today?"

"God, no. I'm not hungry. I don't understand why I'm so nervous. People get married all the time. Maybe you could help me with my hair. I want to braid these strings of gardenias down both sides, and some over the top of my head. You look fantastic, Marianne. The dress is perfect, and your hair looks perfect. Maybe it's too early to do my hair. I don't want the flowers to wilt. What time is it anyway?"

Juan would claim later that he'd gone through a worse case of nerves than Emma. He'd been hanging out in Eduardo's room, waiting for the ceremony to start, and they smoked a huge joint of Maui Wowie. However, instead of calming him, the pot made him paranoid and completely withdrawn. He told Emma later that he felt like an imposter in someone else's life, an imposter who'd been found out. His tongue wouldn't work right—he couldn't speak Spanish, much less English.

Bill backed up his story. Said that Juan couldn't talk when he'd shown up at his room, and he didn't even start to come around until he'd made him drink at least three Rum and Cokes.

So the wedding party and the wedding guests were in roughly the same condition by the time the ceremony began. Just as the sun began to descend over the water, the quartet struck up the Wedding March. Latecomers scrambled for seats as Emma walked down the aisle of chairs with her father. She was so nervous at first that she felt like Ray was holding her up. But she smiled anyway, as she walked in the ancient ceremonial procession, behind bridesmaids and flower girls. Everyone and their mother were there—hundreds of smiling faces, and as she nodded greetings to one friend after another, she began to relax.

In her flowing dress, made from intricate, antique lace, with the gardenias braided throughout her hair tumbling around her face with each step, Emma beamed at her guests. The ushers escorted the bridesmaids to their spots, then took up the four corners of an antique white shawl that had been tied to flower-covered poles, and raised it up above Juan and Ed's heads. When she reached the front aisle, Emma broke away from Ray for a moment, walked over to Stephanie, and popped a kiss on her forehead. Then she let her dad lead her to Juan under the canopy.

The ceremony proceeded as planned, without a glitch. Ed did a great job as minister, read the poem, and the ceremony vows that Juan and Emma had written. The best part for Emma though, was when Juan read her the Pablo Neruda poem, up close, his arm around her waist. She could feel his breath on her face, still sweet through the rum and pot, mingling with the scent of the gardenias in her hair. When they exchanged rings and Ed declared them married, they began their exit down the aisle to boisterous cheering and clapping. Emma was worried that they might get mobbed before they made it to the back, where they were supposed to have some kind of reception line, according to Christina. The wedding party lined up, but it quickly became a free-for-all. The record company people were the only ones who adhered to tradition, trying to form an orderly line. Everyone else just started grabbing and hugging.

All of Christina's efforts to curb the chaos were frustrated. She finally threw her hands up in the air. "That's it, I give up! At some point, you and Juan need to pay proper respects to our record company guests though—they're footing the bill for most of this party, after all. Don't worry, I'll make sure they're happy—and the press, of course…your friends are unruly, Emma—there, I've said it—it had to be said."

"I'm not worried," Emma slurred. "Relax, Christina, have fun."

Dinner was more of the same craziness. The string quartet played romantic chamber music while people bellowed over them. Exquisite food was devoured by the alcohol-fueled crowd—food that Juan and Emma didn't taste, but forced down their throats in the hope of neutralizing all the champagne. People who hadn't seen each other in years swore noisily to never lose touch again.

Old lovers hooked up again, and new lovers stole caresses under the tables. Sentimental toasts, one after the other, flew around the room like a single drunkard's unending stream of consciousness. Juan and Emma were in it together, all the craziness, the unrelenting spot light, the wild dance that their wedding had been for days. There was a peace between them. They had found the worst, opened it up and hurled it at each other, waded through it, and found each other again.

When the last toast had finally been delivered in take-your-own-time Hawaiian fashion, the crowd spilled back out to the lanai to dance. There were enough musicians among the guests to make up twenty bands, so people had to take turns jamming. No less than sixteen musicians took the stage first thing.

"There are way too many people on stage—who am I supposed to tell to get off?" Christina asked Emma worriedly.

"Don't worry about it." That was Emma's standard reply for the night.

"Why me?" Christina said, throwing her hands up in the air.

Appropriately, the musicians started with "Midnight Hour" just as it was closing in on 12 a.m. Ray fought his way onto the stage. As father of the bride, he no doubt felt entitled. The jam began, as it would end, with people who could barely play on stage with some of the best musicians in the world. Not to mention the singers; everyone turned into a singer after midnight. The dance floor was packed with people enjoying what they swore was the best music they'd ever heard. Even the record company execs and their wives looked like they were having a good time. It was impossible to be self-conscious or important in the midst of such mania.

The crowning touch came toward dawn. Emma had gone to the ladies room with Marianne, crammed in with what seemed like about a hundred other girlfriends. The champagne had caught up with them all, and they were just hanging out, brushing their hair and putting on make-up, while waiting their turn to go into the stalls and vomit their guts out. They made way for the bride, surrendered the first available stall to Emma, who fell on her knees, as sick as she'd ever been. In the midst of her violent vomiting, someone exited the stall next to her, and let the door slam with a force that brought the toilet seat crashing down on the bridge of her nose. It caught her in just the right spot to give her a concussion, and leave her with two black half-circles under her eyes the next day.

If there hadn't been so many witnesses to the incident, the press could have had even more of a field day with her black eyes. It made good press, regardless. "Rock and roll wedding ends in injury," the most conservative account would begin.

"Don't worry, *reina,* it'll give them something to write about," Juan consoled her as he applied a fresh icepack to her eyes in the early hours of dawn, their wedding night over. "It was perfect; it couldn't have been more perfect. We have the rest of our lives together. I'll take care of you, *amorcito*, I promise."

...

Emma's publicist, Lauren, had a pretty little press release prepared about the rock star's romantic marriage to a handsome guitar player from El Salvador. Lauren's article described the

Hawaiian location, the flowers, the poetry of the ceremony, and Emma's beautiful wedding dress. It raved about the food and the music, and listed the celebrities who attended. The article got picked up by UPI, and was printed in the Entertainment sections of Sunday papers from Hawaii to New York and London.

The story that made front pages came out on Monday—featuring close-ups of Juan and Emma smiling for the camera, Emma with two shiners, unmistakable, even under the make-up. The official version of the incident came from Lauren, who informed reporters that a wedding guest had knocked into a row of lights, causing them to fall—hitting several people, including Emma. The long bar had fallen from the ceiling and clipped her between the eyes just as she had glanced up, but luckily, no one was seriously injured. It was obvious that none of the reporters bought the story, and Emma couldn't really blame them, but she hoped to God that they wouldn't get the truth out of any of the witnesses. Everyone had a story about a reporter trying to trick them into a statement, but these were people whose lifestyles placed them just far enough outside the law to have learned how to keep their mouths shut when it came to hard copy.

The reporters seemed to be convinced that Juan, the jealous groom, had hit Emma; but no matter how they tried, they evidently couldn't get a single wedding guest to make an official statement. That didn't stop them from speculating though. Rumor circulated that some waitress in a restaurant in San Francisco had told a reporter a few weeks ago that she had seen Juan being violent with Emma, that he had dragged her out of the restaurant. Her statement had been printed as God's truth, so the reporters had evidently arrived in Hawaii anticipating a good story. The only thing Juan and Emma could make of the restaurant incident was that the waitress must have misread a common occurrence—Juan helping Emma out of a place because she was too blind-drunk to walk alone. Lauren said she didn't think much of that explanation as a rebuttal.

Although the majority of the guests had left Sunday morning in order to be back at work the next day, some of them had planned their vacation time to coincide with the wedding, and would be spending another week in the Islands—enough of them that Juan and Emma had some allies. Also, a number of record company execs, including two of Emma's favorite A&R men, John and Carl, had stuck around for the press conference and to talk business on Monday. At least the hotel wasn't completely hostile territory.

...

The alarm went off at one p.m. Sunday afternoon. Emma awoke to Juan caressing her and kissing her gently, whispering,

"Wake up, Mrs. Avelar."

"Coffee," Emma croaked.

"It's on the way. You look so beautiful when you're asleep, *amorcito*."

"I know, it's the only time my mouth is shut, right?"

"I love your wit. I love everything about you. It's too bad we can't stay in bed. You have smudges of dark blue under each eye," he said, dropping light kisses on each eyelid.

Emma opened her eyes, smiled at him, then curled up and pulled the covers over her head. "Go away, I'm too miserable, I'm dying. My head is going to spin across the room. You married an imbecile. Oh God, I'm dying."

"I have a headache, too, which admittedly, I deserve." Juan tugged the sheet off Emma, picked her up and carried her to the shower. "We have to be downstairs in an hour. Lauren threatened my life if I don't have you down there by two." He turned on the water and joined her under the spray.

The shower helped them both, as much as anything could. Room service arrived while they were in the shower, and it was way more than Juan had ordered. There was a note from Sonny's cousin, a chef, saying he had baked the coffee cake special for the first day of their marriage. There was also a bottle of cover-up from Lauren, with a note saying, “Thought you might need this. See you at two o’clock sharp.”

“Jesus, what a Nazi Lauren is,” Emma said. But she was grateful for the make-up.

Emma had the jitters for the second day in a row. The last thing she wanted to do right now was face the press, with their cameras. She looked awful, beaten-up.

Juan came up behind her as she struggled in vain to cover the splotches under her eyes. His arms encircled her waist as he looked over her shoulder into the mirror with her. “You look gorgeous, as always. The dark circles just accentuate your perfect skin, the blue of your eyes. They’re going to love you, don’t worry. Blink your eyes and it’ll be over. All things pass. It’s not important. You are the most perfect human being on this planet, Mrs. Avelar.”

Juan and Emma made their way downstairs, only ten minutes late. Lauren awaited them at a table positioned in the front of the lanai. A flock of reporters and photographers were positioned like vultures around the tables facing the front. It seemed like millions of flash bulbs went off in their faces the minute they walked into the room, a warning to prepare for the worst. And then the barrage hit.

“Tell us Emma, is it true your husband punched you in the face last night because he caught you with your ex-boyfriend out on the beach?”

Before Emma could respond, another reporter yelled out, “Rumor has it that your husband has a bad temper. Is that how you got your black eyes?”

“A waitress in San Francisco states that your jealous Latino fiancé dragged you out of a restaurant, kicking and screaming two weeks ago. Why did you marry him, Emmy?”

“Is it true that your husband has ties to the drug cartels in Columbia—that you met him through your drug connections?”

“Testing, testing,” Emma yelled into the microphone. “Can I get a word in edgewise here? First of all, this is my husband, Juan Avelar, and he plays lead guitar in my band. Secondly, no, of course he didn't hit me. Jesus, does he look like someone who would hit a woman? I'm more likely to hit someone than he is. Take that as a warning."

"Come on Emma, you're the most beautiful woman in the industry and by far the best vocalist in rock n' roll. Tell us what really happened. It's obvious he hit you. Tell us why. We love you. You're the best," another reporter cajoled.

"We heard that your husband's ex-girlfriend stated that he has a violent temper when he gets jealous. Is that what happened last night?"

"Jesus, what a bunch of genius reporters this mob is," Emma whispered to Juan. "Hang in there darling, we'll win them over."

Emma was tempted to veer from Lauren's version of events and just tell them the truth, but she could sense that they wouldn't have believed that either. They were out to get Juan, no matter what. This was his first press conference, and he was the meal. They obviously intended to eat him alive.

"Give me a break here, people," Emma pleaded. "We're newlyweds; we're happy—it was an accident with some lights, just like Lauren told you. I admit I was a little bit intoxicated, and maybe I tripped on the cords. Maybe it was my fault, but my husband didn't hit me. Jesus, lighten up. Please."

"It's always the same story, Emma; the victim blames herself. All these questions about why he hit you reflect the rampaging chauvinism of our male-dominated society. Whatever you did, you didn't deserve to be hit. This is an outrage," a reporter from a women's magazine called out.

"Get a grip, can we just start over? No one hit me!" Emma glanced at Juan, whose expression resembled a deer caught in headlights. Obviously, he didn't think he should have to defend himself against such completely absurd charges.

"Wouldn't you agree that you have an affinity for violent men?" a female reporter shouted. "I recall the incident of the jealous boyfriend who threw furniture out a hotel window last year. What's the attraction to violent men all about, Emma?"

With that question, the floodgates were lifted and volumes of embarrassing incidents from Emma's past came rushing into the room on a tide of speculation. All her crazy, public episodes, one after the other, were offered as possible reasons why Juan had hit her on their wedding night. Every denial turned into a confirmation of what the journalists suspected. It was hopeless.

"A reliable source has just confirmed that you got between your husband and your father in a fight—the blow was meant for your dad, wasn't it?"

"What? My father? Are you crazy?" *My father? That's it. I've had it.*

Emma jumped up onto the table and assumed an aggressive stance, staring down the reporters. She glanced down at Juan and flashed a grin, then whipped her head around to the crowd and began belting out: "*There's no business like show business like no business I know.*" She was vaguely aware of the dropped jaws of the reporters, but she focused on the song. *Everything about it is appealing...Nowhere could you get that happy feeling when you are stealing that extra bow...* She caught Juan's eye and winked, then waving her arms in mock emphasis of the lyrics, she continued to the end of the first verse, threw her arms wide open, Ethel Mermen style, and dropped to one knee as she sang the grand finale line: *Let's go on with the show.*

For a few moments of stunned silence, Emma held the pose, maintaining defiant eye contact with her audience.

Then the applause started and it grew like a wave, until spontaneously, all the reporters and photographers were on their feet, clapping and cheering. This was an audience who appreciated survival mechanisms.

"Okay, please let me introduce you to my husband, who is an amazing person and a gifted guitar player," Emma announced to the room. "He is from El Salvador, attended Brown University, and dropped out of law school at UCLA to play music. You're going to love him almost as much as I do."

Now the reporters became interested in Juan and turned their attention to questions like, "How did you meet? What's it like to be married to Emma Allison? Where are you going to live?" Inquiries pertinent to covering a wedding.

Their articles would be full of false accounts of what really happened, how Emma really got the black eyes, but after Emma's extravagant performance, and listening to Juan's thoughtful answers to their questions, the theories had moved from Juan being the culprit, to blaming a jealous ex-boyfriend—with countless speculations as to just which ex had hit her. God knows, she had enough ex-lovers to choose from. Along with the juicy story of the black eyes, the handsome newlyweds would be presented in a romantic light, as survivors of a violent mishap on their wedding night. All things considered, Lauren and the A&R men thought the press conference had gone well, and congratulated Emma on thinking up such a clever diversion. As if thought had entered into it.

"Well Emma, you are full of surprises," a record company bigwig said to Emma, as she and Juan tried to beat a hasty retreat from the press conference. "Maybe we should investigate the possibility of a Broadway show, to add to the mystique of the next record. It was really good. I didn't know you could do that kind of material."

"Wow, thank you. That's really kind of you. So glad you liked it. I'll be happy to consider whatever you come up with. Thank you," Emma replied. "Jesus, what a moron," she said to Juan, as they made their getaway.

"Listen, Mrs. Avelar, you were brilliant in there. It took all of my self-control not to burst into laughter, and so many people took it seriously, it was unbelievable. You are very funny, on top of your other talents. You single-handedly turned them around. No wonder you're a big star; you're brilliant. I love you, *mi querida preciosa, mi esposa.*"

"I'm afraid to say it out loud, that I might jinx it, but I think that was it for a while. I think we're free. I love you, too, baby. I love you more than anything. We can do whatever we want now. Let's go back to Hana, or do you want to see the other islands?"

"What I'd really like to do is spend a week in bed with you," Juan was saying, just as they ran smack into Margie and Sonny.

"Hey, it's the lovebirds." Sonny eyed Juan suspiciously. "I had to leave early last night, take my Aunt June home, but I heard about your face, Emma. Man, it's worse than I heard. It looks like somebody messed you up good. Shit, girl, I'll kick their ass, you give me the word. Nobody's gonna mess with you like that."

"God," Emma said, "even you, Sonny? It was an accident. Give Juan a break, will you. God. The fucking toilet seat fell on me while I was throwing up, okay? I'm an idiot. Jesus, he's going to be sorry he married me."

"No shit? I heard about that, but I thought it was just some kind of weird rumor. Wow, a toilet seat gave you those shiners? Sorry, you gotta admit it looks bad, huh Juan? No hard feelings, hey, right?"

Margie gave Sonny a playful swat on the shoulder. "Quit while you're ahead, Sonny. Which was yesterday. Shut up. Just put a lid on it." She turned to Emma. "You okay little *haole*; you gonna be okay?"

"Don't sweat it. I'm great. I'm married to this man, for Christ sake. How bad could it be? I'm lucky I didn't crack my skull."

"Yeah, and how 'bout you?" Margie asked Juan. "You gonna have to kick Sonny's ass?"

"I'll let it go this time," Juan laughed. "You can't believe how happy we are to see friendly faces. Give us a minute to go change into bathing suits, and we'll meet you out at the bar."

In the elevator, they encountered another old friend of Emma's, Wade, from Rolling Stone magazine. "That was a good laugh, Emma," he said. "I think I should write a review on your tabletop performance. It was the best thing I've seen you do yet."

"Fuck you, too, Wade." Emma smiled and tossed her hair back. "Jesus, it was good to look out there and see your face in the midst of all those hacks. This is my husband, Juan. Juan, this is Wade, one of the few real writers in rock n' roll journalism."

"Good to meet you, man," Wade said, shaking Juan's hand.

"Emma, it's flattering that you hold my profession in such high esteem. But I should warn you that I actually do know how you got your shiners. Cynthia was in the bathroom when it happened. I'm open to bribes, though. How about if I do an interview with you and Juan later this afternoon?"

"Yes, absolutely; God, that would be great. Can you join us down by the pool for drinks?"

Juan and Emma returned to their room to find the message light flashing. The amount of messages was daunting, so Emma called Christina and asked her to come over and return calls for her. All she and Juan really wanted to do was collapse on the beach and take a nap, but they knew that wasn't in the cards this afternoon.

...

When they got down to the poolside bar, Sonny and Margie were sitting at a table with Bill and Marianne, Ray, and Stephanie. "Come and sit down, you lovebirds. We saved you seats," Stephanie said. "How about Bloody Marys? That's what we're drinking."

"Sounds good, Stephanie. How about you, darling? Sound good?" Emma asked Juan.

"Yes please, that would be great," Juan said to Emma. And to Stephanie, "Perfect choice, you read my mind."

When their drinks arrived, along with seconds or thirds for the others at the table, Stephanie proposed a toast to the newlyweds. "May you be as happy as Ray and I have been together, and may we have a grandchild soon."

Emma threw back her head and laughed. "Whoa, are you just now telling me that babies really do come from a man and a woman getting married?"

"Well, it's a start, honey."

"I'd say we have a few years to think about it. And anyway, how fair is it to bring a child into a world that's this fucked-up!"

Juan face darkened. He stood up and stretched. "It never occurred to me that you might not want children."

Stephanie laughed. "She's just playing the pessimist, Juan. Em, honey, you needn't worry about the state of the world. Life finds a way. In fact, Ray and I always felt like having you was a defiant act—a slap in the face of logic. It's the ultimate expression of faith really, that no matter how screwed up the world is, there's always the possibility of it getting better."

"Yeah, you made the world better just by being born," Ray added.

"I'll drink to that." Juan lifted his glass.

Emma took a playful bow. "Oh sure, you guys; yep, that's me all right."

"Why don't we go lie on the beach for a while?" Juan suggested. "They'll bring us drinks and food out there. I'm hungry again."

Friends were scattered around in little groups on the beach, sunbathing, and no doubt nursing hangovers. Kids were playing in the surf and bringing back buckets of water to pour on their parents' backs, throwing balls, and building sand castles. Emma watched Juan interact with the children effortlessly, returning their balls, helping with the castle moats, and a visceral feeling stirred in her stomach. She wondered if it could be a maternal instinct. Juan pulled stuff out of her that was so hidden she didn't know it was there. Why did he get peeved at her for saying she didn't want to bring a child into the world? She had only meant it in a light-hearted way. He said it had never occurred to him that she might not want children—which meant what? That he wouldn't have married her if she didn't? She thought about bringing the subject up again, but for once, thought better of it. It had been too long a day, and they had all the time in the world to sort these things out.

By the time Wade joined them on the beach for the interview, the Bloody Marys and some fine Maui pot had done their job. Juan and Emma were relaxed, and Wade kept the conversation flowing smoothly with the type of questions he asked. Emma knew only too well that he could be a scathing critic, but he was also a thought-provoking writer who knew a lot about music.

As the sun began to set, everyone agreed to meet in the lobby at nine to go to dinner at The Blue Max, in Lahina. People went back to their rooms to get ready for dinner. Juan and Emma finally had a couple of hours to themselves.

Emma was sleepy, but Juan was wide-awake. She could tell he had entered that stoned zone where your thoughts crystallize and time slows down so much you can hear it grinding to a stop. She knew that totally sober, Juan could hold the threads of a number of lines of thought, weave them together in different ways, examine the end result, then start over again; but when he was really stoned, his mental processes seemed to speed up. Of course, intellectual exchange was never a problem with Juan—expressing his feelings was a different story. Yes, he was romantic and could turn her on without trying, but any kind of conflict and his ability to communicate seemed to shut down entirely. Emma wondered where he was, what he was thinking about.

Emma propped herself up on a pillow and tapped Juan lightly on the shoulder. "Talk to me, baby. Did I do something? Are you mad at me? You seem so detached."

Juan turned to face her and took her hand. "Sometimes your beauty renders me incapable of speech," he said slowly, thoughtfully. "It is as though your soul manifests in your behavior…the light and the shadow in a continual match that neither can win…the balance continually correcting itself. Like a guru, you bring me into the present, and I am humbled by your light."

"Wow, that must have been good pot! I'm buying you a kilo of it—no, a ton. Where did you get it?"

"You joke, but I am serious, Mrs. Avelar. You tend to drink too much, and you can become irrational, yet also, without thought, you can clear a path through illusion into the very heart of what is real—and the way you honored your mother with a kiss during our marriage ceremony, you blessed our marriage."

"Whoa, hold on a minute. You've got me confused with someone else." Suddenly a thought occurred to Emma, and she turned serious. "Are you feeling bad about not inviting your parents?"

"I am ambivalent."

Juan always came across as a calm, aesthetic person, but Emma was beginning to be able to detect the hidden storms, and to realize that she wasn't the cause of all the turmoil. He was so beautiful that he stopped her heart just to look at him, but his charisma was deeper, more nuanced—the way he held himself so proudly upright, coming across as casual and coolly self-confident but not arrogant…the way he made her feel soothed and stimulated at the same time in his presence. All these things and more, she wanted to say to him, but everything she thought of seemed trite.

So she just said, "It'll work out, baby. Why don't we take a shower together?" She figured he'd had enough self-disclosure for the time being anyway.

…

Dinner was on the A&R men, John and Carl, and everyone took full advantage of it. Locals who hadn't been able to make it to the wedding showed up at the Blue Max, swelling the guest list, filling the place. After dinner, the crowd milled around, hanging out, talking—some of them ending up on stage playing music. The restaurant was more than happy to stay open for the free-spending crowd.

Juan and Emma were happy to get back to their room that night. It was late, and they were tired. Side by side, they brushed their teeth over the one sink. Juan seemed to suddenly notice that Emma was staring at him in the mirror. "What is it?"

Emma felt a great, hovering spirit of tenderness descend and envelop the room. The cackling of the demons that lurk in corners stopped abruptly. She heard them gasping as they suffocated in the sacred mist. Emma inhaled deeply, felt the air suffuse her body and produce tears. “I love you just as much as you love me, baby. You know that, don’t you?”

“Why are you crying, *amorcito*? Here, let me kiss away your tears.”

Juan picked Emma up and set her on the bathroom counter. He brushed her hair back from her face and stroked her cheeks. She laid her head on his shoulder and breathed in his scent. Slowly, he moved in between her legs and down onto his knees. When her orgasm came, the spirit shook the room and lights twinkled. Emma saw a tunnel and she fell into it, dropping through stars, past planets, into a new universe, one where Rob didn’t exist. She was floating, and in the midst of the timeless journey, Juan entered her body, and she moved with him effortlessly. When she came again, this time Juan did too.

Later that night, as they lay side by side, Juan said, “Tell me about Carol.”

The light of the new universe shimmered softly in the darkened room. Emma sighed. This was a gigantic step into intimacy that he was asking her to take…probably more than he realized. He already knew how Carol had died—Roger and James told him. But he obviously wanted her to pull out her heart and dissect it in front of him, just to see it bleed…no, that wasn’t true—he wanted to heal it.

Jeannette Sears

Chapter Seven

Emma, 1974: A Walk Around the Block

That press conference was a nightmare. Usually, I don't give much of a shit what those reporters make up. But my wedding, for Christ sake, you'd think I could have managed to not turn that into a circus. It was amazing, though, being with all our friends together in Hawaii. The music— first the Mozart, and then the crazy jam—my dad up there on stage having the time of his life, everybody singing all night. The romantic poetry…Juan.

I thought that things between us wouldn't change much. It was only a ceremony, after all. But it has changed. I swear to God, I can do no wrong in Juan's eyes now—him calling me Mrs. Avelar all the time, as though he can't say it often enough. It's weird, but I really like the sound of it, as though it makes it official that we belong together.

I feel like someone's got my back, like I have a best friend again. Looking at Juan, flashing on how he's my husband now, not just my old man, is an amazing trip. Jesus, after all the "do your own thing" stuff, here I am, married, and digging it. I should have smelled a rat with Ray and Stephanie—with their big rap about personal freedom, and them being married all these years. They've always been each other's best friends and I've never had that with a guy before. The only best friend I ever had besides Juan was Carol.

When Juan asked me to tell him about Carol, I felt myself shrinking inward, closing in over the memories, literally clamming up. It's such a perfect expression, "clamming up." Shutting the shell for protection, attempting to keep the center safe from predators. But it's ridiculous, because Juan is no predator. It's all my own bullshit—stuff I don't want him to know. I don't want Juan to look at me differently. Then again, I've done enough already to turn him off, and he's still here, so maybe it's my own judgment that's worrying me, not his.

•••

I can't come up with a specific reason why I started up with heroin. It just sort of happened. It's not like anything was wrong in my life. I didn't have the childhood from hell, like Carol, and I'm not going to pin it on Rob—that would be giving him too much power. My career was going great, I felt good—no shortage of guys, no heartbreaks or anything. I have no excuse to pin it on.

I'm not sure exactly when things got so out of hand. Carol was bummed about her brother getting strung out again. I was back in the studio in New York, working on Changes that fall of '68, and Carol went back to the Bay Area for a while. Said she needed a break from the East Coast. Needed a break from her brother, is what I thought. I didn't mind her leaving because I had a thing going with this songwriter, Brian, and he was taking up all my spare time. He and I were doing a lot of coke, staying up all night, writing songs together. After the success of Projections, the record company would have put me up at The Plaza, but I wanted to stay in The Chelsea. I found it inspiring to be around all that crazy energy.

Brian and I didn't make it to the end of the record, but four of our songs made it onto the album. I wrote the other six songs with Bill, who was a second engineer on my record back then. I flashed out on Bill while I was still with Brian, and we started sneaking around at the studio, making up excuses to stay late. When Brian figured out what was going on, he was pretty laid back about it. Didn't make much of a scene—probably because he didn't want me to dump the songs we'd written.

Bill and I kept things light, or at least we tried to. He knew I would be going on tour in December for at least six months, and he had been asked to produce an album in L.A. for a new band. I figured we could pick up where we left off when the time was right, if we both still wanted to. Don't get me wrong; I was really into Bill, but what was I going to do, ask him to give up his big chance as a producer to come along as a soundman on my tour? Or give up my career to go live in L.A. with him? We were both really young and into our own trips. The timing was off, and anyway, I never loved him the way I love Juan. I knew he was more into me than I was him, but he never tried to guilt-trip me about it, and so we managed to stay friends all these years. That first album Bill produced was gigantic. It kicked off his career.

We finished *Changes* in November, and I was back in San Francisco in time for the holiday season. I had moved from the Haight because the neighborhood had changed fast when the press publicized what a party it was. Speed freaks and runaways had crowded out the artists and musicians and intellectuals who had given the place its reputation. I had bought a Victorian house in Pacific Heights instead, with the royalties from Projections. This would be my first holiday in my own home.

Carol had been house sitting for me, and of course, it was natural that she would stay on as a roommate. The house was too big for just me, anyway. But when I got home, I felt a funny vibe right off the bat. Part of it had to do with the fact that Carol had already spent some time there and I hadn't. Her vibe was permeating the house and it made me feel like an intruder. I told myself that I was just feeling territorial, and I didn't want to give in to that. Looking back on my homecoming, I don't see how I could have missed what was actually going on: The long, beautiful scarves hanging over the towel rack in the downstairs bathroom, the matches alongside the teaspoon sitting on the counter. Carol nodding out when I was the one who was jet lagged. Unmistakable signs if I'd known what to look for.

Two days after I got home, I walked into the house to find Carol and two other chicks sitting around the table, stoned out of their gourds. Another mutual friend was just stumbling out of the bathroom as I came in, a junkie chick. I was pretty stoned on pot, so the reality of the situation dawned on me in slow motion. Mumbling some excuse about needing to use the bathroom, I went to check it out. I could smell the burnt matches buried in the wastebasket. Picked up the teaspoon and found that it was still hot.

Carol must have felt my energy, because she was waiting for me in the hall.

"It's not like you think," she said, putting her hand on my arm.

I shrugged her off. "Get fucked, Carol. How do you know what I think?"

She reached for me again. "You're so uptight, Emma. Let's talk. It's groovy, baby, everything's fine. I'll tell them to leave. I didn't know you'd be back so soon. You're just tired."

I couldn't bear to even look at her. "What does it mean? Just tell me what it fucking means. After everything you've been through with your brother, how could you?"

Carol threw her head back and put her hand on her hip, in that model-like way she had of standing. "You've been on the East Coast too long. You're making a big deal out of nothing."

I had been trying not to scream, but I finally let loose. "I come home to find you shooting up in my house, and you tell me it's no big deal? Christ, what is a big deal?"

Carol's bottom lip jutted out. Her voice was low and accusing. "You don't have to go on a power trip. I'm well aware that it's your house, Emma. I'm not using again. We're just getting high—playing around. You could try a little yourself; maybe you wouldn't be so uptight. You don't get strung out from just trying it. You don't understand 'cause you've never tried it."

I was on the verge of tears…who was this person? "Fuck off, Carol. You sound like a goddamn pusher or something."

She gave me one of her cooler than thou smiles. "Okay, fuck you, too. I just thought maybe you could use a little taste of soul, that's all."

I stormed up to my bedroom and slammed the door. There was no way I was going to argue with her while she was in that state.

Jesus, telling me I needed "soul." That bothered me more than I'd shown. I could hear doors opening and closing downstairs, people leaving, and then Carol came tapping on my bedroom door. She came in and sprawled out at the foot of my bed, started crying.

"I'm sorry, Em. I don't know what to do. I'm all strung out again."

"Don't worry," I told her, stroking her hair. "We'll get you cleaned up by Thanksgiving."

The next day, I drove her down to a rehab clinic in Santa Cruz. While she was gone, I had the house scoured from top to bottom. Then I got some Lakota religious leaders to do a spiritual ceremony to cleanse the house of any remaining bad vibes. We smoked some weed together, and they started doing their thing—chanting and waving burning sage in the air. I was digging it. I closed my eyes and breathed in, inhaling the sage, and when I opened my eyes, there was something in the room that hadn't been there before.

It was a dark shadow, a blackness compressed into an indefinable entity that emanated pure evil.

Alarm bells went off in my head.

I glanced around, wondering if anyone else was seeing the demon thing. If they were, they didn't let on. I closed my eyes again, hoping it would go away, but it didn't. It hovered in the corners as we moved through the house, avoiding the smoke from the burning sage. I was freaked out, but I kept telling myself it wasn't real—just another bum trip.

I was determined that Carol and I would have a fresh start in my new home. She had gotten off on the wrong foot because I wasn't there. Everything would be fine now that I was back for her to hang out with. We'd look out for each other, as usual.

After a week in rehab, Carol was clean again and I drove down in my Porsche to get her, taking the coast route. It was a beautiful fall day and I was driving along singing to the radio, when out of the fucking blue I got the creeps, big time. Someone, or something, touched my shoulder.

I glanced in my rearview mirror. Nothing.

It was the middle of a sunny afternoon, for Christ sake. But I couldn't shake the image of the demon thing I had seen at the house cleansing. It crossed my mind that maybe it was following me. Or maybe I was just having a bad acid trip flashback. I rolled the windows down, tried to let the bad energy out and some fresh air in. My hands were sweating.

Carol was skeletal and her skin looked yellow when I picked her up. But she was in a mellow space, loaded on the Methadone she'd been given to wean her off heroin. We spent the trip back to San Francisco planning our Thanksgiving Day party, going over the menu, who we would invite, how we would seat everyone. We were both excited about entertaining in the new house, but more than that, we were just happy to be back in each other's good graces.

We stopped at a great Mexican restaurant in Half Moon Bay for dinner, but Carol didn't eat a bite. It worried me. She was way too thin, and I like thin, but she was over the top. I found myself nagging her to eat, which made me feel old, like somebody's mother, for God's sake. The irony of me trying to whip somebody else into shape wasn't lost on either of us.

Our Thanksgiving Day party was a riot. Bill came up from L.A. and the house filled with friends. Even the dark corners had people lounging in them. Stephanie made a perfect turkey, but it ended up on the carpet when Bill tried to carve it. I had put it on a TV tray, and the thing collapsed. We ate the turkey anyway, and the whole episode was captured on our home movie camera. No shadow entities showed up on the 8mm film.

...

Early December, my band was out on the road for three weeks, promoting *Changes*. Even though it shipped out gold, most of the audience was still unfamiliar with the new material and they wanted to hear all the old songs they recognized. It was the first time I'd experienced that, and I found it frustrating. I was sick of the songs from *Projections* and just wanted to move on. Talk about naïve. I'm still doing some of those songs. You have to give your audience what they want.

Carol was on a very low dose of methadone that allowed her personality back into the picture. She'd put on a few pounds and was back to model-thin, rather than concentration-camp-thin. She seemed happy doing her publicist thing, and we both gelled with this line-up of musicians. After the shows, a big party scene would develop in the hospitality rooms, with groupies, drug dealers, visiting musicians, and anyone else who'd managed to obtain a backstage pass.

The guys all knew each other pretty well by now, too. Instead of disappearing to our own, private scenes after the shows, we all hung out together, like we used to in *Altered States*. The first week, we pretty much slept wherever we ended up. Carol and I went on Christmas shopping sprees in Chicago and Boston, combed the antique stores for treasures to bring home, and even went ice-skating on Lake Michigan. We were all drinking a lot and smoking pot, but staying away from hard drugs.

When we arrived home a few days before Christmas, the album had gone platinum. Of course I was riding high, but at the same time, I just took it for granted. I was used to strangers talking to me wherever I went, and I never forgot that the fans were on my side; they were my audience and for the most part, they were cool. But I didn't spend any time marveling at my success or even being particularly grateful for it. My attention was always focused on what was right in front of me—relationships, sex, furnishing the house, writing songs, buying clothes, getting high with friends. It seemed like every day held some excitement, not just for me, but for everybody I knew.

The San Francisco bands had all taken off, gotten record deals, and the music was totally alive and innovative. Altered States had broken up, but all the guys were in other bands now, bands that were making it. There was always something to do, day or night. The city was bustling with mimes and minstrels, clowns and street theatre. Bands played every night, and there was improv comedy and creative hippie dance performances, even though the Haight-Ashbury was still crumbling before our eyes. I was happy to be back home, even if it was only for a short while.

Carol and I spent Christmas in Sausalito with my parents and a few of their friends. It was a low-key day, the only one in that time period. Bill came up from L.A. the day after Christmas, but left the next day because we got into a fight. I think the reality of it being our last time together for a long time got to us. He accused me of being cavalier about our relationship, and I suppose I was acting that way. I've always hated break-ups. That was the last time we would be together as lovers. We made up by phone, but we were too busy to see each other. Two days later, I was back on the road, first coast to coast, and then twenty dates in Europe.

Winter tours can get dreary. Once New Year's is over, all the holiday decorations come down, the weather outside California and Florida is soggy, and the audiences are back to slogging away in school after their holiday break. Except my audiences weren't exactly tied to their desks that winter. They were actually exploding all over the place, occupying administration buildings, forming picket lines, protesting racism, putting pressure on The Man to stop the war. It seemed like every college town had something going on, and we ran smack into a face-off between the students and police at the University of Massachusetts. We were lucky they allowed the show to go on that night.

The college towns were one thing, but Jesus, those Eastern industrial cities were another. Between their giant smoke stacks creating dirty air, and miles of dingy, dilapidated high-rise apartments, they got fucking depressing. After going from one to another of those cities, you start forgetting where you are. They all start looking the same.

The shows are always a rush though, no matter where you are. We gave it our best on stage, every show. And the truth is we were concerned about the reviews; no matter how cool we tried to be about it, they made a difference to our morale. But the charts mattered more. It was a huge boost to see record sales rising steadily.

We were all pretty partied out after the last tour and the holidays. I started spending a lot of my free time writing songs with George, the new keyboard player. He could come up with music as fast as I could write lyrics, and he was an experienced lover. I got so involved with him that I didn't notice what was going on with Carol, or how tight she and James had become.

One night we were all hanging out in some hotel bar after-hours, and Carol was wearing this velvet outfit that had a matching jacket with long, draping sleeves. George knocked some God-awful, sticky drink over onto Carol's jacket, and without thinking, she pulled the jacket off to go rinse it out in the bathroom. I followed her in to help her, and saw the tracks on her arms.

My stomach went into a spasm and I felt like I was going to throw up. I grabbed her shoulders, trying to get her to look at me. "Jesus, Carol, you've got to be kidding. What are you thinking? Not again, not fucking again."

She pulled away and started scrubbing at the stupid stain as though it was the most important thing in the world. "You're over-reacting, Emma. You make everything into a big dramatic production. Please, just give it a rest. I know what I'm doing."

I was flipping out. "Christ, Carol, you think I want to see you end up dead? Look at your brother, look at all our friends who've used. It's a dead-end street; you know it is."

She looked at me in the mirror, coolly, from behind half-closed eyes. "You know Emma, sometimes I really feel the age difference between us. You think half the musicians we know don't use sometimes? What about the jazz greats, your hero, Billie Holiday? Honestly baby, it's under control. We're just using occasionally."

"We? Who's *we*?" I said, trying to keep the desperation out of my voice. "Who the fuck is *we*? Who are you shooting up with? Tell me."

Carol started humming a Billie Holiday tune under her breath as I stared at her in disbelief. Suddenly, I knew who it was. "James, isn't it."

"Ain't nobody's business," Carol sang, glancing over her shoulder at me. At that moment she was as far away from me as Billie Holiday.

"That's it? After everything we've been through? It's not my business? Jesus! It fucking well is my business!"

"It ain't always about you, little Emma." Carol closed her eyes and continued the Billie tune, improvising words. "It's my house, it's my career, whatever I need, I want you here, cause I'm the center of, this whole goddamn crazy world." She opened her eyes to half-mast and murmured, "Baby, you're just jealous of James and me. That's what this whole thing's about."

"I'll tell you what it's about. You're fired, and so is James."
I stormed up to my room, assuming Carol would come after me, but when someone knocked on my door, it wasn't Carol. It was George.

"Emma, what's going on? I heard you and Carol had a big fight. What happened?"

Now the tears came. "Carol's using again. I fired her, and James. I can't watch it happen again; I've had it."

"That's heavy shit, all right. But it'll blow over. You know it will. It's not worth blowing the tour for."

I asked him to leave.

James was coming in as George was leaving. He came over and casually sat down on the edge of the bed. "Can we talk? Carol told me about your conversation. Did you mean it? Talk to me."
I dried my eyes. "I don't know, I'll figure it out tomorrow. I just need to be alone. Why didn't Carol come?"

"She thinks you're trying to run her life, Emma. I'm sorry, but that's what she said. And what was that about us being fired? We have a show tomorrow, right? How can we be fired, baby, how would that work?"

I saw his point, of course. How could I fire him when we had to play a gig the next day, and Carol was needed to handle the press. It was a pointless tactic on my part. Anyway, I didn't want them to leave.

"Tell her I didn't mean it." James left and came back five minutes later with Carol. The three of us sat on my bed and talked things out. Their basic argument was that their personal habits weren't affecting their ability to carry out their jobs. I had to agree with that. I mean, Jesus, I hadn't even noticed they were using until I saw the tracks. They ended up crashing in my bed that night, all of us cuddled up together like it was a pajama party. Without the pajamas.

A precedent was being set that night, without any of us really being aware of it. Now, instead of just Carol, it was Carol and James, the couple that I hung out with. It wasn't a threesome or anything, just a friendship. And James was easy to be around—hip and laid-back offstage, exciting in performance. He'd shoot a mixture of cocaine and heroin, called "speedballs," before the shows, which would give him a lot of energy on stage. Then he'd switch to plain heroin afterwards, so he wouldn't be hyped up and doing that mad, cocaine-rap thing. Carol and James were a couple for sure, but they were usually too loaded to want to fuck, so they'd hang out in my room after the shows. A few other friends or band members would come by, too, but it was mellow. Not a big party scene. I got used to seeing Carol and James disappear into the bathroom to shoot up. After a while, I took it for granted. They were maintaining, so it was okay. As long as they didn't run out of the drug.

Which happened in Philadelphia. Christ, what a scene. James went off to score with some sleazy looking guy. Carol was worried about him, and as hours went by, grew increasingly nervous about getting her fix. Neither of us had any idea who the connection was or where they'd gone. In fact, James missed sound-check, a first for him. So much for the habit not affecting his job. Ed was having a conniption fit, and Carol was frantic when they hadn't returned by late afternoon, but what were we going to do, alert the police? Finally, just before we had to leave for the gig, James called and said he would meet us at the venue, not to worry.

When we arrived at the gig, he was already there with an entourage of Philly hippies. They all hung out after the show and ended up coming back to the hotel with us. One guy in particular, Richard, was very outgoing, offering me heroin and coke, and coming on to me big-time. My anger around the fiasco dissipated as I snorted coke with Richard and the others in my room. When the phone rang, I picked it up, assuming it would be somebody asking to come up. Instead, it was the front desk calling to alert me that the narcs were on their way up, and that they had directed them to Ed's room. Immediately, we started gathering together the drugs, intending to flush them down the toilet, but then Richard pulled out a gun and a badge, ordered us to stop and put our hands up, just like in a movie. He then pulled a walkie-talkie from his backpack, and within minutes, the police burst into the room. They took us all in. Ed had us out within two hours, but not before the press caught wind of it.

Rock n' roll's Sweetheart Arrested On Drug Charges," the headline read the next morning.

"Jesus Christ, haven't they got anything more important to write about," I fumed. I hoped that we hadn't been such big news in the Bay Area, but figured I'd better call Ray and Stephanie anyway.

The charges against Carol and me were dropped, but James had a trial ahead of him, as did the sleazy connection. Evidently, Richard had been undercover for some time with that group of people, and James just happened to get led to the wrong place at the wrong time. The biggest problem that the whole mess created was that James and Carol started going through withdrawal, and we had a show in Detroit day after next. They were both pretty sick by the time we got to Detroit, but some kind soul of a dealer had read about the bust and was waiting with a nice, fat stash for them at the hotel. Ah, the perks of notoriety.

By March, I had a healthy cocaine habit going. James and Carol had managed to keep us in drugs pretty easily since the Philadelphia fiasco. I'd usually drink a lot of champagne after the shows, then snort some coke to counteract the downer effect of alcohol. It seemed like a winning combination, one drug to go up, another to come down. Cocaine was an expensive drug in 1969, hadn't hit the streets in a cheaper form yet.

Speed had already wreaked havoc with the street scene, and cocaine was doing the job with the musicians. Cocaine was an elitist drug. Lines weren't passed to just anybody, like joints always were. You had to have something the person with the stash wanted in return, or you were out of luck. No problems for me; as a rock singer, they'd give me all I wanted. Or if you were a pretty girl, those dealers would give you coke just to have you around because your beauty gave them status or something.

When the last gig plunked us down in New York mid-March, we had a few days off before leaving for Paris. Since nobody in the band shared my affinity for the Chelsea Hotel, we were in the Plaza, whooping it up, celebrating our having survived the winter tour, celebrating the advent of spring—celebrating just to celebrate. We had played to sold-out houses, the record was at the top of the charts, and advance sales on the European gigs were exceeding our expectations. One of my old boyfriends from my first recording sessions introduced me to the New York art scene, which seemed to take to me in a big way. For my part, I was flashed out by these ultimate artists—by their art, and the far-out studios and lofts of Greenwich Village. Their life-styles were just way more Bohemian than the California art scene. There was also more heroin—so much in fact, that I seemed to be the only one not doing it.

Hanging out with a small group of ultra-hip people in a famous painter's loft one night, surrounded by art, engaged in lively, interesting conversation, I snorted heroin for the first time. It was laid out in lines, like coke. Since I was pretty wired from the coke and these people weren't junkie stereotypes, I decided to go with the flow and snort it to even out a bit. Carol had told me that it's not very addictive if you just snort it, and I didn't want to be perceived as some naïve, unsophisticated little West Coast straight chick. It was bad enough that I was the baby of the crowd; I wanted to hold my own with these heavyweights.

...

So that was how I started with heroin. Sounds pretty lame, doesn't it? Embarrassing really, that when it boils down to it, it was peer pressure that seduced me into crossing that line I had drawn for myself. Not stress, or heartbreak, or the Viet Nam War. Not assassinations, or a bad childhood, or even fuck-head Rob. After all I'd seen with Carol and her brother, with James, and other junkie friends, I ambled into heroin use as if I were going for a walk around the block.

Chapter Eight

The Honeymoon, December, 1974

Emma was silent for a while after Juan asked her about Carol. Someday she would tell him all about what happened; she wanted to, but now wasn't the right time to break open that piece of her past. This was their honeymoon, a brief interlude that should be exclusively theirs. Finally, she said, Let's not talk about the past. Let's just be with each other here, in this moment, in the present, like you said. The truth is I wasn't even alive before you. I have no past, not really. Nothing is important but this moment. That, and where we're going tomorrow. We've got to decide."

"You decide then," Juan said. "You know the islands; where should we go?"

"Well, we could go touristing all over the place, and that would be fun, or we could just go back to Hana and chill out in the sun for the week. It's up to you."

"I think I detect that you would like to spend the time in Hana. You need to relax, *corazon*, so let's go let the sun make us chilly, as you say."

"You wouldn't say the sun makes us chilly, even though I said we… wait a minute, you're teasing me, you snob. You perfect-English-grammar egghead, I'll get even; you better be worried. But are you sure? I'd love to show you Kauai and the big island."

"I'm also agreeable to seeing these new places. Whatever you like."

"Jesus, at this rate, we won't make it as far as the door. One of us has to decide."

“Very well, let’s just go back to Hana, and reserve our energies for the tour. We can go to the other islands on another trip, when we have more time.”

The next day, Juan and Emma drove her parents to Lahina where the art gallery owner who was handling Stephanie’s paintings was waiting for them. After numerous goodbyes with hugs and kisses, Juan and Emma were finally alone. They were both pensive as they drove past miles of pineapple and sugarcane fields, turned onto the coast road toward Hana. The car twisted its slow, bumpy way across the island, and Emma finally broke the silence by bringing up a sore subject.

“Listen baby, I really dig the way you were with my parents. You made them feel like you weren’t taking me away from them. You knew what to do. I want it to be like that with your family. I’m afraid that the longer we don’t tell them about our marriage, the more left out they’ll feel, and the more they’ll build up resentment against me. It’s important to me that your family likes me. I’ll keep it together around them, I promise.”

“Emma, why can you not understand that it has nothing to do with your behavior!”

“Probably because I have a very fine-tuned bullshit detector.”

“You’re wrong about this. It’s inconsequential whether or not my parents would approve of you; they don’t approve of anyone, least of all, me. You were lucky to have been raised by non-judgmental, open-minded artists.”

“Oh God, don’t start that again.”

“But you’re so close to them. I can’t relate to my parents at all. It is the harsh reality. We will never have their approval…unless you give up rock n’ roll to have babies, and I go back to law school.”

“Law school? When the hell did you go to law school? Oh right, UCLA—you did tell me, but there are huge chunks of your life I know nothing about.”

“I thought you said we shouldn’t talk about the past on this trip.”

"I've changed my mind now."

"As you wish. You direct the conversation, and I will most willingly follow."

"Okay, when was the last time you saw your parents?"

Juan glanced at Emma, and then turned his attention back to the road. He was smiling. "At my graduation from Brown. We fought the whole time. They said they couldn't understand the man I had become, that they regretted sending me to such a school. They were convinced that I had been misled by my liberal education. I told them I wanted to be a musician, but they objected emphatically. To them, music is a hobby, not a profession."

"Except classical, right?"

"Yes, I suppose, although even classical guitar would be frowned on. My parents wanted me to start law school immediately, but I refused—told them I wanted to travel. They agreed to let me spend a few months in Europe. Travel is a matter of culture, after all. And so I took off with my guitar and backpack, and basically drifted from one country to another for over a year. I had no desire to settle anywhere…yet I dreaded returning to the life my parents had planned for me."

"Somehow I find it hard to imagine that you were alone for a day, much less a year."

"I didn't say I was alone."

"Another Cheryl isn't going to put in an appearance here, is she?"

"No, not a Cheryl. But in Majorca, I met a Dutch girl and went back to Amsterdam with her. I was tired of drifting. I lived with her for almost a year."

"So, were you in love with her?"

"I wouldn't call it love. Our mutual love of marijuana was the big attraction—that, and her attraction to other women, which could be very stimulating. It was a crazy time."

"I bet it was. Do you wish I was bi, too?"

"Do I detect a hint of jealousy?"

"In your dreams. I'm not the jealous type—never have been. Should I be?"

"No one compares to you, *reina*. Marieke and I lived together, but we weren't really a couple. It was more a relationship by default—I didn't know where I wanted to be, only that I didn't want to go back."

"But you did go back, right?"

"Eventually, yes. I couldn't go on living on an allowance like a child forever. I rationalized that since reality, as we perceive it, is only illusion anyway, one path is as good as another, so I might as well please my parents and go to law school."

"Jesus, that just sounds so fatalistic. I mean, Christ, of course one path is not as good as another."

"It was immaturity on my part…and laziness—not wanting to take responsibility for my choices. Of course, it was also a perverting of Hindu philosophy to justify my own inertia."

Emma squeezed Juan's leg. "You're talking to the right person here. I've always used any excuse known to man to justify my behavior. But honestly baby, I don't think you're in the same league as me when it comes to self-deception and just general craziness."

Juan looked at Emma out of the corner of his eyes as he maneuvered the windy road. "You're not as crazy as you'd like me to think you are. I'd say, by anybody's standards, you've managed your life pretty well."

Emma broke into laughter. "That shows how well you know me. I married you under false pretenses, that's for sure. If I'm your rock of sanity, you're in big trouble."

"In some ways, you're the sanest person I've ever met, *amorcito.* I was dead before I met you. You brought me to life."

"Sell that to someone else. You looked pretty alive when I met you. You didn't seem to be lost between worlds in Maya Land or anything."

"But I was. When I started classes at UCLA, I felt as if I had become imprisoned in my parent's version of reality. I went through the motions that first year…biding time, playing guitar to keep my sanity, but I was very unhappy. And then, the next year, my beloved grandmother died and she left me enough money to become independent. So naturally, I quit school immediately and moved to Venice Beach. My parents have never forgiven me for dropping out."

"We can win them over. It'll be different now, with you in a big band and everything."

"It was never a question of popularity or economics. It is our lifestyle—who we are. You are never going to fit their image of a proper Salvadoran wife…thank God."

"I'll wear modest clothes. I won't drink. And by the way, I'm willing to have babies—if you are. We could get a nanny to go on the road with us. You do want to have children some day, don't you?"

"I want twenty children, and all of them to look like you, *reina*. But if the earth should allow us to replace ourselves with two children, I would be grateful. I would be the happiest man on earth."

"We can start working on it any time, or at least practicing." Emma ran her hand lightly along the inside of Juan's leg.

"You're not making it easy to concentrate on driving."

"You said you want children."

"Yes, I like being around children." Juan was trying to keep his eyes on the road. "I miss my niece and nephew. I've been negligent in my responsibility to my sister's children. I didn't even attend my nephew's baptism."

"Well, we'll make it up to them. I'll help you. I can keep it together when I have to. I just have this strong gut instinct that we should wire your family or call them or something, to let them know we're married. I don't want them to think that I'm the one who didn't want them at our wedding. Don't you see that?"

"They would not assume that it was your decision, I promise you. But okay, we'll do it. We'll send a telegram announcing our marriage if that will satisfy your sense of propriety. Anyway, I'd love to call my brother and sisters. You'll like them, especially Catarina, the baby. She's only sixteen, but very intelligent, and interested in everything."

"Now I'm nervous. How will I talk to them? Fuck, I've got to learn Spanish right away. I'd love to say "hi" to your family. Maybe you can teach me a few basic sentences so I don't sound like a complete idiot."

"Don't worry so much. Everyone in my family speaks English, except the babies. My parents don't speak very well, but they understand basic ideas."

"But you led me to believe that I wouldn't be able to communicate with your family. You did, you know you did. You lied to me, you jerk."

"Based on the premise of communication, I did not lie to you. Indeed, I assure you that you will not be able to communicate with my parents. I grew up speaking the same language as them, and I can't communicate with them. It's a different world."

"What a cop-out. Look at how you use debating tactics to slip out of admitting the truth—that you're a liar. Pull over at the next waterfall and I'll show you how I deal with masters of deception." Emma began tickling his ribs, kissing his neck and face. The car swerved crazily.

Around the next bend, a river split the rainforest and a waterfall poured over boulders into a small, clear pool. Juan pulled the car off the road under the flowering trees, and grabbed Emma.

"Wait baby, let's go swimming first. I'm all sweaty. We've got a picnic lunch. Aren't you hungry?" Emma murmured, as Juan kissed her face, her neck, her breasts. "Maybe we should take our towels down by the pool."

"You started this." Juan eased her bikini bottom down and off, then pulled her onto his lap in the front seat of the jeep.

Emma looked around. "What if another car comes by?'

"What if it does?"

...

The freshwater pool was refreshing, and after a swim, they picnicked by the waterfall before resuming their journey. The mood in the car had changed, and they stayed off serious subjects, content just to take in the beauty as they slowly made their way along the long road to Hana. They arrived at the Hana Resort Hotel at sunset to find that Margie had arranged for dinner in their bungalow, complete with candles and champagne. And this time, the place wasn't swarming with visitors. Apparently, everybody knew it was their honeymoon, and they were giving them some space.

At Emma's instigation, Juan called the front desk, got Margie, and asked her if she would arrange to send a wire to El Salvador. With a deep sigh, he gave her the information, told her where to send it.

Emma started laughing. "Jesus, it's not like you're sending a notification of death or something." When Juan didn't return her smile, Emma changed her tone, began rubbing his neck. "It'll be all right, baby, you'll see."

Juan shook his head. "I'd like to put them out of my mind now. The last thing I want to do on our honeymoon is think about my parents. Even their long reach can not touch us here."

The next afternoon, as Juan and Emma lay on the hotel's private beach, Alana came bouncing up to them with some fresh leis and a telegram from El Salvador. Emma was excited about it, and demanded Juan translate it immediately.

"It begins with a formal congratulation, but there is an implicit accusation in the wording. They go on to say that it is unthinkable that their son would marry without their approval, without even their knowledge. Of course this would be their reaction…I tried to warn you."

"It's okay, baby; don't get negative. We expected it. They'll come around. Let's go call your sisters and brother now, before it gets too late. It'll cheer you up. We can get them to run interference with your parents. Come on. I think the sky's about to open anyway."

Back in their bungalow they ordered Piña Coladas, and Juan dialed his sister Marta's number.

"*Si, gracias, Carlos*," Juan said into the phone. "Good to talk to you, too." Covering the phone with his hand, he whispered to Emma, "That was her husband, Carlos; he's calling Marta to the phone now…Marta?"

Emma watched as Juan conversed with his sister and her children in Spanish. The look on his face told her she was right to make him call his family.

Again, Juan whispered to Emma, "Marta says our marriage is the most exciting thing she has ever heard of, and she has two of your records, and she can't wait to meet you. She's asking one question after another about you; do you want to talk to her?"

"Yes, of course."

Juan said into the phone, "Do you want to talk to her now? Will you speak English?"

Emma took the phone, and Juan went to the door to let room service bring in their drinks. "Hi Marta," Emma said. "Thank you so much. Wow, that's so great to hear. Wait till you hear the new one with your brother playing on it. Yeah, thanks. How are the children? Uh-huh, can't wait to see them. Really? Wow, he sounds so smart. No, we won't be able to come until spring because we've got to do a tour. Yeah, promotional. Uh-huh, the new album. Me too. Well, why don't you guys come to San Francisco for Christmas?"

Juan nearly dropped his Piña Colada. He had turned white. "No, no," he mouthed, shaking his head vehemently.

Emma ignored him. "Wow," she said to Marta, "you really think so? God, that would be great. We could take the kids to The Nutcracker. Yeah, I hope so. Okay, nice talking to you, too. See you soon." Hanging up the phone, Emma turned to Juan, reached for her drink and took a sip. "Guess what? Your whole family may come for Christmas!"

Juan's face stiffened up. He blinked in disbelief. "That was an impulsive invitation, Emma. You should have asked me before suggesting such a thing."

"Jesus, you can be so negative. Marta and I hit it off. Her English is great. It would be fun. You said you miss the kids."

"It would be delightful to see Marta and the kids, but Emma, we will now have to invite my parents, as well. An impossible situation has suddenly developed."

"Well, you've got to face them sometime, and it will be festive during the holidays. We can buy the kids a bunch of presents and take them to see Santa…oh, lighten up; it's not the end of the world."

"My only hope is that Marta will be unable to accept the invitation. How could you do it, Emma? Do my wishes mean nothing to you? Your rash behavior is intolerable…I'm going to have a cigarette."

"You're just using this as a lame excuse to break our pact—no smoking before dinner, period end. If you do, then I will, and we'll both be right back up to a pack a day. You're not really that mad at me, are you, baby? I just want you to patch things up with your family; you'll feel better if you do…how about if I roll you a joint?"

Emma went into the other room, fumbled around, came back with a lit joint and placed it between Juan's lips. Juan took several tokes, then passed the joint to Emma. They both watched as the pot smoke swirled in colorful patterns in the air made humid from the warm rain. "Can we talk about it?" she asked softly.

"There's nothing to talk about. I overreacted."

Emma wasn't going for the "overreacted" explanation. In spite of all Juan's protesting that he didn't care what his parents thought, she was pretty sure the opposite was true. Why else would the unflappable Mr. Avelar get so bent out of shape at the mere thought of confronting them. "What's the worst that could happen if they come?" Emma asked.

"Nothing, nothing at all. It's all in my head; I know this, Emma. I don't want to talk about it—they'll probably come, and it will be fine. It's all illusion anyway."

"What, you're not going to start with the "all illusion anyway" business again, are you! Feelings are powerful, even if you don't acknowledge them."

"Feelings are unreliable, but I concede that they're powerful. I'm sorry, *amorcito*. I should not try to make you feel bad about being gracious to my family."

"I don't forgive you."

Juan pulled Emma into a tight embrace, and whispered into her ear, "I don't blame you. I'm a fool."

"All right, I forgive you if you're going to be that way about it." Emma melted into him.

Juan pulled back and looked into her eyes. "You did the right thing, *reina*; you always do. Let's call my brother in New Haven and invite him, too. Then we'll call my parents, and we can talk to Catarina."

"Now?" Emma stepped back into his embrace. "Can't it wait? I'm feeling somewhat distracted at the moment."

Later, they put in the call. Ricardo seemed thrilled with the invitation—told Emma he would much rather come to California for the holidays than go back home. He'd read about the marriage in the newspapers, so he wasn't surprised, but his feelings were hurt. Even though he understood why Juan hadn't invited the family, he wished he could have been at the wedding. He also told Emma he was a fan, and that she wouldn't have married Juan if she'd met him first.

Emma hung up the phone and turned to Juan, laughing, "Your brother is a flirt."

"You can't blame him. He loves your music and you are so beautiful. All right, let's do it. Let's call my parents."

"Okay, now I'm getting nervous. I don't want to blow it for you. What do I call them? What are their names? You've never even mentioned their names."

"The culture in my country is formal. You should address them as Mr. and Mrs. Avelar at first, but they will probably tell you that you may call them Don Gilberto and Doña Margarita because you are a family member. Don't worry, they'll be polite. I've probably blown this up into more than it is. And they already know we are married, anyway. Ricardo told me that he called them after he read the news."

Juan dialed his home number as Emma stood nervously shifting from one foot to another. "*Hola, Mamá.*" *Si Mamá, gracias. Hola* Catarina, did you grab the phone from *Mamá*? His body visibly relaxed as he talked to his sister "*Si*, I love you, too. Will you speak English? Yes, it is true that I married Emma Allison. No, I wouldn't say I'm famous now. Ah, Ricky told you. You'll meet her very soon. What is she like? Yes, you can come to a concert. Is she very conceited? What kind of question is that! Will she like you? Here, why don't you ask her yourself, since you're obviously not interested in your brother anymore—only his famous wife." Juan handed the phone to Emma.

"Thank you." Emma took the phone and her face broke into a huge smile. "Of course I'll send you a copy of the new one. Your brother is brilliant on it. God, I'll send you a hundred copies so you can give them to your friends. Thank you, I can't wait to meet you either. I always wanted a sister. No, I'm an only child…whenever you want. Absolutely, maybe at Christmas. I can't wait either."

Then Margarita Avelar was on the line, welcoming Emma into the family. Emma thought she sounded charming, really nice. With a thumbs up to Juan, she handed the phone over to him. Juan spoke in Spanish to his mother, so Emma didn't understand what he was saying, but she deduced from his tone and manner that his mother was giving him a hard time.

"What did she say?" Emma asked as soon as he hung up the phone. "I knew she would be pissed off that we didn't invite them to our wedding. I knew it."

"She asked if we were married in the church by a priest, and when I told her we weren't, she said she was relieved because the marriage is not valid. She said we could have it annulled easily."

"Really? That's what she said after being so nice to me! Fuck. She sounded so charming, and the rest of your family seemed to like me. Well, I can't say you didn't warn me."

"It's not personal, Emma. She probably did like you—how could anyone not like you. She's stuck in the Colonial mentality, that's all. I am the first son, and as such, I will inherit the family home and coffee plantations…it was expected that I would marry a girl from one of the families of the oligarchy—for the connections…for power, and to uphold the traditions of my family. It makes me crazy. Let's light another joint."

Emma lit a joint and took a long, deep drag. "So, your mom's a hypocrite. Hey, no one's perfect. Ray and Stephanie have their moments, too. They're your parents, we'll deal with it."

"Yes Emma, as you say, no one is perfect; but it's not like my parents just have bad habits or annoying mannerisms. They have deep-rooted beliefs and customs that impoverish and enslave the indigenous people of my country. And they have no perspective on how backward they are, how cruel."

"Well, people change. Look, I'm just trying to make you feel better about them. Maybe we'll be a good influence and they'll change their attitudes; and your brother is cool—maybe together we can make a difference. You've got to have hope."

"Yes, but you've also got to be realistic. My parents don't want change—it's a threat to them. They believe it is in their best interest to maintain the status quo, and in my country it's maintained through intimidation, through military police…and through making deals with the United States. My family is powerful in El Salvador. My father is a ruthless man…but even so, he is my father, and I love him. I love both my parents, but I don't respect their way of life. It exploits and oppresses the poor. It's a no-win situation."

"Nonsense, there's no such thing. Maybe we'll be part of the solution. Where there's life, there's hope. Come on, the sun is shining again. Let's go back out on the beach; the rain has stopped."

...

The week played itself out in a lazy succession of days at the beach, and nights of hanging out with friends, or holing up in their rooms, exchanging opinions on everything from trivia to politics and religion—and making idolatrous love day and night.

Just when Emma and Juan felt like they had totally relaxed into the laid back rhythm of Hana, it was time to leave. They would only have a few days at home before starting the tour.

On the plane ride back to San Francisco, Juan said to Emma, "I think we should move. Buy a house together, start out fresh."

"What, don't you like my house? Do you think there's something creepy about it?"

"It's not that I don't like the house. It's that it's your house. I want to start our life together in a house that belongs to both of us. I want to buy you a house, not live in yours."

"This isn't about what I said when I was mad at you, is it? God, baby, you know I didn't mean that, don't you?"

"No, it is as I say; I want a house that is ours. I have enough from my inheritance to buy us a nice house. What about in Marin County? You're always saying you'd like to live in Mill Valley. Let's buy a house there."

"Everybody else has moved across the bridge; we might as well, too. It's just so weird because I grew up in Marin. It's like I'm going home or something. But it would be out-of-sight. We could have a pool and a big garden with redwood trees, and a studio. Yeah, let's do it. I'll sell my house. It has bad vibes anyway, always has. We could pool our money, get a big place with lots of room for kids, and guest rooms for your family. Are you sure? You want to do it?"

"Anything that makes you this animated has to be a good idea. Let's do it right away."

"I know who can find us the perfect house: John Cipollina's dad, Gino. He lives in Mill Valley, he's a realtor, and he's very cool."

...

The day after they got home, Juan and Emma met Gino in Mill Valley to look at houses. He had one in mind that he was sure they would like, but he showed them a few others first so they could make comparisons. Winding up the narrow roads of Mill Valley to the top of Mt. Tamalpais at the end of the afternoon, Gino pulled into a long, wooded driveway that led to a large Brown Shingle built around the turn of the century. There were two cabins, a swimming pool, and five acres of redwood trees. The view was spectacular, with the rolling hills, the bay, the City, and even the tip of the Golden Gate Bridge. They made the decision to buy it on the spot.

Out on the road, in Kansas City, their offer was accepted and the house went into escrow. They were in Dayton, when they phoned El Salvador and found out that Juan's family had accepted Emma's invitation—they were coming for Christmas. Things were moving right along on the home and family front.

Things were going great with her career, too. Emma felt that the new band, with Juan on lead guitar, was the best she'd ever had. They were playing to packed houses, the album was climbing the charts fast, and the single, "*Close To Your Heart*," was at number 1.

...

The tour became a major period of adjustment for the newlyweds. Emma was used to running the show, and as much as she had always tried to maintain a hippie, communal atmosphere within the band and crew, everyone was aware that they were working for her. She always got what she wanted. But things were different with Juan. He always seemed more interested in music and ideas than the material world, but he'd made it clear that the concept of working for his wife was unthinkable. They had agreed that he would join the band as an independent contractor.

Some of the entourage were jealous of him, and they would get in little digs whenever they could—insinuate that he was living off his wife's talent. Perhaps it bothered Emma more than it did Juan. He seemed able to shrug things off, but she took note of the comments and where they were coming from—mainly, Roger, who had it in for him because he had replaced James. Although it was true that Emma had catapulted Juan into the limelight, that didn't detract from the fact that he had spent years studying music, refining his guitar playing skills. He wouldn't be on stage with Emma if he weren't good enough, and Emma was sure he knew her well enough to realize that.

Juan seemed able to always keep his cool—basically just ignoring the negativity and keeping a low profile in band politics. He smoked a lot of pot and meditated. Emma teased him to no end about the meditating, but secretly she admired the way he stayed detached from all the band crap. And when she drank too much and got too crazy, he would retreat to his own hotel room—which drove her crazy, but she understood.

For her part, Emma tried to tone down the drinking and keep things on an even keel. She knew the male ego way too well to ever override Juan's decisions or contradict him in public. Juan had an easy rapport with the road manager, Ed, and most of the band. For the most part, they respected Juan's musical abilities and his casual, cool persona. The press was a different matter.

Although the majority of the reviewers praised Juan's guitar playing, there were always a significant number of critics who seemed to feel that the only good review is one that contains heaps of sarcasm. Juan got to be their target this time around.

"Latin lover should stay Close to Allison's Heart and away from her concerts," read one of the reviews in Cleveland.

There was an element of racism in some of the reviews that took Emma by complete surprise. But not Juan.

"The stereotypes are abundant. Positive or negative, they're still there. At least he didn't suggest I go back to washing dishes," was Juan's reaction to the article.

Juan's influence was evident in the music on the album, evident in the band in concert, and evident in Emma's earnest attempts to reshape her behavior.

"Allison has never sounded better than she does on this tour. No longer the whimsical flower child, Emma has blossomed into full-blown womanhood, as gutsy and complex as the wide array of material she offers in concert. Her husband, Juan Avelar on lead guitar, steers the band into uncharted territory, recharging Emma's old standards with a new consciousness, a Latin-psychedelic-blues sensibility. Just the electricity between them on stage makes the show worth catching," another critic in Cleveland reported.

The tour generated enough in album sales for the record company to recoup their promotional expenses and the wedding expenses within a few weeks. Emma knew she was an enigma to the record company businessmen—a pain in the ass, actually. But she also came through where she knew it mattered most to them—in their bank accounts.

Chapter Nine

Emma: Christmas, 1974

It was pretty hectic when we came home from tour. We only had two days before Juan's family was coming in and I hadn't even finished Christmas shopping. Plus, we had to start thinking about what we would do with my house—sell it or rent it. And then there was packing and sorting through stuff that also really needed to be done. It seemed so overwhelming that I decided to just shine it all on and not worry about it. Juan and I went shopping together for his family instead. It was one of our best days together, ever. The City was so festive that it snapped him out of his dreary brooding about his parents' visit. Jesus, he could be morose sometimes. But on that bright winter day in San Francisco, we were like an ad for the city, riding streetcars, walking through the crowded streets together arm in arm, enthusiastically buying presents like nobody's business.

Juan and I were learning how to skirt around each other's hang-ups. I was trying my damnedest not to party too much and get crazy on him, and he was trying to be more communicative with me about what he was feeling. I'd get fucking worried when those green eyes of his would focus on some distant place that I couldn't reach. It would make me want to get wasted. And he said that he felt like he couldn't reach *me* when I was drunk, so there it was. At least the problem was that we wanted to maintain contact with each other, instead of either of us feeling smothered.

I got Christina to organize getting the house cleaned and decorated for Christmas. Juan and I went out for a Christmas tree, came back with one so big we had to cut it down to fit in the house. Then we cut it too much, so it ended up shorter than we wanted. It was beautiful, though. Everything was ready by the time Ricardo arrived on the night of the 22nd. What a flash that was. He was too young for me, and I was already in love with his brother, but talk about a lady-killer. Ricardo was as handsome as Juan. And I don't say that lightly. He was also a little more full of himself than Juan, but I liked him. He was my brother now.

I went to bed early that night to give the brothers some time alone together. They hadn't seen each other in ages. That was hard for me to understand. I had always imagined that if I had brothers or sisters, we would hang out together a lot.

We hired two stretch-limos for his family's visit because we couldn't cart everybody around, even with both our cars. Besides that, parking is a bummer in San Francisco, and even worse during the holidays. There would be seven people coming in at the airport, plus Ricardo, Juan, and me.

Catarina was the first to come bounding through the gate, straight into Juan's arms, then Ricardo's, and then mine. Gorgeous, just like her brothers, Catarina had the exuberance of a child, with a playful, intelligent glint in her eyes. She smothered me with kisses, then hooked her arm through mine possessively. Probably felt my low-level tremble as I greeted her parents politely, shook hands with Mr. Avelar, received a kiss on the cheek from Doña Margarita.

Both of Juan's parents were excessively well-groomed people. Attractive enough, but straight-looking beyond belief, just like Juan had said. His dad was dressed pretty much like the straight dudes here, in a sports jacket and dark trousers, short hair, close shaven, handsome, but something unattractive in the lines around his eyes and mouth. His mom looked like an aging beauty queen in her tailored, navy-blue pants suit, with her shiny black hair pulled taut into a chignon at the nape of her neck—perfect make-up, and plenty of it—plenty of gold jewelry, too. They both were hard to read, as though their attire were designed to let them check you out while making it impossible for you to assess them.

Marta was pretty, but she was dressed like an old lady in a pants suit that looked like an olive-green replica of her mother's. I knew she was a year younger than me, but she looked older to me.

But she and her husband, Carlos, were friendly—kissed me and seemed sincere in congratulating us on our marriage. They were exhausted from the flight, harried, trying to keep track of their kids who were so happy to be out of the confinement of the plane that they were running in circles. Two-year-old Oscar had to be picked up to keep him from taking off, and he screamed in protest. Four-year-old Silvia eyed her uncles with reserved curiosity, until Juan scooped her up and began throwing her up into the air and catching her, causing her to shriek with laughter. It was a trip for me to see Juan with his niece. He was just so natural, so at ease.

It was one of those rare days at the airport when everyone's luggage actually arrived, and I took that as a good omen for the visit.

I wanted to come across as the perfect wife and all that, so I'd hired these two hippie housecleaners, Deanna and Cathy, to get a dinner together while we were at the airport. They were to make lasagna, salad, and garlic bread. That was it. Get it done, have the kitchen cleaned up, and be gone by the time we got home.

Not exactly how it panned out. I knew something was fucked-up the minute we pulled up to the house, because Deanna's car was still in the driveway. There she was at the door, greeting Juan's family as though they were her long-lost friends, trying to hug even his standoffish father—drunk on her butt and speeding on meth, too. You could smell the alcohol a mile away. Then Cathy strolled into the room, trying to act casual and normal, grinding her teeth, trying to keep her equilibrium.

"We got into the wine while we were cooking. Had to open it anyway for the sauce. You guys were gone so long we had to open another bottle. Did you have a good flight?" Deanna said to the room.

Cathy grabbed at my coat and purse. "Here, let me help you, Emma. It's such a gas to be here. Do you guys know how far fucking out this chick is? Emma is the best; she's the best," Cathy announced, breaking into tears from the gush of alcohol-induced emotion. "I love her. I love Emma. She's out-of-sight. I fucking love her."

"Right on," Deanna said.

I was stunned. Here Juan had given me a big lecture about not saying "fuck" in front of his parents, and not getting wasted, and I had done everything I could to be cool and impress the shit out of them. And we come home to psycho drunk chicks on speed. It was all I could do not to start laughing. What the fuck, you know? You do your best, and then life throws one at you. Jesus! Both Cathy and Deanna were too drunk to drive, so we had to send them home in one of the limos and have the other driver follow with Cathy's car. So much for making a good impression on Juan's family. At least the dinner was good.

And before she went to bed that night, Catarina told me that it was worth anything to have seen the look on her mother's face when Cathy tried to hug her father, and when she came out with all the bad language. "It's good for my parents, Emma. They are so…hard, I think you would say. They need to become more modern. I'm very happy. I love you."

The day before Christmas was sunny and cold, with a sharp wind that bit through your clothes. After a light breakfast, we took Juan's family sightseeing in the limos. We hit all the usual places—Fisherman's Wharf, Ghiradelli Square, Union Square. The city was all lit up, music on every corner. We ended the day taking photos of the Golden Gate Bridge, then crossing it to go to my parent's pad for Christmas Eve dinner. Juan had smoked a little pot with his brother during the day, sneaking off like they were two naughty kids. It cracked me up. I was glad he did because it made him chill out. After all his worrying about his parents, things had gotten off to such a crazy start that I think he just gave up. He let me do the worrying instead.

Juan's parents rode in the limo with Marta and Carlos and the kids on the way to Sausalito, which gave Ricardo and Catarina and Juan and I some time alone together.

"Go ahead and smoke your marijuana," Catarina said with a sly grin. "I already know you do. I'm not a child. I know what you've been doing."

Ricardo lit a joint. "Cata, you're too smart for us."

I'm usually the first to start fucking around, but this was over the top. "Jesus, you guys, you're going to get busted. What if your father smells it—won't he know?"

"No, he doesn't know what it is," Cata stated smugly. "Ricky, give me a cigarette; come on, before we get there. I like to smoke. They know I do sometimes; it's okay." Then out of the blue, she turned to me.

"Emma, teach me how to say bad words in English, like the girls said when we arrived. I know the words, but I don't know where they go in a sentence. I want to make my parents frown like that again. It is so good for them. They are too much controlled."

"No, *hermanita*, you must not do that," Juan said. "It's already hard enough for Emma and me. If you start to use bad language, they will blame us."

"No, because I'll tell them it is Ricky's fault," Catarina teased her brothers. "But this is serious to me, Emma, because I want to be free, like the women here. You said this word when my parents were in the store. You said *fuck*, and I think this is good to express what you feel. Why is it so bad, my parents cannot tell me, only that it is dirty?"

Christ, there was no way I could have seen this one coming. "Listen Cata, I don't want to do anything to offend your parents. For God's sake, don't go saying *fuck* in front of them."

"Okay, I promise, if you will explain."

"It's hard to explain. It's kind of a philosophical thing here, using words like *fuck*. I mean, I was brought up by pretty loose parents and they were into this whole Lenny Bruce, beatnik thing. Like words aren't dirty or bad, but things people do are bad—like hurting each other, like racism—these things are bad. But words in and of themselves are not bad. They only have the power you give them."

"Yes, I think I know what you are saying. If a person does bad things to people, but he doesn't say bad words, this does not make him good. So you can say bad words and have a good intention, yes?"

"Exactly. And the idea is that you also have to strip words of their power to harm you. Do you understand? If you can't say *fuck*, then you're basically saying that sex is so bad that you can't even say the word. Fuck, I'm getting lost here. Let me have a hit, if you guys are doing it anyway. Okay, Cata?"

Cata reached for the joint. "I want to try it, too."

"No, absolutely not," Juan said in a weird, authoritarian tone of voice that jerked my head around. "You couldn't handle it in front of them. Another time, Cata. Maybe at the beach, with just the four of us, but not now."

I like Emma better than you men." Cata's bottom lip went into a pout. "She treats me with more respect. And she's smarter than you."

That did it for me. I passed the joint to Cata. I could see what a pain in the ass these big brothers were to her. I was getting high at her age and I sure as shit wouldn't have wanted someone telling me I couldn't. Anyway, I didn't think Mr. And Mrs. Avelar would even notice—what with the little kids to look after, and meeting my crazy parents and everything. Besides, you don't really get high the first time you smoke—you have to learn how to do it right. Sure enough, Cata spluttered and coughed on the couple of hits she took—didn't keep much smoke down.

"What is lenny bruce?" Cata was trying to maintain her dignity and keep the conversation going. But suddenly we were pulling into my parent's driveway, and the guys were snuffing out the joint, all of us trying to change gears fast, to cop a straight face. I had a bottle of lavender water in my purse, and I sprayed us all down before we got out of the car.

Being with Juan's parents, stoned, was a bizarre trip. They were like aliens. When we all piled out of the limos at my parents' funky, arty house, they both looked over at me, and the way they looked at me made me paranoid. I finally understood what Juan had been going on about. Their eyes had the dark, cold intensity of Artic waters. I had to get it together fast because I had to do introductions and everything, and I didn't think I was going to be able to pull it off. And then little Silvia pulled away from her grandmother and came leaping into my arms. Put her little arms around my neck, and pulled me back from that paranoid space into her sweet presence. "*Te quiero, tia,*" she murmured into my neck.

With all fairness to Gilberto and Margarita, they were fish out of water standing there at my parents' doorstep, inside a huge metal sculpture entitled, "The Universe Inside You," which served as the front porch. Abstract redwood sculptures, scattered throughout a Japanese rock garden that was interspersed with ferns and flowers, made up the rest of the front entrance. All in all, it was as disparate and wildly artistic as both my parents. Gilberto and Margarita's manicured appearance, their carefully cultivated mannerisms, stood out in stark contrast to my own parents' way of being, even before Ray and Stephanie opened the door. As I took in the scene, in stoned, slow motion, I noticed Margarita's eye twitch, watched her try to gain control of the traitorous nerve. It dawned on me then, that beneath their armor of sophisticated geniality, Juan's parents were nervous about this meeting, too. I felt a twinge of regret that I had gotten high, that I had, in fact, just turned their daughter on to pot.

"My mother's friends did most of these sculptures," I said like a tour guide. "My parents have been collecting for years. Some of these artists are in the big museums now, but my parents got their stuff before they became well known." I was prattling on, grasping at reasonable conversational material as we waited for someone to come to the door. Jesus, it wasn't like they weren't expecting us.

Finally the damned door opened, and there stood my mother, looking beautiful in the antique velvet gown I had given her for

Christmas last year. Silver highlights glinted in the tangle of tight, brown curls that frizzed around her face and down her back. She greeted each of us in her usual fashion, hugging and kissing right off the bat, even Gilberto and Margarita. Stephanie smelled like vanilla, and nobody ever seemed to mind her hugs and kisses, including Juan's parents.

The house smelled like cedar and salt water, like sandalwood incense and roast beef, and like the pine of the huge Christmas tree that dominated the living room. Three walls of the living room were window, which made it seem like the blue water of the bay and the boats in the harbor, the distant city lights of San Francisco and the little Victorian shops of Sausalito, were all part of the house. I knew my family's scene was probably a million light years from the Avelar's, but I didn't see how they could fail to dig it.

My dad swept down on everybody, taking coats, kissing the children, putting out pots and pans and my old toys for Oscar and Silvia to play with. Stephanie disappeared into the kitchen, and reappeared with delicious looking hors d'oeuvres. Ray followed, carrying his special holiday mulled wine. Juan and Ricky and I, who had the munchies, dived for the food, and Cata was right behind us. So much for not getting stoned your first time.

Marta and Carlos seemed grateful to Ray for diverting the kids, and everyone relaxed as the wine worked its way through our nervous systems, through our distinctly different planetary genetic codes. Ray and Stephanie put dinner on the table, got us all seated, offered up thanksgiving to the Great Spirit of Compassion, then asked Juan's parents if they'd like to say a blessing. Gilberto recited what sounded like some standard prayer, and I dug it. It made me feel like we had achieved some familial harmony, in spite of our being from different planets.

On Christmas morning, after getting the turkey in the oven, the whole troop of us bundled up warm and went to the beach. It was freezing, of course, but also invigorating. The kids got to run their energy out, and we all had a nice, long walk. By the time we got back, Ray and Stephanie had come over, and friends had started dropping by. It turned into a jam, with Juan and Ricky on guitar, Ray playing sax, friends playing percussion and singing. I shooed all the friends out at dinnertime though—wanted it to be just family.

We did the whole holiday thing, singing Christmas carols, feasting, opening presents. It was good will to all, like a storybook Christmas. Everybody but the kids drank a great deal of wine and champagne and cognac. Getting wasted together helped us bridge the significant chasm that was actually the centerpiece of our first holiday together as one big, happy family.

So that was me on the domestic front. I tried; I gave it everything I had. But I had New Year's shows coming up, big stadium affairs, double-billed with another band, and I got edgy as the days wore on with the Avelar's. I had to watch what I said and did twenty-four fucking hours a day, and I started feeling stifled. Juan got it. I mean, he grew up feeling that way. Ricky just pretty much zoned his parents out, got into a thing with one of my friends, and started crashing at her pad every night. But Cata was ripping through ten years in ten days. It was like she'd been saving up her energy, awaiting the opportunity to explode into full-fledged rebellion—to express her total disdain for her parents' values and conventions. You can guess who Mr. and Mrs. Avelar blamed for that. And to a certain extent, they were right. Cata was ready and we provided the time and place.

We took Cata with us to rehearsals on the 29th. I could see her hanging out with a roadie from the other band, drinking tequila and smoking pot while we were on stage. Juan was vibing the guy as we went over our songs, and during the break he stormed over and snatched the shot glass out of Cata's hand. I did a double take. Juan was majorly pissed off at her and the guy, which I thought was unfair, because, Christ, they weren't doing anything outrageous. She should be allowed to have a good time, too.

Sometimes Juan was like a fucking carbon copy of his parents, and I told him so. He got so pissed off at me that he just split and left us there at the rehearsal hall.

It was the same old jive shit from him—split at the first sign of conflict. Well, I figured, fuck it—two can play the same game. So Cata and I split in the limo with her cute roadie and Greg, who sang with the other band. They were from the East Coast and I knew him from when I was recording in New York. I'd had a thing with him a long time ago, but I made it clear to him that I was with Juan now, married in fact, and that Cata was my sister-in-law. He was fairly cool with it. The four of us went out to dinner, talked, tried to outdo each other with road stories. No sex, although I could have, of course. Got home around ten, not too late. Jesus Christ, you'd have thought we'd been missing for days. I wasn't the one who'd fucking left us there in the first place, but Saint Juan was at his most self-righteous, accusing me of humiliating him in front of his family, in whispers, you understand, since the house was full of people. Cata came knocking on the door. She'd sensed the tension and wanted Juan to know that I hadn't flirted with Greg or done anything wrong, and that she was on my side because he was the one who had stormed off and left us.

Juan and I made up later that night, when I had sobered up. Both of us apologized and he actually thanked me for being so good with his family.

The shows helped me regain some of the ground I had lost with the family after bringing Cata home drunk and stoned. They all seemed to enjoy the flash of the huge concert, getting to hang out backstage—a special room for the kids with a clown and babysitters and balloons and toys. Lots of diversions for Ricky and Cata, too—beautiful babes and dudes, plenty of drugs.

The tension between Juan and I dissipated as we got back into our gig routine and the shows went well. It's always harder doing hometown gigs. You want to sound good in front of all your friends. And every person you've ever met has been calling you, wanting a backstage pass, and the backstage area becomes an intense scene in itself. Sometimes it can jinx you, having all your friends at the side of the stage. Not to mention your in-laws from the planet El Salvador. But the shows went well for us. New Year's Eve was extra high energy. Juan played some killer solos that levitated the stadium, and my voice held up through a million encores and an all-star jam at the end of the evening.

I felt like we partially redeemed ourselves with the good *Señor* and *Señora* for our wicked influence on Cata. That fucker, Ricky, never did get any of the blame for his sister's sudden descent into degeneracy. He knew how to play his parents. Didn't take them seriously the way Juan did. But in all fairness to Juan, he had all the first-son bullshit to contend with, and besides, he just wasn't a player like Ricky.

Thank God Margarita and Gilberto didn't have a clue about a lot of shit, or there would have been no redemption for any of us. Cata accidentally on purpose got dosed with acid backstage at the New Year's show. I knew the culprit had to be that cute roadie, because it wasn't like acid was in every beverage backstage like it is at the Dead shows. You had to want it to get it, but I didn't say that in front of her big brother, my virtuous husband. She actually had a great trip, sitting with the roadie on the opposite side of the stage from her parents, digging the music. And her parents went home with the kids after our set, didn't stay for the jam, so Cata's trip escaped their notice.

It was obvious that given the opportunity, Cata could turn into as wild a child as I had been. That seemed okay on one hand, but scary on the other. Jesus, it was like I was getting old, wishing I could warn a young girl about what to avoid, hoping she wouldn't go through some of the stuff I went through. That line of thought led straight to Carol, but I struggled to push it away.

There had been some surprises during the holiday visit. The first one was that I formed such an attachment to Cata. Jesus, she was smart and so fucking sassy—my kind of person. The other thing was that you couldn't help noticing how much Juan's parents loved their family. However straight they were, however different their take on life, no one could say they didn't love their kids and their grandkids. I even started feeling as if maybe they loved me a little bit, too, by the end of their visit. I was part of the family now, and I think they accepted that fact on some level.

When the family left, taking the kids to Disneyland before heading home, I was both sad and relieved. Juan and I could breathe again. We only had a few days alone before we were off on a two-and-a-half month tour.

Every day we drove over to Marin to look at our new house. We'd get burgers to go and then park near the house to eat—just sit in the car staring at the house, like we were at a drive-in or something. We couldn't get enough of it.

One day we were sitting up there smoking a joint, fantasizing about the recording studio we'd put in the house, and wouldn't you fucking know it, someone must have called the cops, because there they were, tapping on the window. Juan was holding the joint, and the car was full of marijuana smoke. I thought we were busted for sure, but the cop turned out to be a fan and after I dragged an album out of the trunk and signed it for him, he left us with a warning to be more discrete.

We hit the road with a degree of enthusiasm I hadn't felt since my first tour. The visit with Juan's family had made us closer—chalk one up to my instincts. Those gray cities had lost their ability to depress me, and it was like the audience picked up on our vibe. Juan and I were floating miles above the monotony of the road. My intellectual, low-key husband had turned into a kick-ass performer, bringing all the intensity of his cerebral space onto the stage, loosing it on the band and the audience. I was having a ball up there, and there was no place I wanted to be but with him. I'd caught a glimpse of serenity from the closeness we shared. Most nights after the shows we'd hang with the band for an hour or so, then go back to our room, make love, and then write songs. It wasn't a new pattern of behavior for me, but everything felt new with Juan.

Juan and I got so close that we could feel the world through each other's skin, tune in to what the other was thinking, finish sentences for each other. This was particularly good for song writing—the phrasing, the melody and words flowing naturally from the music, or vice-versa. We tried to learn everything there was to know about each other. The only thing I held back from him was stuff that I didn't think he could handle. Like the sheer number of guys I had slept with. Like my life as a junkie. Like Rob.

Chapter Ten

Moving to Marin: 1975

The band closed the tour in Ft. Lauderdale, March 10th. Emma's old friend, Linda, showed up at the concert and invited Juan and Emma to come spend some time at her house in West Palm Beach. It was an irresistible offer, despite the fact that they were both itching to get back to California for the big move into their new house. Their escrow wasn't due to close for a few more days, but they wanted to start packing, getting ready.

However, Emma and Linda had been close at one time, and Emma hadn't seen her since the wedding, so she wanted to spend some time with her. Juan encouraged the idea—said it was good for Emma to connect with her girlfriends, to be around people who didn't put her on a pedestal because of her fame.

Linda and Emma had kicked around San Francisco together, but eventually Linda moved east to be able to earn a better living doing astrological charts and readings. When Emma had visited her in New York, Linda was still struggling. She told Emma it was too fast paced for her and she couldn't get used to the weather. Emma had suggested Florida, and judging by her house, which was an enormous, if somewhat dilapidated, Spanish style mansion right on the beach, Florida had worked out well. Juan showed great enthusiasm for the musty old manor house—said it reminded him of the beach houses in his homeland.

Of course, the first thing Linda did when she got the newlyweds back at her house was gather all the vital stats on them so she could do their charts. Juan went along with what he obviously considered a parlor game—gave her his birth date, and time and place.

"I thought you already did my chart years ago. What, did the planets shift or something? Do they look different here than they did in California?" Emma teased her friend.

While Juan and Emma relaxed on the beach, Linda stayed in her study to work on their charts. A couple of hours later, she appeared on the beach bearing wine and a cheese plate with fruit, and two ornately designed charts.

"So, you got them done." Emma sat up and dusted the sand off her hands. She reached for a slice of pineapple, took a bite. "What do you think? Do we have a shot at making this work? Are the stars in our favor?"

Linda poured them each a glass of wine and handed it to them. "Yes, you're definitely right for each other," she said, but she looked troubled.

Emma searched Linda's face. "What's the matter? Are we going to end up murdering each other or something?"

"Nothing like that." Linda looked down at the charts, apparently studying them for a minute, and then glanced back up at Emma. "When did you get so paranoid? Your suns are in trine, which is the most compatible relationship."

"Oh, thank God." Emma lit a joint and passed it to Juan. "I've been worried about it all day," she said, teasingly.

Linda ignored that. "Not only are your suns in trine, but your moons are conjunct, which means you're on the same wave-length, that you can live together easily because you instinctually relate to life in the same way."

"Yeah, okay, but we have our moments, believe me. Tell her, Juan."

"I'm staying out of this."

Linda carried on. "And you've got to have a hot sex life because the significators of passion and love, Mars and Venus, are all in harmonious relationship. You're soul mates. Count your lucky stars you found each other."

"Good one, Linda. 'Thank our lucky stars'—I like it." Emma passed her the joint, and noticed a fleck of worry in her eyes. "So what else do you see? Does my self-proclaimed genius show up in my chart?"

"I'll do a whole reading for you in the house, but we better put these away so the sand doesn't wreck them." Linda rolled the charts up, fastening them with a rubber band.

"Wait a minute, I want to see something in the charts," Emma said.

"Later. Look, the sun is starting to set behind my house. Doesn't it look cool? Wait till you see the moon over the manor. Trippy, looking out on the ocean and it not being west, isn't it?" Fidgeting around nervously, picking up the beach things, Linda continued, "It's so great to have you guys here. My old man and I split up right after Christmas. Saturn was opposing his Mars and he got really wigged, so I had to kick him out."

...

After they got back from dinner, Linda laid the charts out on the coffee table and went over all the aspects to show them how perfectly suited they were for each other. She lost Juan after a few minutes. He excused himself, and went up to the bedroom to lie down.

"Good night, and thank you for hosting us in your home," he said to Linda. And to Emma, "Take your time, *reina*, I'm going to read for a while. Be with your friend."

When he was out of earshot, Emma said, "Okay Linda, thanks for the pep talk. It helps when you're telling people what they want to hear, doesn't it? But come on, tell me what this means. What's all this stuff globed together in this one house? It must have some special significance."

"Some heavy shit for you, Em. I think you probably already know."

"You mean about Carol?"

"Yes, I think so. Also, look at where this is. That could indicate addiction. Neptune was squaring your ascendant in the late sixties. It's probably the period when you were strung out."

"What about all this in Juan's horoscope, too? The same as in mine. What does that mean?"

"I'm not sure, Em. It could be a problem in your relationship, something you're keeping from him maybe. Yeah, that's probably what it is. Have you told him about everything that went down with Carol—that whole trip?"

"Not yet; the right time just hasn't come."

"Oh good, that's it then. Saturn can be really heavy, but I think you've already been through the worst of it. You better tell him. Yeah, that's this build up of Saturn, all right."

"Fucking Saturn. Fine, I was going to tell him when we got home anyway, but if it's in my stars, that's the sealer, right?" Suddenly Emma felt edgy. She got up from the couch and started prowling around the room. "Have you got some tequila or brandy? Ah, found your stash. Here, have a drink with me."

She poured snifters of Hennessey for both of them. "Come on Linda, let's forget the past. Tell me what's going to happen in the future. Should I invest in the stock market? Will there be rainbows day after day?"

"Very funny, Emma. I'm not doing fortune cookie readings."

It came back to Emma then, how Linda had always liked to be the big authority on what would happen in peoples' lives. She loved to attribute everything to this sun sign or moon trine, or whatever. Emma didn't really believe in astrology, but she suspected that nonetheless, there was something in it. At the very least, she recognized that it was a good way of expressing intuitive feelings in symbols. And in spite of her skepticism, that brief, disturbed look of Linda's bothered her.

If Linda was aware of Emma's doubts, it didn't seem to bother her much. She probably chalked it up to something in Emma's chart. "Hey Em," she said, changing the subject, "a friend of mine called, and I told him you're here, and he offered to take us into the everglades tomorrow. I've been with him before; he knows how to spot the alligators. Do you want to go? I have to call him back tonight."

Emma downed the rest of her drink and poured another. "Sounds cool, as long as you're sure that wasn't the Saturn disaster you spotted in my chart. If a shark gets me, that's one thing; but I refuse to be eaten by a creature with a brain smaller than a peanut."

The everglades excursion was made extra trippy by some mushrooms that Linda shared with Juan and Emma. She said she had been saving them for a special day and figured that day had arrived. For Juan and Emma, it was both their first psychedelic trip together, and the first time either of them had done psychoactive drugs in a long time. Linda was a perfect companion, and the guide, Sam, turned out to be a guide in more ways than one. He did indeed get them very near some alligators—so close that the three tripping people all said they felt like they had crossed eons, gone back to prehistoric times when jungle and beast dominated the earth. As the day wore on, Sam brought them down gradually—fed them oranges and plums, and cold white wine from his cooler.

Still stoned when they got back to Linda's house, Juan and Emma went up to their bedroom. It was a first for Juan, making love on a psychedelic, and a first for Emma—making love to someone she loved while tripping.

…

As soon as they got back to California, Juan and Emma drove to Marin to see their house.

This time, they didn't have to sit outside and look at it. They wandered through the rambling old house, planning what they would change, where they would put things, what colors they would paint the walls. The entire spring was taken up with the renovating and the move, as well as rehearsing a new band four afternoons a week. But they were in their new home by the end of June, with four days to spare before they had to be back on the road for a big summer festival tour.

…

The new band was cooking. Emma had hated to let her bass player, Roger, go. He'd been with her since the beginning, but his resentment of Juan had created dissension in the band throughout the last tour. His replacement, Daryl, was handsome—looked a bit like Jimi Hendrix, and played a funky slap bass. Her drummer had also been negative about Juan. She could have tolerated his backbiting, but he brought his problems onstage too—deliberately fucking with the beat. She'd replaced him with Daryl's band mate, Stuart, who had the reputation of being both solid and creative on percussion. Sam was still on rhythm guitar, and a young piano player from Marin, Neil, rounded out the line-up. Her road manager, Ed was the one constant, and he knew the ropes inside out by this time.

Ed was a big, burly guy, with long hair and a fuzzy beard that disarmed people, led them to believe he was a stoned-out hippie, when in fact, he was the most together person on the tours. Highly intelligent and articulate, with a wry sense of humor, Ed was in charge of every aspect of the band's travel. It was his job to make sure everybody got where they were supposed to be on time, collect the money after the shows, and make sure everything went smoothly, from hotel accommodations to limo service. Emma trusted Ed, and relied on him. He never hit on her either.

Emma was excited about the new band. The gospel & soul influence of the rhythm section, and the Latin influence Juan brought with him created a new sound—the realization of the change Emma had been hoping for. That summer they were playing enormous venues, with a stage setup so huge that they needed two semis to lug the equipment. Stuart and Daryl were both married with kids, and liked to bring their families on the road, so between band, families, and crew, they were up to about thirty people. It was like a traveling circus, but the energy was good.

•••

Arriving back in Mill Valley on July 28th, Juan and Emma had only three days to get it together to leave for San Salvador. Juan was quieter than usual, and Emma could tell he wanted to talk. "Okay, what is it?"

"Emma, there are things you need to prepare for."

"Besides my bathing suit, my new Bermuda oh so proper shorts, sandals, no saying fuck, what? God, you're so serious. I was fine with your parents. Don't be so uptight."

"Of course you were. You're better with my parents than I am. But that's not what I'm concerned about. Come sit down and talk to me." Juan pulled Emma down into the oversized chair he was sitting in. "Listen, you need to know…San Salvador is like a blow to the heart; it is more savage than any place you have been before."

Emma wriggled out of the chair, laughing. "More savage? You mean like Tarzan and the Apes? What? It's cool, baby. I'll like it, don't worry."

"Emma, I want you to be serious."

"Jesus, okay, I'm serious. Seriously getting bored with you being so serious. Lighten up, for God's sake. It'll be okay."

"No Emma, listen to me. My country is poorer than you can imagine. You will see sick people, old people and children with malnutrition begging at the airport. They will surround us in swarms as we wait for our luggage. You don't understand…people live on the downtown sidewalks, and they live in newspaper shantytowns, in filth. You need to be prepared."

"You could write a travel book: 'Places Not to Go, Juan's Sightseeing Bum Trips'."

"Listen to me Emma, you're not going to Club Med. Everywhere we go in El Salvador, there will be human suffering…and there is no solution. You could give away every dime you have and it wouldn't be enough." Juan hung his head and sighed deeply. "There is a hopelessness that is tangible."

"Oh God, baby, I'm sorry. I didn't realize. You know, I thought you were just nervous about your family. Really, is it really so bad? I've been to Mexico. We have slums here. I've seen poor people. I can handle it."

"No, it's not comparable to Mexico or the inner city ghettos of North America. Our downtown streets are full of people, and they have diseases you've never seen. They have sores on their bodies; many are missing limbs, or have a nose or an ear rotted off from leprosy. It's a disgrace that we don't care for our poor—a disgrace I grew up with, and I am ashamed to take you there."

"Why should you be ashamed? It sure as shit isn't your fault. You have more conscience than a fucking saint."

Juan shook his head. "No, Emma, I am culpable. My family lives behind protective walls to avoid interaction with the poor, but they are our servants, our gardeners, the people who grow our food. The magnitude of their poverty is immense."

Emma took Juan's hands and massaged them as she spoke. "Jesus baby, it sounds terrible. Maybe we can do something to help. Don't be so down about it. We'll deal with it. It'll be cool. We can do something. I don't know what, but we'll figure it out. Don't stress so much."

"You wouldn't be so optimistic if you had any idea what I'm talking about." Juan eased his hands away from her, got up and started pacing. "You've led a charmed life, Emma. What can I expect you to know of these things, these bitter existences? You're going to have a rude awakening, that's for sure."

Emma stared hard at him. "Well fuck you, too. You think I don't know about suffering just because I wasn't raised on the other side of the moon like you were? You're so goddamn pompous. Suffering has many faces, you know, and I've seen a few of them, too."

"I don't want to fight with you. I'm going for a walk."

Emma jumped to her feet, and got right up in Juan's face. "You always do that, you fucking cop-out. You always leave. Don't you walk out that door or I won't be here when you get back."

"Very well, let's both go for a walk. Come on, it's beautiful out. I don't want to fight with you."

The trails on Mt. Tam, lit by moonlight on a warm July evening, were just what they both needed to calm them. They walked hand in hand.

"I didn't mean to imply that you haven't suffered," Juan told her. "I know I get too emotional when I speak of my country. It's only that I want to warn you. I don't want you to be taken by surprise when we get there."

"It's okay, baby."

"*Reina*, talk to me about Carol. You are always so mysterious when you mention her. It is always in connection with suffering. Tell me, please. I want to understand everything about you. Why do you carry this pain so secretively?"

"It's not a secret; I just don't like to talk about it. Carol was my best friend for years. It's a long story."

"We've got all night."

"Things got really crazy. You know what it's like on the road. Carol was my publicist, and well, she died. I don't want to talk about it."

"Emma, I already know she was a junkie, and that you were for a while, as well."

Emma stopped in her tracks and jerked her hand away from him.

"Who told you that?"

"What does it matter? It doesn't change anything. I know she died of an overdose...Roger told me." Juan pulled Emma close. "We will face our demons together, *corazon*." He laid her back gently under a tree, in the tall grass by the trail, and began kissing her.

Emma's body responded automatically to Juan's touch, but the old loop in her head had wrapped itself around her heart. If only I'd taken Carol to lunch—if I'd taken the time to be with her...she always said I was self-centered...if I hadn't been so wrapped up in my own trip...if only I'd called her. I loved her. I'm a monster.

Chapter Eleven

Emma, 1975: Heroin Hell

Juan had a knack for chasing the demons away. We made love that night under the redwoods, slowly…so slowly that time seemed to stop. The demons must have gotten tired of watching, because they split. But I knew they couldn't have gone far; they never did. By the time we got back from our walk they were already there at the house, waiting for me, hiding from Juan. We lay in our bed that night and talked for hours, the French Doors open to the cool Mill Valley summer mist. Juan already knew about Carol and that strung-out period of my life. At least he thought he did.

That European tour, spring of '69, I got strung out. All through the winter tour, I had been on Carol's case for shooting up…yapping at her about her problem as I snorted lines of coke and heroin. By the end of that tour, I was used to her doing it, and I started telling myself it was no big deal. She and James were my closest friends, and I couldn't keep acting like I was their mother. People do what they're going to do. You can't nag somebody into change, and it wasn't like I could go back and repair Carol's messed up childhood.

James was actually a pretty together dude. I think he just liked the drug. I don't know, maybe he was locked in a closet as a baby or something, but he was a fucking great guitar player, and Carol was obviously in love with him. He was pretty in a craggy sort of way, and cool to hang with, but I was never attracted to him.

James quickly rose to become counselor-in-chief of our own little junkie circuit. He saved my skin when we arrived in Paris and the whole band got searched, all the way down to personal cavities. Of course, the standard search only escalated to that level because they found “drug paraphernalia” in the drummer’s suitcase. And when they made us take off our coats and jackets, they saw the tracks on James’s and Carol’s arms. I wasn’t carrying, thanks to James insisting that Carol and I go through all our stuff and dump our drugs before we left the States. He assured us that he could score anything we wanted in Paris, first hour we were there. He made good his boast, too.

By the time we cleared customs, after Ed convinced the agents that our drummer had asthma and could only smoke tobacco through a water pipe, and offered them each four free tickets to our concert, we got to our hotel around six p.m. By eight-thirty, I was snorting alternate lines of coke and junk, while Carol and James nodded out after their fifteen long hours of deprivation. James’s contact, Mathias, was a Dutch cat, very hip and beautiful in that ultra-European, glitter and flash kind of way. I dug him, but I kicked him and everybody else out of my room early that night. I was just fried from the long trip and the time change.

The very next day, I hooked up with Mathias—strolled all over Paris with him and James and Carol. We went to the Louvre, dined at a bistro on the Seine, had coffee in the Latin Quarter—all the usual tourist stuff. I tried to take everything in stride, but I really was flashed out. The city is just so fucking gorgeous; you have to fall in love with it. Mathias was the perfect guide. He knew all about art and architecture—gave us the background on everything we saw.

Looking back on it, I think I was equating Mathias with Paris, so I thought I was falling in love with him. But we had a problem: he couldn’t get it up. We spent the night together doing drugs, drinking, and trying to get it on, but it didn’t happen. Of course it was the heroin, but I didn’t know that at the time. Hadn’t done that little dance myself, yet. I was happy in his company during that period, though. We made a great romantic couple, even though the romance was more with the city and the drugs than with him.

The show in Paris supposedly went over well, but you could have fooled me. It was one of those off nights, where no matter how well you perform you don't feel like you've really got your audience. I was struggling through the whole set, and I could see the guys were feeling the same way. I was sure that we liked Paris better than it liked us. Mathias translated the reviews for us the next morning, and to our surprise, they were positive. What the fuck, you can't always tell.

Mathias came with us to Amsterdam, where John Lennon and Yoko Ono, who had just married, were doing this demonstration thing—lying in bed all day and talking to people about peace. I had a message waiting for me that I had been invited to drop in on them, and, of course, Carol wanted to come. She had met John before, when she lived with Ritchie—had told me how smart he was, and hip. I was intimidated about going to meet him and his New York-arty wife, but damned if I would let that show. Carol and I put on our finest velvet and lace, fortified ourselves with lines of coke and smack, and presented ourselves at court, which was a hotel bedroom. It was a pretty weird scene, like a big ego trip, but it was also totally cool. They were sincere. They cared. And however you express that, it has to be good. I, for one, loved their naked album cover. It was just fucking outrageous. And you sure couldn't call that an ego trip. I would never do it because I'm too vain. I wouldn't want to be as exposed as they were willing to be.

The scene in their room was relaxed. We talked about this and that—their convictions, which I agreed with. God, it could have been my parents talking. We snacked, sang some songs, smoked some pot, just hung out. Nothing intimidating about it. I'd met a lot of celebrities, but meeting John was special, because of his music and because of the kind of person he was. I respected him, and Yoko.

There was, however, a backlash to the John and Yoko thing for me. It felt as if when you stripped away all the hype and bullshit, I was just some lightweight hippie who happened to be in the right place at the right time. Who looked right—nothing to do with talent—just dumb luck—good genes, not something I deserved. I wasn't prone to getting into funks, but I fell into a hole. In retrospect, I know now that heroin was the hole.

Mathias did me the favor of shooting me up my first time, good friend that he was. I'll never forget his Dutch accent and his off-center way of phrasing things as he prepared the heroin. "Here Emma, this makes you feel better."

"I don't know, man. It's a big step. Maybe I'll just snort it."

"It's better if you shoot it. You won't believe it."

Images of Carol and James nodding out ran through my mind. And Billie Holiday singing, stoned out of her mind on TV. She sounded amazing. I wanted to try it just once. "Okay, you do it…just a taste…not too much. I don't want to get strung out."

"Don't worry. You can handle it. You are artist. You create your own universe. A bohemian does not pay attention to the bourgeoisie and their little morality." He tied my arm off with his scarf, and held the needle out to me. "Do you want me to shoot you up? Don't be afraid, baby."

God, the rush. I still can't think about it, because if I do, the craving comes surging back. It's always lurking just around the corner in the shadows, sharing space with the demon thing. Interchangeable with fucking Rob, and Carol, and the depths of despair I so casually decided to explore.

When the heroin hit my bloodstream that first time, I felt like I was in the heart of life, understanding the human condition. We're all *down*; we all need our fix. And of course, that's also literal. You actually do need your fix, on time, at regular intervals, or the high of *down* turns into a nightmare fast. After that first rush, you know you're going to do whatever it takes to get back to that space. For me, it wasn't too hard. I had Mathias, who seemed to have connections in every country in Europe. I didn't have to use a lot to get high. A little went a long way, like it does at first. I felt like I was in top form throughout the tour.

We hit twenty cities in two and a half months. Had a little time to trip around in each one. What got me was how culturally different all the countries were, even though most of them were closer to each other than San Francisco is to Los Angeles. Each beautiful, old city had its own personality, a fresh surprise. There I was, being welcomed with open arms into all these incredible places, high on the excitement of the trip—and choosing to journey to the center of down. Hanging with a gorgeous, cosmopolitan lover, who never wanted to fuck—a guy who spoke a million languages and knew everything about everything, including how to shoot up in veins that don't collapse easily or show in sleeveless clothes.

Having the time of my life, and feeling more down than I had ever been. Not to mention being with Carol, who was on the same wavelength as me, as usual. She was keeping it together, arranging interviews, keeping the foreign record company execs happy. Charming each member of the press into feeling more important than the others. Doing her job. And we had stepped into a new level of intimacy with each other. Not only sharing our childhood memories and our deepest feelings, like we'd always done, but also sharing our heroin. Sharing our needles. Carol and James, and Mathias and I were a tight little foursome.

We all got sick at the same time, too. At the end of the tour, luckily, but that wasn't unusual. Your body seems to wait for the end of a tour. You know you can't get sick when you've got shows, but the minute you fucking let your guard down, your body collapses. We all hung in there for the duration of the tour, getting high, staying well, sight seeing, playing to packed houses. And in the midst of all the activity, I was writing.

In cafes, in parks, bars, coffee houses, everywhere we went, I was inspired. Lyrics came tumbling out so fast I could barely catch them. I didn't even notice how dark my thoughts had become. I thought I was composing the material for the next album, as usual. One of my gems started out like this:

Through the mists of shattered dreams
The hollow eyes, the distant stare
Ghost images come marching
All the legions of despair
They march on me when the sentry's gone
When reason flees and the demons throng...

Christ, when you're there, when you're doing it, you don't see it. I did use some of the material, but most of it was morose, rambling shit that nobody would want to hear.

As cool as Europe was, we were all ready to come home by the end of the tour. I was nervous about Mathias coming with us, because I knew he was going to expect to stay with me, and I wasn't ready to have him in my house. But I didn't know how to tell him that. Part of it was just being stoned all the time. You let things go—take the path of least resistance.

When we got back to San Francisco, we had him with us. Got him into the country on a visitor's visa and Ed even managed to get him a temporary work visa, presenting him as my new personal assistant. For the first time, I had a guy living with me. Carol went to stay with James over in Marin, so it was just Mathias and me, and we were both pretty sick and run-down after the tour. We were just lucky it was only the flu, and not hepatitis.

Living with Mathias got old fast—especially considering he had no connections here, and we had to rely on James and Carol to score. This guy who had seemed so charming showing us all over Europe with his million language skills looked completely different in the California sun. He looked like a goddamn ghost; he was so pasty white. And he didn't drive, which blew my mind. It had never come up over there, with us taking taxis or limos, or walking everyplace. But back in California, land of the freeways, it just seemed ludicrous.

I could have put up with hauling him places, but he never gave me my space. Christ, I'd be off on my own in the garden, writing a song, and he'd just come flop down next to me and start talking, with no fucking clue that I wanted to be alone—no awareness that I was trying to do some of the "creating" that he supposedly respected so goddamn much. Plus, he used more than his share of dope. And he was a terrible fuck—when he actually managed it. It got to the point where he just got on my nerves so bad I couldn't stand it. I didn't know how to handle the situation, so I called Carol. Told her what was happening.

Carol was matter of fact. "Just tell him to leave, Emma. It's simple."

"I can't. Where will he go?'

"He can come over here and stay with James and me until he goes back to Holland. Have Ed talk to him. That'll solve the problem."

And it did. But then, I was lonely. I wanted Carol to move back in. Don't get me wrong; it wasn't like there was any shortage of people to hang out with. But it wasn't the same as the easy space Carol and I occupied together. My house turned into Grand Party Central that July, but I was lonely in the midst of it. Also, I was nervous about shooting up alone. The ante on my habit had been steadily going up and you heard all these stories about people overdosing, and I didn't want to become another heartache cautionary tale. Brian Jones, of the Rolling Stones, had died earlier in the month, found dead in a pool. It freaked me out. Carol kept better tabs on my habit than I did, checking the strength and purity of the stuff they got for me. She didn't want me to buy from anyone they didn't know.

We were back to our triangle, James and Carol and I, and it suited me fine. Carol hung out while James worked on songs with me. I had that mountain of lyrics from Europe, but they were mostly shit, so I had to write new lyrics, and I just couldn't seem to come up with any decent music. Bill was busy with an L.A. band—wouldn't be available till we started recording in August, so James was co-writer by default. I liked James's playing, but as it turned out, I wasn't crazy about the music he came up with. It just didn't seem to mesh with my writing. As the month wore on and the songs weren't ready, I was really glad that Bill was going to be engineering the record—that he would be there to help whip the songs into shape.

I hadn't heard the last from Mathias either. Toward the end of the month, I got a MasterCard bill that was way over my credit limit. They had graciously extended my limit to accommodate me—for a charge, of course. It turned out that I had paid for Mathias's first class around-the-world ticket, as well as for clothing from some of the most expensive shops in San Francisco, and six separate cash advances, amounting to God knows how many thousands of dollars.

He had used the official papers we had put together to get him the work visa—the ones that legally verified that he was my assistant. Used them to justify signing my name. And he pulled it off. It hurt my feelings more than anything else. I mean, I wasn't broke or anything, and the credit card company couldn't make me pay for the fraudulent charges, but it was a real slap in the face. Hey, wasn't it me who used to tell people never to trust a junkie!

Then, in the middle of ruminating about how fucked the human race is, how we're all heading for hell in a hand-basket, the astronauts walked on the moon and I saw some hope for us. The moonwalk sent me off on a Science Fiction kick that would influence the record more than the heroin did. I started reading all the sci-fi I could get my hands on.

I arrived in L.A. to start recording the first week in August, and the songs weren't even close to ready. Carol and James came with me. She would handle publicity, as usual, and he would help with writing. And score heroin for us. We had sublet a house in the Hollywood Hills on a month-to-month basis, instead of staying in a hotel. I was looking forward to spending time with Bill again, working on the music together, bantering in the studio, maybe hooking up with him.

Big crimp in the plan. First of all, Bill had an old lady. Jesus, talk about my timing. He'd been dying for me last time I'd seen him. Then there was the fact that he freaked out about me using.

"What are you doing?" he yelled. "Are you completely crazy? Look at your arms. Why, Emma, why? You could die. People do, you know. All the time. I've seen too much of it."

"Jesus, Bill, lay off. I'm okay. Christ."

"You're not okay; you are definitely not okay. I find you here nodding out like a junkie and you tell me you're okay? Where's that at, Emma?"

"Why don't you just lay back, man? You're coming on like a straight dude…it's all cool. Let's get some work done."

"You think you can stay conscious long enough to write? Somehow I doubt it."

"Fuck you, Bill. You're such a drag. It's not your place to pass judgment on what I do. It's my record, and…"

Bill cut me off mid-sentence, "Your record?" he yelled. The veins in his neck bulged and his face went red. "Your record? Oh no, I don't think so. My name will be on the thing, too. And if you think I'm going to produce some piece of shit just to please you, you've got another thought coming."

"Well fuck you. I'll get another producer. Fine." I stormed out of the house, and went and sat by the pool. Bill let me stew for a few minutes, then came after me.

"Come back, Emma; let's finish our conversation."

"I thought it was finished. I thought you just fucking quit."

"Come on, Emma, let's go back inside and talk." He gently took me by the arm and steered me back into the living room. "Let's compromise, sweetheart. Why don't we take a few days off while you clean up? You can detox, and start methadone treatment. Then we can get down to work."

"I can start work now. God, you're making a mountain out of a molehill."

"I know you can sing. You can always sing. But I'm speaking as a friend, Emma. I'm worried about you. I don't want to see anything happen to you. Please, try to kick. I'll help you."

Bill talked himself blue in the face, but I wouldn't budge. He eventually agreed to do the album on my terms, because he could see I'd give him up before I'd give up the drug. Also, I think he thought I would be safer if he was looking out for me. Yeah, he was still in my pocket, old lady or not.

"These are good, a lot of potential," Bill said, when I showed him the lyrics I was working on:

Been on a road
I thought I'd never travel
Stood on a mountain
I thought I'd never climb
Walked through a valley
Where only a fool would venture
Sat at a table
Drank a poisoned wine…

"Do you hear what you're saying here, Emma? Well, it shouldn't surprise me. You've always been able to describe what you're going through. What about something like this?" He began playing a guitar line.

The chords were just right for the words, but some of my phrasing wasn't working. "Let's drop the "where" in the sixth line. I think it'll sound better…"Only a fool would venture."

We had started the afternoon fighting, and by midnight, we had a song. It was the first and only thing that went smoothly in the production of *Coattails of a Dream*. Everything else was a struggle, from getting the songs written, to recording my vocals, to fighting over the mixes. In retrospect, I'm lucky Bill stuck around to see it through to the end.

That first week in L.A. got off to a pretty scattered start, in every possible way. I was trying to work on material, and people kept coming by. Everybody and their brother wanted to write with me because my last albums had sold so well. There was good money in publishing royalties. You couldn't blame them for trying. These were people who needed the bread to support their habits.

I didn't feel like I had to settle down and pace myself for the studio at that point. I was going to New York for a few days in the middle of the month anyway, to play at some big outdoor concert in Woodstock, New York. So there was that, kinda scattering the energy.

But the real kicker came on August 9th, when this actress, Sharon Tate, and her friends were murdered in their own home, not far from our house in The Hills. Then, the next night, there was another grisly murder. It was all fucking creepy, with messages scrawled on walls in blood, and Sharon Tate being pregnant and everything. When it turned out that a hippie-type dude, Charles Manson, had done it, along with his "family" of ghouls, paranoia set in big time. For all we knew, the "family" might have "visited" us instead. They could have come to one of our parties during that first week, and we wouldn't have thought twice about it. They were just a bunch of young girls—young girls who murdered people. Apart from the paranoia, it was upsetting—a complete nightmare. I kept trying to wrap my mind around how humans could be capable of such barbarity. I mean, there was Sharon Tate, pregnant, happy, just minding her own business, and they killed her in cold blood, just like that.

James and Carol, and Bill and I followed the murder case closely. It was terrifying and tragic, and impossible to ignore. Especially since a number of the members of the "Manson family" were still at large. I was more than a little relieved that I got to get out of L.A. on the 14th.

Carol came along with the band to New York, of course. The next day, we rode up to a Holiday Inn in this off-the-beaten-path town, named Liberty, of all things. Took fucking hours to get there, and when we did, we had to stand in line to get the keys to our rooms. It was like old home week in that line though. The Grateful Dead were there, Janis Joplin, Joan Baez, and the Jefferson Airplane. Half the goddamn San Francisco music scene was hanging out, waiting for room assignments. We all more or less ended up in the bar that night, playing poker and throwing down whiskey and tequila like it was going out of style.

They helicoptered us onto the site late morning of the next day, Saturday, and we were all blown away by the sheer size of the festival. It seemed like everybody I knew was on the bill. And in spite of the soggy conditions, everyone seemed happy to be there—listening to all the incredible music, feeling the good vibes of an audience that had swelled to about four hundred thousand-plus.

We were scheduled to go on late afternoon, and I was nervous before the show. The band hadn't played together since Europe, so we weren't going to be as tight as we would have been just coming off the road. We should have rehearsed, but, well, things hadn't panned out that way, so we just got up there and gave it our best shot. I sang, and danced all over that rain-soaked stage, with this incredible cameraman, Dave Myers, apparently capturing my every move as he swayed to the music, doing his own sort of dance with the camera, but never getting in the way. It wasn't the best set we'd ever done, with the terrible weather and everything, but I felt like we could hold our heads up afterward.

I was so relieved when our set was over that when Bear, who made the best acid short of Sandoz, offered me some I took it without hesitation. As I was coming on, the weather was growing progressively worse. It was dramatic as all hell—the wind howling and rain pouring down. But the vibes were good. Then again, I didn't have to perform in those conditions. I tripped around with Carol backstage, waiting to see the Grateful Dead go on at midnight. They had to contend with thunder and lightening, and Bob Weir got shocked so bad you could see the electricity zip into his lip. But they pulled their set off anyway, like the pros they were.

LSD can be a bumpy flight up; jagged edges on your nerve endings can create sensory overload, but I had a smooth trip, thanks to the heroin in my bloodstream counteracting the hyper effects. I just coasted the whole night, listening to the Dead's set, hanging with friends, flashing on the colors of the rain.

Carol and James and I got back into L.A. on the 18th, to find that the Manson murders were still dominating the front pages. Back to freaky shit and our now freaky house in The Hills, that no longer seemed safe. Happily, our connection was there as well, and after a few hours, we felt no pain—only normal, drug-connected paranoia.

After a few days of recuperating by the pool from the rush of Woodstock, I started songwriting with James and Bill again, and I spent my spare time with a sun-tanned, blond actor named Tom, who was a total health-nut. We were an unlikely couple, but at least he didn't have a habit. All through September, we worked on material. Didn't get any tracks laid down. The stuff I was doing with James was okay, but no grabbers. Even Bill and I were having a hard time writing together. And I didn't feel like recording stuff until I was sure about it. This album had to be good because my contract would be coming up for renewal, and I wanted to get a better deal this time around. My track record being what it was, I had the upper hand, and I wanted to keep it. I suppose I psyched myself out—created a cycle of indecision that left me open to everybody's opinion, which dragged the process out.

Bill finally broke the cycle in early October. He let me know that he was booked to do another band in January, and that if I wanted his services, it was now or never. I reacted badly to his ultimatum at first, as usual, but I came around eventually. And after we made up, he wrote the music for what would become the title track, "*Coattails of a Dream.*"

The dust devil twirled through a garden of roses
In the heat of the desert fell rain
A whirlpool formed in a murky dark pond
And nothing was ever the same
Our dreams have been of temples
Building blocks of stone

Jeannette Sears

When the fortress was completed
I was all alone

Going to let those temples crumble
And build steps up to the sky
To where we want to go
Going to build them high
Take me up, won't you take me too
I want to climb those steps
Find my way to you
High in the clouds, we'll find higher ground
High in the clouds, never coming down

I was pulled through the night
On the coattails of a dream
Where angels cried
And their tears ran upstream
As if my heart was overflowing
I could feel it in the rain
As if my heart was flying
As if something would remain

Felt the breath of the beast
Burning in the cold night air
Felt eyes boring through my back
When I looked, nothing was there
We won't be swinging
On the wrecking ball
When the last tree goes
We won't hear it fall
We'll be flying through the night
On the coattails of a dream
Fleeing to that place
Where water runs upstream
Pull me through the night

On the coattails of a dream
High above this scene
High in the clouds, up on higher ground
High in the clouds, never coming down

The song broke my writer's block, and we decided to go ahead and lay down basics. Bill's reasoning was that it would inspire me to get off my ass and finish the rest of the songs. I was so psyched about the album starting to come together that I decided we should celebrate after the session. I came home with magnums of champagne, full-party mode, shot up a speedball with James and Carol, and then started drinking the champagne. Ended up getting violently ill and passing out.

I found out later that when Tom couldn't rouse me from the bathroom floor, he got scared and picked me up, put me in the car, and drove me to the emergency room at UCLA. I woke up in the hospital and ended up spending a week there, enduring endless admonitions about mixing alcohol and drugs. Luckily for me, the doctor was a fan, so the incident didn't turn into a legal problem. I came out of the hospital having kicked, on a methadone program, and ready to work. But I didn't stay straight long, in spite of Tom and Bill's best efforts. Even Carol thought it would be better if I laid off while I was recording. But I started in again before a week was up.

The last week of October, we got held-up. James had gone to score from a trusted contact, and there were these guys waiting outside for him when he got there. They had ripped the dealer off and were nabbing the guy's customers as they came to score—customers with their pockets full of cash to pay for the dope. That would have been bad enough, but James still needed to score, so he came home to get more cash. They followed him, and held us up. Stole every dime in the house, plus instruments and recording stuff, and even jewelry. We were afraid to call the cops because of the tracks on our arms.

Then we got paranoid about staying in that house—worried that the robbers would come back. We split the next day, and moved into Tom's house for a few weeks. Then we moved over to the Landmark Hotel, where we stayed until we finished the recording, right around the holidays. Bill and I had hashed out an agreement that he would postpone his next project for a month and give me all of January to mix.

We knocked off at the studio for a week at Christmas, and I went home. It was good to be back in Northern California, away from the constant hype of Hollywood. It had been groovy for a while, but eventually started grating on my nerves. Tom had to hang with his family in Newport Beach that week, and James and Carol went back to his house in Marin, so I was on my own for the first time in ages. I was actually a little freaked-out about being alone, after all the weird shit in L.A.; so I called my friend, Linda, the astrologer—asked her to come stay with me. I was grateful for her company. She wasn't into smack, but she certainly wasn't adverse to coke. She'd snort up lines, I'd shoot up, and we got along fine.

I spent Christmas day at Ray and Stephanie's that year. They had to have known what was going on, but they were cool about it. It was the first New Year's Eve I didn't have a gig in years. It hadn't seemed worth it to pull together and rehearse a band for just one night, and besides, I needed a break. So Carol and James, and Linda and I went to Winterland to see *Quicksilver Messenger Service*. My old buddies, John Cipollina and David Freiberg, were in the band. They were on the bill with the *Airplane*, and *The Sons*, and *Hot Tuna*. A great fucking line-up and very groovy people to be with. Linda and I dropped some acid backstage, in the safety of old friends, and brought in 1970 tripping.

•••

Back in L.A., problems developed in the studio. Bill had played some rough mixes for the A&R men just to get them off his back, to show them we had something, and they went and got fixated on the rough mixes. So when we brought them in to hear some final mixes, they had a fit. Wanted us to change them back to the way they were, which was just fucking ridiculous. The only reason the assholes had any leverage at all was because we'd gone way over schedule, and budget. So they held things up even more by trying to put in their two cents, when they didn't know what they were talking about. Ultimately, the record company backed us up, but with great trepidation. *Coattails of a Dream* shipped out gold and had sold over a million copies by the end of our spring tour. Talk about vindication.

We were on the road March through mid-May, playing a lot of college towns. The students were still out protesting the War and the Chicago Seven verdict and stuff—trying to make themselves heard. And they had the Heat coming down heavier than ever on them. But the tour rolled along relatively smoothly, with the exception of a few incidents with James, when he shot up too much—nights when Carol and I had to keep him on his feet, moving around the hotel room—afraid he'd die if he fell asleep.

I didn't give the student unrest much thought until we reached what was supposed to be the laid-back surfer school, UC, Santa Barbara. Then I got pissed. The students there had been protesting up a storm, and our cowboy Governor, Ronald Reagan, actually told the press, and this is a fucking quote, "If it takes a bloodbath, let's get it over with." He was talking about university students, for Christ sake, who were, you know, citizens of the United States with the right of free speech. That wasn't the end of it, either. Toward the end of the tour, the National Guard opened fire on protestors at Kent State University in Ohio, killing four students. And we now had troops in Cambodia as well as Vietnam. So much for protesting. The Man had more power than ever.

In the middle of the tour, we became preoccupied with another problem. It suddenly hit us that we were going to be leaving for our first tour of Japan a few days after we finished this tour, and we hadn't put the slightest bit of thought into how we were going to score over there. We'd just been under the assumption that it would be like Europe, that somebody would have a connection. But as the departure date closed in on us, no magical being had come out of the woodwork to arrange things. And everyone who'd been there said there was no way you could smuggle drugs into the country—that customs was too uptight over there.

So Carol and James and I came up with a brilliant plan a couple of weeks before we left. We'd have the dope sent to our hotel in Tokyo, so it would be waiting for us when we got there—hidden in with some promotional materials, and addressed to our publicist, Carol. I shouldn't have let her do it, of course. James and I both let her take all the risk. Let her insist. Let her argue that the band could go on without her, but not without James and me. Like the cowards we were, we let it all fall on her. And it did fall, because of course, she got busted.

Wigged out from the long flight, in the Twilight Zone of the neon of Tokyo, dazzled by all the fans that had turned out to greet us, we got to the hotel and found the police waiting for us. All of us were searched, and Carol was arrested—hauled off to jail, exhausted and needing a fix. We all would have been hauled off too if the promoter hadn't intervened; I'm sure of it. Thank God he had so much money riding on us or we might all still be rotting in jail there.

James and I had to kick cold turkey, too. There was simply no dope to be found, or at least we didn't know how to get it if there was. And we were under constant surveillance by the Japanese Heat. Withdrawal was hell, but at least we had a few days to get through the worst of it before the tour began. And we had plenty of good prescription downers to take the edge off, which was no small thing, because we couldn't even get any pot. Ed and the promoter managed to spring Carol after a few days, under threat of my canceling the tour if they didn't let her out. But they immediately deported her. James and I didn't see her until we got back from that miserable tour.

It was too bad things turned into such a bummer, because I really dug Japan. The people were amazingly friendly, and my albums had always sold well over there. If it wasn't for the goddamn dope, we could have all had a blast. The Japanese record company took me to Niko on my birthday. It was a beautiful village in the hills, surrounded by forests of what looked like the redwood trees back home. At the edge of town, there was a long path of stairs leading up to a temple. The weather was gorgeous, and we took our time on the path, tripping on the mellow vibe. The temple itself was mind-blowing—an ancient, ornate shrine. I was surprised to recognize one of the carvings—the "hear no evil, speak no evil, see no evil" monkeys. I lit some incense in front of a giant Buddha, and thought about Carol. She would have loved the place. Afterwards, the company took us to a restaurant back in Tokyo for a surprise party. They tried to make up for the terrible bust, I'll give them that; but it hung over us like a cloud.

We got home the end of June to find Carol had cleaned up while we were gone. She was in a very positive, up state—not pissed off at all—which just made me feel like a complete jerk, that she had taken the rap for us. Of course I insisted on paying for all her legal costs and her back salary. Fucking big of me. I thought James should have felt worse than he did. I mean, for Christ sake, he ran right out and started using again, and got Carol back into it with him.

I had all of July off to write songs for the next record, so I tried to stay clean. Went to Maui for the month. It rained all the time and the humidity was unbelievable, but hiding out at the Hana Resort off-season, hanging out with friends who didn't use, was the best thing I could have done. I built my health back up and got a ton of lyrics written—was ready to go down to L.A. and work on the music with Bill by August, right on schedule. Still in my sci-fi phase, a lot of my lyrics were rambling speculations on the interconnectedness of physics and metaphysics.

Carol and James and I were booked into the Landmark again. We'd had enough of renting houses in Hollywood after last summer's gruesome events. Tom came around, but after having spent a month in Hawaii with sun- tanned bodies, I was bored with them. James's friend, Stevie, another musician of course, interested me more. I was in Hollywood about a week before I started using again, shooting up with Stevie.

Carol and I picked up where we'd left off, no weirdness between us at all. Not on her part anyway. I still felt guilty about the Japanese fiasco. I wanted to make it up to her somehow, but some things you can never fix. We spent our days together, laying out by the pool, or hitting the boutiques on Sunset and Santa Monica Boulevards. I bought mountains of beautiful clothing for both of us. We'd put on our new finery at night and make the club scene with James and Stevie. I also found time to work on material with Bill, and yeah, I was writing with Stevie, too. By the end of August, we had started laying down basics. Carol would come into the studio and sit through hours of boring takes just because I wanted her opinion. It's the kind of friend she was. And she'd arrange press things here and there—kept the publicity happening.

September, the weather turned even hotter, the Santa Ana winds scorching your lungs with every breath. You had to be indoors during the day, which was fine for me. I'd just go straight from the hotel to the studio. Carol went back up to San Francisco for a couple of weeks when she couldn't take the heat anymore. During the weeks she was away, we got a lot of work done in the studio. And Stevie scored us some heroin that was so pure that even after we stepped on it heavily, it was still stronger than we were used to.

You'd think I would have recognized the breath of the beast in those Santa Ana winds. My shrink friend over at UCLA told me that those winds make people crazy. That the emergency room fills up when they start blowing. But the signs were all in shadow, and I didn't even catch a glimpse of the demon until it was too late.

The day Carol came back from San Francisco, September 20th, James and Stevie were in the studio with me. I sent a limo to pick her up. She stopped by the studio briefly to say hello, then went back to the Landmark to hang by the pool. Carol always had a key to my room, as I did hers. It was a long-standing tradition with us.

We knocked off work at the studio around ten p.m. and James said he was going back to the hotel to be with Carol. Stevie and I went out to dinner. We were hungry because we'd skipped lunch.

When Stevie and I got back to my room around midnight, I asked him to leave. I wanted to spend some time with Carol. He understood, went back to his own place. I took a shower, a goddamn shower. Put on comfortable clothes, then rummaged around for my stash. It was time for my fix. In the beaded bag with my stash was a note from Carol: "IOU, I was desperate. See you later tonight. Love you, C."

There was a chilly cramp in the pit of my stomach, and I didn't know why. *What if James didn't go straight back to the hotel? What would it matter? Why am I feeling so uneasy?* I laid back and slipped into the rush.

Coming out of the rush, maybe ten minutes later, adrenaline hit me and my stomach knotted again. What was it about that note that was bothering me? Something was grabbing me—what was it? *Oh Christ! Carol didn't know how strong my stuff was.*

Probably not a problem. I dialed Carol's room. No answer. *Okay, probably not a problem—probably nodding out.* I fought back panic. I shoved my stash under a pillow, slipped on thongs, and padded over to Carol's room, knocked softly. No answer. *They could be making love.* All I could hear was the TV.

I let myself in with my key. The room was dark, lit only by the glow of the TV. James was asleep in a chair by the door, and Carol was sprawled on the bed.

I let out a breath I didn't know I'd been holding. "Hey you guys, you sleeping already? Get up. Come on. What a couple of bores."

James nodded awake, then closed his eyes again. "Give it a rest. I just got back."

I flopped down on the bed beside Carol. "Hey Baby, wake up. Come on, I haven't seen you in ages."

I reached over and stroked her hair. The palm of my hand grazed her cheek. It was cold under my touch. Instinctively, I felt for the pulse at her neck. Nothing.

"Jesus, James, she's not breathing! Call 911. Do something!"

I rolled her over, pinched her nose and started trying to blow life back into her—pressing down on her chest, expelling only my own air. Crying, blowing into her mouth, sobbing with each breath. "Carol, it's Emma. Come on baby, you've got to breathe. Come on, you can do it. Breathe, sweetheart, breathe for me."

I jerked around to look at James. He hadn't moved.

"Get up, you fucker! Call 911," I screamed. I was counting out the beats between blowing and pressing. "Come on Carol, don't do this. Come on, breathe. Please, baby, please don't do this. Breathe."

James continued staring at me blankly, and then suddenly he got what was happening. "Stop screaming, Emma." He looked more irritated than concerned. "We've got to get rid of the stuff before we call the ambulance. We've got to think clearly."

My hands were busy on Carol, press and release, press and release, and at that moment I thought, *Why couldn't it be you laying here instead of Carol! I wish you were dead.*

James was on his feet, finally. "I'm going to go get your stuff, too. I'll hide the kits around the back, in the bushes, and then I'll call 911."

The door slammed behind him.

I held my best friend in my arms, desperately trying to will her back to life, as I waited for sounds of sirens in the distance.

Chapter Twelve

Demons & Deaths: 1975

When they returned from their walk on the mountain, Emma popped into the shower. Afterward, she joined Juan on the deck. He'd poured them each a glass of chardonnay. When they were both settled comfortably into the pillows of the wicker couch, Juan put his arm around Emma. "Tell me about Carol's death. I think it would be good for you to talk about it."

Emma felt a twinge of resentment at Juan's intrusion into her past. She looked out at the redwood trees, then back at him. When her eyes met his, the resentment vanished. "It wasn't suicide, if that's what you're thinking. It was a disastrous chain of events. Carol would never have killed herself. She was too full of life, too radiant."

Juan nodded. "I never thought she did. I know her death was accidental."

Emma smiled. "She was amazing, Juan; you would have loved her. And she had this wicked sense of humor. We had running jokes, you know? Just stuff between us that would crack us up and nobody else would know what we were laughing about."

"I wish I could have met her. It sounds as if you two were like sisters." Juan pulled Emma into a close embrace. After a long pause, he whispered in a choked voice, "It's a dangerous drug. I am quite selfishly thankful that you survived it."

Slowly, agonizingly, Emma laid out the details of Carol's death for Juan. "The heroin was too strong," she concluded, fighting back tears. "I didn't warn her because I didn't know she was going to take it, you understand? I should have warned her."

"Don't do this to yourself, Emma. It wasn't your fault. It was an accident, a tragic accident."

"The coroner said she died at about three in the afternoon—while we were in the studio, without a clue as to what had happened. You'd think you'd know when somebody important to you leaves this world, wouldn't you? I'd have thought you'd know. I mean, I loved her, and we were all fucking oblivious." Emma buried her face in her hands and gave way to pent-up tears.

Juan put his arm around her. "I'm sure she knew you loved her, and of course you had no way of knowing."

Emma wiped her eyes angrily. "That's what kills me about it, don't you see? We were going about our day, absorbed in our own little fucking world in the studio, and there she was by herself—dead in the hotel room…all alone…and I didn't know it. She just fell asleep and never woke up. I found her, you know, and fucking James was sitting there in the room and didn't even realize she was dead."

Juan looked incredulous. "I understand your anger. It's inconceivable that anyone could be so unconscious! Do you think she could have been saved if James had reacted immediately?"

"I don't know. Probably not—she was evidently already gone by the time he got to the room."

"Roger told me you were arrested?"

"Yeah, James and I both got busted. He had hidden his stash and some of mine out in the bushes. But he didn't know about the kit I'd stuck under my pillow. The police searched my room and they found it, of course."

"So you were arrested on possession?"

Emma nodded. "James was busted too, because he had been in the room with her. But they dropped those charges the next day, when they realized that we were in the studio at the time of her death."

Juan got up and refilled her wine glass. "That, at least, was a small mercy."

"It was, really. They definitely had me on possession, and the truth is if I hadn't had such a good attorney, they could have charged me with complicity, too. I mean, I was crazed when the police got there. I was crying and screaming that I had killed her, that it was my fault—my heroin had killed her. And it was, you know."

"But it was an accident, Emma; it wasn't your fault. You realize that now. Tell me you do."

"Define *fault*. I was at fault, as a matter of fact. We all were, and it didn't matter to me about the charges. Nothing mattered to me. They threw me in jail, but I was out before I started withdrawals because I had the bread for bail. And that's what it comes down to—money."

"It's not true—you can't believe these things."

"But it is true. Ray and Stephanie posted bail. They came and got me, flew with me back to San Francisco, took me home to their house. I kicked my habit there in my old bedroom, going crazy, screaming, just freaking out for days on end."

"Your parents are wise. My respect for them continues to grow."

"Yeah, great," Emma said sarcastically. "But in this case you're right; they deserve it." Her voice softened. "They looked after me night and day. I made life hell for them—it was hell for all of us…and just when the drug had quit wrecking havoc on my body, and I was trying to face the fact that Carol was gone, Janis Joplin died. Bill phoned to tell me. She overdosed at the same fucking hotel as Carol."

"And she also was your friend?"

"Not close like Carol, but yes. It felt like the end of the world. Like everything in life had suddenly become tenuous. Janis had always seemed invulnerable to me, with her powerful voice, and her…well, her presence. Just the way she laughed. The way she could shoot pool, and spit on the stage, and move you to tears the minute she began to sing. And you realize that Jimi Hendrix died just a couple of days before Carol, don't you?"

"I was aware that he died the same year as Janis. It was a great loss for the world—both of their deaths, and Carol, too, obviously."

"It was like the sky was falling. All the deaths just piled on top of each other into a doomsday mountain. But, I kicked because of Carol, and I stayed off it because of her…I hated heroin after her death. It was instantaneous. I went from loving it to hating it, as if it were a living entity."

Emma was trembling so hard her wine splashed out of the glass. Juan took the glass from her hand, and pulled her close. Murmuring words of consolation, he tried to soothe her, but she was out of control.

She pulled free of him and began to pace. "I kept hallucinating this demon monster that was like the source of all evil. It had killed Carol, and it was trying to possess me. I kept freaking out because I'd see it just on the edge of my vision. I'd sense its malicious presence, and I'd start screaming. And then when my parents would come running and get me calmed down, I'd start to worry that the thing had Carol."

Emma sank back into the couch, weeping. This time, when Juan sat down and offered her comfort, she didn't pull away.

"Withdrawal was a piece of cake compared to the reality that Carol was gone, you know? It's like you sleep and pretend that waking life is the dream, and even there, between worlds, you can't escape the truth. I'd wake up within the dream and realize that I had been dreaming, that she really was gone. Do you see?"

"I see that this death broke your heart." Juan gently stroked her hair. "I grieve with you. It's too tragic to bear. But you do know your friend, Carol, is not really with a demon, don't you? You understand that the demon figure is an archetype, a psychological construct. And it sounds like it's a very accurate representation of heroin."

"Jesus, Juan, you can be so goddamn condescending." Emma drew away from him, wiping her eyes. "I'm not stupid, you know—just because I didn't go to some Ivy League college. I've read Jung, for Christ sake. I know what an archetype is."

"Emma, you're angry at me because you're in pain. I wasn't implying that you didn't know. Only reminding you, because you describe things as if they have objective reality. It worries me."

"You think you're so goddamn analytical, but you don't know everything. You don't know anything about objective and subjective reality. Nobody does. The difference can't be scientifically measured, can it? The whole 'if a tree falls in the forest' bullshit!"

"I'm sorry, Emma, but please don't scream. Your voice gets shrill."

"One minute you love me more than the universe and the next minute, my voice is shrill?"

"Stop it, Emma." Juan reached for her again, pulled her back into a close embrace. "You always attack when you're hurting. I'm sorry, *amorcito;* let's don't fight. I do love you more than the universe. You teach me every day. I don't mean to sound that way. I think I too am afraid of pain, so I try to retreat to logic. I try to hide from my emotions. I'm sorry."

"Yeah, you do. And it's bullshit. But I understand. I wish I could find a way to hide from my feelings." Emma's tears came back. "I should have warned her—if only I'd thought to tell her how strong the stuff was."

"You must not blame yourself for this tragedy. Promise me that you will not do this." Juan stroked Emma's hair again and massaged the back of her neck. "Go ahead and cry, *mi querida preciosa.* You'll feel better. It's good to cry, and to remember your friend, to honor her with your tears."

Emma did feel better after talking to Juan about Carol. After he had fallen asleep that night, she lay awake. Her mind was racing, but she wasn't depressed. She thought about Juan trying to tell her about archetypes, and smiled to herself, remembering her mother's lessons in Tarot. When Emma was a child, Stephanie had spent two years painting the entire tarot deck. And Emma had been subjected to lengthy dissertations on the esoteric meaning of every single symbol on each card in the deck. She'd grown up discussing the nature of reality with her parents and their friends...not to mention all the acid trips spent flashing on the interconnectedness of physics and metaphysics.

Emma snuggled up to Juan and listened to his even breathing. One thing she hadn't mentioned to him was that Carol's parents didn't so much as come to the memorial service. They lived in New York, and they didn't even bother to come get her body from San Francisco—just wired instructions that she was to be cremated, and her ashes sent to them. Bill officially identified Carol's body and made the arrangements for the memorial service. While Emma was in the throes of withdrawal, Bill had helped Ed handle the press, and stayed in contact with Ray and Stephanie, as well as Carol's brother, Evan.

Bill had met Evan at the airport and put him up in a hotel for a week. It was Bill who also carefully coordinated Carol's memorial so that Emma would be well enough to attend. Emma thought that Carol would like to remain in the Bay Area, so Bill took part of her ashes from the box before entrusting the remainder to Evan to take back to their parents. He chartered a 103-foot clipper ship for the service, and organized a sunset sail to scatter her ashes in the bay.

October 15th was a sunny day, with a strong wind blowing, especially out on the bay. The graceful wooden ship was big enough to accommodate more than the seventy guests they had limited the memorial service to. On board was an interesting group of people, indicative of the person Carol had been. Artists, musicians, hippies, and beat poets stood clustered in little groups, trying to speak softly, but having to raise their voices to be heard over the wind. Emma could see the loss of Carol in each person's eyes—that little flicker of the eyelid that happens when people are trying to blink away the permanence of death.

The sail was as hauntingly beautiful as Carol had been. There was music and food and wine, lots of poetry and tearful tributes to her life. Carol's old boyfriend, Ritchie Brown, had come over from

England to be there. He had obviously cared very much for Carol, but Emma couldn't shake her underlying resentment of him. He was the one who had first introduced Carol to heroin. She knew it wasn't fair, but she blamed him for Carol's death as much as she blamed herself.

As the sun fell into the thin line of the horizon, bathing the sky with pink and lavender hues, Emma and Evan scattered Carol's ashes into the sea while everyone sang, "Amazing Grace".

All these years later, Emma still felt grateful to Bill for the way he took charge after Carol's death. He had done it all in the same laid-back, highly efficient manner that had put him on top as a record producer. If you wanted the job done right, you called Bill Rothman; if you were lucky enough to have him for a friend, you could be trapped in hell and he'd find a way out for you. Bill understood artists, and that was no doubt the reason he was able to function at a high level in the chaotic world of rock and roll. And although he was a musician and songwriter himself, if he was prone to the same extremities of temperament as his clients, he kept those inclinations firmly in check. She would never have come out and said it, but Emma admired Bill. Carol had loved him, too.

...

In the hour before dawn, Emma once again came to terms with Carol's death. Not that it was all right. It would never be all right. But it was a fact, a grim reality. *Bad things happen to good people and that's just the way of the world,* she thought—which led her to thinking about the stuff Juan had told her about El Salvador. She tried to picture the scenes he had described. Somehow, she just couldn't imagine Juan's parents walking down a street filled with mutilated beggars. Not Margarita, with her perfect hair-do. Eventually, she fell asleep clutching Juan's hand.

Emma and Juan had promised his family that they would put aside the month of August to visit them in El Salvador, but once they were home, they didn't really want to leave again. Their house in Mill Valley seemed like the most perfect place on earth. Fog swept in from the ocean and hovered low over Mt. Tamalpais, providing respite from the heat of July. They hadn't had much time alone together, much less any time in their new house. But true to their word, they were back in a plane on August 1st, bound for El Salvador. I'm going to see Cata, and Silvia, Emma thought, and felt a wave of love wash over her, both exciting and calming.

...

The entire Avelar family was there to greet them at the airport. Silvia, carrying a bouquet of flowers and bouncing with joy at the sight of them, came running into their arms. Cata was the next to embrace them, all smiles, but her smile seemed forced. Warm greetings, and hugs and kisses ensued profusely from the rest of the family. Emma was so delighted to see everyone that she completely forgot about the army of beggars Juan had told her to expect—until he whispered to her significantly that he couldn't believe how much his country had changed in just a few years. He looked bewildered as the family walked together to the luggage claim without being accosted by so much as one beggar.

Three cars were there to transport the family back to their home, and over Cata's protests, Juan and Emma were put in the car with Don Gilberto and Doña Margarita. Conversation on the way to the house was rather formal and stilted, even though Juan's parents were obviously overjoyed that their son had finally come home for a visit. Juan told them of the success of the tours, and of settling into their new house. Speaking English, he inquired politely about the health of each of his relatives.

Emma listened to them talk, thinking, *There simply can't be that many people in a single family, extended or not.*

The Avelars answered Juan's inquiries in English, reverting to Spanish only occasionally. Emma continued to keep an ear open to their dialogue, responding when it was expected of her, but she was more interested in the city they were driving by. She was especially keeping a lookout for the tin and cardboard shantytowns

Juan had described. They reached the gates of the Avelar mansion without Emma spotting any barrios or hordes of poor, starving people.

Well, Emma decided, *maybe it's like him thinking his parents would never accept our marriage. He can be so negative, and here we are now, visiting them, and we're all getting along okay. There weren't any limbless beggars with leprosy at the airport, and this place doesn't look so bad. I've seen worse.*

When they pulled into to the Avelar estate, Emma upgraded her initial assessment of San Salvador to astonishingly beautiful. Entering the grounds through huge, wrought iron gates, opened by two smiling men in straw hats, the procession of cars wound their way through acres of manicured gardens. European flowers grew next to tropical plants and banana trees, and giant avocado trees spread their shade over lush lawns. High, Spanish style walls covered with flowering vines surrounded the entire estate.

"Are we actually still in a city? This is just so beautiful; it's like a dream. My goodness, you must have a lot of land here—at least five acres, am I right?" Emma asked.

Mr. Avelar looked pleased. "Thank you, Emma, but you flatter us. It is not so nice as the United States, but we hope you will be comfortable in our home."

"I think I'll survive," Emma said, then quickly amended her words. "I mean, of course I'll be extremely comfortable. I'll feel like the Queen of Sheba." Then, noting their quizzical responses, she added, "Sorry, it's just an expression. It means your house is so beautiful that it looks like a palace. That I'll feel like a queen staying here."

"It's all right, *reina*, they understand you," Juan said. "The house is as massive as a castle fortress and it can feel like one, too. I think we have approximately eight acres. We all appreciate your enthusiasm for our home. Don't we, *Mamá*?"

Mrs. Avelar nodded politely. "It is our great honor to receive you, Emma. We enjoyed our visit in your country very much. Your hospitality was appreciated. We are happy to welcome you to our home."

Numerous servants ventured forth politely to greet Juan and meet his bride. They were shown to a spacious bedroom with a private sitting room, and left alone to freshen up before dinner. Gauzy white curtains billowed at French doors in the sitting room, and in the bedroom stood a king-size bed, canopied and hung round with the same gauzy fabric. The doors of both rooms were opened wide onto a balcony, allowing the thick scent of gardenias and roses from the garden to permeate the air. Emma flopped on the bed, delighting in the excess of the romantic quarters.

Juan paced around the room, walked out onto the balcony, and came back in. "It's obvious that I've come up in my parent's estimation by marrying you, Emma. This is the first time they've given me this room. Usually it's reserved for 'important' guests,"

Emma's response was a slight shrug and a provocative stretch. "Maybe we have time for a short nap, *Don* Juan."

Juan answered the invitation with a look that got things started before he even reached the bed.

...

Dinner was at nine, which Emma thought was wonderfully civilized. These were hours she could relate to.

"But," Juan informed her, "everybody gets up at dawn, too. You work all morning, and then take the afternoon off to sleep—a *siesta.*"

Emma did some last minute primping in front of the large, ornate mirror. "How do I look? Modest enough? Okay, I'm ready; let's go down for dinner. Come on, I don't want to be late. They'll think it's my fault."

Despite her tiredness, Emma enjoyed the camaraderie of the large family dinner. Don Gilberto and Doña Margarita retired shortly after dinner, but the four siblings, and their spouses and children moved into the living room and kept up a lively conversation until well past midnight. The children finally fell asleep, curled up on the couch, Silvia with her head in Emma's lap.

Emma sensed something different in Cata. She was cheerful, but her behavior seemed forced—not her usual easy-going, chatty self.

When they got back to their room that night, Emma said to Juan, "Something is wrong with Cata. Did she say anything to you about it?"

"No, but I know what you mean. It's probably a boyfriend problem. At her age, that would be normal, right?"

"There you go again, acting superior, like a big brother. I don't know Juan; I think she would have whispered something about it to me if that's all it is."

"I *am* her big brother, Emma. Let's go to bed. She'll tell us tomorrow."

Just as they were drifting off to sleep there was a soft knock on the door.

Cata's voice was hoarse. "Please, can I come in?"

Juan pulled on his pajama bottoms and went to the door. "*Hermanita*, what is it? Why are you crying?"

"Come sit beside me and tell us what's wrong." Emma pulled the sheet up around her and patted the center of the bed, propping up pillows.

Cata sat down heavily. "I'm forbidden to talk to you about it. *Papá y Mamá* have forbidden it."

Emma handed her a tissue. "It's okay, Cata. Whatever it is, it'll be okay."

Cata wiped her eyes with the tissue and blew her nose. She shuddered, and pulled herself together before speaking. "Have Papá y Mamá said anything to you about what happened day before yesterday? I am certain they are aware of it."

Emma could tell that Juan was just as perplexed as she was. "Give us a hint, sweetheart," she said, gently pushing Cata's hair back from her face.

"The students." Cata tossed her head back wildly. Evidently she could tell from Juan and Emma's expressions that they didn't know what she was talking about. "Dozens of students were killed and even more were taken." Cata's eyes were like saucers, deep brown with flecks of yellow. They welled with tears that spilled down her face as she spoke. "They say you don't come back if you're taken. That you are 'disappeared' and your family doesn't ever find out what happened to you. And many people are in hospital, with terrible wounds."

Emma put her arm around Cata. "Slow down, honey. Who got killed? Who killed them? Why? We don't know anything about it."

Cata gulped. She looked like she was going to say something, but buried her face in her hands instead and cried silently. Every once in a while, she'd glance up at the door.

Juan sat down on the bed on the other side of his sister and tried to comfort her. "Don't worry, Cata. *Mamá* and *Papá* have gone to bed. No one can hear you but us." When she calmed down a little, he asked, "Are you talking about University of El Salvador students? Were friends of yours involved?"

"*Si*, my boyfriend was part of the protest. I wanted to go, but they wouldn't allow me out of the house. They locked me in my room. Can you believe it?"

Juan looked alarmed. "Yes, I can easily believe it. Who is this boyfriend of yours?"

"He is studying to be a doctor. He's very intelligent and he believes in equal opportunity for the masses." Cata smiled through her tears, obviously unable to conceal her pride in her boyfriend, and in her own worldliness.

"Where did you learn to say *the masses*?" Juan glowered. "It is a dangerous idea that your boyfriend expounds. No wonder they locked you in your room."

"What do you mean *it's dangerous*?" Emma looked at Juan accusingly. "You believe in it too. You always say you're an egalitarian." His expression made her pause for a second, but only a second. "Why are you whispering?" she demanded. "Jesus, things got weird all of a sudden."

"Because this is a dangerous subject, Emma. Please, keep your voice down. It is considered a Communist idea, and people get shot here for less than that." He turned back to Cata. "Who is your boyfriend? Do *Mamá* and *Papá* know him? Do I know him? Who is his family?"

"You don't know him, Juan, but he is the friend of our cousin, Ramon Bernal. He is the second son of a businessman—textiles, I think. Uncle Bernal has business with his family. I met him at a coffee house after we came back from San Francisco." Cata sighed deeply and turned to face Emma. "He speaks good English," she said proudly, "and he's very handsome. I am in love."

Emma raised her eyebrows at Juan. "That's great, Cata. Wow, we're happy for you…aren't we, Juan! What's his name?"

"How old is he?" Juan asked quietly.

"His name is Carlos Sanchez, and he's almost twenty." Cata smiled innocently, but there was a hint of slyness in her eyes.

"Why has he got you mixed up in radical politics?" The room went silent. Juan dropped into a chair by the bed and hung his head. "I can see that you're not going to answer me—obviously, there is no good answer."

"What's going on here?" Emma demanded. "Jesus, Juan, she's not a child for you to scold."

"You're right, but I fear for her." Juan looked up thoughtfully, and spoke softly and slowly. "There was a protest march here in San Salvador? I can't believe it. The situation has changed a lot since I moved away."

Emma struggled to keep her voice down. "Can we back up? Who shot who? Is Carlos okay?"

Cata's smile had vanished. "Carlos got away, but many students didn't. They were marching down University Avenue, a peaceful demonstration, protesting the government oppression. Carlos was there in the crowd. He said everything was going as planned, until they reached the area around Rosales Hospital. Suddenly there were armored cars and troops, and they attacked the students."

"Who attacked the students? I'm having a hard time following you," Emma said.

"The military." Cata stared down at her hands as she spoke. Her voice was a low vibrato, quivering, on the verge of tears. "Carlos said it was hard to escape because the military had the protesters surrounded. They had also been waiting behind La Asuncion High School, and they moved in on the students—they shot them, and they also killed them with machetes…it's true."

Cata sniffled, and struggled to retain a modicum of composure. "Carlos told me that at first, he knelt like the other protesters. He knelt to indicate submission, you understand—that they were peaceful. But when he saw that people around him were getting killed, he began to run. He was lucky he wasn't in the front or the back of the crowd."

"Wait a minute." Emma glanced from Cata to Juan and back again. "You're telling us that *dozens* of students were murdered just two days ago? Here, in this town? It must be in the papers back home by now. We must have just missed the news."

Emma suddenly stopped short as the impact of Cata's words hit her. When she spoke again, her voice was trembling. "Oh Cata, thank God you weren't in that march. You could have been killed." She shook her head in disbelief. "Jesus, this is unreal. It's too fucking crazy."

"I don't think it would be in your papers, Emma; it wasn't even in the papers here. They made an announcement on TV that eleven students had been arrested. That's all they said about it." Cata's voice was steady, but the muscles in her cheek twitched crazily. "I didn't know about the deaths until I saw Carlos last night."

"You saw him last night?" Juan spoke softly, but there was barely-contained rage in his tone. "Do you realize the danger of being involved with a subversive?"

"I don't care. I love him." Cata locked eyes with Juan in a defiant stare for a long minute. She was the first to look away, her body slumping.

Juan's body was rigid. He said nothing. The silence burned between the two siblings. Emma came up beside him and placed her hand on his shoulder. "She loves him, baby."

"She's too young to know that," Juan said, but his voice was gentle.

"Tell us what happened," Emma said to Cata. "Where did you see Carlos?"

"I snuck out to meet him. Ricky and I told *Mamá* that we were going to the cinema. Ricky knows what happened—he was there when Carlos told me about it. Please don't be mad at him Juan."

"I'm not mad at anyone, *hermanita*—only concerned for your safety."

Emma put her arm around Juan's waist. "Of course he won't be mad, Cata. Tell us everything."

"It was a planned ambush. The military had ambulances—they had come prepared." Cata stared down at the floor as she spoke in a monotone voice. "The soldiers murdered people…and then, Carlos said he saw it, they threw their bodies into the backs of the ambulances that were there waiting. They wouldn't let the doctors help people who were wounded. Instead, they hit them with machetes…and just threw them in with the dead—left them to die. They did this so there would be no evidence left of the murders. But Carlos said that many people witnessed it."

"It sounds like he's lucky to have lived to tell the tale," Emma said, then immediately regretted her words when she saw the blood drain from Cata's face.

Cata gasped. "I would die if anything happened to him! Oh Juan, there's something else I haven't told you! We are worried about Ramon. He's…missing. His parents called Carlos, asking if he'd seen him."

Emma could tell by the look on Juan's face that this was serious news. She reached for Cata, and hugged her, rocking back and forth. "Thank God you're okay. Don't worry, baby. Those bastards won't get away with it. Your boyfriend will be alright. And I'm sure your cousin is okay. He's probably hiding out some place. He'll show up in a few days. Have you talked to your parents about this? They'll help you; of course they will.''

"Emma, no matter how many times I've told you, you don't seem to get it." Juan's voice was bitter. "Tell her, Cata. Tell her about the kind of help you can expect from Mamá and Papá."

Cata looked into Emma's eyes. "They knew; don't you understand? They knew what was going to happen. That's why they locked me in my room. My mother's brother is the General in charge of the National Guard. My parents know everything that goes on here."

"I'm sure they didn't count on Ramon being in that march, though." Juan's face had turned yellow-grey, but his voice was firm. "If he is still alive, Papá will have him released. Don't worry about him, Cata. But your boyfriend will surely be arrested if it comes to Papá's attention that he got you involved. Does Papá know about Carlos?"

"No, I told them that I saw a pamphlet advertising the march on a stop sign near the university. He doesn't know that I know anybody involved. At least, I don't think he does. He might. You know Papá."

"Emma, Cata should go back to her room now." Juan's voice left no room for argument. "We must be careful. Cata, try to stay calm. We don't want them to know that you're aware of what happened. It would be too dangerous for your friends. We will arrange an outing, just the three of us, and Ricky, tomorrow. We'll go someplace where we can talk without worrying about them hearing us. Okay, *hermanita*?"

Emma took a deep breath when Cata left the room, and let it out slowly. "Jesus, Juan, everything slipped into full fucking paranoia mode all of a sudden. Do you think your parents have spies in the house or something?"

"Nothing is normal after what Cata has told us. They probably *are* having her watched. I had no idea that the situation here had escalated to such a point. Please Emma, understand that you must say nothing of any of this around my family, especially my parents."

"Oh, I thought I'd bring the subject up over breakfast. Jesus, you must think I'm really stupid."

...

"Morning" came for Juan and Emma at about one in the afternoon when a maid knocked on the door, then entered with a tray of coffee and hard rolls. As she moved around the room pulling curtains, opening the windows and French doors, the pretty maid batted her eyelashes and spoke to Juan in Spanish. It seemed obvious to Emma that they must have been lovers at some time—not that she particularly minded, as long as it was a thing of the past. But she couldn't resist teasing Juan about it after the girl left the room.

"She's very pretty." Emma sat down across the table from Juan. "So, what are her other duties, besides bringing you breakfast? Seemed like you two knew each other pretty well." Emma laughed at her own humor, leaned over and tried to tickle Juan.

But instead of laughing, Juan avoided her eyes and his face colored. "I am ashamed, Emma. What you suggest in jest is too close to the truth. I should never have slept with Ana. It was unfair."

"Oh come on, don't get so heavy. I'm kidding; I don't care. It isn't like you married the Virgin Mary here. I didn't mean to make you feel bad. I'd have my nerve."

"It's different, Emma; don't you see that? The circumstances are too unequal. It's because she works for my family—because she is poor, and her family depends on her salary to stay alive. I didn't see it when I was younger. I took my position for granted, and I thought of these poor women in abstract terms—as sluts."

"I hate that fucking word." Emma poured coffee for Juan and herself.

"When I was at Brown, I was surrounded by feminist women. I attended seminars with them; we had lengthy conversations, and at first I thought that they were too extreme, that they were unfeminine. But as I began to get a bigger picture of the world through my studies, I started to see things in a different way…and I saw a picture of myself that I didn't like. That's when I got into meditation and started trying to change."

"So, does this mean I don't have to worry about you fucking her?"

Juan looked puzzled for a moment, and then started laughing. "You are a most incorrigible woman, Mrs. Avelar."

Emma smiled and took a bite out of one of the breakfast rolls. "I've always done as I damn well please." She tasted the strong, black coffee, then added cream and sugar. "God, this is good coffee. You know, those feminist women get on my nerves. They're too serious about everything. I've been around more men than women in this business, and I've always gotten by. You just do it, you know? You take what you need. Don't whine about it; just do it."

"Yes, I've noticed," Juan said with a wry grin. "But you come from a place of privilege, the same as I do. Of course you can survive in a man's world. You could survive anywhere; I'm sure of it. But you're missing the point."

"No, I understand what you mean. I just don't agree."

"Let me give you an example. A young girl from the slums comes to work in a nice house. She makes more money at her new job than both her parents do working the fields. Her employer's son wants to have sex with her, and she is a virgin. It is against her religion to have sex before marriage, but she is afraid to refuse the son because she can't afford to lose the job. If she loses the job, her little brothers and sisters may starve. Does this girl have a choice? Can she take what she wants? Can she do as she pleases?"

"Jesus, Juan, go back to your feminist friends. Christ, of course not. It was a stupid thing for me to say. But if you're talking about that maid who was just here, I'd say she got the better end of the deal. I doubt that she went through any serious changes about sleeping with you—employer's son or not. I mean, contrary to what they're trying to sell you down here, women like sex, too. With you, anyway."

"It's not the point, but thank you." Emma watched Juan's mood shift, and his eyes take on a different kind of intensity. "I think I'll take your advice quite literally. The *just do it part*," he said, and reached for her.

•••

By the time they made it downstairs, siesta time was over and Don Gilberto had already returned to his business affairs. Doña Margarita was upstairs resting with a headache, which made their getaway easy. As beautiful as their home was, Juan, Ricky, and Cata all seemed relieved once they were finally outside the confines of the estate. Their steps became lighter as they turned left at the big gates, out onto the city streets.

The air outside the garden walls was thick with the smell of fried foods, grease, meat, and corn tortillas. An underlying odor of animal and human waste was also detectable through the stronger scent of automobile exhaust fumes. It was humid air, still hot and sticky at six-thirty at night. They moved quickly through increasingly crowded streets, heading toward the downtown area.

Emma was intrigued by the occasional indigenous women she would see walking by in brightly embroidered blouses, carrying baskets and bundles of all sorts of items, from chickens and fruits and vegetables, to clothing. She made the assumption that these were the poorest of the poor that Juan had told her about. "You know, baby, these people don't look so bad off to me. Their clothes are incredible, and they don't look hungry or sick or anything. In fact, they're beautiful."

"I agree; they *are* beautiful. Those are village women come to market, not slum dwellers; and they're not wearing authentic typical clothing. I think they copy those designs from Mexico or Guatemala, I'm not sure, but they're machine-made—not the real thing. The Indians here are afraid they'll be targeted as subversives if they wear their traditional clothing. You wouldn't have seen even this touristy, mock-indigenous clothing in the city a few years ago. I don't know what's going on in this country anymore."

As they turned into the downtown area heading toward the central market, Emma saw soldiers with machine guns on every corner. She whispered to Juan, "Whoa, fuck! You weren't kidding about the guns. Jesus!"

At each intersection a jeep was parked, with several armed men eyeing the passers-by with suspicion and even outright hostility. Emma noticed that the Avelars kept their eyes averted and that surprised her. She had assumed that with their social position they wouldn't have to defer to anyone. Following their example, she avoided looking at the soldiers directly, too, but she found it unnerving to be stared at so intently by the violent looking men. She wondered what would happen if she innocently approached them and asked for directions or something, but she pushed the thought aside. Juan would kill her, if they didn't.

Turning a corner and climbing some concrete stairs, suddenly they were in the narrow passageways of an open market, mingling in a throng of people. Emma was struck again by the beauty of the indigenous people, who offered their wares in bold colored displays overflowing from open stalls. It was a noisy and chaotic, completely new and exotic place to Emma. She wanted to buy everything, eat all the food, take it all in at one time. But Cata steered them through the market, out to a side street, and into a small, empty café.

"We can talk here," Cata said. "Carlos knows the man who owns this place."

They ordered Cokes and *papusas* from a young girl who took their order and then quietly slipped away into the kitchen. The small table was covered with a vinyl, floral print tablecloth that had seen better days. Emma found herself wondering why they would put such an ugly thing on the table when she'd just seen such beautiful fabric being offered in the marketplace for next to nothing.

Juan glanced around, and seemed satisfied that no one was listening. "Ricky, what do you know about all this?" he asked in English. "The university students protesting, and this boyfriend of Cata's—what do you think?"

Ricky shifted in his seat. "It's very bad; worse than ever. A lot of things have happened this summer. I don't know how to say this because it is so terrible, but I think Ramon is dead."

Cata gasped and covered her mouth, wide-eyed. "I can't believe it. Not Ramon."

Emma, fighting back sympathetic tears, bit her lip and curled a protective arm around Cata. Juan seemed to struggle to find his voice, but when he spoke, his words were to the point. "Are you sure he's dead—not just kidnapped? How did you get your information?"

"I met some friends for coffee this morning—they told me. But they can't go to Ramon's parents and tell them they saw him die, because then they would be admitting that they had been in the protest. You see the problem."

Cata looked up from Emma's shoulder and brushed tears from her eyes. "Carlos told me that they're arresting people even *suspected* of having participated." Her face froze in horror as if she had suddenly realized something. "Oh God, what if they find out about Carlos!"

"Shh…it's okay, honey." Emma pulled a tissue out of her purse, and wiped Cata's face with it. "They won't find out. Don't worry, he'll be okay."

"So it's definite?" Juan asked Ricky. "Your friends are sure he was killed? Not just wounded?"

"He's dead," Ricky said flatly. "They told me he was shot several times. They tried to carry him out of the crowd, but he bled to death, and they had to leave him there. The police were closing in on them, firing shots and slashing with machetes."

Emma listened in disbelief. "Jesus," she murmured.

"Do you think Papá knows about Ramon?" Juan asked Ricky. "Surely, he would notify his brother if he knew."

"Who's your dad's brother?" Emma asked, totally confused.

Cata pulled away from Emma's arm and stood up, her eyes dry now and flashing anger. "He's Ramon's father, Emma. He's a very powerful man. The students thought that having people like Ramon among them would ensure that the army would not fire on them. But they didn't care." She spit her words out loudly, apparently no longer caring who might be listening. "*Los hijos de perras* fired anyway. They won't get away with it. *Tio* Daniel will bring charges against them. I think we should tell him."

Ricky put his arm around Cata. "Quiet down, *hermanita,* and don't say such crazy things. Here, sit next to Emma." He pulled her chair out for her, and she sat down, leaning against Emma, who again gathered her in close. Ricky continued, "You know we can't tell him. If they would dare to do what they've done, they had to have been authorized by someone at the very top. *Tio* Daniel can do nothing, and *Tio* Fernando, he will not accept responsibility for Ramon's death. He'll say it is the fault of Communists. He'll blame Ramon for being in the crowd."

"Jesus God, this is a nightmare," Emma said. "I give up. Who the fuck is *Tio* Fernando? Your uncle, right? Is he your dad's brother, too?"

Juan reached over and stroked Emma's hair. "No, *corazon,* he is our mother's brother, the general I told you about last night. Ricky is right. I don't think we can expect any help from *Tio* Fernando…but Ricky, I think we have to tell *Tio* y *Tia* Bernal. They have a right to know what has happened. They must be very worried by now."

"I don't think so." Cata sat up straight. She seemed almost calm. "They probably think he is with his friends at one of the beach houses. Nobody told their parents anything about going to the march. I don't know how Papá found out I was going. But I agree with you, Juan; we should tell them what we know. We don't have to say who told us." Suddenly, her body slumped and her voice broke. "I can't believe Ramon is dead. It is not a reality to me."

"I can't believe it either," Ricky said. "I knew he was involved in those activities, but I didn't believe they would dare to kill him." His voice trailed off. "I was a fool."

The Avelar siblings continued to mull over the events in muted voices as they ate their snacks and sipped their drinks. Emma picked at the food. She understood what they were feeling all too well. Any death always brought her back to Carol. She knew about the mind rejecting horror, about trying to re-invent reality. Of all the things about his country that Juan had tried to prepare her for, the murder of a cousin and a bunch of students wasn't one of them. She realized now, that far from exaggerating the situation in his homeland, he hadn't known the half of it.

A cold, hard knot formed in her stomach as it dawned on her how close death had come calling again. It could easily have been Cata missing, too. She didn't blame Juan's parents for locking her up. Whatever those students were protesting about, it wasn't worth Cata's life.

"And what happened to all the beggars who lived on the streets downtown?" Juan was asking Cata when Emma tuned back into their conversation. "They were always lined up at the airport and all along these streets. Have they been rounded up and re-located? There were so many. Where did they take them to?"

Cata was ashen-faced and whispering. "Carlos said they were killed. Nobody knows exactly what happened, but the soldiers were seen picking them up in their trucks. They took them somewhere, and nobody knows where—Carlos said it is because they killed them. I don't think *Tio* Fernando would allow that, but it is so hard to know what to believe now."

Juan lit another cigarette. "Obviously, we are going to have to reassess our perception of what is possible."

Ricky nodded. "I heard the same thing as Cata, but it could be just a rumor. It's hard to say. I've heard the family talking about how the country needs to build up the tourism industry. And I know they saw the "Miss Universe" contest as a good opportunity to attract tourists. I think they probably just wanted to get the beggars out of the downtown section while the contest was going on. That's the most likely explanation."

"If that's the case, where are they now?" Juan's tone was fatalistic.

"Wait a minute. What are you saying?" Emma looked from Juan to Ricky and back again. "That the police murdered people because of a beauty contest? This is starting to freak me out."

"Don't be upset, Emma. I'm sorry," Cata consoled Emma.

"Oh honey, you don't have to worry about me. And you've got nothing to be sorry for."

Cata took Emma's hand and spoke softly. "I had so much fun in San Francisco, and I wanted to show you the beaches and hike up the volcano, and take you Salsa dancing…and instead, I have made you so sad."

Juan put one arm around Cata, and the other around Emma, pulled them both close. "It's not your fault, *hermanita*; we will still do all those things. Emma understands."

Emma leaned into Juan and pulled herself together. "You're not bumming me out, Cata. It's life, isn't it? It's just fucking life. You don't have to apologize for it. It's sure as shit not your fault. Anyway, I'm your sister now. Of course you should tell me what's happening. I can handle it. I'm sorry about your cousin."

"When was the beauty contest?" Juan asked Ricky.

"It was held here in the middle of July, about three weeks ago. There does seem to be some connection."

Juan's brow furrowed. "Maybe the students were protesting the actions of the police—all the beggars being 'disappeared'. That would make sense. Do you think that's a possibility, Cata?"

Cata stared down at the table, her face coloring. "I don't know. We didn't even talk about that. I'm sorry, Juan. I didn't notice that the beggars were gone until you pointed it out. There have been so many things going on; and sneaking out to meet Carlos has been so difficult lately. I'm sorry."

"Cata, quit apologizing," Emma told her. "Of course you're going to be thinking more about your boyfriend. It's only natural. Everything will be okay, don't worry."

Emma knew what she was saying was pure fluff—something to say because she couldn't stand seeing her in pain…one of those little white lies one falls back on when there's nothing left to say.

She caught Juan's eye over the top of Cata's head, and saw her own thoughts mirrored there. Of course it wasn't going to be okay. The cousin was undoubtedly dead, and the country was in a worse state of turmoil than the United States. Things don't always turn out okay. That much she knew from first hand experience.

Chapter Thirteen

Emma, 1975: The Way of the World

In the beginning, right after you lose someone, there is a sort of numbness, a feeling of unreality.

Sitting there in that dingy little café, I watched Juan and Ricky and Cata trying to absorb the fact that their cousin had been killed—that things weren't going to return to normal. "Normal" had been altered, permanently, but that hadn't sunk in for them yet. I said all the same things to them that people had said to me after Carol died. It was awful because there wasn't a goddamn thing I could say or do to help them, anymore than people could help me after I lost Carol.

The smallest thing could flash me back to those dark days after Carol died, much less another death of a loved one. Suddenly, time would lose any semblance of linear reality; it would begin to shift and groan, intersecting with bits and pieces of the past, both real and longed for. After Carol's memorial service, I inhabited that time loop pretty much continually. People were understanding, but they were on a different continuum. Yeah, they gave me some space, a time to mourn, but they seemed to feel like they could put it into a time frame. Like it's okay to grieve for a certain amount of time, that they determine the length of, naturally, and then it's abnormal.

I was supposed to snap out of it after a few months and get back out on the road to promote the album. At that point in time, I had about eighteen people who were depending on the upcoming tours for their income. As Herbie was quick to point out, if I didn't go on the road they couldn't support their families. I felt bad about it, but I couldn't do it. Herbie looked like a gargoyle to me. I could see greed seeping out of his pores.

Evan and I had gone to get Carol's things from James's house before the service. We sorted through her personal effects, picked out keepsakes for ourselves, and let James take what he wanted to keep. The rest of her stuff, we piled into big plastic bins and brought them on the ship with us. For me, all of her clothes held memories that vividly pinpointed episodes in our lives together. Irrationally, I didn't want anybody to so much as touch her things—things that still smelled like her, that you could bury your face in and pretend that she was still there with you. But I just watched as people picked out things they wanted, and shared stories with them about occasions when she had worn this or that thing. You do that. You share little moments with people as you walk those well-worn footpaths of sorrow. There's nothing else you can do.

I left for Hawaii shortly after the memorial service. Bill came with me. He was the only person I could stand to be around. With him, I didn't have to talk or let him try to console me. He just helped me get where I wanted to go. Which was Hana, of course. He got me set up in a bungalow, stayed with me a few days, and then left. It was during those awful months that I eventually got so close to Margie and Sonny.

After Bill left, I developed a routine. I'd start my day at about one in the afternoon with an Irish coffee, or two or three, and about ten cigarettes. Then I'd stumble down to the secluded part of the beach with a book in hand. A book I'd never read. I'd lie in the shade until the sun receded a little, then I'd move out to the sand. About that time, Sonny would show up with a pitcher of Piña Coladas and some sandwiches. He'd leave them for me at a little distance, like you'd leave food for a wild animal you were trying to tame. I'd get a little drunker, then go snorkeling for a couple of hours. Underwater was the only place I could really lose myself. It was the only place I felt peace.

One afternoon, after I'd been there about six weeks, my routine was abruptly disrupted. I came out of the water to find a couple of A&R men, decked out in Hawaiian print shirts, waiting for me on the beach. After being under water for so long, everything seemed surreal anyway, and those guys were so out of place that I thought maybe I was hallucinating. They had that kind of overly chummy vibe that straight record company dudes have, invading your space without a second thought. They jumped to their feet, all smiles. I completely ignored them—walked right by them as if they were a mirage. But they didn't go away. They knocked on my door at regular intervals throughout the afternoon and evening.

The next day, they started in again. I complained to the management about them, but they had told Margie that I was suffering a nervous breakdown, and they had come to help. I don't blame her for believing them. I suppose they were right. I guess you could call it a nervous breakdown, that the only living beings I wanted to communicate with were fish. So I had to talk to them. Of course, what they wanted was not to get me into therapy or something. Oh no; what they wanted was to get me back to work. They argued and pleaded, and when that didn't work, they threatened.

"The company will have to sue you for breach of contract, Emma. You know no one wants to do that. The record is selling great, sweetheart. All you have to do is give us a date, and we'll make all the arrangements. You're obligated to tour to promote your record."

"Emma, be reasonable," the other A&R guy said. "This album is a monster. It could be your biggest seller yet. Your fans are dying for you…oh, I didn't mean to say that," he stammered, turning red.

I had him then. He was so flustered by his poor choice of words that he backed down. I moved in with the clincher that got them off the island. "You know, guys, I haven't been just hanging out here doing jack-shit. I've been writing songs. If you'll stay off my back for a few more months, I'll have enough material for another record in the same vein as *Coattails*. I could go out and promote both albums at once."

It was the "in the same vein as" line that got them. That's how they think. Then again, maybe they just felt sorry for me. I found out later that they had gone back to the label and really gone to bat for me. When I finally did go back to work, those two guys, the mirage cats, Carl and John, became my true allies in the record company.

Around Christmas, the hotel filled up and it became difficult to find a deserted stretch of beach. I had to rouse myself to drive to more private places. Which wasn't easy, considering how much I was drinking. Sonny had this Aunt Nell who owned a beautiful parcel of land, with fresh water pools that spilled down into the ocean. You had to walk through her cow pasture to get there, but it was worth it. Talk about paradise, it was fucking Eden. It was so secluded that I only saw Aunt Nell once, when she came to bring me some fresh fruit, and check me out. I loved her instantly. She had a heart as big as her body, which was just enormous. She was worried about me drowning, and nobody there to even know it. Started to give me a lecture about not swimming alone, and then got it, without me saying a word. Understood that I didn't care.

"Hey," she said, "maybe you don't care about your own safety, but it's my land. You understand *haole*? I don't wanta get sued, something happens to you. You be careful for my sake, okay? No problem, you wanta swim in the pools, but you stay outa the ocean. I'm responsible here. And you should come to church with Margie. I wanta see you there Sunday morning. You need some God in your life."

With that, Aunt Nell turned on her heels, and marched off in her thongs into the lush vegetation just this side of the cow pasture. I felt like I had encountered some person from another level of consciousness. She actually saw me, and didn't have to say much about it. She brought me back to the reality of responsibilities with her gruff reminder that I was placing her in jeopardy by endangering myself. She left me thinking about how interconnected we all are. Carol would never have wanted me to harm someone like Aunt Nell, or anyone else, for that matter.

That night, I called my parents and asked them to come for a couple of weeks. There was no available space at the resort, but Margie knew of an apartment for rent, right on the bay. I asked Stephanie if that would be okay.

"We'll sleep on the floor, honey," she said, with a sob in her voice. "It will be so good to see you. Ray's got a job going, so we can't get away until the 24th, but if you need me there sooner, I can come."

"No, Mama, the 24th is fine," I said.

They arrived late in the day on Christmas Eve, tired from the long plane ride and the interminable drive to Hana. I took them over to the apartment and helped them get settled. I felt a return to some semblance of normalcy in their company. It was like emerging from a fog.

But the stark shape of things also clearly delineated the parameters of loss. While I'd been unconscious, I hadn't grieved. Now, I felt Carol's death with an acute awareness of the permanence of the grave. It finally hit me; I wasn't going to emerge from the fog and find that it had been a bad dream. I knew Ray and Stephanie understood what I was going through—they had loved Carol, too. We attended the Hana Resort's big Christmas bash that night, me holding onto my mom and dad like lifelines.

Somehow, we got through the holiday season together. Margie had a family event at her place on Christmas Day. The Hawaiian sun shone bright in the clear skies. It was a cultural experience for our family, not because of the Hawaiian-Mainlander thing, but because of how Christian their Christmas celebration was. We had always celebrated Christmas as a sort of Winter Solstice thing—like a Pagan holiday. It was weird, how bought into the birth of Jesus they were, considering it was the Christian missionaries who fucked things up for the Hawaiians. Margie's family loved the Christian God, the Baby Jesus. It was obvious that any cynicism would not be appreciated. So Stephanie and Ray and

I just went with the flow, sang the carols, and were thankful for the company of these generous-hearted friends.

New Year's Eve was harder. The smallest thing, like the rainbow spectrum you get when you squint your eyes in the bright sunlight, would bring on an acid flashback. Would flash me back to last New Year's Eve, when I was on acid with Carol. Here I was, still experiencing the sensations that we had shared, but she was gone. There is an innate injustice in the fact that life goes on after someone you love dies. Death is the one thing we can count on, and it's just totally unacceptable.

I tried to come to terms with everything that had happened, but any great truth that there was out there, well, it eluded me. So, I just lay around on the beautiful beaches of Hawaii and drank myself into oblivion every day. I never hit bottom because that's hard to do when you're bathed in sunlight, the trade winds blowing softly on your wounds.

Ray and Stephanie went home after a couple of weeks, and I started hanging with Margie and Sonny, and their families. Margie liked to pray for me, which was kind of weird and kind of far-out, at the same time. It wasn't like I didn't believe in God, or Goddess, or an eternal being—whatever. You can't run the white water rapids of LSD and come back without some perception of a higher consciousness. I was sure that there were plenty of beings more evolved than me, and that there was a prime source, but I never did have any kind of epiphany or anything. What happened instead was, I got bored with myself eventually. Decided I might as well get back to work.

I wasn't ready to go back to the mainland immediately, but I called Carl, gave him the go-ahead to book studio time in June. I thought that having a deadline would help me be more disciplined in my songwriting. And it worked; I started writing again. Carl called me back about a week later, though. Told me that the company would rather I did a big summer tour to promote *Coattails* first. Said it had been selling steadily, and that they didn't think it had reached its sales peak yet. I balked at first, but

Carl was persuasive, dangling the prospect of huge guarantees. So I agreed to it, not without trepidation. The biggest thing about going back on the road, of course, was the fact that Carol wouldn't be with me.

Lyrics were coming to me, in bits and pieces, but at least they were coming. And my writing still wasn't as negative as it had been when I was strung out. I tried to just get my feelings out on paper first. Started some lyrics that eventually became a song:

We just go on
Running in a prolonged fall
Sometimes that's all
That we can do
The overseer
Might change the call
But we just go on
Running in a prolonged fall

Margie brought out some sandwiches, and joined me for lunch just after I had written those lyrics. She picked up my notebook, and scanned it, glanced up at me appraisingly over the top of the paper, and then went back to reading again.

Finally, she said, "I understand this Emma. You're right. Sometimes that's all we can do. Keep moving. It's life, hey?"

"Yeah," I said. I was flattered beyond reason that she liked my lyrics. I had always connected with her on a basic level, but I didn't think she would care much for my thoughts—mainly because of her Christian thing. I thought she wouldn't get it.

"My dad's got cancer. I don't know if he told you. It's bad, because everybody on his side of the family dies in their forties of cancer. Now he's got it in his stomach; he won't be here much longer. My heart is broken, but I've got my kids, and so I've got to keep moving, like you say. The overseer is God, hey?"

"Yeah, that's what I meant. God, or fate, or the laws of nature. It's all the same."

"No, it's not all the same. You're wrong about that. You got to get right with God, girl."

"Oh God, Margie, don't start. I respect your faith. Whatever. God then, okay."

"It's different, because one thing is impersonal, like all your 'whatevers." Fate doesn't care about you. Laws of nature don't care about you. God cares about you. God is love. How you gonna keep from falling if you don't believe God cares for you?"

"Considering what the missionaries did to your nation and your culture, it's hard for me to understand your views. How can you be so into a God that decimated your own gods?"

"Hey, what did you just write about the overseer changing the call? You gotta go with what you've got. You think I should be bitter? You think you could do better at running the world than God? With all these people running around with free will, it can't be easy. People get to choose. And God, he lets them go with their choices. This is the life I've got, right now. I choose to try to be happy in it. Don't have time for no bitterness. Just hurts you, girl."

"You're a saint, Margie."

Margie floored me. Underneath her hale and hearty manner, she had the mind of a philosopher. She loved that I was interested in the legends of her ancestors, and she filled me in about Hana, which is supposed to be a holy place, with the seven sacred pools and everything. I was with her on that one.

"If you want to understand Hawaiian spirituality," she told me, "you have to pay attention to the everyday lives of people. You see it expressed in the way people respect the '*aina*, the land. The way they respect their ancestors, and each other. You can see it in the hula, how every dance has layers of meaning. The same dance, it might tell the story about how an ancestor struggled for power, but it's also bragging about how good he was in bed—you understand? *And* at the same time, the same dance is worshiping God. Life can't be boxed into one tidy package. There was always one God. He just took on many names in the old ways. The face of all the gods can be seen in one God now, in the great Jehovah."

I found her take on things fascinating, and it helped me focus on something other than morbid thoughts.

•••

When Hana became flooded with tourists at the beginning of Easter Week, I knew it was time to leave. The flight home was practically empty. I was going against the tide, as usual. Arrived home to rainy, cold weather, with a notebook full of lyrics. Ray and Stephanie picked me up from the airport and drove me to my house.

"Are you sure you don't want us to stay with you for a while?" Stephanie asked.

"Or, you could come stay with us, Em," Ray said.

I felt like I should try to face it on my own. Ray and Stephanie had cleaned the house and filled it with bright flowers, turned on the central heating, and stocked the fridge with essentials. It was fun, re-discovering my own habitat—re-appraising the numerous bits and pieces of art and nostalgia scattered throughout the house. But that evening, after my parents had gone, it was a different matter.

I walked into the kitchen to get a glass of water, and out of the corner of my eye, something moved. The air felt electric. My heart started beating fast, and I thought, *run*!

But I couldn't move.

My eyes were drawn to the hallway. I didn't want to look, but the density in that corridor gave me no choice. I recognized it at once. *No! It's not real*. I groped for the hall light, feeling like I was moving through molasses. All the hairs on my body were standing up, and I was drenched in sweat.

When the light snapped on, it seemed like a miracle. I had a queasy feeling that something horrible had just oozed around the corner out of sight, but at least it was gone.

That encounter creeped me out so bad that I called friends—got a party going my first night back. I invited Roger over, but made a point of asking him not to tell James that I was back. I knew it wasn't his fault, you know, about Carol, but nevertheless I couldn't handle seeing him.

The surprise guest that night was Grant, my old boyfriend from *Altered States*. He'd been playing in a popular band that had just broken up. Well, that seemed like cosmic timing. I sure didn't want to be alone in that house, and, I needed a new lead guitar player. Even Herbie thought Grant was good. He'd called him the best musician in *Altered States*.

After drinking champagne half the night, Grant and I hooked up again. He owned a house over in Marin, in Larkspur, but he started spending most of his time at my house. He was helping me get music together for a lot of the lyrics I had written in Hawaii, and we were back to being lovers again, so we fell into a routine of spending most of our time together. It wasn't exciting or anything, which was just fine with me. I didn't need any more excitement—just someone to help me get through the long hours of the days and nights back in that house where Carol and I had spent so much time together. Where her spirit was still rattling around…and something else, too.

Between us, Grant and I knew enough musicians to put together a hot band. I wanted to keep Roger on bass. He was a great player and easy to be with. Carol and I had both fucked him on the first tour, but we were pals now. He knew how to be on the road, and he didn't use hard drugs. Herbie called me up, pushing for me to use these new guys—Sam, on rhythm guitar, and Leigh, on drums. He also had a bass player in mind to complete the rhythm section. I stuck to my guns on Roger, but agreed to audition the other two guys. They were great, of course. Herbie is a weird fucker, but he knows talent. My old piano player, George, rounded out the line-up. We rehearsed five days a week for a month, and by June, we were ready for the road.

The record company had found me a new publicist—even offered to pay her salary for six months. I kept putting off meeting her until a couple of days before the tour started. Even if I'd hated her, it would have been too late to replace her at that point, but

Lauren was alright. Nothing at all like Carol. She had a degree in journalism from some East Coast college, and was way more formal and businesslike than anybody else in my fucking crazy rogue's gallery. She addressed me as Ms. Allison, for Christ sake.

It was a big, summer festival tour. We had top billing, so we usually went on around nine o'clock and were done by midnight. I developed a routine of waking up around noon and starting the day with some brandy in my coffee. By late-afternoon sound-check, I'd have a pretty good buzz going, and then I'd even out with a good sized dinner around seven o'clock. I'd drink tons of water before and during the show, then switch to champagne and brandy or tequila afterward. Grant didn't seem so boring to me now that I was older. He'd get stoned and I'd get smashed. It worked fine. For a while.

We were in Hartford when things got weird. I had to do a photo shoot for a major magazine, and the photographer, Pierre, was a very sexy cat. We flashed on each other all through the shoot, and ended up getting it on in my dressing room. It was my night off, and I wanted to spend it with him. I thought about telling Grant what was up, but decided it was my own business. It wasn't like we had a commitment to each other, or anything.

I went out on the town with Pierre and then brought him back to my hotel suite. We were pretty wasted, so we snorted some coke to keep going. Just as we were starting to get it on again, Grant came knocking on the door. I was going to ignore him, but when I told Pierre who it no doubt was, he said, "Oh, let's let him in. It could be fun."

So I opened the door, and Grant came stalking in. I braced for a scene, naked under a sheet wrapped around me, but ready to do battle. Pierre was cool as a cucumber—poured a glass of champagne and offered it to Grant, who accepted it with what looked like a flirtatious grin. Wow, how had that escaped me all this time!

Pierre and Grant brought their champagne over to the bed and sat down on either side of me. Pierre was the first to get things going. He leaned over and kissed me full on the lips, then leaned over further, and kissed Grant. Okay, this was a first for me, but I wasn't going to let on that it blew my mind. I tried to just go with it as the two men cozied up to me and to each other. Before long, the three of us were getting it on. I got a lot of the attention, but certainly not all of it. Grant and Pierre were as into each other as they were me.

In the spirit of trying anything once, I hung in there while they got each other off. It turned into an ordeal fast, not because it shocked me, or anything, but because it got boring and I didn't feel like I could walk out while they were doing it. Weird, because I'd gotten it on with chicks a few times, more for the sake of the guys than an actual sexual attraction, and you better fucking believe the guys weren't bored.

Waking up together, in the harsh light of sobriety, we were all pretty awkward. Pierre didn't even stay for breakfast. Without discussing it, Grant and I just copped an attitude like nothing out of the ordinary had happened, but we drifted apart after that night. Oh well, wasn't it me who had complained about him fucking the same way, every time!

I fell back into my old routine of doing whatever felt good at the moment. Took to hanging out in the hotel bars after the shows, trying to out-drink the guys. Bringing any cat who took my fancy back to my room with me. There was never any shortage of gorgeous guys on the scene. Between the musicians from the other bands and the steady stream of fans and guests, there was always a party rising up like a whirlwind around me. The downside of playing musical beds in different cities, of course, was that the clap could trail you like the tail of a kite across the tour, and you wouldn't even know you had a venereal disease until you ran into your band mates at the clap clinic back home. What the fuck, it's always something. Anyway, a shot of penicillin, and your worries were over.

The guys in my band were responsible professionals who didn't trash hotel rooms, and even got to sound checks on time, which made Ed's life easier. They were all good looking, too. We had swarms of groupies backstage at every show.

A week or so after Grant and I broke up, I fell into a thing with Sam, my rhythm guitar player. All the groupies were after him, which led me to believe that there was probably more to him than met the eye. We were both drunk on our asses one night, trying to help each other stagger back to our rooms. We made it as far as his room, and sort of fell in the door. Later, when I came to, I was naked on his bed and he was pouring ice-cold vodka down the front of my body. When I opened my eyes, he began to lick up the vodka. A romance made in heaven, obviously.

At least I didn't have to worry about Sam being possessive. He wasn't about to give up the groupies. He was mine whenever I wanted him, but it was a free-for-all the rest of the time. So I started getting it on again with my piano player, George. By the end of the tour, everybody was playing musical beds, including the road crew. Even Lauren had loosened up and gotten into a thing with Leigh. The fun and games worked out okay with that group of people. After all, it was a three-and-a-half-month tour. We didn't want to bore each other.

Of course, for me it really had nothing to do with boredom and everything to do with diversion. I couldn't think about Carol. Which pretty much meant that I couldn't be alone—or sober. Oh yeah, I was running alright. Engaging in sex as escapism, absolutely. But at least I made it through the tour.

•••

My schedule left me only ten days off before I had to be in L.A. to begin recording. The minute I got off the road, the party began at my house. People came up from L.A. to hang out, even though I was going to be down there in a matter of days. One of my artist friends had taken up tattooing, and that became a big attraction at my parties. It was pretty twisted, for a hippie activity. All of a sudden, my house was turned into a sadomasochism parlor. Chicks would be writhing in pain as Big Boots applied his needles to the soft flesh of their inner thighs, just this side of their exposed crotches. Of course, their legs would be wide open, providing a perverse, erotic, sideshow for entertainment. I wasn't really into it, but you know, you can't put your trip on other people. Do your own thing, and all that…even though it was *my* fucking house. And I wanted those people there. I would put up with anybody who could keep the demons at bay. I think Big Boots scared them off.

…

Bill met me at the Burbank Airport, and drove me to his house in Laurel Canyon. He had a little guest cottage on his property where he thought I'd feel safer than at some hotel. Also, it would be easier for us to work on material with me being just outside his door. He was living with his old lady now, an L.A. sit-com actress named Peggy—big silicone tits, a bobbed nose, fake red hair, and a personality to match. I disliked her immediately, and the feeling was obviously mutual. But we were completely saccharine sweet with each other that first day.

She invited me to dinner, which turned out to be a perfectly prepared, gourmet meal. It was so fucking obvious that she was trying to intimidate me. Or maybe just impress me. Okay, I couldn't cook that well in my dreams, and it probably sounds like I was jealous, which I was, a little—but she was setting it up that way—establishing territory. It wasn't like I was interested in Bill on any level other than as a producer…or at least not overtly. Plus, Bill had to have told her that I was blown away by Carol's death. If he did, it didn't faze her. As the week wore on, she took every opportunity to sneak in little put-downs—catty remarks that went right by Bill. Mr. Oblivious thought chirpy little Peggy and I had hit it off great.

Bill liked the lyrics I'd come up with in Hawaii, and a song I'd written with Sonny. We spent an intense few weeks getting the songs ready for the studio. As soon as we'd finished the writing, I moved out of the cottage. Lauren had arrived in town and booked us into the Beverly Hills Hotel. It was far enough off the old familiar Hollywood beaten path that it didn't harbor any bad memories. If it weren't for Bill, I would have recorded at a studio in San Francisco. L.A. had become a city of tears for me, but Bill was almost superstitious about Hollywood Studios—believed we should stay in our old tried-and-true environment. And instead of using session musicians, Bill agreed that it would be good if I brought my band in to record this time around. We'd performed a few of the new songs on the tour, so they already knew some of the material. Besides, after playing together every other night for months on end, we were a tight band.

I have to say that the A&R men, Carl and John, helped the recording of the new album go more smoothly. Instead of harassing me about duplicating the last record, they seemed really into the new songs. Now I felt like I had allies at the record company. They spent many long hours at the studio, listening to us record—gave us feedback that was actually helpful. I'd been worried about the song I'd written with Sonny, "*Searching for Salvation,*" because the lyrics are heavy. Not exactly your standard, good-time rock song. But not a ballad either, because the music is too kick-ass. Carl and John encouraged us to record it the way we'd written it.

John had been listening with his eyes closed, swaying to the rhythm. He clapped enthusiastically when it ended. "Go for it, Emma. Every track on the album doesn't have to have single potential."

"That's right." Carl nodded in agreement. "It doesn't matter if the music has single potential, and the words don't. A good album needs diversity."

Talk about a fucking first, coming from record company people. I had written the lyrics just as I was starting to emerge from hibernation after Carol's death:

Trapped here, in an empty town

Where cold winds blow, all year round
When I first got here, I heard music
Since then, not a single sound
No familiar faces, no activity
It's not just a ghost town
It's a cemetery
And I'm ambling down this street so aimlessly
Wishing, I had stopped to count the cost
Before I gambled, all I had and lost
Now I feel, like I've been sentenced to damnation
Alone on the streets, searching for salvation

The second and third verses were just as cheery. But, you know, somehow that song made me feel better when we got it recorded. Depressed the shit out of everybody else, but made me feel better. Surprisingly, the song ended up getting quite a bit of airplay.

My title track, "*Way of the World*," was slightly more up. Carl and John defined the song as a "power ballad." I had written the bare bones of the music in Hawaii, and Bill had filled it in. He felt that it was our best song this time around.

There was a time, not so long ago
Our futures stretched before us
Like a big sky road
Thought we'd go on forever
Every cloud seemed lined with silver
Every path with gold
Just like we'd been told
It's very easy to find, so much harder to hold

There's just no way, we could understand
How things can change so fast
How we lose command
While we were riding on that high horse

Fortune rode behind us laughing
As we schemed and planned
We didn't know the power
Hadn't felt the touch, of the hidden hand

Chorus:

So it goes
One door may close
But another door will open in its place
So they say
It's just the way...of the world.
Just the way of the world

Don't you worry, baby don't you cry
Things happen for the best
Though we don't know why
Shadows lengthen before they fade away
One day the dark clouds part
And we see the sky
Love has given us
Another chance, we can't let it go by

Repeat Chorus.

We had the album wrapped by late October, just in time for a Christmas release. It got early rave reviews, so the company decided to pump money into promo. Which was fine with me, because all the appearances took up time—during the goddamn depressing holiday season.

One publicity thing I did was a talk show with this famous TV dude. He was kind of handsome in a super straight way—definitely not my type. But for some perverse reason, I decided to fuck him. It was the first time in my life that I'd fucked somebody I didn't think was hip. Well, I went home with this cat, and I blew his mind without trying. No woman had ever given him head before—hard to believe, but true.

We were out on a short tour in late December, then back for a hometown New Year's Eve gig. San Francisco had changed a lot that year, and I'd have to say that by the end of '71, there were no more hippies, really. I didn't fit the description by that time either. Hippies were people who believed in consciousness expansion. My consciousness had been buried by my affair with heroin, right along with my guilt over what happened to Carol. I sure as shit wasn't going to drop acid and go tripping around. I'd probably have jumped out a window.

Now I was into a "mercy" drug that blotted out consciousness—alcohol. Enough alcohol would stem the steady stream of invectives that assaulted both my dreams and my waking life. But alcohol extracted a price, too.

...

The gig had gone great on New Year's Eve, and I'd ended up having friends over afterward. The party lasted all the next day, with people bringing over food and just hanging out. January 2nd, I'd cleared the house—feeling like I needed some peace and quiet. Then I regretted doing it because the house was too quiet. And, it was a huge mess. There was the other, darker undercurrent going on, too. I drank another bottle of champagne in an attempt to snap myself out of the Twilight Zone, but it didn't work. So, I decided to go visit Stephanie and Ray.

I went tearing out of the garage in my Porsche, heading for Marin, got to the entrance of the Golden Gate Bridge, miscalculated my approach to the narrow clearing, and went slamming into a tollbooth at about sixty miles per hour. Talk about blotting out consciousness, I'm lucky I ever regained it. I got a massive concussion and whiplash, but because I had my seat belt on, the sturdy German car protected my body. I was fucking lucky that I didn't injure the tollbooth operator or anyone else.

Luck is such a weird thing. You know, if you'd told me I'd use lucky to describe a car accident that almost killed me, I'd think you'd lost it. But after something terrible happens, we slip into thinking we're lucky that it wasn't worse. Like the way we live, we assume that nothing bad is going to happen to us. And anything bad that happens to anyone else, well fuck, that's his or her bad luck.

But apart from all my bullshit here, I think I was lucky, all things considered. I woke up in a hospital a few days after the accident, looking like shit. My face was black and blue, but nothing was broken. Just a few loose screws—nothing new for me. Ray and Stephanie were freaked out, of course. They'd been camped out in my room for days. I felt really bad about putting them through so much worry.

I was in big legal trouble. My alcohol level had been just ridiculously over the limit. My attorney, Bev, was there to help me with the drunk driving charges, but even she couldn't work miracles. The judge ordered me into an alcohol rehab program. The winter tour had to be postponed, which didn't make the record company happy. But I needed the time to recuperate from the accident anyway. I chose a place in Sonoma County to go for the mandatory six-week program.

The first few days, I had a constant headache that aspirin didn't even touch. They were afraid to give me better painkillers because of the concussion, and also because it was supposed to be, well, a drug-free environment. And I had to do therapy, for Christ sake. The whole concept of tracing everything back to your childhood and blaming your parents for your fucked up life seemed so straight. I understood what the guy was getting at, of course. I felt guilty about Carol, and was indulging in self-destructive behavior as a result. Okay, got that. Now what? You can diagnose from here to eternity, but it doesn't change shit. It doesn't bring Carol back, or erase Rob from the story of my life.

So, the January tour started in March, and only lasted a month and a half. I'd become reacquainted with the bottle the minute I was popped from rehab, and I had a buddy with me. Doug was one of those trust-fund kids from Marin County who had the world by a string, but didn't know what to do with it. He'd been all over the world, had an MA in International Studies, knew a little about everything, and couldn't commit to anything, except getting wasted. He'd had so many DUIs that they'd given him a choice of either jail time or rehab. He was about as into giving up drinking as I was. We hooked up, helped each other pass the time on the inside, and hit the town together when we got out.

In May, I was back on the road for a three-month stretch, with the same line-up of musicians. Doug and I had plenty of time to get to know each other, after the forced penance we'd both been subjected to. I'd been around a lot of crazy dudes, but Doug fucking took the cake. He was out of it twenty-four hours a day. I never knew what the hell he was talking about. He'd been so articulate when we were in rehab that it came as a total surprise. He'd just ramble on about weird shit, and at first, I'd try to stay with his monologue. Figured what he was saying would make sense eventually—it never did.

But there were compensations. I liked getting it on with him for one thing, and for the other, he didn't expect anything at all from me on an emotional level. It was just physical and that was good enough. It didn't last long though. I lost him in the middle of the tour. He got tired of all the traveling. Hated having to get up at a specific time and be somewhere on time. He said he was tired out from the physical demands of touring—that he needed to be on his own schedule. I thought it was pretty funny, actually.

Besides, we were playing at big venues, and there were plenty of guys to take up the slack. Beautiful cats, hanging around backstage, waiting to meet me…acting like I was the woman of their dreams—it made me want to kill…that's what I was to them: a dream. They had no fucking idea who I really was.

July in Manhattan was a nightmare. I was bowled over by the rank smell of the city, the trash on the streets, the proximity of too many people moving through stale air—air that hung motionless, damp and gritty between the suffocating, tall buildings. Not to mention the memories that were trapped in those streets. All those hotels and clubs and shops where Carol and I had hung together.

Then, to round things out, Evan showed up at the gig—strung-out bad. He came into the dressing room, eyes at half-mast, slurring his words, and my first impulse was to ask him to leave.

Yeah, I hated heroin, but that didn't mean I wasn't still attracted to it. But I couldn't blow him off. I saw Carol in the planes of his face, a little down turn of the right corner of his mouth when he smiled.

He needed money, as usual, but I honestly don't think that's why he came to see me. He had loved Carol, too, and I was his link to her. He had no other family.

So I let him come back with us to the hotel bar and hang out. As the evening wore on, he needed a fix—wanted to use my room to shoot up. I drew the line there. I gave him a check for five thousand dollars, and told him to leave. The look on his face was pure Carol, and it tore at my heart, but I couldn't be around the junk.

The tour ended in Maine, so I took my Aunt Mildred up on her offer to use her beach house on the Cape. It was a perfect respite from the haunted corridors of my home—all those darkened doorways where anything might be hiding in the shadows. It was all white and sea-bright blue in my mother's older sister's house.

Aunt Mildred had been married to a right-wing religious fanatic, but she was a widow now, and we connected when she came to her summer home to see me. She prepared crisp green salads and brought trays of fruit down to the beach—made me feel sheltered. While I was there, regenerating in the clean white sand and sky-blue ocean, Evan was back in Manhattan, shooting up, over-dosing. The same way his sister had.

Of course, I didn't find out about it until later. Lauren had left a message with my service to call her when I got home. She had come across a letter from a friend of Evan's when she was screening my fan club mail, telling me he had died. You might fucking know the letter wouldn't be from his parents. It was another blow to the heart, without a doubt, but certainly not unexpected. At least he died in a boarding room, rather than in some goddamn alleyway, thanks to the money I'd given him. Of course, I'll never know if the money I gave him helped him score stronger heroin, too. I didn't beat myself up about this one though.

You can't win for trying with junkies. I loved Evan because he was Carol's brother, and I felt sorry for him, but I wasn't fucking responsible for his habit. He was already there, long before we crossed paths.

...

It was a beautiful late summer in San Francisco. I filled my life with parties and an entourage of lovers and friends and musicians, usually intertwined with each other. We all hung out over in Sausalito at the Trident for dinner and drinks, then moved the party to the No-Name bar, or some out-of-the-way dive in The City. Often we'd go over in the afternoon to downtown Mill Valley and rummage around for esoteric stuff at Village Music, where you could find albums that none of the corporate stores carried. John Goddard, who owned the place, knew everything about blues and jazz, early R&B, rock, whatever. He could tell you who anybody had played with—any obscure bit of background on somebody's drummer or piano player. One time I said, "Hey John, my friend here thinks Janis Joplin was the first to record "Piece of My Heart," but he's dead wrong. It was Erma Franklin, and her husband wrote it for her, right?"

"You're half right," he said, without missing a beat. "Erma recorded it first, but my friend, Jerry Ragovoy, wrote it with Bert Burns." John knew all that kind of shit. He loved the blues and knew all the great legends, but without a doubt, the huge soft spot in his heart was for Janis. He kept a big poster-size photo of her in a glass display case on the wall outside his store, her breasts naked beneath a see-through blouse. And Mill Valley was just the kind of place that would allow that.

We'd usually go from the music store to a funky little diner down the street, and then end up at John Cipollina's house, where we'd snort coke and make music all night. His home was this trippy old redwood house nestled in a wooded valley at the foot of Mt. Tam. Spider webs crisscrossed from his walls to the ceiling, and hung in shimmering patterns from every doorway, lacing the antique furniture and hi-tech recording equipment into a mock-macabre lair of iniquity. John loved vampire lore, and he styled himself as a kind of debonair Dracula. He'd greet you with his long hair falling over one eye; invite you to enter if you dared. But it was all in good fun. He was actually a very kind person.

And in the middle of the constant party I had turned my life into, I was lonely. It was pathetic. For all my supposed huge number of friends, the only people I had ever been really close to, besides Ray and Stephanie, were Carol and Bill. Carol was dead, and Bill was living in L.A. with Perky Peggy who hated me. And I owned the big Victorian dream house in Pacific Heights, a house I was afraid to be alone in.

But sometimes there is fuck-all you can do but put one foot in front of the other and not give any thought to direction. I had created a blinding maze of craziness in my life on more than one occasion, but I got through it.

I always found my way back to the music, and somehow, in spite of the total insanity of my life, I had eventually stumbled into Juan.

The situation in El Salvador now looked like another entrance to a maze.

Chapter Fourteen

El Salvador, 1975

Emma sat in the tacky café with the ugly tablecloth, listening to the Avelar siblings discuss their Cousin Ramon's death. She had to consciously resist the temptation to look over her shoulder every few minutes.

Juan got up and walked over to the doorway for the third time, glanced around, then came and sat back down. He sighed deeply.

"Are you sure we wouldn't be better off back at your parent's house?" Emma asked.

"I've told you, there is no place on our parents' estate that is safe to talk," Juan said.

"We live in a cage," Cata added.

Emma set her drink down so hard it sloshed onto the table. "Well, fuck that!"

Juan shook his head. "We can't dwell on that right now. We need to concentrate on the problem at hand. I don't see any way around it; we're going to have to tell *Mamá* and *Papá* that Ramon is dead."

Cata looked stricken. "We can't—what about Carlos. They'll turn him in—you know they will."

Emma saw the fear in the siblings' faces…and she was beginning to understand their fear. As much as she wanted to jump into the conversation with a solution, she couldn't think of a single helpful thing to say. She squeezed Juan's hand.

Juan responded with a soft caress on her arm, and then turned his attention to Cata and Ricky. His voice was calm and authoritative, but Emma could feel his tension. "Don't worry, we won't give them names. They can't force us…and for *Papá* to mention our involvement to the General would put us at risk—he won't do it. His wrath will be immense, but his hands will be tied."

Cata's face brightened suddenly. "I have an idea. Why don't we have Emma come with us when we tell him? *Papá* won't want to lose face in front of her. I mean, she's not really part of the family…" Cata suddenly stopped; her face colored. "I'm sorry, Emma. I didn't mean it like that…only that my father might feel he should be polite in front of you…oh, don't listen to me!"

"Hey baby," Emma told her. "You don't have to watch what you say around me. I've got thicker skin than an elephant."

Juan smiled at Emma, then turned serious again. "Actually Cata, you bring up a good point. Although I don't relish the thought of bringing Emma any deeper into this, her presence just might diffuse his anger. *Papá* will probably want to present a compassionate front to his North American daughter-in-law." He turned to Emma. "It's not fair to ask you," he began, but Emma cut him off.

"What is with all the kid gloves suddenly? I'm in—I'm in for the fucking count, whatever it is—Jesus!" She hoped she sounded angry rather than nervous. "I think you're right about your dad; he's probably too proud to lose it in front of me."

Ricky sounded grim. "I wouldn't count on it."

…

After dinner that night, when the family had retired to the living room, Juan asked his father if he would dismiss the servants so they could have a private discussion. Don Gilberto looked askance at Emma, and then nodded toward his study.

"No, *Papá*. We all want to talk to you and it must be private. *Mamá*, I don't know if you want to hear this. It is bad news."

"I will hear what you have to say, Juan," *Doña* Margarita replied. "Cata, go and make sure that the servants are not listening."

"We have received reliable information today that our cousin, Ramon, was killed in the student demonstration." Juan's voice was flat. "There were eyewitnesses who saw him die. We have reason to believe that *Tio* Daniel and *Tia* Evelyn have not yet been informed of his death. We need your council, Papá."

Doña Margarita broke in. She sounded more indignant than upset. "Who would kill Ramon? My brother would execute them. They would not dare. Who do you suggest has done this thing?"

Juan seemed frozen by his mother's outburst. It was, after all, evidently her brother who had ordered the army to fire on the students.

Since Juan appeared to be at a complete loss for words, Emma stepped in. "The way I understand it is Ramon was part of some peaceful demonstration a couple of days ago, and your army, or National Guard or something, shot a bunch of unarmed students. And your nephew was one of those who were killed. Right?" she asked.

The sudden silence was deafening. Emma felt *Don* Gilberto's gaze slicing through the thick air, telling her that she had overstepped her boundaries, that she should not have opened her mouth. That she was no longer welcome here.

Well, at least they can't kick me out now that I'm part of the family, she thought. *I'm Juan's wife, and I'll say whatever I want.* But she said nothing more.

Finally, *Don* Gilberto broke the silence. "Who knows about this? It was wrong for you to have involved Emma. She knows nothing of our country. But as she is already here, I ask you to speak. Who knows about this? Who told you these things?"

Ricky spoke up. "Some friends of ours told us that they saw it happen, *Papá*. You know we can't give you their names. They were only there out of curiosity. They didn't realize it would be so serious. They weren't involved."

"Were you involved in this demonstration, Ricardo?" Don Gilberto was clearly furious. "You must tell me the truth. I can do nothing if you lie to me. I already know that Catarina was planning to go. Did you involve your sister in this?"

"No Papá. I haven't been back in the country long enough to know what's going on. And I don't know why you would think Cata was involved." Ricky turned to his sister. "Did you know about this Cata? Is what *Papá* says true?"

"This sounds like The Inquisition," Emma blurted. "What does it matter who knew what? Your cousin is dead. The army killed him. Somebody's got to do something about it…and you don't have to look at me like that, *Don* Gilberto. It's not like I don't respect family. I just can't stand all the beating around the bush. Your nephew got killed. What does it matter if your kids went to a protest? God, you wouldn't last five minutes in The States."

Silence fell like an ominous threat, cutting off the air supply. Emma felt the implicit warning in *Don* Gilberto's tightened lips, in *Doña* Margarita's downcast eye. Emma knew she should lay back. But she couldn't.

"I'm part of the family now. You can get pissed off at me, but I have to say what I think. You can't intimidate me with your high and mighty, Lord of the Manor trip." Emma turned to Juan, "Sorry, baby. I'm out of here."

Cata moved toward Emma. "If Emma leaves, I'm going, too."

"All of you, sit down," Don Gilberto ordered. "No one is going anywhere. We will face this as a family. Emma, I will forgive your bad manners because you do not know our culture. But please, keep silent."

"Papá, you can't give my wife orders." Juan was bristling exactly like his dad.

Emma looked from Juan to *Don* Gilberto, and she felt her heart softening toward the older man. He had, after all, raised her husband. "I don't think your father meant any harm by it, Juan. I'm sorry *Don* Gilberto. It's an American thing, you know? Cutting to the chase. I don't mean to be rude."

"I loved Ramon like a brother," Ricky whispered hoarsely.

Cata put her arm around Ricky's waist. "I did, too."

Juan spoke up, his voice gentle and respectful. "What do you think we should do, *Papá*? *Tio* Daniel y *Tia* Evelyn deserve to know, but for certain they will ask the same questions you have asked. We cannot give names, *Papá*. Innocent people would be dragged into it because they tried to help us."

Don Gilberto was no longer bristling, but his brow was furrowed and the veins in his neck bulged. "I will speak to my brother about this matter. You are not to discuss it with anyone. If you are asked, you know nothing. It is important that we arrive at the same story together, as a family. Already your Uncle Fernando has questioned me about Catarina's friends from the university."

Doña Margarita spoke up, charging the atmosphere with her anger. "My brother would never have ordered the army to shoot at those students. And most certainly, he would have protected Ramon if he had known he was there. The crowd was full of Communist agitators. This is their fault. You will, none of you, speak of this outside the family."

Emma watched as her mother in law's face crumpled and tears began to fall.

All her children rushed to her side. It was clear to Emma that *Doña* Margarita was not a woman who shed tears often. Juan put a protective arm around his mother, while Cata took her hand gently, but *Doña* Margarita pulled away from her children and sat up straight.

"It is your *papá* who has lost his own flesh and blood," she said coldly. "He needs your comfort more than I do."

Don Gilberto had obviously been thinking. "You will go to the beach house at La Libertad tomorrow, as planned. Much of our family will be joining us there on the weekend to meet Emma. You will behave as though you know nothing. It is unlikely that any of them will have news yet." He glanced from face to face. "Do you understand?"

"But what will we say to *Tia* Evelyn and *Tio* Daniel, *Papá*?" Cata asked.

"They will not be there," Don Gilberto replied. "I will speak with them in the morning. You must be cautious now, Catarina. You cannot behave like a child."

Cata's eyes filled with tears, but her tone was defiant. "You treat me like a child though, don't you. You don't care that Ramon is dead and all those other students killed. Only that we don't embarrass you. That's all you care about. I hate you."

"You will apologize *a tu padre* at once," Doña Margarita snapped.

"I will not!" Cata turned on her heel and ran out of the room.

"It is the liberal influence of these friends from the university. She does not know what she is saying." *Doña* Margarita fixed her sons with accusing eyes. "I will speak to her."

When Juan and Emma were finally alone together, they collapsed on the bed.

"Now you understand why I tried to keep you away from all this," Juan murmured into Emma's hair. "I'm sorry. It's worse than I thought. I'm very worried about Cata and Ricky." He stroked her hair back and kissed her neck. "You should leave tomorrow. Go home and rest while I try to sort things out here."

Emma jerked upright in the big bed. "I'm not leaving. Are you crazy? You think I'm that fragile? That's bullshit. I'm involved, okay? It's my family now, too. I'm no deserter, Juan."

"You are impossible, Emma."

"I'll show you impossible," Emma whispered into his neck.

...

The next morning, the family packed into three comfortable sedans for the trip to La Libertad. Four of the household servants accompanied them, as well as the drivers. Emma quipped to Cata that it seemed more like a migration than a trip to the beach. Cata smiled, but the usual sparkle in her eyes was gone.

"Forgive me, Emma. I'm not good company today. My mother gave me a lecture last night that went on for years. She's crazy—you'll see."

"Don't sweat it, sweetheart." Emma patted her hand. "I understand. It's not exactly been a cakewalk for you lately, has it."

"I don't understand 'a cakewalk'."

"Not important…just an expression that means it ain't been easy…you walk around in a circle…" Seeing confusion on Cata's face, Emma said, "Oh, never mind."

As the caravan reached the city outskirts and turned onto the beach road, Emma straightened up and took notice. Filthy cardboard and tin hovels lined the highway, exactly as Juan had described. Ragged children, looking dirty and hungry, wandered the roads with no apparent adult supervision. Every time the cars slowed down at an intersection, these children, as well as older beggars, swarmed toward them with hands outstretched, pleading, "*Dame*."

To Emma, the sight was both heartbreaking and repulsive. Her first impulse was to roll down the window and give them money. But there were so many of them, and they looked like they carried every germ known to man. Immediately, she felt guilty for the thought. These weren't middle-class kids in the Haight who would rather beg than work, and obviously Juan hadn't been kidding about how bad off they were.

As she fumbled in her purse for some small bills to give them, Cata addressed her sharply. "Don't do it Emma; they'll be all over us."

"Hey, open your eyes, Cata. They're already all over us. What's it to you if I give them a few bucks? They look like they need it pretty fucking badly…I mean…*really* badly. I'm not supposed to say *fuck* while we're here, even if your mother is in the other car." Emma tried to get Cata to laugh by tickling her.

"Roll up your window. Now!" There was urgency in Cata's voice, and pain, too. "I used to think my parents were just being stingy when they'd tell me not to give the kids money from the car. But I found out the hard way. I was out with my friends, and my parents weren't there. I gave the kids money and they all started fighting over it. They chased our car down the street in both lanes. There was a car coming the other way…"

She stopped and took a deep breath. "Some of them were killed."

Emma's stomach churned. "Jesus, you don't think of shit like that happening."

She rolled the window up. Shaken by Cata's story, it occurred to her that while the situation in this country was new to her, the concept of hurting somebody while trying to help was neither unique to this culture, nor alien to her own experience.

At the entrance to the beach house, the drivers honked impatiently and two men ran out and opened the massive wooden gates. As they drove into the walled compound, indigenous people of all ages came running out to greet them, waving from the side of the narrow road. The Avelars nodded at their workers. Emma smiled and waved enthusiastically. She found the people beautiful, despite their dirty clothes and the distended bellies and swollen faces of the children.

"They don't look well, yet they're so lovely," Emma murmured to Juan. "And they look so trusting, pure and innocent—like flowers, so close to nature."

"That's a perfect 'Ugly American' observation, Emma." Juan's voice was laden with contempt. "Romanticizing the plight of the underclass. That's exactly what people like my parents say about them—innocent like children, content to play in the dirt."

"Well, fuck you too," Emma shouted.

Both Ricky and Cata looked startled. Juan looked out the window, ignoring Emma.

"What's going on, you guys?" Cata looked from her brother to Emma. "What happened, Emma? Is Juan being stupid?"

"Stay out of it, Cata," Ricky warned his sister.

"There's nothing to stay out of." Emma's voice spiraled out of control. "I'm out of here. Stop the car. I'd rather get out and go play in the dirt with the people than stay in the car with this asshole. Sorry about the fucking swearing, Don-Fucking-Son-of-a-

Bitch-Juan. Sorry Cata. Come on, get out with me. We can walk the rest of the way. Sorry Ricky, you have no idea what a self-righteous asshole your brother can be."

"On the contrary, I do," Ricky said. "If you're getting out of the car, I will escort you."

"Stop the car," Emma shouted. The driver looked at her worriedly in the rear view mirror and shrugged his shoulders. She stomped her foot and shouted louder. "Will somebody please tell him to stop the fucking car before I jump out of it?"

"*Pare aqui*," Juan told the driver.

The driver brought the car to a halt, and Emma stepped out as elegantly as she could manage given that she was shaking and on the verge of tears. Juan stepped out behind her. She heard him say something to the driver in Spanish, and in a terse tone tell Ricky and Cata, "I will escort Emma the rest of the way. Please say that she wished to take some air."

Juan actually had to run to catch up with Emma. He seemed more furious than she'd ever seen him, but she didn't care. Neither of them spoke as he fell into place beside her, matching her angry stride but obviously trying to appear casual, as though they were out for a late afternoon stroll. Emma was sure he was mainly worried about what his parents would think—how it would look to the family—and she was sick to death of how this family was so intimidated by their parents. What did Juan have to be so pissed off at her about anyway? All she'd done was comment on how attractive his fellow countrymen were.

"It was wrong of me to have said those things to you." Juan's gaze was fixed on the ground.

Emma stepped up her pace. "You're goddamn right it was wrong."

"Will you please slow down," Juan pleaded. "It's not really you I'm angry at. It's because I can't change anything, Emma; don't you see that? I'm helpless."

Emma wheeled in her tracks and slapped Juan.

Juan put his hand to his face. He looked stunned, but glanced around to see who might be watching. Emma flew at him with her fists.

"You bastard. Is it my goddamn fault you feel helpless? Don't you ever talk to me like that again. You think just because we're married, you can say shit like that to me? Did you ever fucking hear of divorce? Fuck you!"

She was screaming, beating on his chest, giving in to the sobs she had been too angry to release. Juan let her pound on him until she began to cry, then wrapped his arms around her and began to cry, too.

"Don't baby, don't." Emma held on fiercely. "It's okay. You're not helpless."

Juan held Emma's hand over his heart as they began walking. "No matter how much I try to distance myself from the injustices and inequalities of my country, I find myself right back in the center of the problems. The truth of it is like dirt in my mouth."

"You're not part of it, Juan. You're the most decent human being I've ever known. How can you say that!"

"Because it's true. It makes no difference that I disagree with this oppressive social order; I perpetuate it by my very existence, and there's nothing I can do about it. It fills me with rage…and hopelessness."

"It's all this terrible stuff you've come home to that's getting you down." Emma lifted Juan's hand to her lips. "You're not helpless—far from it. Just don't take your anger out on me. I love you, you bastard."

"I love you, too, *corazon*. I'm sorry."

She squeezed his hand. There was peace between them again as they walked down the flower-lined road, but Emma could tell Juan was still troubled. "What is it?" she asked him softly.

His answer took her aback. "Tell me, Emma, how can I look at my Uncle Fernando—knowing what he did? He ordered his soldiers to open fire on those students, on his own nephew. He might come here this weekend. He could be here already. How can I look at him?"

"We'll get through it, baby," Emma answered calmly.

Juan stopped in his tracks and turned to Emma, looking stricken. "Emma, if he is here, you will have to be very careful about what you say. You must be careful anyway, but with him, it's imperative. Only small talk, promise me."

"There you go again. Jesus, what do you think I'm going to do—accuse him of killing Ramon? God, you must think I'm stupid."

"Just don't drink, Emma. You lose your judgment when you drink too much."

"What do you want me to do? Gain wisdom through smoking pot, like you do? That would go over big, wouldn't it! Hello Uncle Fuck-Head. Got any marijuana? My husband, the illustrious, ever-so-pious pot-head has ordered me not to imbibe any spirits, so I'm hoping you can get me high with some good Central American shit."

"Let's don't start again, Emma. I'm sorry. You know that's not what I mean. You're fun to be around when you drink—up to a point. I don't care about you being outrageous. I love you." He paused. "I should never have brought you here."

"Hey, you didn't. I dragged you here, kicking and screaming, remember? I don't mean to be flippant about the situation. It's just that you act so goddamn superior, and it infuriates me. Of course I'm going to be careful. Jesus!"

By the time they reached the house, they had fallen into a calm, easy pace. To anyone watching, they no doubt looked like a typical honeymooning couple enjoying the beautiful scenery.

The beach house was a crumbling stucco colonial mansion, surrounded by tropical gardens and a stretch of lawn with wavering palm trees on three sides, and on the other, a pristine, gravely beach. Pale pink and decorated in aqua trim, its best feature was the wide verandah that completely encircled it. Cozy looking wicker furniture was strewn everywhere, providing a huge, wrap-around outdoor living room.

A group of about twelve of Juan's relatives and friends sat in rockers and pillow-laden sofas, or lounged in hammocks strung from the rafters. As Juan and Emma approached the house and started up the stairs, everybody sprang up to greet them. The men and women, dressed in their tennis whites, had been sipping cocktails, waiting to see their long-lost relative and his *gringa*, rock star wife. There were cousins in their late teens and early twenties, children of all ages, one of Juan's aunts, a few of his parents' friends, but no Uncle Fernando, at least as far as Emma could tell from the introductions. Everyone seemed so friendly to Emma, who was relieved that they all spoke English.

After much hugging and kissing and trying to make a mental list of names, Emma flopped into a hammock. One of the cute cousins brought her a rum and coke and leaned low over her to light her cigarette.

"Oh oh," a pretty cousin named Maria spoke up teasingly. "You better watch him Juan. Otto already has his eye on your wife."

Juan laughed. "Emma can take care of herself. Let me assure you that she's used to being looked at."

As she sipped her drink from the comfort of the hammock, Emma relaxed into the comfortable banter around her.

"Did you see 'Jaws'?" Maria asked Emma. "Otto saw it in Miami, and he says it's very realistic and scary."

"Don't speak for me, Maria." Otto pulled his chair over near Emma. "I said it would scare *you*. Not that I was scared by it."

"It scared the shit out of me, actually," Emma said. "It's enough to make you never swim in the ocean again."

"There are no big sharks like that in these waters," Otto declared, still giving Emma the eye. "You don't have to worry about that. We've never had a shark attack around here, and anyway, I would save you."

Maria scoffed. "You talk so big! He's just trying to impress you, Emma. He's a chicken, really."

Otto tossed a pillow at his sister. "Shut up, Maria."

"Both of you shut up. You two are monopolizing the conversation," a cousin name Flavio said good-humoredly. "Let's talk about something important. Emma, what about Arthur Ashe beating Jimmy Connors at Wimbledon? Could you believe that? Who is your favorite tennis star this year?"

Emma laughed lightly. "I haven't given it much thought. Chris Evert, I guess."

"Oh yes, she's good, but Billie Jean King is the best," Cousin Ana volunteered.

The conversation dallied on movie stars and tennis stars for a while, and then moved on to soccer. An endless discussion of the last World Cup and soccer's greatest players ensued, with everyone agreeing that Pele of Brazil was the best soccer player who ever lived.

A young maid continually made the rounds among the group with Rum and Cokes on a silver tray. Maria took a drink from the tray, but Otto snatched it from her and downed it in one gulp.

Maria laughed and swatted at him, then took another drink. "You're such a pig! How can you act like that in front of Emma Allison!" She jumped to her feet and held her glass up. "A toast everybody—a toast to the biggest star of all. She is here with us right now; can you believe it!"

"Sit down before you fall down, Maria," Flavio said.

Maria settled back into the cozy whicker chair somewhat woozily. "Honestly, I like your music the best, Emma. But what is your favorite band—the *Beatles*, or the *Rolling Stones*? Apart from your own band, I mean."

"Do you know them? The *Beatles* or the *Stones*—other famous people?" Flavio wanted to know.

Emma took another Rum and Coke. "Well, I hung out with John Lennon and his wife, Yoko, in Amsterdam. Oh, and the

Stones have come to my gigs, and I've been to theirs, and I know Ritchie Brown. Does that count?"

Flavio raised his eyebrows. "I'd give my life to meet John Lennon! What about the San Francisco bands? Did you ever meet Carlos Santana, or Grace Slick?"

"Yeah, we've been on the same bills together. And we see each other around."

Flavio whistled. "Grace is so beautiful…not as beautiful as you, of course, but almost."

"I love *Jefferson Starship*." Maria sighed. "*Miracles* is the most romantic song ever."

By her fifth Rum and Coke, Emma had been informed of everybody's taste in music, their favorite bands, movie stars and sports stars. She began to feel like a character in The Great Gatsby, surrounded by handsome young people who were adept at small talk, and completely incapable of discussing anything of real importance to their lives. It began to grate on her nerves, the constant, empty chatter. Juan obviously recognized the look on her face, because he signaled her with his eyes, a worried, pleading glance, but it came about a second too late to divert the conversation.

"So what are we all talking about here, really?" Emma suddenly demanded, trying to get out of the hammock without falling on her butt. "We're like characters that have already been written—impossible to change. Is that it?" She stood up unsteadily and looked around the porch at everyone. "We're all doomed to an eternity of trivia, while Rome is fucking burning, right?"

"Excuse me?" Flavio looked confused. "I don't think I understand. Is it a song you're writing?"

"Emma is deliberately enigmatic. It's the way artists are," Ricky said, smiling as he stepped through the doorway and accepted a drink from the small servant girl.

"Oh, there you are," Emma said. "Where the hell is Cata, anyway? What's she doing? She should come hang out with us. I'm going to go find her."

"She's probably up in her bedroom thinking about her Communist boyfriend," Otto said, laughing, but with a touch of derision in his tone.

Emma saw Juan and Ricky exchange alarmed glances, which only swelled her sense of outrage at what Otto had said. She turned to him, glaring. "If she's thinking of anything, it's probably more thinking than you've done in your lifetime!"

"Don't get mad at me; I was only teasing. I am your servant; I would throw myself under a truck for you. I would feed myself to sharks…forgive me, Juan, but she is so beautiful. My life is hers."

"You're too late, Otto." Juan put his arm around Emma. "Come on *amorcito*, let's go find our room and take a siesta."

"I'm not tired." Emma reached up and kissed Juan on the lips, then shrugged his arm off her shoulder. "Maybe I could get another drink. Jesus, it's so hot."

Ignoring Juan's glare, Otto sprang up to get Emma her drink, handed it to her with a courtly bow. "Friends again, yes?"

"Leave Emma alone, Otto; you're annoying her," Maria said.

Ricky took Emma's arm lightly. "Actually, Cata was just asking for you, Emma. You and Juan are in the room right next to mine, and Cata is just down the hall. Come on, I'll show you two lovebirds to your room."

"Yeah, okay." Emma pulled away from Ricky, finished her drink in one long swallow, and then lit into Otto. "What the fuck do you know about Cata's boyfriend anyway, Otto? What's it to you if he's a Communist? It's a free country…" She stopped short for a second as she suddenly realized what she was saying. Her voice dropped down to a mumble as she finished her sentence. "…isn't it?" She got the picture, and it had an immediate sobering effect on her. "Jesus, I'm stupid," she stammered. "Never mind, I need a nap." Turning to Juan, she said, "Let's go upstairs, baby."

With Emma and Juan's exit, the group on the verandah began dispersing for siesta time, too. As out of it as she was, Emma distinctly heard Flavio drunkenly whispering behind her back—something about how all artists and musicians are Communists. "I know, I know," she said, trying not to slur her words, as she and Juan followed Ricky up the stairs. "I should have just let it ride. I promised you. I'm sorry. I'll get it together. I want to see Cata. Where is she? Have they fucking locked her up again or something?"

"No, no, she's in her room," Ricky said. "Of course you can see her. She's just pretty down, that's all."

"Maybe we should rest first," Juan suggested, nuzzling Emma's neck.

"I want to see Cata first, make sure she's not a prisoner or anything."

Juan knocked softly at Cata's door, called to her gently. There was no answer, so he tentatively pushed the door open. Cata was curled up in a little corner of the big bed, sleeping noisily, gasping at air, panting, expelling large breaths at intervals.

Emma pushed past him. "She's having a nightmare. I'm going to wake her up." Crossing the room unsteadily, she knelt beside the bed and stroked Cata's hair, whispered, "Wake up, baby, it's only a dream."

Cata blinked into consciousness, and teared up immediately. "I wish it were just a bad dream. Stay with me, Emma; I'm so tired."

"Go on you guys; I'll stay here," Emma said, and began taking off her shoes. Stripping down to her underwear, she fell into the big bed and passed out beside Cata.

...

In the middle of a very deep sleep, something wakened Emma. She was burning up, and an insistent pain in her stomach forced her to her feet, searching for a bathroom. In the unfamiliar room, she opened the closet door instead, and then it was too late. She began to vomit uncontrollably where she stood. Cata woke up and ran to hold her, screaming for help at the same time. A young maid was the first to respond, then Juan and Ricky right behind her.

"No, get out of here," Emma choked between gagging. "This is repulsive; I don't know what's happening. Go away, I'm okay."

"Go send for Dr. Cortez," Juan said to Ricky. "Bring some warm towels," he said to the maid. "And get *Doña* Margarita. Cata, help me get her to the bed."

"No, I need a bathroom," Emma moaned.

The bathroom was just down the hall, but Emma didn't make it there before her intestines began to empty and her stomach turned inside out again. She had never experienced anything like this before, and it freaked her out. She couldn't think straight; her mind seemed inaccessible, as thick with humidity as the tropical air. "I didn't think I drank that much, baby; I'm so sorry," she said to Juan.

"You're sick, *amorcito*; it's not because you drank too much. You've probably picked up some bacteria somewhere. I shouldn't have let you eat that *papusa*. You'll be fine; the doctor is coming. I'm going to carry you to our room."

"No, I'm disgusting, stay away from me. Just get me to a bathroom."

Despite her protests, Juan scooped Emma up and carried her to their room, which had a private bathroom. There, he turned on the shower, adjusted it to a cool temperature, and stepped into it fully clothed with his wife. Cata helped him undress Emma and wash her, and then brought a fresh terrycloth robe to wrap her in. No sooner were they out of the shower than Emma was sick again. *Doña* Margarita came bustling into the room with another, older maid trailing her.

"Let Eva help her, Juan," Doña Margarita ordered. "She knows what to do. You go and wait for the doctor."

Emma felt like she had not a single shred of dignity left. "I'm sorry about the mess, *Doña*…" she began, but her mother-in-law shushed her. And then an angry fist in her stomach forced her onto the toilet, right in front of *Doña* Margarita. Tears of pain and shame streamed down her face, and she began to vomit again. The maid put a wastebasket under her face, so at least she wasn't soiling the floor.

Doña Margarita was unperturbed, all business, like a nurse. "I've raised four children, Emma; this is not the first time I have seen this sickness. Be brave, it will pass. You will be alright. Catarina, give her some peppermint tea to rinse her mouth. Eva, let's put her back in the shower now to clean her."

By the time the doctor arrived, Emma was lying in bed in a cotton nightgown, soaking the sheets with sweat, shivering uncontrollably. Her teeth clacked on the thermometer that the doctor stuck in her mouth; her body shook with each spasm of pain.

"One hundred and four, point one," the doctor said. "We have to bring it down. Run a cool bath. Margarita, send a girl to my office for supplies; we'll have to start an I.V…these American girls are too skinny; they get dehydrated fast."

When the medicines finally entered Emma's bloodstream, she succumbed to a merciful unconsciousness that lasted two days. On the third day, she woke in the late afternoon, disoriented and paranoid. She couldn't remember where she was at first, and when she saw Juan sleeping on a couch next to her bed, she started crying out of sheer gratitude. The nurse, who had been attending her throughout her illness, immediately wiped the moisture from her face, and stuck a thermometer in her mouth. She wanted to cry out to Juan, but she could only mumble. Nonetheless, he woke immediately and came to sit on her bedside.

"Don't try to talk, *amorcito*; you're better now. *Esta bien, esta bien."*

"One hundred and two, point three," the nurse read aloud. "Here, put these cold towels on her forehead," she instructed Juan, as she began sponging down Emma's arms and legs.

"Everything is hungry," Emma said to Juan.

"You're hungry, *reina*? This is so good that you're hungry. I'll get you some soup and maybe some crackers. Does that sound good?"

"No, no, not what I said," Emma muttered, as she slipped back into an incoherent delirium. "Just waiting, everything hungry."

In spite of the doctor's conscientious ministrations, the fever lasted seven days, and when it finally broke, Emma was too weak to move for another few days. Most of the family had gone back to San Salvador, but Juan, Cata, and *Doña* Margarita had stayed to look after her. When Emma was finally able to eat normally and take walks on the beach, *Doña* Margarita announced that she would be leaving to go back to the family home, and that Cata would, of course, be going with her.

A shift in Emma's relationship with her mother-in-law had occurred during her illness. *Doña* Margarita had treated her like a member of the family, like a daughter, and Emma was grateful. She hugged her with genuine warmth when they said good-bye, thanked her for her care. But now that Emma was back on her feet, *Doña* Margarita had slipped back into her mantle of insularity, her emotions pulled back as tight as her carefully groomed hair. She felt stiff as Emma hugged her, but Emma kissed her cheek three times anyway. *Doña* Margarita smiled and responded with a perfunctory air kiss, but Emma saw something more in her eyes.

Cata's eyes pleaded for rescue, but there was nothing Juan or Emma could do for her. There was just no way her mother was going to let her out of her sight.

Juan and Emma had the house to themselves except for a couple of servants, but the vibes felt weird to Emma. The house was too big, for one thing, and it didn't feel secure. She thought maybe the military had wired it or something, to eavesdrop for information. *Jesus, how fucking paranoid am I right now*! She shoved the thought to the back of her mind, but it nagged at her. At least she was feeling stronger—and she wanted to take advantage of the private beach to get a full-body tan.

"As much as I'd like it, I wouldn't advise it," Juan chuckled. "Every eye in the countryside would be on you—you might not see them, but they'd see you."

"Fine, I'll wear a bathing suit like a proper Salvadoran wife." Emma found her bikini and put it on, then grimaced as she caught sight of herself in a mirror. Her ribs were sticking out and her breasts seemed half their usual size. "I look like shit."

"No, you're beautiful, as always, and just think—you're safe from being considered a food source by ravenous animals or wicked witches—too skinny, no meat on the bones."

"That makes me feel so much better—thanks a lot!" Emma smiled. "Let's hit the sand before the sun goes down."

Juan rubbed tanning lotion into Emma's back, then stretched out beside her on the big beach mat. Emma smiled to herself, happy to be back in her body. She stirred sensuously—rolled over onto her side to face Juan. "So, what happened after I got sick? What's been going on? Did anything get resolved with your cousin's murder? Did your parents find out about Carlos? Jesus, I was so out of it. And that doctor was coming on to me—did you know that? I swear to God he was—I wasn't that out of it. Jesus."

Juan pushed his sunglasses up and raised an eyebrow. "Dr. Cortez? I don't believe it. You're too irresistible; it's a problem."

"So that's it? You're not going to challenge him to a duel or anything?"

"It's not a crime to admire a beautiful woman." He ran his eyes up and down her body in an exaggerated leer. "But seriously, Emma, did he offend you? Was he disrespectful?"

"No, Christ, it's okay. He was out there though, the old lech. So where is everybody? What happened after I threw up all over everything and went into a psychotic delirium?"

"So much happened…Marta and Carlos came to see you. The kids were disappointed—I promised them we'd come to their house when you were better." Juan's face darkened. "My Uncle Fernando was here, too."

"The General uncle? No shit! He had the nerve to show up?"

"He came the day after you got sick. Ricky said that he acted like he had just received the news, as if he had nothing to do with the murders. And he informed the family that it was his responsibility to tell them that Communist insurgents had caused Ramon's death."

Emma's jaw dropped. "Did everybody believe him?"

"No, I don't think so, but it was a thinly veiled warning. Everybody was shocked, and no one would dare disagree with him." Juan sighed deeply. "I don't believe that he would have intentionally harmed a member of the family, but then again, he made no apologies. My mother kept Cata in her room while he was here."

Emma sat up suddenly and hugged her knees to her body. There was panic in her voice. "He's not going to hurt Cata, is he?"

"No, you needn't worry about that. She's his own flesh and blood. He won't hurt her. But her friends are in danger, especially her boyfriend."

Emma let out her breath and lay back down. "Somebody better warn him, don't you think?"

"I'm sure he knows. It was terrible, *amorcito*. I didn't have to go downstairs because I was tending you, and *Mamá* used that as the excuse to keep Cata upstairs, too. But Ricky said everyone had to sit at dinner and make polite conversation, and mourn for Ramon, as though his death were a fluke accident, when, of course, it was obviously murder."

"And nobody dared confront him! What about your mom? He's her brother—couldn't she say something to him?"

Juan shook his head. "You don't understand, Emma."

Emma sat up again. She couldn't keep her voice from rising, too. "I'm sick of you telling me I don't understand things! Why don't you explain it to me then—just spell it out."

Juan sat up and began drawing shapes in the sand with his finger, his eyes on the emerging patterns. "The General has a lot of power, and he protects my family's interests, but there are other factions vying for power who would use any suspicions of Communist influence within the family to…well, as an excuse to seize power from us."

"*Us*? Did you just say 'us'?" Emma's voice went up another notch. "You just used your family and the General in the same sentence!"

Juan looked up at her. "He *is* part of my family, Emma. And he would argue that everything he does is for the good of the family. How do you think my parents maintain their power and protect their wealth?" His eyes dropped to the ground and his face colored. He couldn't seem to look at Emma. "Now you see why I didn't want to bring you here—I tried to tell you."

The look of shame on Juan's face cut right through Emma's outrage. Her voice softened. "Yeah, you're right, you did tell me, and I'm not sorry I came. Never mind… we'll see this through together—that is, if I can quit throwing up all over everything."

Juan reached over and took her hand. "No, things are too crazy now. I've got to get you out of here as soon as you're well enough to travel. We have to go see Marta and the kids, but we could be out of here in a few days." He stroked her hand, and light came back into his eyes. "I've been thinking that we should go to Guatemala for a vacation. What do you think?"

"You're changing the subject."

"Yes, of course I am. You need to recover your strength." He smoothed her hair back from her face and kissed her forehead.

"What do you think? Are you up for it?"

Emma flopped back down on the mat and stretched in the bright sunlight. "I'll be okay, don't worry. And yeah, I'd like to see Guatemala. It's supposed to be really mystical—Mayan ruins and Indian villages and everything. One of Ray and Stephanie's friends went there. I saw pictures. My parents have always said they want to go there. We'll check it out for them."

"Would you like to invite them to meet us there?"

"Not this one. Let's just go on our own. We need some time alone after all this, don't you think?"

Juan dropped a kiss on the hollow of her belly, between her prominent hipbones. "Absolutely, we will make a getaway, my little skeleton. There is a huge lake up in the mountains—Lake Atítlan. Aldous Huxley wrote that it is the most beautiful lake in the world. It's surrounded by twelve Mayan villages that are supposed to be relatively unspoiled by the twentieth century. I wanted to go there when I was a teenager, but my parents never considered it an appropriate holiday destination." Juan's face suddenly went serious again. "But are you sure you're feeling up to it? It might be pretty rugged traveling."

Emma laughed. "Jesus, I haven't turned into an invalid just yet. It sounds great. Let's go to the ruins first. I want to see the pyramids. We should get a travel book."

...

The next day, Juan and Emma went back to San Salvador. In spite of the beauty of the Avelar home, El Salvador seemed to Emma to be crumbling around her. The volcano she had thought so fascinating when she first arrived now seemed ominous—as though it could erupt at any moment, carry away the entire country in molten stone within minutes. The smell of rot was in the air, and while the scent of gardenias in the Avelar home might mask the odor, it could not eliminate it. There was too much of everything, and not enough of anything. Outside the walls of the estate, garbage festered—malodorous piles of scraps that people riffled through, looking for bits and pieces of shelter and nourishment: plastic, newspaper, a little melon left on a rind. A few of the people had more than they needed, and everyone else swarmed around scavenging for leftovers. Even when they visited Marta, and Silvia and Oscar scampered onto her lap and rode on Juan's back, Emma couldn't escape the sense of peril and decay.

...

When the plane took off for Guatemala City, Emma felt a tug in her stomach, an uneasiness about leaving those she loved behind.

"Don't worry so much, *reina*," Juan said. His voice was unconvincing. "The family will be okay."

Chapter Fifteen

Emma: 1975—Flash Backs: '72 & '73

When I was so sick in El Salvador, I remember lying there thinking that everything was waiting for me to die. Everything was hungry, it was just the way of the jungle. The insects that the Avelar staff worked so hard to keep at bay were winning the battle. They were persistent and they knew instinctually that I was dying. They wanted my body, wanted to crawl over my flesh and take what they needed to survive—leave the rest of it to decompose, to feed the hungry plant life that hovered just outside the window, and peeked in the French doors, testing the waters, gauging my condition.

My body was hot, and the air I was breathing was too heavy. I was fermenting, going to compost, losing the tenuous thread that ties us to this planet, to this plane of existence. Lizards crept into the room, crawled the walls, tried to stay camouflaged in the shadows, but I saw them, knew they had come for the insects—for their part of the food chain. I didn't seem to have any claim on priority treatment in the scheme of things in the tropics. I was just another energy source. But it wasn't like a nightmare or anything. It was life in its perfection, without the human ego trying to gain the upper hand, trying to cheat Mother Nature. It would really be okay to die and become part of the whole process all over again.

And in the middle of all that, Carol got resurrected. I remember having a whole goddamn conversation with her. She appeared as a snake on a huge leaf of a vine that was furtively encircling the room while Juan slept. She rose up dancing, as if a snake charmer were playing for her, and she was wearing this very slinky, shiny dress, her hair in coils around her face, only she was still a snake. I asked her how it was possible to be both things at once, but she didn't answer—just continued her beguiling dance, with a mysterious smile on her face.

"So, where's the music coming from?" I asked her. "At least tell me that."

Suddenly the vine became part of the snake, part of Carol's body, and it began twining itself around my body until Carol's face hovered directly above me.

"It's coming from you, baby. It always did," she said. And then she began to recede, to shrink, and I was reaching for her, begging her not to leave.

"Stay back," she hissed. "It's your life now. I can only be true to my nature. I will sink my fangs into you if you reach for me again. Play your music for the living; you don't belong here."

She slithered and shimmied, grew smaller, and disappeared out through the window. And then, just at that moment, a small black bird with a bright yellow breast came fluttering into the room and lit on top of Juan's head. That part really did happen…I think…because Juan woke up and shooed the bird out of the room.

But not before I heard its song, the song that broke my fever.

Of course, once my fever came down, I was back to my old way of thinking. I had no fucking desire whatsoever to become insect food or plant fertilizer. But a lot of it was real, you know. What I was looking at there was the reality of death and life feeding on each other. Carol was gone, and even though I missed her, I had to let her go. The fever brought me face to face with the reality that I would be "gone" some day, too. Smashing my head into the Golden Gate Bridge tollbooth hadn't been enough to bring that home to me. Jesus, I'm so fucking oblivious. Then again, I'd exerted so much energy trying to keep things blotted out that it's no wonder I had to go toe to toe with death before I'd concede my own mortality. I lost so much weight in that match, you could see every bone in my body. There really wasn't much left of me for the hordes of insects anyway.

That doctor told me it was my own fault I almost died because I was too thin, which was just absolute bullshit. Jesus, I've always been healthy, despite my best efforts to fuck things up. And I've always been thin. It's because I'm always moving—even when I was strung out on heroin, I danced through all my sets.

…

Stephanie started me in a pre-ballet class when I was about three. We'd get out there on the dance floor with scarves and gauzy fabrics and leap around, imagining we were fairies dancing in the forest, or elves or unicorns. There are home movies of my childhood performances, and when you compare them to the way I dance on stage now, there's really not a lot of difference.

I remember a gig at the Filmore—I was dancing and laughing, high on LSD, and moving through air that was almost solid. The guitars were wailing rainbow colors, and the drums were pounding out the more vivid shades, and I was moving through all those bright molecules, my body instinctively following the patterns, weaving its own design in the process. It was fairyland, absolutely. Even when I quit doing psychedelics, my sensibilities had been permanently altered.

I got back into dance big time after that grueling three-month tour in '72, when Evan died and I was so down about everything. I had been just kind of rattling around my house, trying to fill my time off with constant activity, and then Roger brought over this dance teacher, artist chick, Sandy. She was putting together an experimental movement and color thing and wanted to know if I'd dance for her, sort of freeform, with paint on my body. I would be in a room hung with paper, some colored, some blank, and I would move to the movement of the colored paper, and make impressions on the blank paper. Or something like that. It was a pretty out-there idea, so of course I was interested. I devoted a lot of time to her project, which really didn't come to anything, but she got me back into a heavy-duty dance regimen in the process. We were trading—my participation for her giving me dance lessons. I got the better end of the deal. All that focusing on precision in form and technique helped get my mind out of the rut I'd been carving for myself that summer.

By the time I was back out on the road in late September, I was in top shape, thanks to Sandy's fascist-style, disciplined routine. And I dug her, you know. She was kind of crazy, but in a very far-out, creative way. I suggested to Roger that he bring her on the tour. It was only a six-week stint; you'd think he could maintain a monogamous relationship that long. But it was too much of a commitment for him. Fucking men, Jesus. So, I invited her to come on the road with us as my personal assistant or something. Hey, I was the boss. It was a cool tour, Pacific Northwest, Colorado, Montana—laid back places, not a lot of pressure. But Sandy started wigging out after a few gigs, got progressively weirder. Instead of her centering me, like she'd done in San Francisco, I had to cool *her* out, and it became an energy drain fast.

A few gigs into the tour, I met up with Daren, a musician I had known in the Haight who had moved to Portland and become an attorney, for God's sake. We hit it off, and he showed up at the gig in Seattle, too.

Sandy took an immediate dislike to him. Then, when I came down to meet her in the hotel gym the next afternoon to practice the new techniques she'd taught me, she was all mopey. I assumed it was because Roger was fucking other chicks, and Christ, that's hard. But she was gorgeous—could have gotten it on with plenty of other dudes, there was no goddamn shortage. I tried to cheer her up, but it was hopeless. As the tour progressed, she became just a total drag to be around. And in spite of her looks, none of the guys went for her. Things finally came to a head in Bozeman, when I slept through one of our practice sessions and she came unglued about it.

The phone rang at about four-thirty in the afternoon, which startled me because I'd asked the operator to hold calls. "Emma, I'm sorry to wake you, it's Lauren. Something has happened to Sandy. She slit her wrists."

"Christ, is she okay? Is she alive? She's not dead, is she? What happened?"

"Ed is with her. And a doctor is there now. He says the cuts are not deep, that she's going to be alright. But she's acting really crazy. Emma, she's saying that you drove her to it. We've already got a situation with a few fans in the hallway hanging around outside her door. The doctor gave her a sedative, but she keeps insisting she wants to see you. I'm sorry, Emma, but I think you better talk to her."

"What? She's that pissed off at me? I missed *one* practice. Oh Christ, this isn't about me, but I'm coming. Hold on."

"I'll meet you outside your door."

I pulled on my jeans and a shirt and went flying over to Sandy's room, which was two floors below mine. Of course the fans spotted me and wanted autographs.

"Later," I said, shrugging them off.

"Ms. Allison is busy. She'll be happy to sign your t-shirts later." Always on the job, Lauren.

When I walked into her room, Sandy looked at me reproachfully and began to cry. The doctor, who was a young dude, was all over me in a minute, telling me how much he liked my music and how happy he was to meet me.

"She's stabilized," he assured me. "I really like your latest album, but my favorite is still your first one. I saw you play in '68. What a great concert! I wish I could have been there last night, but family obligations, what can you do."

At a nod from Ed, Lauren swung into action. "Thank you Dr. Mead. I'll get you a signed copy of the album, but would it be alright for Ms. Allison to see the patient in private for a few minutes? Why don't we go to my room and get a copy of the album for Ms. Allison to sign."

Dr. Mead dutifully followed Lauren out the door, and I turned my attention back to Sandy. "What happened?" I asked gently. "Was Roger being a jerk, as usual? You shouldn't have done this. He's not worth it."

"It has nothing to do with Roger, and you know it." Sandy's voice was laden with accusation.

I sat down on the side of her bed and tried to take her hand. She jerked it away.

"Quit torturing me," she said.

I looked around the room to see who she was talking to, but there was only me. "Me?" I said. "Because I missed a rehearsal? Jesus, Sandy, you need to lighten up."

"You broke my heart," she said quietly. "You don't care about me. You never did."

"What are you talking about? Of course I care about you. Jesus, what a heavy trip. I don't think this is really about me, you know."

"Oh, but it is about you, Emma. You always think everything is about you, and now, when it actually is about you, you want to evade the issue. The truth is, you invited me to be with you on this tour and then you dumped me for the first man who came along. You're worse than any dude, crueler than Roger ever was."

"I didn't dump you. I've invited you to hang out after every show. You're here now. What are you talking about?"

"I'm talking about the way you let your breast graze my arm when I was showing you moves. About the way you leaned into my body when we were choreographing the art show. You led me to believe that something was happening between us. And then you invited me to go on tour with you…"

"Jesus, Sandy. I don't believe this. I'm sorry you got the wrong idea. I'm not gay. I'm not even bi, actually. I thought we were becoming good friends like…never mind. I'm sorry if I hurt you. I honestly had no fucking idea that you're gay."

"I'm not gay, Emma. Isn't that a most convenient label for you to put on a complex situation. I thought it was a special thing between the two of us, but I was wrong. You don't care about anybody but yourself. You're the most self-centered, egotistical person I've ever met."

"Come on, Sandy, that's not fair."

"Oh really?" Sandy rose up onto her knees and waved her arms around for emphasis as she screamed. "Because I'm not kowtowing to you the way everybody else does? No one ever calls you on your bullshit, Emma, and it's nothing to do with art. It's just economics. You pay the bills. You have the power. It's just as jive as the straight world. I hope I never see you again." Sitting back down on the bed in perfect Lotus position, Sandy dropped her voice to a low growl. "Just get out of here. I can't stand looking at your perfect little hypocritical face, you bitch."

Wow! That was a stunner. I thought I better obey her and wait outside for the doctor to come back. At least he liked me. Anyway, I didn't want to get her all fired up again—she could start bleeding or something.

I was standing out there in the hall, shaking, when the fans over by the elevator caught sight of me. I was signing their shirts and shoulders, answering their questions, when Lauren got back and rescued me. But not before I'd signed the doctor's album. She rode with me in the elevator back to my room, so she was there for the next crisis. The door to my room was open, and when I walked in, a cop said, "Are you Emma Allison? Is this your room?" Then, without waiting for my reply, he told me to put my hands behind my back. Slapped fucking handcuffs on me.

"You're under arrest for possession of marijuana. You have the right, blah, blah, blah," he said.

They had already arrested Daren, and were in the process of searching the whole band's rooms, and the crew's. Even Lauren's Ivy League, take-charge-of-the-situation manner didn't keep her from getting searched, too. She was clean though, the only one of us who was. Thank God, because she had to spring us all from jail, and try to do damage control with the press at the same time. By the time we arrived at the jailhouse, the reporters were there to meet us. We all got fingerprinted like real criminals, even Daren. It wouldn't have been so bad, just another band getting busted on drug charges, but the press ran with the story.

"Rock Star Lesbian Affair Ends in Suicide Attempt," read the local headline the next morning. "Emma Allison left her lesbian lover bleeding to death while she went back to her hotel love-nest to smoke marijuana and continue her clandestine affair with a married man." News to me. Daren had, of course, neglected to mention to me earlier that he was married, the bastard. I felt sorry for his wife. I mean, it didn't matter much to me that the gossip rags ran lurid stories about our supposed "love triangle" with Sandy. People expect as much from a rock singer. But it was probably hell for her—all her friends reading that shit, and everything.

All in all, it was a depressing fucking episode. Sandy turned out to be deranged, this guy I thought was so together turned out to be a goddamn liar, and Montana is a notoriously bad state to get busted for pot in. Those mid-western states way up north are a country onto themselves. The cops in Wyoming were all riled up after the Nordic-News had alerted them to what degenerates we were. I looked enough like them to fit in, with my blond hair and everything, but they had my number; they knew I wasn't one of them. Extra security awaited us at our hotel in Casper, and people were patted down for drugs at the gig like it was a matter of saving the country from rack and ruin.

We were happy to move on to Colorado because Denver has enough of its own shit happening that we weren't such big news there. Denver is always fun, and the last gig of the tour, Boulder, is hippie-heaven-mid-west. Nobody hassled us there. They had their hands full with the students getting high.

Some guys I knew in a bluegrass band there in Boulder came along to the show, invited me up to the mountains to hang with them the next day. They were all living together in a big old wooden lodge in the mountains, a commune type thing.

The Rockies in October look like a psychedelic painting. The leaves are all these outrageous colors, extravagant purples and reds and pinks, and they crackle in the wind, creating their own music. I was sitting up there on the big front porch of that lodge, in a rocking chair, no less, getting stoned on good weed and Irish coffees, listening to the guys doing these amazing banjo and mandolin licks, with a fiddle coming in and leading the melody on a chase, and I swear the leaves were crackling along with them. Carl, the mandolin player, could do runs that were so fast they took your breath away. And he had a great voice. I started harmonizing with him on his songs, and before you know it we were writing a new song, Carl playing the chords, and me plunking out a melody on an old, out of tune, upright piano. The guitar player, Joel, joined us with his finger picking style, and the tone of the song changed—became a ballad. These guys were amazing musicians, and their life style was way laid-back. They just played all day long, every day, and you could hear it in their music. I knew they were going to be giants in the music scene soon, and as it would turn out, of course, when they eventually did come down from the mountains, they were signed immediately.

We all went for a long afternoon walk, ambling through the singing trees, our cheeks bright red from the cold mountain air, and it was a sweet moment while it lasted; but I started thinking about Sandy and it was all downhill from there. I couldn't believe the things she had said to me. After I'd brought her on the tour, after I'd done her stupid project with her. I'd really liked her, you know. It blew my mind, the way she turned on me—it actually brought back memories of junior high, when Cynthia and Olivia quit speaking to me…and that led to me thinking about Fuck-Head Rob. So I was knee-deep in shit as we walked back to the lodge, but when we climbed the front porch stairs, I turned around, and all the negativity instantly vanished. The sun was setting and the sky was turning shades as vivid as the autumn leaves.

"Nice sunset tonight, huh," Carl said.

"It's just heartbreakingly beautiful," I responded without thinking. And then, suddenly, I had the lyrics to the song we'd been working on earlier. Had to run for paper and pen, and catch them as they came spilling out. "*Heartache Sunset*," definitely.

Well I hardly thought of him at all today
At least not more than once or twice I'd say
But now the golden spots are getting smaller
Big black shadows growing taller
Should I just break down and call him
All my resolve seems so far gone
And I feel another heartache sunset coming on

The sun seems like a traitor every night
Leaving me to face the pale moonlight
Another night of wishing you
Were here and I was kissing you
Can't keep myself from missing you
Being here alone just feels so wrong
And I feel another heartache sunset coming on

(chorus)

Coming on and over me
Sunset colors blinding me
Evening wind is damp and cold
Without you here for me to hold
And you know it's been this way since you've been gone
And I feel another heartache sunset, another heartache sunset
I feel another heartache sunset, coming on

Sunset was the best part of the day
We'd sit and watch the colors till the sun would fade away
Then we'd lie back in the evening wind
Night sky held us like a friend
We were so in love back then
Don't you know my love is still as strong
And I feel another heartache sunset coming on
(repeat chorus)

It was funny how writing those tearjerker lyrics made me feel better. Who was the song about, is a question I'd get asked a lot in the future. And, well fuck, it wasn't about anybody, you know. But I would never say that to critics, oh no. I'd just say that the lyrics were as much as I'd care to divulge, and I'd look sort of forlorn as I'd say it.

That night was actually far from a heartache sunset. Carl and I were both really jazzed that we'd whipped out a song in a few hours, so of course we had to celebrate. The party raged into the night, and I woke up late the next afternoon in bed with Carl and his old lady. I hope we had fun, because I don't remember a goddamn thing. I had missed my flight, my head was a blur of pain, and the slightest bit of noise or light seemed downright evil.

A few Irish coffees later, I felt significantly better, but I was antsy, wanted to get out of the density of the commune, down off the mountain to where the air was not so thin. Carl informed me that part of the headache was probably a mild form of altitude sickness. Fine for him to call it mild. Somebody had some painkillers, which I downed with a few slugs of whiskey, and then over everybody's objections, I took off in my rental car. How hard could it be to find your way down a mountain, right? Just point down, follow the road. So that's what I was doing, cruising along at a reasonable speed, when I suddenly become aware of flashing lights in my rearview mirror. Evidently the cop had been tailing me for quite a while and I hadn't noticed.

"What did I do, officer?" I asked the cop in my most innocent voice. "I'm sure I wasn't speeding, sir."

Busted again. The cop claimed I was weaving all over the place and that he smelled alcohol on my breath. He recognized me, and said he didn't want to arrest me, but that he had to do it for my own safety. And get this, he wanted an autograph.

"Fuck you," I said.

"There's no need to take that kind of attitude, Miss Allison. We don't necessarily have to press charges, but I've got to get you off the road. You're liable to kill yourself in your condition."

Okay, that changed my attitude fast. "I think I have altitude sickness, officer. Couldn't you take me to a hospital; that's where I was headed. I need to get down to a lower altitude. This headache is killing me."

"You're not fooling me for a moment, but we can play it that way. I'm a big fan. I don't want to see you in the tank with those low-lifers. Do you think you can cooperate with me on this?"

"Absolutely," I assured him.

It looked like I wasn't going to be busted after all, but my fortune took another turn when the ambulance showed up. The paramedic was this totally anal straight chick, all business. "The suspect is drunk as a skunk," she said. "I'm going to draw some blood for analysis."

That did it, of course. At least I didn't have to spend the night in jail; but I did end up with another D.U.I. and drug charges for the prescription painkillers I'd taken. I spent a few days holed up in the hospital, and during that time I made friends with a young doctor who gave me a script for the drugs. He wrote a letter to the court explaining that he had given me the pills as samples, so the drug charges were dropped. I had to pay a hefty fine for driving under the influence, and agree to attend traffic school, but that was it.

...

I was relieved as hell to get back home to San Francisco. Of course Stephanie and Ray had read about both busts, and I had that to contend with right off the bat.

"You're partying too much, Em." Ray's hands were clenching the steering wheel as he drove me home from the airport.

Stephanie spoke up next. "You know we don't like to interfere in your life, but we're worried. You could have been killed driving drunk on those mountain roads."

I could feel her trying to catch my eye, but I sullenly stared out the window. "Give me a break, *please*. I'm tired. The newspapers exaggerate. I wasn't drunk, okay?" There was silence, so I plowed on, trying to lighten things up. "What's been going on? I haven't talked to you in ages. Any new paintings, Mom?"

"Talk to us, sweetheart." There was desperation in Stephanie's voice.

It didn't move me though. "There's nothing to say. It was a brutal tour. Sandy had a nervous breakdown or something. I don't want to talk about it."

Now Stephanie dug in. "Maybe you *need* to talk about it though. A very hip guy came to the club the other night when Ray was playing. We both liked him, right Ray?"

"What? Are you trying to arrange a marriage for me or something?" I joked.

"Very funny, Em," Stephanie said dryly. "I'm trying to tell you that he's a therapist, and we got a good hit off him. Maybe you should go talk to him."

"I'm not going to go talk to some fucking therapist! About what? Okay, I admit it—I drank too much and shouldn't have been driving. I'll be more careful. Jesus! Back off."

"You shouldn't talk to your mother like that," Ray said, eyeing me in the rearview mirror.

Stephanie turned in her seat and looked back at me accusingly. "We're both worried about you."

"Well, it's a little late for that, isn't it?"

Stephanie looked like she was going to cry. "That really hurts my feelings, Em. We're your parents—of course we're always going to be concerned for your well-being. We love you."

That stopped me in my tracks. I was about to hit them over the head with Rob, but I just couldn't do it. The anger drained right out of me, and I said, "I know, Mom; I love you, too. I'll settle down and quit fucking-up…but I'm not going to a therapist—okay?"

"We've always tried to do what's right for you, and I'm sorry if we've failed you," Ray glanced back at me, tears in his eyes. "You're the light of our life, little girl."

"I know, Ray. You're both the best."

We pulled into my driveway and I had the car door opened before Ray turned the engine off. Ray carried my suitcases into the house and Stephanie followed with some small bags. I said, "Don't worry about me—it's just been a bad patch…love you both…I'm tired…goodnight."

Marianne was there at the house—she'd been house sitting while I was on tour. I didn't mind her being there; in fact, I was glad to see her. She'd just been through a hellish break-up and was lying low. After five years with this dude, suddenly he tells her he needs his freedom, that he feels tied down—as though she's the one who invented the law of gravity. You know, we all want to fly, but there's gravity, isn't there. What an asshole. He's one of those self-righteous jerks who thinks he deserves a Pulitzer for being macrobiotic. Marianne, on the other hand, is totally far-out—she's an amazing, creative designer—makes all my stage clothes, and she's way cool to be around. She and I opened a bottle of champagne and flopped in front of the T.V. and, you know, she didn't ask me a single goddamn question about the busts or anything.

So, Marianne wasn't a blast to be around like Carol had always been, but I dug it that she was mellow. Since I wasn't alone, I didn't feel like I had to turn the house into a circus right off the bat. It had been an insane tour, and I was content to just fall into a laid-back groove. Marianne was sick of guys at the moment, and the last thing I needed was another lying bastard to put some trip on me, so *we* just hung out together—dined at the excellent Italian restaurants in North Beach, and then came home fairly early every night. I'd started writing for the next album already and Marianne was busy sewing into the wee hours.

One night, our little routine was rudely interrupted. We came home from dinner to find a total stranger sitting on the couch, eating a pear. He didn't get up when we came clanking in noisily and then stopped in our tracks in surprise—he just kept dissecting the pear with a sharp looking pocketknife, glancing up at us every now and then rather casually.

"Okay man, what are you doing here?" I said, but not in a mean way.

He didn't even look up—just muttered, "Is that any way to talk to your old man?"

I still had my keys in my hand. I glanced toward the door, signaling Marianne: *Run*! We jumped into my car, locked the doors, and took off. It's the weirdest damn thing that when you're looking for a cop, you can't find one. If I was drunk or stoned, I would have seen them on every corner, but when I actually needed them, they were off eating doughnuts or something. Finally, I stopped and used a pay phone to call them. When we got back to my house the police were there waiting for us. I thought the guy had probably split by now, but no, he was still in there, trying to convince the cops that I had invited him over, that he was my boyfriend.

"Miss Allison," the cop said, "would you mind stepping into the house with us. The suspect is restrained, but he claims to be your guest. We need a positive I.D. that he's your intruder."

So I had to go in and listen to the crazy fucker say that I was lying—that we were lovers, and I was just pissed at him. Thank God I had Marianne to back me up or they might have believed him. They took him off, told me I had to go in the next day and press charges and get a restraining order. It was bizarre because the dude seemed to really believe what he was saying.

The cops helped us look around the house to determine how he'd gotten in. He'd broken the lock on the sliding glass door to the patio, which threw me into paranoia, big time. It brought home how easy it is to break into someone's life, how breakable lives are. How morbid I can be. Jesus, just when I thought I was breaking the cycle of coming home and getting freaked out, here I was looking into closets and cupboards again, trying to find the maniac before he found me. That episode helped me decide that it was alright to jump ship and go back to Hana to write. It wasn't just ghosts that were plaguing me, but genuine maniacs that other people could see, too.

•••

Margie had been holding my favorite bungalow for me. That was a leap of faith on her part, considering November was her busy season. She said she knew I'd come. It was one of my rare good decisions, to go back to Hana. In spite of how unhappy I'd been when I was last there, I had come through it, and some of my most prolific songwriting had gone down in that cabin. It has something to do with the trade winds, which are about as different from the Santa-fucking-Anas, as you can possibly get. No matter how hot it gets, no matter how heavy things are, those winds cool it. The Spirit of the Islands is in those winds; you can feel it.

The wind also blew something besides spirits in that time around, just a few weeks after I got there. I was lying on the beach, down quite a way from the other guests, sipping from a thermos of Piña Coladas, trying to catch some inspiration. I was just chilling in my Hana haze, staring out to sea when a shape manifested on the waters—a beautiful yacht, with beautiful cargo, too. I watched lazily as the ship dropped anchor and a few people boarded a motorboat, headed right toward my spot. As they got closer, I could see that there were three guys, all hip looking, with long hair and gorgeous bodies. One of them was the best thing I'd seen in a long time.

Normally, I would have gotten up and found a more secluded stretch of beach, but I was definitely interested in what the sea was delivering that day. Hashish, as it turned out, and lots of it. I should have guessed, but I was too busy flashing on the pretty guy with long corkscrew curls to wonder what he was up to. I offered him hits of my drink, he gave me hits from a pipe, and the relationship was off and running.

The other two guys took off down the beach with walkie-talkies, obviously trying to sort something out. Time began passing in that sort of suspended animation way that you get from good dope, where everything is strange and funny. At some point, a couple of fishing boats entered the harbor and moored right near the yacht, and the two guys with walkie-talkies motored out to meet them. I could see that they were unloading something from the yacht, packing it into the smaller boats, but I didn't get it. It was like I was watching a mystery movie that was also a comedy.

My leading man began to get fidgety. Started pacing around the beach until the movie was over and the fishing boats left, his two friends with them.

"How are you going to get back out to your boat now?" I asked him.

"Looks like I'm going to have to swim for it. Are you game? I can whip us up some great Margaritas, and I've got chips and salsa."

Wow, I was tempted, but I honestly didn't think I could swim out that far, as wrecked as I was. "I don't know. You could be anybody. You could sweep me off to God-knows-where. I don't think so," I said, leaning toward him in what I hoped was a seductive way.

"Would that be so bad?" He trailed his hand up my arm suggestively. "How about if I swim out and come back for you in the motor boat? Is that a better proposition? You relax—but don't leave me. I'll be back soon."

He flipped me the peace sign as he went crashing into the waves, and I watched him get smaller and smaller in the vast scale of the sea. For a while I thought maybe I had hallucinated the whole sequence of events, and then I got too tired to think about it, and nodded out in the warm sun. But when I woke up, he was lying beside me, reading my book. When I blinked up at him, he snuggled up close and kissed me. His mouth tasted salty, and his hair smelled like ocean.

"Are you ready for your Margarita now, Emma?" he whispered.

"Did I miss something? How come I don't know your name, and why do I remember the sea delivering you to my feet? How do you know my name?"

"It's Elliot, and you know more about me already than most people do. How do you think I know your name? Is there a famous rock singer out there posing as you, using the same name?" He laughed, and his teeth glinted white in the sunshine. "You were the siren on the sand, calling me to my doom. I'll follow you anywhere, but you've got to come back to my boat with me and let me make love to you. You don't even have to swim."

I went for it, of course. I couldn't resist someone ballsier than me. The cabin of his boat was decked out with plush cushions and an amazing sound system. He put on Dylan, always a good choice, then led me into the kitchen, where he had everything all set up. Pretty damn sure of himself, but I liked that, too. He was as handsome as my old movie star boyfriend, and much better in bed.

Afterward, my body felt gritty with sand and sex, so I asked him if his floating palace included a shower, which I knew it must, of course.

"Don't wash it off, baby; I like the funk," he said, his eyes still sending out sparks. "Just lay back and let me lick the sand off you."

One more time, great fucking sex, and then I definitely wanted that shower. The hot water felt so good on my body that I stayed under it until it began to cool. When I walked back into the bedroom, the atmosphere had changed. My mellow lover was tearing around the room, picking things up, throwing stuff overboard.

"The coast guard is going to be checking us out, Emma. Do me a favor, baby, and tell them I came here to see you, that I'm your old man. I'll explain later. Will you do that for me?"

"No problem, I can handle it. I'll just wing it. But what's your last name? I should probably know that. What did you do, smuggle dope or something?"

Jesus. Of course he did. Where had I been? Apparently they had loaded the fishing boats right before my eyes, only I hadn't noticed.

"But how do you know they're coming?" I asked.

"The load went down. The boat on point got a message through to me while you were in the shower. The coast guard will be investigating all the ships in the area. Don't sweat it, we're clean. I buried the last kilos under the palm tree by where you were sleeping this afternoon. We should be in bed when they get here. Or I'll tell you what, I'll make dinner. Pasta, you like pasta? And a salad. I have plenty of food. It's better to be doing something. Just act casual."

So we were prepared when the coast guard showed up. Elliot was just putting the food on the table when floodlights washed over the boat. Two guardsmen boarded and asked us a bunch of questions, looking around suspiciously. When they realized who I was though, their attitudes changed, got a lot friendlier, fast. If they'd done a background check on me, they probably would have arrested us both on the spot. Instead, they bought the romantic story of Emma and Elliot, and moved on in their search.

I saved his ass that night, absolutely. But I really didn't want to sleep on his boat. For all my bravado, I was kinda creeped out by having another close call with the law again already. Jesus, it seemed like every time I turned around, I was attracting weird energy.

So, Elliot took me back to shore and slept in my bungalow with me. But during the night, his walkie-talkie started squawking and I could hear him whispering to someone in a worried tone. When he finally came back to bed, he stroked my forehead gently until I fell into a deep sleep.

Early the next morning, around eleven a.m., Elliot woke me.

"I'm sorry, Emma, but I've got to cut out of here. I let you sleep as long as I could. I'll never forget what you did for me last night."

"Which part?" I said, wanting him again.

"Save it for later, beautiful. I've got to meet some people in Lahina. I'm going to dock the boat there, and if it's cool with you, I'll come back tomorrow."

"Don't you want some breakfast or something?" I asked, wanting to keep him with me as long as I could.

"No, I've got to split. But I'll see you tomorrow. Will it be okay for me to stay here a few days?"

"Anything you want. I've got connections here. Just come back soon."

But he didn't come back. The sea took him away as suddenly as it had brought him. Days came and went, and nothing, not a word. I asked Sonny to put out feelers, but none of his people knew anything about Elliot. I couldn't believe it was just a one-night-stand kind of thing for him—felt it had to have been trouble. I tried not to think about him—worked on songs, hung out with Margie and Sonny and the gang, and time passed as it always did in Hana, every day beautiful in some way. And when Elliot didn't come back in over two weeks, Sonny decided to go investigate the spot where Elliot had told me he hid the remaining stash. Two kilos of Afghani hash, which Sonny decided to take charge of, and maybe smoke a little as payment for looking after it. And then a letter came. Margie brought it to me on the beach, sat down beside me and watched as I opened it, waiting for an explanation.

"Yeah, it's from him," I said. "Jesus, Margie, let me read it first. I'll talk to you later."

"Okay, be like that."

Well, it didn't make me happy, but at least I found out what had happened. Basically, he explained that the Heat had closed in on him. He'd had to hightail it to California, which was where the letter was postmarked, and then leave the country. He said he'd be back when things cooled down, and that he'd find me. And, oh by the way, he'd given me a false name—he'd had to. Didn't even sign the letter. Jesus, Elliot wasn't even his name. It pissed me off. I spent days writing vengeful songs about retaliation, and then I moved on, started some lyrics:

We lost each other in a tunnel
As long as from here to a star
Colder than the first angry words from a lover
Damp like a dungeon and darker by far
Dancing alone in the ruins of a temple
Under the stars in that once mystic place
And all the sweet words that once lay between us
They had vanished without a trace…

When word made its way to Sonny that Elliot, or whatever his name was, wasn't coming back, he couldn't hide his delight. "It's your consolation prize," he said, as he passed me a pipe of sweet smelling hash.

"Fuck you Sonny," I said, but I took a hit anyway.

Sometime before Christmas, some very stony time, I might add, I got the lyrics to "*Walk on the Water*," which became the title track of my next album. The Elliot episode got mythologized, and I was able to have fun with it. Just more fucking crazy bullshit.

Mist rising from the raging sea
See a man walking straight toward me
He said I was here before the dawn
Been waiting but it took so long
(Now the morning's almost gone)

Mystery man called out to me
You only believe in what you see
What you see can make you blind
Better leave what you know behind

Walk on the water
Come on now, girl, you won't sink
Miracles can happen
When you don't stop to think

Step out now, walk on the water
You've got to believe
You've got nothing to give
If you can't receive
Walk on the water
Come on, walk with me
Walk on the water (repeat, out)

Ray and Stephanie joined me for Christmas in Hana again, only this time we had a bungalow reserved for them at the resort. Ray fell right into the rhythm of the place, jamming with the guys after hours, getting high. Stephanie was holding back, doing her something-is-wrong, but-I'm-not-going-to-tell-you-what-it-is number. At first I tried to ignore her undercurrent of disapproval, and then I tried getting her to talk about it, but all I could get from her was, "It's okay, darling. I'm fine. Don't you worry." Which meant, of course, that she was pissed at me.

"Okay Mom," I finally said. "What's going on?"

"Why don't you tell *me,* Em? You hold the answers, not I."

Christ, no wonder I turned out so weird. Stephanie could be the most cryptic person on earth. But in spite of my feigned ignorance, I knew what she was pissed about. She'd already told me on the way home from the airport after the last tour. It was because of the busts and D.U.I.s and everything—and because by the time she'd see me on the beach, I would already have had more than a few drinks, and would be ordering another. Personally, I felt like I was more together than I'd been in a long time, but it obviously didn't look that way to my mother.

We ended up having a big argument one night, and she almost left the next day. Luckily, she couldn't get a flight, due to the busy holiday season. I couldn't remember what I had said to her, but Ray told me it was bad—that I'd called her names and accused her of being a terrible mother—told her that she hadn't protected me…blamed all my problems on her. I guess it blew her mind. Ray said that neither of them could figure out what I was so mad at her about. Obviously, she had no fucking clue about Rob, and I wasn't about to spell it out for her. Besides, why did I blame it all on her, when he was Ray's best friend? Maybe Ray seemed too fragile to be able to take it, or maybe I was more afraid of losing his love.

I tracked her down on the beach that afternoon and tried to make it up to her. Told her I didn't mean any of it, and promised to stop drinking so much. It broke the ice anyway. She quit sulking, and I tried to cool it with the booze around her. At least she liked to smoke pot, and once she didn't have to be a shining example of sobriety for me, we were soon back to enjoying each other's company. We brought in the New Year in Hana, then Ray and Stephanie took off for the other side of the island where they would be talking to galleries about representing her art.

•••

I went back to San Francisco mid-January with enough material for two albums. Marianne was still at my house, which was fine with me because I had to go to L.A. right away, and would be gone for months. She just sort of ended up living with me, or I should say, house sitting, because I was never there.

•••

It was rainy in The Bay Area, but L.A. was sunny and relatively clear. I was booked into a suite at the Hyatt House, right on Sunset Boulevard, not too far from Bill's or the studio. All the bands had started staying there, so there was always some craziness going down, always people to hang out with. Bill took me to dinner my first night in town, cute little Peggy in tow. She was just oozing sweetness, hanging on every word I said like I was some goddamn casting director or something. Obviously, Bill had told her to be nice to me. Jesus, what a favor. Luckily, I didn't see much of her during the following months, as Bill and I got the songs finished and arranged, and eventually recorded.

I tried to stay focused on making a good record during that time, not getting too out-there. I still had legal hassles from my previous busts so I didn't want to bring the Heat down on myself again, but what the fuck, you know? You try, and then shit happens.

I was at some goddamn party in Beverly Hills one night in March, some rock band was renting the house, and the Hells Angels showed up, which was okay. They'd been invited, but I guess they made the neighbors nervous with their loud choppers, and anyway, somebody called the cops, who made a raid out of it, like they were really snagging some criminals this time. Got a bunch of us on possession, which was no big deal, except that I still had the other legal shit to contend with and didn't need one more thing. But for the most part, I kept it together and we brought the album in on time, and on budget. Of course, that had a lot to do with Bill.

...

I went to New York and booked myself into the Plaza for a couple of weeks. I felt like it had been long enough that I could be there again by myself without wigging out, and anyway, my old buddy, Jack Riggs, from the big English rock band, *King Snake*, was in town recording and had asked me if I'd put some vocals on one of their tracks. Besides that, Herbie had been saying he wanted to spend some time with me, too, and you know, New York is perfect in the spring before it gets so hot and oppressive. There's also the fact that you don't drive there, so I wouldn't have to worry about getting another goddamn D.U.I. As long as you've got someone to pour you into a cab, you can get by in New York. I didn't have to worry anyway though, because Herbie hired a watchdog to hound me.

It was Christina, and she actually turned out to be okay. At first, I couldn't stand her. She fussed about everything, like I was some imbecile who couldn't keep it together if she didn't nag me non-stop. I told Herbie to get her off my back or I was going to kill her, but he defended her, insisted that she was one of the most competent rock 'n' roll publicists in New York. So much for a holiday with her around. She set up a constant stream of interviews and arranged for me to make appearances at plays and parties and late night T.V. shows.

I got it in for her because she followed me everywhere, trying to moderate my behavior as though she was some kind of expert on social interaction, when in fact, she was totally up-tight, without even the slightest sense of humor. I'd have three drinks and she'd start pursing her lips in disapproval, and on my fourth, she'd be clicking her tongue, making comments like, "Do you really think you should?" And the long-suffering expression on her face, oh God, it became comical after a while. But Herbie saw her as a perfect buffer between the press and me, so that was that. I had to put up with her.

The sessions with *King Snake* were easy; they loved everything I did. And hanging out in New York with Jack Riggs and the other band members was a trip. We were on the art scene, going to theatre, late suppers, and all-night clubs—never a dull moment. Everybody in that group got as wasted as I did, so I sure couldn't see that I needed Christina following me around with them. But there she was, every time I turned around. So I felt like it served her right when she tagged along to this artist's house in Soho where there was a party going on that was actually more like an orgy. She got stuck right in the middle of about twenty people going at it in every imaginable way, and a couple started coming on to her, rubbing up against her. I was wasted, laughing so hard I kept falling over, and I wouldn't have fucked any of those people anyway; so I snuck out the back door with Jack—left her there alone. I thought she was going to be majorly pissed at me the next day, but she didn't even bring it up. We were at this little luncheon with Herbie and a company exec, and I couldn't resist teasing her.

"Did you have a good time last night, Christina?" I asked innocently.

"Why, yes I did, thank you," she replied. "And how about you? Did you enjoy your evening?"

That was boring, so I brought it up again, after a few Mimosas. "Which one was best Christina? Which one did you choose, or should I say ‘ones’? I thought maybe you liked the chick with the diamond stud in her nose.”

Christina glared at me. “I don’t think this is an appropriate time to talk about it, Emma.”

“Oh come on, you’ve got no sense of humor. Does she, guys?”

“I understand that you think it’s funny, Emma.” She turned to the guys. “She’s talking about an artist orgy event that we attended last night. Apparently the idea of me having sex in public is pretty funny to Emma. It is pretty funny, actually. Well, actually, I didn’t, but it was funny anyway. Look Emma, there’s an item about the luminaries who were at that orgy in today’s paper, in this column right here. These events make good press.”

“Oh come on, you’re kidding,” I said, anxiously reaching for the paper.

“Got you,” Christina said wryly.

I respected her more after that one. Apparently she did have a sense of humor after all. You just had to really dig for it. By the time I went back to San Francisco, I had hired her as my assistant publicist. Things had gotten so crazy that I really did need someone in New York to hold things down while Lauren was out on the road with me. It was also becoming obvious to me that I was going to have to take my attorney, Bev’s advice, and hire some people who would answer to me personally, not to management or the record company. My contract with Herbie was expiring in October, and he was leaning on me to sign with him for another five years; plus, my record deal was almost up. He and the record company exec had planned our little lunch date to talk about how much I needed them, to point out how beneficial it would be for me to sign sooner than later and not have to think about all the legal stuff. Their rap convinced me that I needed to pay some attention to the business side of things. And as much of a pain in the ass as I had thought Christina was at first, I discovered she was smart and meticulous, and I wanted her on my side.

…

Back in San Francisco, I had a series of meetings with Bev to discuss my contract with Herbie. He had been a good manager, so I didn't see any reason to leave him, and Bev agreed, but she pointed out that I was now in a position to negotiate a much better contract with him. For one thing, I wouldn't have to agree to his stipulations this time around. The biggest change was that I'd get to keep all my mechanical royalties by setting up my own publishing company, instead of going through his. It really just boiled down to a bunch of paper work, but amounted to a lot of extra money. She also insisted I have an audit clause in my contract, giving me the right to hire an independent accounting firm to investigate both the record company and management's books.

It was a mellow May. I lay low, took care of biz, and actually managed to go more than a month without a brush with the Man. Mid-June I was back out on the road for a three-month tour. I had the same boys in the band, with the exception of George. We were on the bill with two other San Francisco bands, so it seemed like it was going to be a fun tour. But then everybody got sick—the singers, the musicians, all the crew, everybody. We turned into a goddamn traveling virus manufacturing company.

By August, I was in trouble big-time with my throat. It started with a fucking cold that went into my chest. I couldn't so much as take a drag of a cigarette without a coughing fit, and all the coughing made my throat completely raw, so I ended up with laryngitis, which just can't happen on a tour. It wasn't like I had another singer on hand to cover vocals for me. You can't just cancel a show either. The promoters have so much money tied up in production that you could ruin them by canceling. Not to mention that you could have the shit sued out of you. Well, not if a doctor says you can't go on; they can't sue you then. Which is what happened to me in Columbus. I had been squeaking by for a week on throat lozenges and hot lemon and honey drinks, taking steam baths, and decongestants and antibiotics, and even refraining from smoking, for God's sake—but I got progressively worse. The doctors kept telling me to rest my voice for a few days. Yeah, right.

Then it just got me. I woke up in Columbus after a travel day, and found I had no voice. There was no pushing it—nothing there to push. My temperature was high, and I felt like I had run into the Golden Gate tollbooth again—no energy whatsoever. I was supposed to perform that night, and you better believe that when Ed contacted the promoter, he had a doctor at the hotel immediately. My throat was just about totally closed up; had to have a shot of Prednisone, and even then, there was no way I could sing that night. The doctor said the steroid was a quick fix, that I had to promise to go in for treatment when the tour was over. Turns out I had the bane of a singer's life, polyps on the vocal cords. It was the only time in my career that I canceled a show.

Chapter Sixteen

From Guatemala to Europe: 1975

The scene at the airport in Guatemala City was exactly like Emma had envisioned San Salvador, based on Juan's description. "Jesus," she whispered, "maybe all the poor people from your country moved here." She regretted her comment the moment she saw the look on his face. The last thing she wanted in the midst of the bustling chaos was another fight about her insensitivity to the poor.

Beggars followed them as they made their way through the airport to board a smaller plane to Tikal, their high-pitched voices a continuous whine. Indigenous people in dirty but beautiful handmade clothing begged them to buy their wares, and hordes of children peddling clay whistles shaped like birds whirred around them in dizzying circles.

Emma reached for her purse and felt Juan's hand clamp hard on her wrist. "What are you doing?" he hissed. "Do you never learn?"

She met his eye. "Learn what? Not to care? I get it with my head, but not with my heart."

Juan let go her wrist and Emma knelt down to buy some whistles from a band of kids, and soon found herself surrounded by a still larger group a few steps later. There seemed to be no end to them. She handed out money until she ran out of cash—and they'd only been in Guatemala twenty minutes. Finally, Juan spoke sharply in Spanish, and the persistent beggars turned their attention to a new target.

"What did you say to them?" Emma demanded. "Something about the police, right? Oh come on, you didn't threaten to call the cops on them…you did, didn't you?"

"Very good, Emma. You are beginning to understand many words in Spanish now. Let's get going. We don't want to miss our plane."

The check-in section for the plane to Tikal was outdoors, more like a stall than a reception desk. It was immediately obvious to Juan and Emma that their luggage was completely out of proportion to the size of the plane—an old DC 3 that had seen better days. They decided to go spend the night in an expensive hotel in Guatemala City, one that would let them store most of their luggage there while they traveled.

The taxi ride to the hotel made Emma wonder why they had come there. The armed soldiers on the streets were a terrifying echo of El Salvador. She didn't say it to Juan, but she could see why Guatemala wasn't high on his parent's idyllic holiday list.

The fancy hotel stood out in stark contrast to its surroundings, and she was grateful for it. They rose early the next morning to catch the first flight to Tikal.

Both Juan and Emma had been in small airplanes before, but this plane was like nothing they'd ever seen. The seats were literally coming apart at the seams, spilling their innards onto the stained, threadbare carpeting. The overhead cabinets rattled and shook ominously as the plane lurched off the ground, and when Emma, feeling sick, went to the toilet, she discovered a hole in the floor, big enough for a small child to slip through.

I don't want to know, she thought, and returned to her seat. "Don't ask," she told Juan. "Just don't ask."

The short flight was uneventful until the landing. As they swooped low over the jungle, Emma thought the landing strip looked impossibly short and narrow. The crashed airplane rusting at the strip's mouth didn't make it look any safer.

"Are we going to make it?" Emma asked. "It seems like something's wrong."

Her question was lost as the pilot applied full throttle and the plane jerked back up into the air for another go around. The pilot had indeed overshot the runway. Second time around, the plane bounced safely into a little clearing and deposited its passengers in the ruins of Tikal.

Emma felt the dense, muggy forest like a hush against her skin. The air was heavy with the life of the rainforest, of another time. The ancient jungle city was alive with birds and insects, and the clamoring of monkeys. Mayan pyramids reached to the sky, their structures intact despite centuries of the jungle's attempts to reclaim the land. The constant encroachment that had buried the city had also kept its secrets.

They spent the day climbing the massive pyramids with steps so steep and narrow that even Emma's small feet were almost twice as big as the stairs. They explored the ruins until nightfall, and then took the plane back to Guatemala City. Emma had a different attitude about the country and its citizens by that evening.

"I guess we probably fucked them over too, just like we did the American Indians, don't you think?" she said to Juan over dinner and a couple of bottles of Chilean wine. "Of course the conquistadors were probably your ancestors, right?"

"You don't have to remind me. It's life, isn't it? We are a strange and often brutal species. But I want to make love, not war, Let's go to bed, *reina.* I'm tired."

"Yes, but don't you see how incredible these people are. I can't believe it. We were nomads when they had cities with plumbing. It's incredible, it's just fucking amazing, don't you think, baby? Wasn't it even better than you could have imagined? Grander? Let's order another bottle of wine. Can you get our waiter over?"

"Emma, we should go to bed. We have to get up early to drive up the mountain. It's too dangerous to drive at night. You can have a nightcap from the mini-bar in the room."

Later, just before he fell asleep, Juan whispered into Emma's ear, "I am as enchanted with this country as you are. It was a perfect day, pure poetry. I will never forget it."

Out on the open road, the scenery changed dramatically. A volcano, green with dense foliage, dominated the landscape, and colorful little villages dotted the roadside. Fruit-stands and funky outdoor cafes stood grouped with dilapidated gas stations on the outskirts of the villages, and everywhere were bus stops. Even when Juan turned the Range Rover onto the road up to Panajachel, there in the most remote spots stood tiny bus stops at the intersections of dirt paths.

Juan, normally so patient, began to get visibly exasperated when they kept getting stuck behind the buses on the narrow roads. He and Emma could barely breathe in their wake of noxious belching, but it was difficult to pass them on the steep, winding road. He had to time it to be ready to tear ahead when it pulled over for passengers, but each victory would only be short-lived. Five minutes later they'd be stuck behind another bus.

The aggravation of the bumpy ride through exhaust fumes proved a small price to pay for the view awaiting them at the summit. As they rounded a particularly perilous hairpin turn, the mountain pass opened onto a panoramic vista, and Lake Atitlan lay before them. Emma gasped.

"Pull over, Juan. You have to be able to enjoy this view without us going over the side."

Juan and Emma got out of the car and walked to the edge of a cliff. There below, three volcanoes rose up from a huge lake's shores, reaching into the clouds like silent sentinels, protecting the pristine beauty of the place. Emma had never seen Juan look more excited. "It's even better than I expected," he told her.

As they wound their way down to the village of Panajachel, they passed miles of terraced gardens lush with vegetables, yellow rows of corn, and everywhere, bright flowers. Emma wasn't about to comment that anybody looked like a flower, but she was totally blown away by the people she saw. The Mayan men were dressed in straw cowboy hats, western shirts, and brightly embroidered short pants. "The book says that the pants are called *calzoncillos*," she told Juan. "And the women's blouses are called *huipiles*. All the different patterns are unique to each village. The women do all the embroidery, and they weave the cloth. Fucking self-sufficient, I'd say!"

"They're the inheritors of an advanced culture." Juan kept his eyes on the road, stealing occasional glimpses of the people and scenery. "The indigenous people in my country used to dress like this, too—before they were forced to either abandon their culture or die. Obviously, these people still have a modicum of freedom."

"Thank God! You know, baby, I had no idea that there were still people like this in the world. Well, I mean I knew logically, from National Geographic and stuff, but to actually be here—it's like a dream." Emma vacillated between staring out the window, and thumbing through her guidebook frantically for names of things. "Look Juan, they must be so strong." She pointed to the small men trudging along the side of the road. Carrying huge bundles of wood on their backs by a strap around their foreheads, they walked leaning forward, into the mountain.

"I'm sure they are…and they must be, too," Juan said, nodding toward some women and girls, dressed in embroidered *huipiles* and wrap-around skirts, walking proudly alongside the road. Large baskets of produce were balanced on top their heads, sitting on headdresses of long scarves wrapped round and round into bright colored halos.

Juan and Emma had reservations at a lakeside hotel that was small and rustic by American standards, but must have been the Hilton by Mayan village standards. The only high-rise on the lake, it was a mere two stories, but even that seemed an outrage to the natural beauty of the place. As soon as they got to their room, Emma stretched out on the bed, happy to be out of the car after the long, bumpy journey. "I'm starting to get the whole siesta thing. Let's take a nap, shall we?"

"I would never refuse to come to bed with you, *mi reina*."

While Juan and Emma had slept, word evidently got out that Emma was in town, probably through the North American hotel receptionist. Pana, as the locals called the village, seemed to have a burgeoning hippie, ex-pat population, if the small hotel restaurant was any indication. Juan and Emma took in the packed place, and decided to eat elsewhere. Emma couldn't imagine that the hotel owner would be a fan, but his behavior was definitely deferential when they made inquiries about restaurants. He tried to insist that they join him in his private quarters for dinner—to avoid the masses, he said. Emma was relieved when Juan adamantly refused. She would rather have been with "the masses" than him.

Emma turned to the receptionist, whose nametag read, Cathy, for advice. "The guidebook sure lists a lot of dining options for such a small village."

"Yeah, there are lots of groovy places to eat now, what with so many tourists coming through…people are making a lot of bread. Me, I'm thinking of moving over to San Pedro cause it's getting too built up here."

Emma looked at Juan and rolled her eyes. "Right, too built up. Well, can you suggest a café that serves Mayan food?"

"Sure. Sausage Michael opened a new place down by the dock with Pie Mariah. It's really good—great pies. Or you could go over by the bridge to the "Sloper's Joint"—get it? The joint? The Slopers always have a good stash of organic vegetables they grow themselves."

Emma, who was used to counter-culture lingo, was lost. "Who or what are the Slopers?"

Cathy smiled condescendingly. "The Slopers live on the slope outside of town. We don't use last names here because you are what you do…dig? I mean, you're not what you do, but you are who you are, and your last name has nothing to do with who you are…dig?"

"Got it. So you are Receptionist Cathy, then?" Emma asked with a straight face.

Cathy put her hands on her hips. “Of course not. I’m *Hotel* Cathy!”

As Juan and Emma strolled around the town, they saw goods from all over the Highlands offered for sale in street stalls. Emma was starting to recognize the various patterns from different villages, and she couldn’t resist buying one of each. They ended up dining on “typical” food, fish, rice, and black beans, at a haphazard Guatemalan-run beachfront café—sitting at tables in the sand on the lake’s edge, watching the sun set in lavish colors over twin volcanoes.

...

The next day, they took a boat across the lake to what the guidebook described as an authentic Mayan village—Santiago. As the boat approached the town, they saw clusters of women washing their clothes and bathing in the lake. Many of them were washing their hair while children splashed around them in the shallow shoreline water. The minute the boat docked, a flock of unkempt children surrounded Juan and Emma, hands out, begging, like the kids at the airport.

“Don’t even think about it,” Juan warned Emma. “You know what will happen. We can make a donation for the poor at the local church.”

“I can’t just ignore them, Juan. They’re children, and they look hungry.” She handed out all her coins and small bills, but just as it had at the airport, the situation got out of hand fast. There were too many kids, too many demands. “Tell them I haven’t got anymore. *No me moleste, por favor*,” she said to the kids, trying out her Spanish—which had absolutely no effect on them whatsoever. The kids followed them as they made their way up the steep, cobblestone street that wound up from the dock into the village.

Vendors, selling beautiful Mayan tapestries and clothing, lined both sides of the street, sitting in front of their round, thatched roof mud huts, hawking their wares. Many women and girls sat in their yards weaving cloth on primitive stick looms.

At a sharp word from Juan, the kids dispersed, and village life swallowed Juan and Emma up. Santiago was no Panajachel—in fact, there were no hotels, just a funky pension that had an outdoor café of sorts. Juan and Emma stopped there for a coke. The lukewarm liquid wasn't all that refreshing, but Emma passed on the ice, fearing it might contain a potent bacteria like the one that had leveled her in El Salvador.

At the heart of the village they found a beautiful old church. They entered the cool stone building, looking for a box for the poor where they could make a donation. A friendly looking priest emerged from the interior to greet them. Father Stanley Rother expressed his gratitude for their gift and assured them that it would be put to good use. "Would you like me to show you around a little?" he asked with a Southern accent. "It's an interesting set-up we've got here."

Juan and Emma exchanged looks and both nodded at the same time.

"You're inside a four-hundred year old Spanish Mission church," Father Stanley explained. In the courtyard, there was an adjacent building. "This is where the local god is housed," he said casually. "We had to come to terms with him. The people here grow their food on the mountainside, weave cloth to make their own clothes, and celebrate their unique culture, including preserving their own god. And here in the central courtyard of the church, the community has gathered since the time of the conquistadors. Now, forgive me, I am needed in a meeting. Enjoy your stay, and thank you for the gift. May God bless you."

Emma watched Father Stanley disappear into the church, and then she turned to Juan. Apart from the dirty kids and a few beggars, the people gathered in the courtyard didn't look as poor as the people at the airport and in Guatemala City had. They seemed to be doing okay. She said as much to Juan, with great trepidation, considering how mad he'd gotten in his country, just because she'd thought the poor people were beautiful. To her surprise, he agreed with her.

"It's true, these people have dignity. It's an ancient civilization, and they seem to have a certain autonomy, probably due to the geography of the region." Gesturing to a crude wooden bench on the broad porch of the church, he said, "Let's sit for a few minutes, shall we?"

Emma was happy to pause in the shade. There was a cool breeze and the temperature was perfect. Juan sat on a low adobe wall looking out at the lake and the volcano. Emma snapped a few shots of him in profile, furtively admiring him through the lens. "I was reading last night," Juan said, staring into the distance, "that these Mayas, the Tzutujils, were the last to hold out against the conquistadors."

"You mean the whole mountain area, or just this village?"

"This village—it's such a remote spot, they probably don't have to worry about the army, even now."

"Wow, that's true. You're right, we haven't seen any camouflage this side of the lake—just the most gorgeous embroidery I've ever seen."

"I know! The work is amazing. And don't you think the patterns are similar to Middle Eastern cloth—like Afghani textiles? It makes me think that the people brought it with them during the great migration—you know, before the ice age changed the continents. I don't see what else explains how people a continent away from each other came up with the same motifs." Juan got up. "Shall we walk? Do you feel okay?"

Emma jumped up and tucked her arm through his. "Great, I feel great."

Wandering through the bustling streets of Santiago, buying gifts for Ray and Stephanie and all their friends, and listening to Juan expound his theories about the origins of Mayan culture, Emma was as happy as she'd ever been. As they sat on a cliff overlooking the lake, just on the outskirts of town, reveling in the feel of the sun, Emma was surprised by a sudden realization. Before she had time to process the thought, it had popped out of her mouth. "I want to have your baby."

Juan's eyes were still, like the lake. "Stop taking the pill, *reina.* Let's do it," he said, his gaze burning down her body.

"I didn't mean right this instant. Jesus, Juan, you're going to get us in trouble here. Stop it," she murmured feebly, as Juan pulled her back onto the grassy slope.

...

Their time in Guatemala was like a second honeymoon, marred only by their dinner with Don Miguel, the hotel owner in Pana. They didn't really want to spend time with him, but the man was pleasant enough, and his English was fairly good, and there was just no polite way to refuse him.

Dinner was a long, drawn-out affair, beginning with cocktails on the patio, and moving into the dining room for course after course, complete with bottle after bottle of wine. Toward the end of dinner, Emma was feeling loose enough to share with the innkeeper how her experience in El Salvador was so different from Guatemala. "Juan kept telling me about all these poor people in his country, on and on, about how hard it was going to be. How he wanted me to be prepared. And when we got there, it was mellow. We didn't see any starving homeless people or anything. But then we heard that the military killed them all. Isn't that fucking bizarre?"

Juan cleared his throat and gave Emma a significant look, which she chose to ignore. Don Miguel started to say something, but Emma cut him off.

"You think the military could round up a bunch of people and kill them, and no one would notice? You think people would just go on with their lives like nothing happened?" Emma slugged down the remainder of her wine and stood up, weaving. Don Miguel hurried to refill her glass, and Juan tried to speak up, but Emma's voice was too loud for him to be heard. "Maybe that's what happened in Germany in the forties; but I never thought it could happen in this day and age."

Juan leaned over and whispered, "I don't think he even understands what you're talking about. Why don't we call it a night? You're tired."

"I'm not tired." Emma pounded the table with her fist. "He understands alright, don't you, Don Miguel!" She paused for a second. "You know what I thought when we got here? I thought maybe all the poor people from El Salvador came *here*." She smiled triumphantly at her own wit, but when no one else cracked a smile, she frowned, too. "Okay, wait, I'm sorry…that was rude. I'm joking, but you know, we were bombarded by beggars at the airport here…Never mind, it's just my stupid sense of humor."

Don Miguel jumped into the conversation full force. He, too, had been drinking wine with every course, which made his heavily accented English even more pronounced. "But you are right, Señora Avelar. It is problem. El Salvador has found the right solution. They clean their streets—kill only the bad people and the *Communistas*—is better for the good people. You don't want to see those people on the streets—is bad for tourism. Guatemala, too, we must be, how do you say…efficient."

Stunned, Emma fumbled for words. "You're kidding…right?" she said feebly.

"No, don't look like that—is no joke…is better for the good people. You don't feel sad, please. A beautiful woman should not concern herself with these things."

Juan seemed to suddenly become interested in the man's point of view. "Are you telling us then, that the socio-political changes in my country are common-knowledge here in Guatemala? If I may ask, how is it that you know of these alleged covert activities?"

Evidently interpreting Juan's interest as approval, Don Miguel confided, "I have many sources in your country. We both know that there exist in Guatemala and El Salvador these Communist revolutionaries, and we should cooperate to stop them. Our business interests are connected, *comprende?* The 'domino effect', as the United States says to us—if one country falls, the other will have danger also. We should be good neighbors, *te recuerdes?"*

"He's freaking me out," Emma told Juan, glaring at Don Miguel.

"You don't understand my country, or the home of your husband," Don Miguel told Emma. "The *Communistas*, they spread their propaganda among the peasants. These *indios* are ignorant; they are lazy and poor, easy to fool. The *Communistas* promise them money to turn them against their own governments—is part of a conspiracy to dominate the world."

"The world? What the hell are you saying?" Emma's voice went shooting up the scales as she shot daggers at Don Miguel. He seemed oblivious to her anger.

"We fight against the *Communistas* to keep the world free. At this table, all our countries are allies; we are all friends… I salute you, *Señora* Avelar," he said, raising his glass to Emma. "Don Juan is a man of much luck."

"So shooting students and killing homeless people is going to keep the world free?" Emma heard herself shouting, but she couldn't stop. "What world are you living in? Jesus! Let's go Juan; this guy is a fascist."

"Fascist?" Don Miguel sounded incredulous. "Do I understand your wife calls me *fascista*?"

"I'm sorry Don Miguel; we will take our leave now." Juan stood up and took Emma's arm. "Thank you for your generous hospitality."

"But of course. No need to apologize. Your wife has been influenced by the Communistas, but she is very beautiful. I can see she is tired; I should not have given her worry with too much talk of politics. Is not good for women, especially beautiful women."

"He's crazy. Get me out of here," Emma said to Juan.

…

The next day, Juan and Emma left the mountains and went down to the five-hundred-year-old Spanish city of Antigua. Emma had a blazing headache. She kept hearing Don Miguel's voice in her head, explaining why it was okay to kill people.

When they finally pulled into Antigua, the city looked surreal in the filtered sunlight of early evening. Although it was only forty-five minutes from Guatemala City, Antigua was light years away in aesthetic terms. Soldiers with machine guns were there, too, but they kept a lower profile and acted less menacing than they did in the Capitol.

Juan and Emma spent five days in Antigua in Spanish-Colonial luxury. The hotel featured a Steinway piano and an indoors swimming pool, and was decorated with the finest Mayan handspun fabrics, and indigenous art. They spent their days enjoying the splendid city, and promenading in the central plaza at night.

It was a relaxing end to an exciting, but physically and emotionally demanding trip. Emma felt her strength return as she and Juan spent leisurely hours in bed planning their future, how they would re-model their studio, fix up their house, and maybe create a nursery...just in case. They both wanted to spend some time at home for a change, and Emma was determined to record the next album in San Francisco, come hell or high water, or Bill's objections. She and Juan agreed: If Bill wouldn't come up North, they would hire another producer, or even produce the record themselves.

...

They arrived home in early September to glorious weather. Even Mill Valley was hot, and free of fog for a change. Their mountaintop home was a haven from the craziness of the music business—but not from news of the rapidly deteriorating social climate in El Salvador. Ricky had gone back to school on the East Coast, so they were able to talk to him on a regular basis. He told them that Cata was being held captive by their parents. Every time a member of Juan's family called, it would be like pulling teeth for Emma to get him to talk about the conversation with her. He would say that he was dealing with it, and that it was all illusion anyway—which by now she recognized as Juan's own personal brand of bullshit.

Juan spent an hour each day in meditation, in one of the little cabins on their property. He said it centered him, and wanted Emma to join him. She tried sitting still and observing her breath, but her thoughts wandered and she got bored. She could do about ten minutes, tops.

They were having dinner one warm night out on their patio when the phone rang. It was Cata, crying hysterically. Juan took the call and came back to the table looking like a zombie. He sat across from her in silence, staring off into space. She gave him a minute, and then snapped at him. "Goddamn it, you've got to talk to me about it. I'm sick of the silent treatment."

Juan sighed wearily. "It's not silent treatment, Emma. I don't want to worry you; surely you can see that."

"I'm already worried—Jesus! Talk to me. What's up with Cata?"

"She's afraid our parents are going to have Carlos arrested."

"Fucking hell!"

Juan sighed deeply again. "You always side with Cata, and I understand why; but if it comes down to her safety or her boyfriend, I'm going to choose her safety."

"What, and I'm not? Give me a break."

Juan leaned across the table and took Emma's hand. "I know. Your instincts are always accurate. I'm ambivalent because while I know that the students' grievances are justified, and I agree that reform is needed, I am afraid that their marches and protest meetings will only stir up more trouble for the indigenous people…and cost more innocent people their lives…and I don't want Cata to be one of the casualties of a revolution."

"Neither do I, baby. Don't think for a minute that I put more value on social change than on Cata's life. Things will work out though; they always do."

Juan smiled into Emma's eyes briefly, then reached for a cigarette, serious again. "In America, yes, that seems to be true. The sheer numbers of your middle class balance the rights of the people. But in El Salvador, there is no middle class to speak of…no body of people to hold the military in check, no congress to demand an accounting of the actions of the military and the ruling class. My family will always act to protect their own interests, and if they see Cata's boyfriend as a threat, I don't doubt that they will dispose of him."

"We've got to help her."

Juan raised his eyebrows. "How?"

"Let's give it some thought."

Later that night, Emma woke Juan. "I think we should have Cata come live with us."

Juan propped himself up on his elbows and grinned at Emma. "You are amazing…staying up late worrying about my little sister."

"I'm serious, Juan. She'd be safe here and she wouldn't be any trouble."

"Oh, but she *would* be trouble…"

"Don't joke; I'm serious."

"My parents would never let her come—but that doesn't detract from your generous suggestion."

"Let's at least ask." Emma was up long after Juan fell back to sleep. *It's time to start planning the next album…and…this might be a good time to go off the pill. How does anyone know when the time is right to have a baby—maybe you just have to go for it.* The decision was made for her when Herbie called to tell her that he had booked a big European tour for the fall and winter months. The money would be very good and it would help boost record sales on The Continent.

"It's been too long since you've been over there, Emma," Herbie told her. "They love the new album. You go over there and knock them dead with Juan on guitar, and we're gonna have an international mega-hit on our hands with '*Close To Your Heart*'."

Emma frowned at the phone. "I'd kind of like to spend some time at home, Herbie. I'm always on the run, and it's making me crazy."

"You've got to strike while the iron is hot, baby; you know that. I've got you booked into the big halls on bills with the European super groups. Tell me you'll do this."

"Alright, but I want some significant time off after the tour—promise me. I need a life. Jesus, Herbie."

...

Emma felt like she had to work a lot harder with European audiences than she did with her fans back home. It made her nervous before the shows. But when she got up there on stage, the nervousness would vanish and she would become totally immersed in the performance. The write-ups were not all great, but she knew to expect that from the foreign critics and tried not to let it get to her.

Juan complained that he wasn't used to his every move being tracked; he said the paparazzi drove him crazy. But the press obviously loved him. Photographs that emphasized the contrast of Emma's blondness with Juan's dark good looks appeared in all the big papers and magazines. The pair was trailed constantly by photographers. That made for good publicity, but pretty much shot to hell any chance at privacy.

The tour was going well, and Juan and Emma were at peace with each other, managing to get along in spite of the road's stresses—until Elliot showed up in Amsterdam. Emma came off stage to find a gigantic bouquet of tropical flowers in the dressing room, with a note that read: "I've waited for this night an eternity and have never stopped thinking about you. Please let me explain. I'll be waiting in the hospitality room. My name is Simon, and my hair is black now, but I'm the same man who fell in love with you in Hana."

Emma knew immediately who the note was from.

Juan had been smoking a joint with Daryl, and came into the dressing room a little while after her—giving her time enough to read the note, freshen up, change into clean clothes, and then conceal the note in her purse. Juan was still sweaty from being on stage, and as he undressed, he kissed Emma and suggested she join him in the shower.

"No baby, I'm cool. I'll take one back at the hotel. I need to talk to Lauren about the radio spot tomorrow. See you out there." Emma fluffed up her hair nervously.

Her eyes darted around the hospitality room impatiently, trying to spot Elliot; but he saw her first. Came up behind her, put his arms around her waist, pulled her close to his body, and turned her around so that their mouths were just inches apart. Before she could gather her senses, he kissed her. Involuntarily, her body responded, and she kissed him back for one second, just long enough for the photographers to snap a few shots. She pulled away from the embrace almost instantly, but not fast enough to avoid the photos. Photos that would be printed with captions like: "Rock star's marriage on the rocks?" Or: "Brother-in-law rocks rocker's marriage." Another one simply read, "Kissing Cousins."

"Jesus, Elliot, or whatever your name is, you can't do that." Emma took another step back from Simon. "I'm married now. My husband is the guitar player. Didn't anyone around here tell you? How did you get back here?"

"It doesn't matter to me, Emma. I don't care that you're married. It doesn't mean things are over between us. I *had* to split; believe me, I didn't want to. We have unfinished business. I felt it in your kiss."

"Oh God, you can't talk to me like that. You can't talk to me at all. You're going to get me in so much trouble with my husband. Jesus."

"You don't have to be afraid of him, Emma. He's not going to lay a hand on you; I'll make sure of that."

"That's not what I meant. Of course he's not going to lay a hand on me. Oh Christ, you must have read that bullshit about the wedding. He's not violent, but he's probably going to leave me over this. We've got to go explain immediately. He's in the dressing room. Come on, I'll introduce you."

"I don't want to meet your husband," was what Simon was saying when Juan walked up to them.

"Why not?" Juan said to Simon. "I can see you're hitting on my wife, but I'm accustomed to such things by now. She's a bewitching temptress," he said, putting his arm around Emma possessively, pulling her close. "This happens at every show, doesn't it? Tell him, *reina*."

"Well, actually, I know him," Emma said. "Why don't we go back to the dressing room and talk?"

"If it's private, perhaps I should give you some space." Juan pulled back from Emma abruptly, a sardonic smile on his face.

"That would be great, man," said Simon.

"No baby, it's not private from you." Emma was trying to reassure Juan, but felt like she was hanging herself with every word. "This is Simon; I knew him a long time ago. Jesus, there's nothing weird going on here, except that he just kissed me, and I think somebody took a picture…shit! Can we go talk in private?"

Inside the dressing room, Juan lit a joint and passed it to Simon. Emma passed on the pot, and opened a bottle of champagne instead.

"Okay, this is civilized," she said. "Let's have a drink."

Emma watched as Juan and Simon got stoned together, scrutinizing each other more closely with every hit. She poured them each a glass of champagne and studied their body language as they studied each other. Simon was gorgeous, no doubt about it, but Juan was the one who made her catch her breath, who rendered her incapable of maintaining any cool. She loved him even more as she compared him to Simon, but she knew she was in trouble. Juan always retreated from the slightest emotional conflict, and his pride would not allow him to squabble over her. She prayed that the kiss had not been captured on film, but she knew that it had been. She'd felt the heat of the flashes.

"Listen man, you seem cool, but I need to talk to Emma alone. Do you mind?" Simon said to Juan.

"No!" Emma shouted. "I don't want to be alone with this guy. It was a long time ago, baby—before I met you—when I was still mourning over Carol…I'm sorry Simon, but you can't come bursting into my life here. Our thing is way over; it's history. There is no 'thing'. I love my husband. You're going to have to go. I'm going to call security if you don't leave immediately."

"But why are you so upset, Emma?" Juan's voice was icy. "Maybe you do have some unfinished business with Simon. Regardless, you shouldn't be so rude to a guest. Do give him the courtesy of listening to him."

"Thank you," said Simon. "I'd like a few minutes to at least explain to her what happened."

Emma was trying to keep it together. "Wait a minute," she said to Juan, clutching after him as he pulled away.

"My wife is free to do as she likes, of course," Juan told Simon. "Take all the time you need. I'm sure it's an interesting story."

Juan's sarcasm pushed Emma over the top. "I'm out of here. You can both get fucked, for all I care," she shouted, and stormed out of the room.

Cameras flashed in her face as she opened the door, but Lauren was there to shoo the photographers away, to escort her to the limo. Emma ordered the limo driver to take off, but Juan and Simon came running, shouting for him to wait. They both piled into the car; Lauren jumped in at the last minute, and then the driver hit the gas.

"I absolutely need to know what's going on," Lauren said, breaking the ice. "I'm going to have to supply some print to go with those pictures or it's going to turn into an embarrassing situation."

Everybody just stared at her in stubborn silence for a while, listening to the sound of cracking ice. Finally, Simon introduced himself as an old friend of Emma's.

Lauren shook hands with him. "Nice to meet you; but listen, the press is going to have a field day with this unless we put out a release right away. Could you give me a little bit of background, something to work with? Maybe I could say you're an old friend of Juan's."

Simon flashed his devastating smile at Lauren and sparks bounced around the limo. Lauren blushed, Emma rolled her eyes, and Juan raised an eyebrow. "Why would the press be concerned about this? I don't think I follow you," Simon said pleasantly. And then his countenance totally changed as the situation no doubt dawned on him. His face turned white and his eyes darted around nervously. "You think they took a picture of Emma and me? Who did, do you know? We have to get the film. Let's go back."

"A little late to think about that now, Simon Elliot," Emma said accusingly. And then it dawned on her why he was so upset. Of course he couldn't have his picture in the papers; he was in hiding. Her voice softened a little. "I think you better explain your situation to Juan and Lauren, *pronto*."

"I can't do that."

"You can't not do it at this point," Emma told him. "Maybe we can come up with a look-alike or something—say it was somebody else."

As usual, Juan obviously gleaned what the problem was from following the conversation, but it had to be spelled out for Lauren, who completely lost it for a few minutes. "Oh my God, you're wanted?" She looked shell-shocked. "This is not good. Didn't you see the photographers move in when you came up behind Emma like that? How could you be so careless?"

Emma reached over and took Lauren's hand. "Hey, it's okay. Worse things have happened, believe me. We are where we are, Lauren. Let's find a solution."

"Emma is right; we have to concentrate on the present." The sarcasm had vanished from Juan's voice—it had become calm and rational. "Something has occurred to me. Simon, with your black hair, you could be my brother. We can say it was Ricky who kissed his sister-in-law in maybe too familiar a manner, but it was because he was drunk. I can live with that. What do you think, Emma?"

"I think you're an amazing person, and I love you more than ever. Honestly baby, this one wasn't my fault. Please tell him, Simon. I don't want my husband to think I'm cheating on him or something."

Simon stared into Emma's eyes briefly, but intensely, and then turned to Juan. "I need to split. Listen man, it's not her fault. I've held onto a fantasy for a long time. I thought she loved me, and I was wrong. My mistake. I'm sorry. I hope we're cool. It wasn't like I'd ever seen you before or knew you. The luck is on your side. Would you drop me off here on the corner?"

"Be careful," Emma said, as Simon jumped out of the car.

"Peace." Simon flipped them the peace sign, then disappeared down the block.

Emma exhaled loudly. "Wow, that was intense. I'm glad he's okay. I never knew what happened to him, except I heard he was on the lam."

Lauren had recovered her composure and was back in her take-charge mode. "I need to make some calls; I'll get right on it."

"We'll talk later," Juan said to Emma as he stared out the window into the night.

Back at the hotel, in the privacy of their room, he faced Emma. "Did you love him? Do you still have feelings for him? I need to know the truth," he said calmly.

Emma fidgeted with the buttons on her blouse, avoiding Juan's eyes. "No. But he was right that we had unfinished business." Matching his calm, she looked up at him directly. "It's finished now. Okay?"

"Did he send the flowers that were in the dressing room?"

"Yeah, they were from him."

Juan's tone was icy. "So you knew he was there, but you chose not to tell me. Why?"

Emma was becoming flustered and angry, but she tried to be honest. “Fuck. Maybe I didn’t know how I’d feel. Maybe I wanted to handle it without you getting jealous. It was a spur of the moment thing.”

Juan nodded his head, but didn’t blink an eye. “Perhaps you need more time to think about it. I’m going to get my own room for the night. See you later,” he said, and walked out of the room before Emma could protest.

“I’m not going to come running after you,” Emma yelled down the hallway. *He could cut me some slack once in a while*, she thought. Pacing around the hotel room, Emma felt like she was coming out of her skin. When Juan didn’t return after about half an hour, she decided to go down to the hotel bar, see if any of the guys in the band were there. Stuart and Neil were there alright, chatting up some groupies and drinking shots of tequila with lime and salt. The group made way for Emma, and the party swelled as fans came by the table to compliment the band. Everybody wanted to talk to Emma, but instead of the tequila lifting her spirits, it plunged her deeper into a somber mood, making her incapable of small talk.

“What’s shaking, baby?” Stuart said. “Did you and Juan get into it? I saw that dude kiss you.”

“You might say that.” Emma shook her head miserably. “It was just a kiss, for Christ sake; it happened, okay? It’s not like I was being unfaithful or anything. Shit happens, you know?”

“Tell me about it. I’ve been married twice—both times a bummer.”

“Jesus, give me a break. We’re not getting a divorce; we just had a fight, that’s all.” Emma forced herself to snap out of her dark mood. “Your turn to buy a round,” she told Stuart. Eventually she went back up to her room and crashed in a drunken stupor.

The next day on the train to Vienna, Juan refused to sit next to her. The band and crew all seemed to know that the couple was fighting—they gave them plenty of space. Emma had begun drinking cognac from a small flask as soon as they boarded the train, so by mid-afternoon she was wasted again. She staggered into the compartment where Juan was sitting, calmly reading a book, and plopped herself down in his lap.

"Don't be mad at me, baby, please; I can't take it," she sobbed.

Juan encircled her with his arms, held her tenderly. "Don't ever do anything like that again, Emma. If you do, I'll leave you. I can't bear the thought of you wanting another man."

"But I don't; I promise you I don't. Nobody but you, only you, baby."

The rest of the tour went smoothly, for a rock band. Nobody missed any shows, in spite of a nasty virus that burned its way through the band and crew. The musicians seemed to be happy to be playing with Emma; Emma was happy to still be with Juan, and the whole entourage got along reasonably well—which Emma knew was reflected in the shows—in the vitality of the music. The audiences in Europe loved Juan's guitar playing; he got tremendous applause on all his solos and was constantly mentioned favorably in revues. It made Emma happy to see her husband receiving recognition as an artist in his own right, and she could tell how pleased he was, even though he never mentioned it.

Carl and John, the A&R men, met up with the band in Italy on Thanksgiving and took everybody out to celebrate at a restaurant in Rome. European sales had definitely been boosted by the tour, so the record company was happy, too.

...

Mid-December, Emma and Juan were finally back home for a stretch of time. They were to do a New Year's Eve show at the coliseum in Oakland, take some time off for writing, and then start recording in February. Their spacious house felt like a palace after being cooped up in hotel rooms for months, and in spite of the rainy, wintry weather, the temperature seemed moderate compared to the northern cities of Europe.

It was a much needed, quiet Christmas for them, with dinner at Ray and Stephanie's—very pleasantly low-key after the long tour and the upsetting visit with Juan's family.

New Year's Eve, Emma shared the bill with some of her oldest friends and, as usual, backstage was a big party. She warned Juan that all the food and drinks in the hospitality room would be dosed, even unopened bottles of wine. The Merry Pranksters liked to inject acid into the bottles through the corks with hypodermic needles. And sure enough, about an hour after they arrived at the stadium, Juan and Emma started coming on to acid. It seemed like everybody else backstage came on at about the same time, too. The greenroom was buzzing with people tripping, and the energy was good. The audience appeared to be as stoned as the bands, to the extent that the entire stadium seemed to breathe and move like a single, organic entity.

Juan and Emma stayed close to each other throughout the trip. Emma felt safe in the intimate space they had created and she felt that Juan did, too.

Making it back to Marin by daybreak, Juan and Emma watched the sunrise from the top of Mt. Tam, with remnants of the acid still causing them to taste colors.

Later, lying in bed on New Year's Day, Emma remembered she'd forgotten to take her birth-control pill. She slipped out of bed, and went into the kitchen to get the packet from the cupboard. She took out a pill, stood there looking at it for a few minutes, and then dropped it, along with the whole packet, into the wastebasket.

Chapter Seventeen

Emma, 1976: From Craziness to Bliss

January 1976: I didn't put a lot of thought into trying to get pregnant—it was more like surrendering to the rush created by the energy between Juan and me. It wasn't that I wanted a baby. It was, specifically, that I wanted Juan's baby. That bizarre concept had lain there in the center of our relationship from the beginning, and suddenly, it was no longer some hypothetical, abstract idea, but a simmering desire. I'd been on the pill since I was sixteen, working non-stop since then, too, and I had no fucking idea how I could fit a baby into our hectic life; but I figured it would be self-explanatory if it happened.

Christ, it'd been three years since I've had any real length of time off, and that wasn't exactly a holiday. When I came off tour in August of '73, I had to go on steroids. I needed throat surgery; my airways were almost closed. The surgery wasn't that big a deal, having those polyps removed from my vocal cords, but the recovery time was longer than the doctor or any of us had anticipated.

They did the surgery in early September. Everything seemed fine until a few days after I came home from the hospital, my throat suddenly swelled up so badly that I couldn't breathe. Stephanie called an ambulance and I landed back in the hospital for a week while they tried to get the infection under control. It was staph, for Christ sake. Then I had problems with hives from some antibiotic they gave me. It was craziness with no small measure of irony that I wasn't able to tolerate legal drugs, after all the random street drugs I had taken with no problems.

When I was finally stabilized they sent me home, with Stephanie as my guard. It was like I was twelve again. I couldn't smoke, couldn't drink, couldn't take any extra drugs at all for fear of drug interactions; and my mom was there to make sure I didn't deviate from the doctor's instructions. Marianne was there, too, siding with Stephanie all the way. I wasn't supposed to even talk for a while, and I sure as hell couldn't sing. They allowed me to read and watch TV, which was just too fucking big of them. I was going stir-crazy until Stephanie bought me a bunch of art supplies and started giving me refresher courses in drawing and painting. It was the first time since I was a kid that I'd had time to get into art, and it was actually pretty exciting to be learning new stuff. When my throat healed, I began other lessons—this time in singing. The doctor warned me that I had to learn to sing without blowing my vocal cords out again. He said the next time would be worse, and no matter how much I protested that I didn't have time, he countered with the argument that I might not have a career again if I didn't take the throat thing seriously. So I began classical lessons, gradually building a voice that was supported deep in the chest, rather than belted from the throat. I was pretty much of a hermit during those months because I couldn't really hang with my friends and not party.

Out of boredom, I got heavier into painting. It helped pass the time, and, it had a side effect: it also brought some of those old, residual demons out of the shadows. Although it helped to have Marianne there, I still wasn't a hundred percent comfortable in my house. It was there, that odious, lurking-around-the-corner thing; I could sense its presence.

Out of self-defense, I decided to try to paint it. Instead of trying to ignore it, or running from it, I kept trying to get a better look at it so I could capture it on canvas. And the weirdest thing happened—it started trying to evade me. It was a macabre game of cat and mouse, but at least I had Marianne or Stephanie there refereeing.

They kept me tied up, sober and quiet for damn near seven months, but at least I was allowed to get back into dance during that long winter of paying dues for having done too much of everything. I needed the exercise after the goddamn steroids, which had rounded my face and body so that my clothes barely fit and my face looked like one of those cherub paintings. Spring broke spectacularly that year of '74, and I joined the disciplined runners along the Presidio, feeling like I had deserted my hippie heritage—sold out for less than thirty pounds of weight loss.

I balanced it though—began smoking on the sly, just so I wouldn't become too much of a health nut. By April, I was back down to a hundred pounds even, so I decided I better start beefing up on champagne and Irish coffees at the bars along the Marina. After receiving a clean bill of health and tentative permission to return to work, I jumped off the wagon, big time.

...

Bill wanted me to come down to L.A. to write for the next album with him. I decided to go early in order to escape the ever-vigilant Stephanie-Marianne team of behavioral police. Got into L.A. early May, checked into the Hyatt House, and put out the word to old friends that I was back in action. It had already turned into summer in Hollywood, so the first order of business was a tan. I started hanging out with some Malibu movie stars, getting high all day, hitting The Corral club in Topanga Canyon at night.

Whenever I'm in L.A, there inevitably comes a point when I find myself face to face with Carol's death again, and that spring of '74 was no exception. Still, I don't hate the city because of it. Carol is never far from my consciousness anyway, and she's never closer than when I'm in L.A. So, although it is a city of tears for me, it is also a source of joy—the scene of some of our best times together. I remember the way she died, but I also remember the way she lived.

There's this thing about L.A., this perception that everybody is gorgeous—and it's true for the most part. Like, the trash man is beautiful, you know? Except the people with power—they wear beautiful things and drive million dollar cars, and they don't have to be beautiful. But all of them are hyping constantly—everybody's got some deal going down. They're like junkies without the powder, druggies without the high. No wonder the ones who can, move out of town.

Malibu is another trip altogether. You sit there in the sand, looking out at the ocean, breathing the salt air, and there's all the bullshit of L.A. at your back, but it doesn't matter, because you're just a few steps from something real—something that connects you with the wider world, that puts the Hollywood mirage into perspective. The Pacific waves roll in murky blue, breaking big enough to surf on, warm enough to swim in, even as early as May.

Something in me broke with those waves, too—started crashing recklessly onto wilder shores, places I hadn't ventured even during the heyday of my strung-out period. Maybe my body chemistry had changed from all the goddamn steroidal drugs or something, but alcohol started having a weird effect on me. I didn't want to admit it, but I was having total blackouts most of the time.

I used to think people made shit like that up because they didn't want to remember making an ass of themselves or something, but I had that dead wrong. There is nothing comforting about not being able to remember something. I would rather live with the memory of any gross humiliation or pain than not be able to access the memory. It scared me, and the more scared I became, the more I drank so I wouldn't be scared. Yeah, another one of my usual brilliant solutions to problems.

So, apparently I was getting pretty nuts up there at The Corral, as spring turned into summer, and I spent my days getting wasted with my Malibu friends, then heading up the canyon at night to drink myself further into oblivion. Why? I have no fucking idea why, anymore than I ever really figured out why I got strung out on heroin. It seemed like a good idea at the time. And I know that sounds glib, but I think it's true.

I was supposed to be writing songs, but Bill's project had gone over schedule, so he had no time for me until July, and I just didn't feel like doing anything that required discipline. I had been so disciplined for years, you know? In spite of my drug use and stuff, I'd always managed to stay on target with recording and tours and everything. I knew how fast Bill and I could whip out songs when we had to, so I allocated myself a little space of time to explore the outer reaches of permissiveness—dumped absolutely every "should" and "shouldn't" that still remained in my psyche into a black hole, into that place I could no longer access, even if I'd wanted to. And I guess I got pretty out there, if you can believe the stuff that was written about me during that time. Lauren joined me in L.A. to do damage control with the press, but even her considerable skill couldn't turn me back into the image that the record company had always banked on.

Some jerk-off guy wrote that he had seen me giving one of my movie star friends head under the table at The Corral, and I thought, *In your dreams, buddy*. But the truth is, at that time there was so much stuff swirling in that black hole where my memory had once been, that it could have happened. I just don't know. But I do remember somebody going down on me, under the table one night. I think it was a chick, I'm not sure, but suddenly I was coming, and I didn't try to hide it or anything. The people I was with thought it was far-out, and I was wasted enough not to give a shit what anybody thought anyway. Another story that came out that summer, complete with photos, had me and a bunch of Hollywood big shots dancing naked in the rain at some guy's ranch in Topanga. So what kind of a shit-head goes to a private party, takes pictures, and sells them to a trashy publication? I wouldn't know, of course, because I don't even remember being at the ranch.

A serious wake-up call was on its way. Emerging from a blackout, I found myself coming back into my body in an emergency room, wading into consciousness through a haze of intense pain, head throbbing, tasting blood, every muscle in my body aching. I guess I went horseback riding through Topanga canyon in a summer dress and sandals, and I must have lost my balance and fallen, because my foot had been caught in a stirrup, and I'd been dragged through some dense shrubbery. Evidently, some kid who knew how to ride a lot better than I did (which actually could describe just about anybody on earth), caught my horse and brought me back to my friends. I'm told she had me riding on the front of her saddle, holding me around my waist, leading my horse back by the reins, too.

And nobody got her name! My friends took me off to the emergency room, and my gallant little rescuer remained anonymous. I have always hoped that she'll show up at a gig and introduce herself one day, but since I have no memory of the incident, I wouldn't recognize her if she was standing in front of me. I was lucky to survive the accident with no broken bones—just a concussion and some scratches and bruises.

I got another DUI soon after the runaway horse incident. Lost my license for a few months as a result, but my luck held, and the judge went fairly easy on me. Part of my sentence included two weeks in a rehab clinic, which wasn't bad because some of the most interesting people in L.A. were in there with me. Also, the doctor got to the bottom of the blackouts. It was so fucking simple—"rapidly rising blood alcohol concentration." The solution? Remember to eat before you drink, and drink slowly. At least that was my interpretation of the solution. I disregarded the part about 'alcoholic tendencies' and 'genetic propensities', all the boring shit. The doctor laid a huge trip on me about the danger of blackouts, blah, blah, and so forth, and I was polite about it all, but actually, he really did help me. Just maybe not the way he intended to.

After that, no matter how wasted I'd get, I'd always remember to eat something; and it worked wonders, enabling me to drink as much as I wanted and not lose myself entirely. I started carrying around protein bars, and little bags of high-energy stuff, like hikers do. Another trick I learned from one of my fellow inmates in the clinic: drink as much water as you do alcohol, and you can keep going indefinitely. Of course, it also cuts down the amount of alcohol you can consume per hour if you're slugging down water, too, so you don't end up with fucking "rapidly rising blood alcohol concentration". So, I actually was rehabilitated. I never had another blackout, or at least, not a total one.

Which is not to say that my days of sticky situations were over. God knows what would have happened if I hadn't met Juan when I did. I thought my life was going to end on July 5th, and it definitely could have.

I had spent July 4th at a barbeque at Bill's house, then gone with some friends to Malibu when I couldn't put up with Peggy anymore. I eventually ended up at The Corral that night. A bunch of bikers showed up, and one of them was so sexy that, over my friends' vehement protests, I left with him.

He drove his chopper fast over the windy roads of Topanga Canyon, me clinging to him for dear life, and we ended up at some funky, little house in the San Fernando Valley. I came to the next morning with somebody slapping me in the face.

"Get up bitch," said a woman's voice. "I'm gonna fucking kill you."

I opened my eyes to a snarling chick with ratted up hair holding a gun to my head, glaring at me angrily through pounds of black eye make-up. "I'll kill you both!" She was waving the gun between the biker and me. "I mean it; don't try anything, bitch."

I was too surprised to even be scared. It just seemed surreal. "Jesus, don't weird out on me. Are you his old lady? He didn't tell me he had an old lady. What's going on?"

"Fuck off, Roxanne," the biker told her. "Get the fuck outta here or I'm gonna take that gun and waste you."

"Don't threaten me, cocksucker. I'm gonna blow you and your bitch out of the water. You're not fucking with me anymore, asshole," Roxanne said, and then she fired the gun into the pillow, right by our heads.

The noise was so loud, it deafened me for a few moments, and in that time, the biker tried to grab the gun from the lunatic's hand, but she fired again. This time she hit him in the arm. She immediately dropped the gun and rushed to his aid, tending his wound, kissing his face. "I'm sorry, you gotta believe me, I didn't mean to shoot. Me and Kevin been waiting all day for you yesterday. You promised, remember? You promised you'd bring him some fireworks. Then I come over and see you in bed with this bitch."

"You better split," the biker said to me. "Where do you live? Maybe Junior'll take you."

I realized then that he had no more idea who I was than I did who he was. "No, it's okay, I'm cool." I hastily pulled on my clothes, grabbed my purse, and made for the door. I left him there on the bed with Roxanne, bleeding where the bullet had grazed his arm, acting as if the whole scenario was just foreplay to them.

Another biker dude, presumably Junior, was still crashed on the couch in the living room. The shots hadn't even awoken him. I made my way to a phone booth outside a 7-11 down the street, and called a cab. Got back to the Hyatt happy to be alive.

I thought about telling Lauren about the scene with the biker and his old lady, but I knew she wouldn't see the humor in it. Carol would have been in stitches. I told Bill about it when we got together later that night, playing up the bizarre story, expecting Bill to crack-up, but he got all serious on me instead.

"You went off with a biker, and no one knew where you were going? He could have killed you, Emma. How would anyone even have known where to start looking for you? Let's face it, you have the judgment of a two-year old, if that."

"Jesus, you've been living in L.A. too long. Why would he want to kill me? He wanted to fuck me, that's all, and he did, for about ten seconds. Lighten up, for Christ sake. You don't see how it's funny that I wake up to this woman from Mars wanting to fight over her man or something?"

"People die over smaller things. It's not funny, Emma. Anyway, you might think more of yourself than to fuck a sleazy biker you just met. You're better than that."

"And I suppose you've never had a one-night stand with a sexy, sleazy woman?"

"It's different, and you know it. I see where you're going with this, trying to turn it into misogyny on my part. Anything to divert us from the reality that a man poses a physical threat to a woman that a woman simply does not pose to a man."

"Oh yes, but that isn't what you said, is it? You put it on the level of my self-esteem, not my safety. It's okay for men to want to have down-and-dirty sex, but not women. Same old shit, free-love not withstanding."

"If we can write as well as we can fight, we could get some serious work done. You have some lyrics for me?"

I wouldn't admit it to Bill, but I knew what he meant, of course. The whole "life is dangerous, most accidents happen close to your home, it's usually someone you know who kills you, greater chance of dying from a bee sting than a shark attack, and so forth," was my rap, but the truth is I didn't really feel that way. My nerves were jangled, like I was running on speed, and I didn't want to crash headlong into another tollbooth or something. Also, I hadn't forgotten the Manson murders. That memory, combined with the fact that my body had taken a recent beating from the horseback accident, and I'd just been slapped in the face that morning, not to mention been threatened with a gun, made me resolve to cool it for a while. I decided to quit running around so much—just hang out in Hollywood, and concentrate on the album. And I was definitely cured of taking off with strangers on motorcycles.

...

So, I was at the Whiskey instead of The Corral that blazing July evening of '74, and there, in the middle of the craziest period of my life, Juan and I found each other. Now I can't imagine not having met him. I can't imagine us being anywhere on the same planet and not finding each other. Thank God I had quit blacking out. What if I'd seen him and then not remembered him!

It's only been a year and a half since Juan and I met, but I feel like Carolina chose us as her parents long before either of us were born...which sounds scarily like something my mother would say. When I decided to stop taking The Pill that New Year's Eve of '75, a baby was still just an abstract idea. But making love with Juan became even more intense because it was the first time in my adult life that I'd had sex without birth control. I welcomed anything Juan wanted to give me, took it to my heart, to my womb, loved it effortlessly. It was a new type of recklessness for me, an abandonment that was scary and exhilarating.

•••

Bill came up in the New Year, January '76, and we started recording at the Record Plant, in Sausalito. Bill stayed in our guest cottage—loved being in Marin County, up on the mountain, in spite of the rain and fog. I felt some guilt that I'd always refused to stay at his place in L.A., but then again, when he'd been with Peggy, it was such a drag. God, I was glad when they broke up. At least Bill and Juan respected each other, maybe even liked each other, in spite of the underlying current of competition that still ran between them.

We started out sketching the songs, music first, unlike previous albums. Bill liked the Latin element Juan brought into the songwriting, even though he felt threatened by Juan's talent. After a few days, Juan and Bill came to me, proud as all hell, with a bunch of completed music and asked me for lyrics. I sat in a lawn chair out by our pool wrapped up in a down comforter, and wrote the words.

"The Sleeping Maiden's Hand"

Watching the sun rise true

A Light Rain of Grace

Peaking on Mt. Tam
I was lying there with you
In the sleeping maiden's hand
The fog was hanging low
Over the Golden Gate
Then it parted like an omen
Come to seal our fate
I want to say, I am so full of gratitude
Forgive me if this sounds
Like a worn-out platitude
But I have to say that it was destiny
And now I want to give you
The very best in me
Because baby, it doesn't get more real
Than being here beside you
Rushing to the thrill
And if you want me for always
Absolutely then, I will
I'd been waiting for a miracle to happen
And I wasn't sure I'd know it if it came along
But there's no way we could have missed each other
I could feel your presence, you could hear my song
I could feel the hand of fate
When you found me
From across the stars
From all around me
Serendipitous
Meant to be
All the things that lovers say
Meant for me, finally
If you went beyond the mountains
I would feel your breath in the wind
I would inhale your love throughout my body
Then back to you my love I would send
And if you went across the sea

I'd wait on the shore for you to return to me
Because you are destiny, meant to be
And I am for you, your destiny too
I'd been waiting for a miracle to happen
And I wasn't sure I'd know it if it came along
But there's no way we could have missed each other
I could feel your presence, you could hear my song

We fell into a natural rhythm of writing during the afternoon and recording at night. Bill and one of the assistant engineers started flashing on each other, and soon he was sleeping at her house most of the time. Ray and Stephanie would often drop by and listen to us recording; the studio was maybe seven minutes from their house, so it didn't require any tremendous effort or anything. For the first time in my adult life, I actually felt kind of normal. I had a schedule, a husband, and a gorgeous house that I wasn't afraid in. I didn't get wasted at clubs and end up with strange men, or get D.U.I.s, or blackout or shoot heroin…just wrote songs and recorded, drank champagne, and made love with my husband. A normal routine, peaceful.

Not for long though. On February fourth, an earthquake struck Guatemala, wrecking havoc, killing thousands of people, leaving a million homeless, without food or medical necessities. In the days immediately following the quake, the news worsened—the water supply was contaminated and dysentery was killing even more people. Over twenty-two thousand people were dead, and more were dying. They needed aid, and they needed it immediately. I put in a call to Bill Graham, asked if he'd promote an emergency relief benefit in San Francisco. Right away.

"It's do-able, when are you thinking?"

"Sooner than later. They're desperate down there. My schedule is wide open. I can probably get Jefferson Starship to play, too. It's up to you, Bill, how soon you can pull it together."

"I'll get back to you. Was El Salvador affected by the quake? Your husband's family okay?"

"Yeah, they're fine; thanks for asking."

Two hours later, Bill called back. "It's a go, Emma. I cleared Saturday, the 21st, at Winterland for you. That only gives us two weeks to promote the show, but it shouldn't be a problem if you get Lauren on it right away."

"You're amazing, Bill. Nobody but you could get it together that fast. Thank you. I'll put in a call to Starship, see if they want to double-bill."

"No need; I just talked to Grace and Paul — they're in."

My next phone call was to some local DJs, asking them if they would run some ads. Everybody wanted to help. I recorded a plea for aid for Guatemalan earthquake victims, and the DJs played it twice an hour. Within a week all the drop-off centers were swamped with goods, and enough money came in to transport the stuff, too.

The problem was, who was going to actually take the stuff down there? Juan and I met with some people who had hastily formed a relief organization, and they had somebody lined up to take supplies down on a big ship immediately. We got a good hit off them, so we decided to entrust all the goods to them, and the ship left before the concert even happened.

Between writing and recording, some last minute rehearsals, and working on all the relief projects, the two weeks until the concert went by in a flash, and I didn't even notice that I had missed my period.

Winterland was packed the night of the gig, with people waiting outside hoping to get in later. There was a very high energy in the auditorium, a sense of the community coming together to do something important. The Bay Area was like that, and still is, actually.

Meanwhile, our big radio relief effort was disappearing down the coast. The fucking pirates evidently sailed right on past Guatemala, took the medical supplies, and food and clothing down to South America, and sold them. That much information got back to us. But it wasn't just the stupid hippies who got taken for a ride.

The fuel for their journey had been donated by an oil company, the same fuel that we had given them the money to buy. At least we hadn't given them all the money. The bulk of it had gone to the Red Cross. And anyway, we didn't know we had been majorly ripped off the night of the gig, so we were all feeling good about our efforts.

Juan and I came home ecstatic about the music and the amount of money we'd raised, and took it out on each other. It was that night, as we lay in bed after making love, that it hit me about my period.

"I think I'm pregnant, baby."

"Are you sure? How do you know? Aren't you on the pill?"

"I stopped at the beginning of January—it's a surprise. Aren't you happy?"

"If it's true, you know I would be the happiest man on earth. But how could you know this soon? Have you seen the doctor?"

"Quit being so rational. Jesus, I just know, okay?"

Juan looked at me like I was the Madonna or something, as if I were psychic, and holy, too. That was a first, and I didn't really deserve it. The explanation for my sureness had nothing to do with any mystical insight—my breasts had become incredibly sore, and my girlfriend who has a kid told me that's the first sign of pregnancy.

My condition was confirmed in March, and while the extended family couldn't have been happier, Herbie had a fit.

"You didn't plan this very well, did you? You're not going to be able to promote this album when you're six months pregnant. What about your career? It's not too late for an abortion. Talk to me, Emma."

"Fuck you, Herbie." I hung up on him.

He called back an hour later with the good news that he could get me out in April for a spring tour—"so at least you won't be out of the public eye so long. I talked to the company; they're willing to release the new album in the fall—you can promote it in the winter. What do you think?"

“We’re not even finished mixing yet. I don’t want to go on the road. I have morning sickness, for Christ sake. Jesus, Herbie, is there a human being in there somewhere? How about congratulations?”

“Work with me on this, Emma. I’m happy for you; sure I am. Congratulations, okay? You’ve got to do a spring tour. Trust me on this. Finish the record, stay in shape, we’ll have you home by the end of May. You can wear loose clothing. Do this tour, and then you’ll have a six-month break to have the baby. What are you hoping for?”

“What do you mean what am I hoping for? I told you what I want.”

“A boy or a girl?”

Jesus, one minute he’s telling me to get an abortion, and the next thing you know, he’s asking me whether I want a boy or girl.

“Christ, I don’t care Herbie. I just want to be able to enjoy this time. I’ve been working hard for a long time.”

“Opportunity only knocks once, Emma. I have to urge you to make decisions that are good for your career. You’re a star, baby. Say you’ll do this tour.”

Herbie got his way, of course. He was right about not losing momentum. The album was finished and we were back on the road in April. I was three months pregnant and still thin as a rail, but by the end of the tour I had a slightly rounded curve to my stomach; and I was starting to look like Marilyn Monroe with the cleavage.

Juan and I both quit smoking cigarettes entirely, for the sake of the baby, and I cut way down on my drinking. I was fairly paranoid anyway because of all the drugs I’d taken in the past. I knew the “psychedelics cause birth defects” line was a crock of shit, but all that stuff I’d heard came back to haunt me.

I brought it up to my doctor when I saw her in May. She was mainly concerned about alcohol—told me to limit myself to a glass of wine a day. It was a tall order, but I tried to follow her directions. I was tired a lot during the tour, morning sickness that lasted all day sometimes, but we put on a show night after night, and then toward the end of the tour, I got energized. Just as the thing was ending, my energy had come back.

...

I got back into painting during those months the baby was growing inside me. Juan and I felt the miracle of life as though we were the first people to ever have a child. We were fascinated by the little nudges of elbows and feet poking through my skin, and awe-struck by the evidence of life in the ripple created as the baby turned in its microcosm. I painted animals and bright landscapes of Mill Valley and Sausalito—the bay, the bridge, the wetlands—everything in full sunlight. In fact, it was such a sunshiny period that it cast no shadows. Events were building up in the shadows alright, but we didn't see it from our bright world.

Juan and I hiked the mountain every day, had picnics, told each other stories. We discussed names endlessly, with the intensity of philosophers. By the end of summer, I'd had a sonogram, and knew the baby was a girl. Juan said she should have the name of one of his maternal ancestors. We settled on "Rosa", his grandmother's name. I wanted to honor Carol, of course; Juan suggested "Carolina", which I loved, and it just naturally got shortened to "Lena", which was perfect, because I didn't want to call her "Carol" as a first name.

Carolina Rose-Allison Avelar was born October 8th, 1976, but don't get the idea that she just waltzed into the world. My doctor and Juan and I had it all set up that I would have a natural childbirth in the hospital, in a private room with candles and soft music, riding the bliss waves until the little one arrived.

Didn't exactly play out that way. After ten hours of excruciating pain, I started begging for drugs. What had I been thinking? The one time I actually did need painkillers, I'd asked the doctor not to give them to me. When they finally condescended to give me a shot of something, it was a joke—did nothing to lessen the pain of my body being torn open. After fifteen hours, they did me the favor of giving me a "spinal block," which is the pleasure of having to hold perfectly still while they insert a needle the size of Texas directly into your spine. But the payoff is enormous—it renders you paralytic from the waist down, so at least you can rest up for the next wave of pain.

Thirty hours after my labor started, Lena was born with the cord wrapped around her neck twice. The doctor knew what to do, and in spite of what felt like the most harrowing experience of my life, apparently everything was fine, normal. Jesus, and they like to pass off the job of mothering as a cakewalk. Yeah, I'd assumed that since women did it all the time it couldn't be that hard. I acquired a whole new respect for all mothers.

Herbie sent a huge bouquet of flowers and the biggest stuffed animal I'd ever seen. Lena and I arrived home from the hospital to a house that looked like a cross between a florist's and a toy store.

Caring for a baby was completely new to Juan and me, and we dug it—even changing diapers. I was absolutely intent on nursing Lena, but that was no piece of cake either. Nobody tells you that you might give birth to a wired little person who'll wake up every two hours wanting to nurse.

Juan and I solved the problem by just letting Lena sleep between us, so I could let her nurse while I slept. We spent all our time looking at her anyway. She still had the universe in her eyes those first couple of weeks—now I knew what my parents meant by that. Stephanie handled all the cooking and household management for us, and she and Juan fought over who got to hold the baby the most. Just as we were adjusting to our new, beyond demanding schedule, Herbie called to say we had to finalize the tour.

"What tour?" I asked groggily.

"Got you booked in Cincinnati November 10th, Emma. Just six weeks, like we agreed on in March. The album is moving fine, but this tour will really boost our Christmas sales."

"What? You've got to be kidding. I'm not going on the road next month. Jesus, Herbie, I'm nursing a baby here. I've got milk;

it leaks you know, on the front of clothes. Can you see me up there on stage leaking milk on the people in the front row?"

Silence.

"Can't do it, Herbie."

"Maybe you should think about putting Carolina on the bottle, Emma."

"Maybe you should go fuck yourself, Herbie," I said, and hung up on him.

He rang back within minutes, and this time Stephanie wouldn't let him talk to me. I heard her saying, "You may be her manager, but I'm her mother…yes, well I think you've got to get your priorities straight. We've got a baby here…"

Christ, Stephanie could be heavy. It was the first time in my life that I saw the strong resemblance between my mother and me. I looked at Lena carefully, wondering which of my personality traits she was going to pick up.

The next day another gigantic bouquet of flowers arrived from Herbie, with a note saying, "Sorry. Please call me. I won't pressure you."

I let a few days go by before I called him, just to show him I was serious.

"Your mother is formidable," Herbie told me. "She would have made a great manager. My wife says I was off the wall, Emma. I'm sorry, okay? Can we move on? How's the baby?"

"She's good, no actually, she's amazing. The most beautiful thing on the planet."

"And I thought you were, Emma."

"Is this charm, Herbie? Christ, now I know you're going to try to talk me into something."

"You set the pace, Emma. Tell me what you want to do. When do you think you'll be ready to go back on the road? I'll work with it, whatever it is."

"I'm thinking summer, probably July. My doctor says babies tolerate other fluids better at nine months, so I can give her a bottle as well as nursing her then."

"Not a problem. I've asked Lauren to set up a photo shoot for next week though. Is that okay? It would be Roger; you like him, right? He'll come to your house."

"I look like shit, Herbie. I don't really want my picture taken right now."

"Roger'll make you look good, I promise. We'll keep you in the public eye this way. You've gotta give me something, Emma."

...

That was that, and I got nine months at home with Juan and Lena, which is not to say that there was no drama. Juan's family came for Christmas to see Lena, and it was obvious that things had deteriorated even more between Cata and her parents. Everyone was polite, but the dissension within the family created an underlying tension that sabotaged our best efforts to have a festive season. I was glad when they left and we were able to settle back into our routine.

Then, in March we got a frantic phone call from Doña Margarita, asking us if we would take Catarina. I listened in on the conversation on the extension line. "Her life is in danger," Doña Margarita whispered to Juan. "Please persuade her to come live with you. Tell her you need help with the baby."

I about fell on the floor. After they hung up, I carefully put my extension down and then ran into the living room. "Did I hear her right, Juan? This is crazy! What the hell is going on? She hates me. She thinks I'm a bad influence on Cata."

Juan grabbed me, pulled me onto his lap. "Settle down, *corozon*. She's never hated you—but you're right that this is crazy. It's the last thing I would have expected from my mother. Things must be really bad. But it's not fair to burden you with my family's problems after you've just had a baby. You need to build your strength."

"Of course she'll come live with us…end of discussion."

...

The minute Cata stepped off the plane I could tell she'd changed. This wasn't the same carefree girl who'd loved to get high and hang out at concerts. But Lena cheered her up immediately. She fell in love at first sight with her niece, and for her part, Lena lit up whenever Cata came near her. However, it was obvious Cata was pining for her boyfriend back home.

We were scheduled for a summer tour and I kept hoping it would be just the thing to snap her out of her depression. I offered to pay her to assist Stephanie with Lena while we were on the road.

At first she refused the money, insisting that she didn't want to be paid, but a couple of days later, she came to me and asked for an advance. "I'll work for the money, Emma. I wouldn't ask, but my parents won't allow me access to any of my inheritance, and I want to bring Carlos here. Please, can he stay here? I miss him so much, and I'm worried about him. Please…you'll like him. We could stay in the cabin. I need to see him; I'm going crazy without him."

Well, Jesus, how could I say no?

"Easily," Juan said, when I told him the plan. "You could easily have said no. My parents will have a heart attack. He's not good for her. They'll never permit it; surely you see that."

"I already said yes, and they don't have to know about it, do they? Anyway, you thought they'd never accept me and we're doing okay now, wouldn't you say?"

"There's no arguing with you, I know that. But it's different. You're not a Communist insurgent trying to ferment revolt in my country."

"I would if I could. And don't forget, they all thought I was a Communist. I think it's just a word they use for anyone who doesn't like the status fucking quo of El Salvador. She's in love, baby. You know what it's like. Let him come."

Carlos couldn't get a visa. I thought we could help him get one if we got an attorney involved, but it didn't work out. There was just no way the Man in El Salvador wanted to let this guy out of their sight. So we sent him the money to come through the underground, across the Mexican border, like other refugees and poor people do. It took a long time, but he finally made it to San Diego by the middle of May.

How to get him past the random roadblocks between the border and L.A. was the next problem. I phoned Bill to ask if he had any contacts who could do something like that, and he offered to go get him himself. And he did. Met up with Carlos armed with Hollywood-hip clothing, make-up, and a bottle of bleach; checked into a border town motel and transformed Carlos into a heavy-metal rocker. They made it past all the security checks with no problem. Bill put him on a plane in Burbank, and Cata met him in a limo at SFO.

This was the first time I'd ever seen Carlos, and to me he just looked regular, which is to say, weird. He had attempted to wash off his eyeliner, but it had smeared under his eyes, matching the black roots evident beneath his badly bleached hair. His shirt had long sleeves with flaps hanging off the sides, and his jeans were fashionably torn and funky. He looked shell-shocked but happy, as he and Cata piled out of the limo onto our driveway. I could see immediately what Cata saw in him. He wasn't elegant like Juan, but he was handsome, with strong white teeth and a very sexy smile.

You could see that he and Cata were dying to get the formalities over with so they could get at each other. Juan put on his big brother tone, inviting them into the house for a drink; but I rescued them—pleaded fatigue, asked them if they would mind getting settled in the cabin and coming to the main house later for dinner. I had put a bottle of champagne and a bunch of snacks in the cabin, so they were set to go. Cata's smile was my reward, and I kept it uppermost in my mind as I turned to face my frowning husband. I wasn't worried; Juan hadn't been able to stay mad at me a minute since Lena was born. I had acquired divinity status in his eyes, and I played it for all it was worth.

In spite of himself, Juan liked Carlos. That first night, I watched Carlos win him over, and I realized why his country considered him dangerous. He was enormously articulate, even in English—presented his views with dynamic force. You could hear his integrity and intelligence in every word, not to mention his conviction. Carlos had principles so high you couldn't miss them, so wide you couldn't get around them, and it obviously turned Cata on. She just beamed with pride and love when he spoke—hung on his every word. When Lena cried during dinner, Cata jumped up to get her, sat her on her lap and fed her little spoonfuls of strained fruit, then danced around happily, jiggling her as we all talked.

Lena was into scooting around and she struggled in Cata's arms, wanting to be put down so she could find some danger to expose herself to. Carlos got up and took the baby, bouncing her in the air. Lena gurgled and cooed with delight.

"Jesus, Carlos, you're studying medicine, you know how to organize unions, and you can take care of babies. That's fucking impressive," I said.

Carlos laughed. "I grew up in a large family and I am the eldest. I always helped my mother, before I got sent to work on the coffee plantations."

"How did you manage to get into university?" Juan asked him.

"It was the village priest. He was from the United States and he was a Liberation Theologian. He wanted to give me opportunity, so he taught me English and Latin.

"I'm sorry, what?" I asked.

"English and Latin," said Carlos.

"No, the other bit, about liberation."

Juan spoke up. "It's a Marxist doctrine, Emma. A lot of the clergy in El Salvador use it to incite revolution."

"When did you get so conservative," Cata said to Juan.

"Please Catarina, do not be disrespectful to your older brother on my behalf," Carlos said. "He is protective of you, naturally, as is correct. But Juan, you misunderstand the intention of the priests. The theology is inspired by the words of Jesus, not Marx."

"It's a dangerous theology," Juan maintained.

"Oh, lighten up," I said. "Let him tell his story."

Carlos smiled. “Jesus was a champion of the poor and oppressed, and if we are to be like him, so we must work to bring about equality in our society. I am fortunate that Father David helped me, but there are so many in our country who have no one to help them.”

“In Guatemala, too,” I chimed in. “You should have heard the way this jerk in Panajachel talked about the poor—like they were dirt. It was unbelievable.”

Carlos nodded his head. “Yes, I understand. That is also the prevalent attitude in El Salvador. And how can we even begin to build a land of opportunity when all the land is owned by a few families?”

“Such as our family.” Cata sipped her wine, looking around the table at each of us. “We have more than we need; we have to re-distribute the land.”

Juan appeared composed, but I know him well enough to know that he was agitated. He kept his voice low and logical. “I do not disagree that reform is needed. Our country lacks social infrastructure.”

“So why do you say that the priests who are on the side of the poor are Communists?” Cata demanded. “How can a Christian be a Communist? They’re godless, aren’t they? Didn’t they close down all the churches in Russia?”

Cradling Lena in one arm, Carlos reached over and stroked Cata’s hair soothingly; but she wasn’t in the mood to be soothed.

“You couldn’t deal with the situation in El Salvador,” she said to Juan, “so you just walked out on us—on your country, and your family. You turned your back on us. If it wasn’t for Emma, I wouldn’t be here now.”

“Whoa, lay back little sister,” I told her. “Give Juan a break. He’s on your side, remember?”

“But that is precisely the problem,” Juan said. “In reality, there is no right or wrong side. When you square off into sides, you perpetuate the illusion that we are all separate. Politics is intellectual delusion. Only action taken with indifference to consequence contains purity of motive."

I looked from Juan to Cata, trying not to roll my eyes. *Oh Jesus, he's using that fucking "I'm talking to idiots" voice again.*

"De veras? Purity of motive?" Cata was practically spitting. "Who told you that? That sounds exactly like something someone would say who abandons his country. Someone who lives in a safe country, while his own country's government is involved in the systematic repression of human rights in all of Latin America!"

"Now wait a minute," I said. "If you're going to get nasty, I want in on the conversation. I don't like my fucking government much either. I don't like any government, actually. Have some more champagne…what are we talking about here? Are you pissed at Juan about something?"

"She's sleeping now; shall I lay her down?" Carlos asked, cradling Lena gently.

"Yeah, that would be great. She'll wake up if we try to transfer her. You can lay her in the playpen for now."

The evening had pretty much worn itself down by that time anyway, so we all went to bed and left the dishes for morning. Later that night, after I'd nursed Lena back to sleep again, Juan and I touched bases on the evening.

"You can see how Cata's thinking has been influenced by Carlos and her other radical friends," Juan told me. "It's not the same as it is here; you saw what happened to Ramon. I do not disagree with her, or with Carlos, but I cannot condone action that could get her killed. I'm troubled and I see no solution for the problems."

"Well, you don't have to solve the world's problems tonight, baby. She's here, safe and sound…and getting laid—oh Christ, don't get mad—she's an adult. But speaking of getting laid, how about we try it on the loveseat by the window, or on the rug by the fireplace…"

•••

Later, we discussed whether we needed to hire a nanny. We were going to be rehearsing heavily, and then going on the road. We really didn't want a complete stranger spending a lot of time with our daughter, and we didn't want another person living in our home either. However, we didn't want to saddle Cata with the full responsibility of Lena during the shows either.

We agreed that if Stephanie and Ray were willing to come on the tour, too, we could get by with just family for now. And as the weather was so beautiful, it might work to have rehearsals at our house. We could have Cata and Carlos keep the baby outside in the sunshine while the music was blasting, and bring her to me when she needed to nurse.

Rehearsals were easy, even though we hadn't played together since the benefit in February. I had put the guys on retainers, so nobody had quit on me, and they were all kick-ass musicians—picked right up like we'd been on the road yesterday. Daryl and Neil had written a couple of great songs that I let them sing; not out of the kindness of my heart, but so I would have more breaks during sets to check on Lena.

Every Friday the band's families would come hang out by the pool and listen to us rehearse, and then stay for a barbeque. The wives and girlfriends all brought food and helped out with everything, pulling together like a family. Ray and Stephanie, a few of their friends, and a number of my old friends also became part of the Friday night parties. The sun poured down golden on our house on Mt. Tam…and the dark fog floated patiently, just beyond our garden.

Chapter Eighteen

1977-78

Allison's Wonderland still has the magic. Comeback tour illuminates Emma's undying star quality, read the August edition of Rock News. A local paper read, *Rocker rocking the cradle no more, Allison brought down the house Friday night in a stunning comeback performance at the Pontiac Stadium. If this is what motherhood does for you, bring it on. ...Avelar's guitar work shone in the band's soulful encore, with Emma's soaring vocal reminding us once again why she remains, as always, Close to our Hearts.*

"Jesus, it's like I'm having to prove myself all over again. You'd think I hadn't been on tour in ten years. Look at this fucking review." Emma tossed the paper to Juan, who was rummaging around the room service table for coffee.

"I already read it, while you were sleeping. It's a very favorable review. I didn't read anything even remotely negative in it."

"You're right, it's just been piling up—all the references to this being a comeback tour. Comeback from fucking where? It isn't like we've been on another planet for Christ sake. I take a few months off to have a baby and they're ready to dub me a has-been."

"I wouldn't take it too seriously. It's not worth it."

"It's just the nature of the business, right? It could be worse; I shouldn't complain. I've seen worse; in fact, I've seen a lot worse."

"The nature of criticism is arbitrary." Juan smeared butter and jam on a croissant as he spoke. "And its value is debatable because it has no substantial basis in fact. In truth, it's nothing short of bias—only one person's opinion, and not always a qualified opinion, at that. You should never give critics the power to hurt you." He broke into a mischievous smile. "But, of course, the critics who write that I am a virtuoso guitar player are obviously quite intelligent, and qualified to make judgments."

Emma took a sip of coffee. "I'm not hurt. They just piss me off, that's all. They think they're the goddamn authority on everything. I don't see them putting themselves out there. Fuck it anyway; where's Lena?"

"Cata and Carlos took her to a zoo. I told them we'd meet them in front of the lion's cage at four, if you felt up to it."

The appearance of their limo in front of the Pontiac, Michigan zoo caused a major stir. They could only be what they appeared to be—rock stars. Emma signed autographs and talked baby stages with other parents for a few minutes, introduced Juan to the fans, then politely got away, explaining that she had an appointment. Seeing Lena across a stretch of green, she ran toward her baby, who stretched out her arms for her *papá.*

"She likes you better than me," Emma told Juan, who had caught Lena up in his arms. "I don't blame her though; she's got good taste, like her mama." Emma wrapped her arms around Juan's waist and pressed up against him and her daughter. Lena responded to Emma's attentions by grabbing a handful of her hair and sucking on it. "I'm just a meal to her," Emma said, laughing, kissing Lena's stomach and sweet-smelling neck.

...

The tour had been the usual one-on, one-off format, but the venues had become gigantic. In many of the big cities, stages had been erected at football stadiums, where it seemed like the audience was miles away. Emma felt like she was singing to the ether, not to actual people.

Emma put in a call to Herbie, complaining about the lack of personal contact in the stadiums, but it was too late to change things—the shows were already booked. Herbie understood Emma's concerns, but pointed out that taking a large show on the road now added up to so much money that she really needed to play the large venues in order to make a profit.

"But what about if we played smaller places?" Emma screamed into the phone to make herself heard backstage at a huge coliseum. "Then we wouldn't need so much equipment and we could scale back on everything and just put on great shows that would promote the record by word of mouth. I feel out of touch with my audience, Herbie. This is not good."

"We'll talk about it when you get to New York, sweetheart. Don't worry about it. You're getting good write-ups and the fans love you; just get out there and knock 'em dead."

At least she had her family on the road with her. Emma felt grounded by Juan and Lena, her mother and father, and sister in-law. She felt anchored in spite of the fact that they were constantly on the move. Without any conscious decision on her part, she had begun drinking less, going to bed earlier, and conserving her energy for the shows and being with her husband and daughter.

The arrangement with family looking after Lena was working out well. Cata and Carlos had plenty of time to explore the American cities. They enjoyed carting Lena around to parks and museums and zoos during the day, and they had the evenings to themselves, to catch the concerts or be alone together. Stephanie and Ray were on duty at night, playing with Lena in the big hospitality rooms backstage, watching over her with that devotion peculiar to grandparents. Stephanie often brought her charcoals to the shows and did character studies backstage, sketching band friends and groupies and critics, as well as the tech people who kept things running smoothly.

In New York, the entourage swelled to over forty people as the rest of the band's and the roadies' families and girlfriends met up with them. Emma liked the chaos—felt an underlying contentment in the midst of all the shifting routines and changing of schedules that the new personalities brought with them. Family was a safe-haven from the hip culture that had lured her and Carol into heroin use, a buffer between herself and the demons that lurked in the shadows of her old hangouts.

Old friends came out of the woodwork in Manhattan—artists and musicians, junkies, people working the AA Program, actors and models—all the old crowd, the ones who'd survived so far. Emma did the dance: accepted invitations to parties and art openings, theatre and dinner dates, but with a once-burnt wariness. Anyway, it was different with Juan in the picture. People treated her differently when she was with her husband; there was a less predatory vibe. Juan held his own in the New York scene—he seemed able to stay focused on the arts and culture, and not let the pretentious bullshit bother him. He also smoked a lot of pot.

Herbie called Emma and tried to insist on having a private meeting with her to discuss upcoming tours and general career direction; but Emma was adamant that Juan be included. He tried to lay down the law to her. "I'm not managing you both, Emma. If he's part of the package, that's your business; but *you* are my client, not him. Bottom line, I'm going to protect your concerns. Period end."

"That's jive, Herbie You can't separate my concerns from Juan at this point. He's not 'part of a package'; he's my husband, for Christ sake. I'm not a solo act anymore."

When Emma and Juan met Herbie for lunch the next day, it was as if the phone conversation had never occurred. Herbie had obviously gotten the message; he was smooth, cordial and fraternal with Juan, careful to include him in his outline for the next year, and to ask his opinion on all the issues they were discussing. Basically, Herbie laid out a case for the necessity of big concert tours due to rising costs and the fact that rock n' roll had become big business now.

"If I book you into smaller venues, it's going to look to the record company like you don't have the fan base to fill stadiums.

The radio stations aren't going to play you as much if they don't think you're reaching a large audience, either. Radio has changed a lot in the past couple of years. You have to think about these things; you have to stay with the times. Business in America is re-positioning itself, and we've got to stay on top of the game."

Emma glared at Herbie. "Well, that's about as soul-numbing as it gets. Jesus, Herbie, even as long as I've been with the company, you're saying they'd drop me if I didn't play stadiums? Just like that? What about art? Wouldn't they make any kind of concession to artistic preference?"

"I'm not saying they'd drop you for that reason. But if you don't play the big venues, your record sales will drop. This is a business, Emma. The record company is not your friend. They love you while you make money for them, and if your sales fall, *hasta la vista baby."*

Juan had been listening intently, and now he spoke up. "Perhaps the stages could be redesigned to give Emma closer contact with the audiences. There is perhaps a solution that will please everyone. But Herbie, you're wrong about the record company people not being Emma's friends; everyone loves my wife."

Juan's comment broke the tension, and the three of them began to discuss ways to make the gigantic stadiums more palatable to Emma.

From New York, the tour swung down through Florida, where two band members got cameras, guitars, and money ripped off from their hotel rooms in Miami. Then it was out to Puerto Rico for a four-day stint, and finally, back up the East Coast, ending up in Maine the first week in September. Afraid of immigration problems, Carlos and Cata had stayed in Florida and gone to Disneyworld while the band was in Puerto Rico, then met back up with them in Boston.

Herbie rented a big beach house in Maine for the whole month of September—told Emma and Juan that they needed a vacation. He was being Mr. Thoughtful, after getting his way about everything. It was a beautiful old house right on the beach, and the weather was perfect. Emma and Juan set up house for a couple of weeks, with the family. Still on a creative high from the energy of the tour, Emma and Juan began writing songs at night after Lena had fallen asleep, creeping out into the living room, where Juan would play acoustic guitar and Emma would play with words. They would often see Cata and Carlos combing the beach in the wee hours, arms around each other's waists. Emma would smile at the sight of them; Juan would frown.

"Why do you have to be so negative?" Emma demanded of him. "They're beautiful together."

"I fear for them," is all Juan would say.

...

Despite the relaxing rhythm of their time at the beach, Emma and Juan were glad to get back to their own home. Riding across the Golden Gate Bridge into the rainbow tunnel that welcomed them to Marin, Emma felt exhilarated. Juan shared her mood, as did Ray and Stephanie; but Cata and Carlos were both somewhat subdued. It was obvious that something was up, and it came out over dinner that night. Carlos had decided to go back to El Salvador—soon.

"It has been the most educational experience of my life, and also the happiest time; I cannot express my thanks to you," he told Juan and Emma. "I never imagined that I would be able to come to the United States, and if I may tell the truth, I had no desire to come here. I had a false idea of what Americans are like, and now I have learned how very wrong I was. But it is necessary for me to go home. I have to start classes at university in December, and I must prepare."

Emma's brow furrowed. "Maybe you could go to school here. Isn't it kind of dangerous for you back there?"

"It's no good, Emma." Tears filled Cata's eyes, but her voice was even. "I've been trying to talk him out of it for the past two weeks. He is determined, and he is right that his country needs him…but I need him, too."

The room was silent. Emma watched Juan as he stood staring out the window. The conversation had wound its way around the room—wound all four of them into a tight knot. She knew everybody felt it, and perhaps Juan more so than all of them; but he appeared calm. He had warned her that it would come down to this moment, and now that it had arrived, she found herself unequipped to handle it.

"He must do what he has to do," Juan said quietly, and left the room.

"Jesus, that was insightful," Emma yelled after him. "Any more words of wisdom?"

There were logistics to consider in Carlos's departure, too. They'd have to smuggle him out of the U.S. and back into El Salvador covertly because the authorities there would surely detain him for departing illegally; and detainment for Carlos could mean death. Since crossing the border into Mexico wouldn't be a problem, they decided to let Cata drive him down to Tijuana in one of their cars, where he would take a plane to Southern Mexico, then make his way by land through Guatemala and into El Salvador. It was a messy plan, but none of them could think up anything better.

The day he left, Juan and Emma stood in their driveway holding Lena, watching the car pull away, and Emma knew that they were both experiencing the same sense of dread.

"I'll just be glad when she's back in the States and has heard from him," Emma told Juan. "I have a feeling it's going to be a long wait though."

Cata phoned from Big Sur to say they had decided to spend a few days there if it was okay with Juan and Emma. They were still processing the reality of their separating, trying to come to terms with the length of time they would be apart. Emma assured her that it was fine for her to take all the time she needed, but admonished her to stay in touch so her big brother wouldn't freak out.

Cata checked in from Bill's house in L.A. After that, they didn't hear from her for four days, until she called to say that she had seen Carlos off in Mexico, had crossed back into the States with no problem, and that she was going to stay at Bill's for a night before heading back up on Highway 5.

Cata was only back a few days before the band took off for Europe. Not enough time had passed for word about whether Carlos had made it back to El Salvador safely. Cata told Emma that they had arranged to stay in touch via Bill—reasoning that he would always know how to contact them, wherever they were. Emma felt that the timing of the tour couldn't have been more perfect for taking Cata's mind off worrying about Carlos. She could see how serious the relationship was—that Cata would no doubt marry Carlos one day—and she understood it, even felt optimistic about it. That Cata was obviously able to think long-term enough to be away from him for a while seemed like a good indication of their level of commitment to each other. And Emma knew that Cata would have plenty to occupy her on this tour, even though Stephanie and Ray were coming along again.

Cata had been to Europe twice with her parents, but Emma was sure that she was going to find the place much more exciting traveling with a rock band. Without Carlos around, she was going to have to fight off the guys. She was no little kid anymore, and she had become drop-dead gorgeous.

Sure enough, guys started coming on to her at the airport before the plane left the ground. Harry, the soundman, obviously had a crush on her. Emma thought it was funny that he tried to hide how smitten he was—deliberately avoiding even looking at her when Juan was around, and following her every move when he thought no one was watching. She told Juan, jokingly, "I think Harry is afraid of you."

Juan raised his eyebrows. "Should he be?"

"I'm talking about Cata, for Christ sake; are you blind?"

"Isn't he a little old for her?"

"She's not that young, but you can relax; she's not interested in him."

"Who's *he*?" Juan asked, furtively gesturing toward a young guy who was falling all over himself to help Cata with her things.

"He's one of the lighting crew—kinda handsome, don't you think?"

"More importantly, does Cata think he is…I hope so. Perhaps this trip will expand her horizons and she will lose interest in Carlos."

"I wouldn't hold my breath on that one, baby."

The logistics of traveling into a different time zone with a baby were difficult. Lena managed to keep all the adults in her life on her schedule, which was erratic to say the least. Right around her birthday, she finally acclimated to the time change and began sleeping at night, which transformed the family dynamic back into a more harmonious state.

The band was in a hotel in Wiesbaden when Lena took her first steps. It was like a major miracle had occurred, with Emma calling the family to come watch, and everybody acting like she was the smartest baby ever born. The awe over Lena's newly acquired mobility soon gave way to a constant state of worry though, as awareness of all the new dangers it had opened to her became apparent. The hotel windows were the first glaring problem. Within a week of walking, Lena had learned to bounce off beds dangerously close to windows, and could reach all sorts of things that had previously been beyond her grasp.

Returning to their room in Brussels, Lena seized the moment while Juan and Emma were inspecting the windows and tucking away cords for safety purposes, to waddle into the bathroom and find something new and interesting. A minute later she came toddling out, drooling blood, with the handle of Emma's safety razor sticking out of her mouth. Emma was certain that she had left it up high, but the maid had been in while they were out, and had obviously left it on the edge of the tub.

"Jesus, how does any child survive past two? How do the parents survive? You have to watch them every single second," Emma said to Juan after they had carefully wrested the razor from Lena's mouth, over her protests.

Luckily, the cuts were superficial, but it was a warning to Juan and Emma that they would have to be even more vigilant. For the rest of the tour, they checked bathrooms for sharp items, had all furniture moved away from windows, glass coffee tables removed from the rooms, dangling cords stapled, and they sealed all electrical outlets with their own stash of little plastic covers.

Juan took the phone call that finally came in late November, in the dressing room in Milan. It was an expensive call for Carlos to make, and Cata came running for the phone from the hospitality room, breathless. After talking to Carlos, Cata loosened up and began to resemble the outgoing girl she had been when Emma first met her—returning flirtations and enjoying the pleasures of Italy along with the rest of the band. When they got to England, Cata even went out with one of Emma's old friends from *King Snake*, which pleased Juan to no end.

...

But when the tour ended, and they were back home in Mill Valley, Cata gave Juan and Emma the news: she was going home. "I'm going to enroll at the University of San Salvador," Cata told them. "As much as I love it here, and will miss all of you, especially Lena, I have to go back. My country is going through many social changes, and I want to help."

Juan's face tightened, but he spoke in an even, controlled voice. "Don't try to be deceptive, Catarina. We all know why you want to go back. If Carlos had stayed here, there would be no question of you returning to El Salvador. It's a foolish move."

His tone of voice irritated Emma. "Give her a break, Juan. She's in love, and she's old enough to make her own decisions."

Juan scowled at Emma. "But she is not considering the consequences of such a decision." He turned to Cata. "All of us have been educated in the United States, and if you want to be in a position to help your country, then you should avail yourself of the best possible education instead of running after your boyfriend."

Cata stuck out her bottom lip petulantly. "I'm not running after Carlos. That's not fair. In fact, we are going to be married soon."

Juan folded his arms across his chest. "*Papá y Mamá* will never agree to it. This is ridiculous; you're too young to make such a decision."

Emma sat down on the arm of the chair by Cata, put a protective arm around her, and glared up at Juan. "Quit being such a downer, Juan. She loves him."

Juan glared right back at Emma. "And you stay out of the affairs of my family!"

"Fuck you. Now it's *your* family? You didn't even stay in touch with them until I invited them to our house. You sound just like your parents."

Cata looked up at him accusingly. "She's right, Juan."

Juan turned silently and started to leave the room, then stopped, turned back, and faced the two glaring women. "I'm sorry…you're right; I'm assuming a false role." He paused for a moment, visibly fighting to control his emotions, then continued in an even, low voice. "I like Carlos, Cata; surely you can see that. But I'm worried about where the progression of events at the university will lead you and Carlos. I think his life is already in danger, and while I used to believe that we had nothing to fear because of Uncle Fernando, after what happened to Ramon, I am no longer so sure. And there is also the danger that you could be kidnapped by the Left." Juan sunk down into a chair and dropped his head into his hands.

Emma thought for a minute that he was crying, and immediately felt terrible about what she'd said. She crossed the room and stood behind him, massaged his shoulders. "It's okay, baby, we understand…don't we Cata?"

"I understand, but it doesn't change anything." Cata shook her head sadly. "I will stay until you find a very good nanny for Lena, but please Juan, don't attack me again. Carlos likes you and respects you. It would hurt him to know you disapprove of our marriage. You won't say anything to our parents, will you?"

"Of course he won't," Emma assured her.

The next day, Emma asked Stephanie if she knew of a suitable nanny.

"Actually honey, I think I do. There's this woman named Trish; I don't think you've met her, but I've known her a long time. She's working as a secretary, but she hates the job. She might be into it."

Emma called her. Trish came by, and they hired her on the spot. The way she talked about how her grown children were all thriving and about how much she loved her little grandson, led Juan and Emma to believe she must have been a good mother, and that they could trust her with Lena. Trish said she'd be happy to move into their spacious house.

Cata left in the middle of December, after she had ascertained for herself that Trish would be good with Lena. Emma knew that the truth was that Cata wanted to be with Carlos for Christmas, and she could tell Juan knew it, too, but he said nothing. Cata told her parents that she was homesick and wanted to be back with them for the holidays after being away so long. The Avelars put some pressure on Juan and Emma to come, too, but there was no way they were budging from their own home after the long back-to-back tours.

"It would be nice to feel like we actually live here," Emma told Juan.

Lena was old enough now to maneuver around the big Christmas tree, pull down ornaments, cut her hand on the glass, and nearly pull the whole tree over on top of herself, in spite of three adults constantly supervising her. Juan and Emma went crazy with decorating the house because this would be the first year that they would do Christmas dinner in their own home. Ray and Stephanie would come, of course, and Ricky was coming, plus Trish's two kids who still lived in the Bay Area, as well as

Marianne, and Daryl, who had nowhere else to go. Then Bill called and said he needed a break from L.A., hint-hint, and somehow, Emma found herself having to provide dinner for sixteen.

Trish got the turkey in the oven Christmas morning, and Stephanie was in the kitchen cooking before Juan and Emma even got up—and all the guests brought pies and casseroles and side dishes, so the dinner was a success in spite of the hostess's limited culinary talents.

Juan and Emma had been awakened Christmas morning by Lena bouncing on the bed, as usual. Trish came and got her, and put her to work banging on pots and pans while she and Stephanie cooked. Later, Juan and Emma watched their baby try to open all her gifts from under the tree, and fall asleep in the process.

The Avelars phoned around noon to wish them a Merry Christmas. Marta and her husband and kids were there at the family home, which made Emma wish she could see them; but talking to Margarita was like going back to square one in the relationship again. She sounded like her old, cold, distant self, and it reminded Emma why Juan had wanted to keep that distance. When Cata got on the phone, her voice was falsely cheery. Emma asked after Carlos, but she could tell that the parents were listening and Cata couldn't really talk.

New Year's Eve was a big show in Oakland again, triple billed with the Grateful Dead and Jefferson Starship. Backstage was like a carnival, with Wavy Gravy entertaining the kids in between introducing the bands. The stadium was packed and the energy celebratory, yet the audience never felt volatile.

...

Bill came back up in January to start working on the new album, and settled into the cabin. Emma had written a lot of lyrics covering a diverse range of subjects, from love songs, to environmental sagas and political denunciations, to Sci Fi, to straight-out rockers. Bill said he needed time to sort through the material, to try to get a sense of the structure of the album.

Emma was adamant that she wanted one of the songs about El Salvador to go on the album. Juan protested at first, but it was a half-hearted protest. Emma felt his ambivalence and zeroed in on it. "Don't you think it would be good for your family and all those jaded cousins of yours to get a glimpse of what they look like to outsiders?"

Juan gave in with a shrug. "You're probably right. Your artistic instincts are invariably good. Go for it."

Do You Know

Took a little trip down south of the border
All the way to Salvador
Where a few people dine with the finest wine
And all the rest eat off the floor
But who am I to criticize
Who am I to cast the first stone
The people in power are our allies
Oh yeah, we train them here at home

(And) What's going on down south of the border
Tell me somebody, do you know
How did it get to be *(chorus)*
That what they reap, we sow
It's been keeping me awake at night
I can't play it any way to make it come out right
The truth is I don't understand
Why their blood is on my hands

They tell us if we let one country fall
Over the next one goes
We're gonna need a Berlin wall
To hold back the dominoes
We've gotta keep the peasants down

Gotta lay them in the ground
It's the way we save a nation
From Communist domination
(Repeat chorus—But what's going on...)

Bill listened to the song intently. "I don't think the song will fit with the rest of the material. It's going to come from out of nowhere, Emma. People won't have the slightest idea what it's about."

Emma put her hands on her hips in an aggressive stance. "Well, maybe they'll get curious then. You must have talked to Carlos and Cata. We're training and funding the military down there—those fuckers who are making war on their own citizens! Don't you think people should know that? I didn't know. That's how those bastards get away with that shit."

Bill put his hand on her shoulder. "Save the lecture, Emma; I'm on your side, remember? Okay, fine. We'll fit it in somehow. Maybe between *Latin Eyes* and *Yours For the Asking*."

Bill and Juan had finally developed a relationship bordering on friendship, and their new level of ease with each other was evident in the writing and recording of the album. Emma knew that Juan was grateful to Bill for all the help he'd given Cata and Carlos, and he expressed respect many times for the professionalism that Bill had always shown. The two men even seemed to be able to fashion songs without stepping on each other's egos now. Emma's newfound contentment was evident in the lyrics she was continually scratching out.

I've been so many places, seen so many faces
And you know they all leave traces, on your sanity
But this time around
I'm gonna take care of the love I've found
No more beating it into the ground
Hear what I say
Love is here to stay

This time around.

The recording was rolling along by the end of January, had gathered steam by February, and was ready for mixing by the end of March. Working in Sausalito made it possible for Emma to keep nursing Lena a few times a day. Every night, Juan read Lena a story and Emma nursed her before Trish took her home and put her to bed. The toddler had a small cot by Emma's side of the bed, and that's where she'd be when they got home from the studio around two a.m. Trish would be asleep in their bed, her hand hanging over the side, on Lena's tiny back. Juan would wake Trish, careful not to wake Lena, who was sleeping through the night now, and Trish would retire to her own room down the hall.

Juan and Emma had become accustomed to being awakened at daybreak by Lena bouncing onto their bed and snuggling down between them, then patting their faces and pulling on their hair until she had their attention. They delighted in the sound of her voice, the scent of her baby breath on their faces, her little hands rousing them from sleep. Emma would nurse her, and they would play games until Trish came to get her at seven. Exhausted, they would fall back to sleep until noon.

"*This Time Around*" was finished mid-April, with the release date set for mid-June. The band was scheduled for a tour June 15th through September 5th, so May was their only stretch of time for a getaway. Emma wanted to go back to Hana and show off the baby, and Juan was game. He reminded her that he, too, had history there now. The Hana Resort was already booked, but Margie found them a beautiful house for rent, overlooking Hana Bay. It was a perfect arrangement. The owners of the house had children, so the home already had everything they needed, including a crib in the giant bedroom and safety gates installed at the stairs.

…

Juan and Emma sipped Pina Coladas on the balcony overlooking the bay, and watched the sun set. “We’re back in paradise,” Emma murmured.

“Pair-a-dice,” said Lena, who was seated on Juan’s lap.

Chapter Nineteen

Emma, 1978—The Dark Planet

Hawaii was an escape from all responsibilities, except the one little awesome responsibility we called "the boss." Yeah, we had Trish with us, but Juan and I spent all our time with Lena. She was starting to make these short, funny sentences, and she'd repeat anything she heard. It was a real wake-up call though when I started hearing my own vocabulary coming back at me out of her sweet, little mouth. I decided to try cleaning up my language, Lenny Bruce or not. Evidently I was a little too late. We were hanging out on the beach one day, and as I leaned over Lena to hand a sandwich to Juan, I dropped it in the sand. "Oh…dear," I said, fumbling for words. "Oh my, I can't believe I did that. Oh fu…for goodness sake."

"Mama," Lena said in her innocent little voice, "you should say *fuck*."

Juan and I tried our best not to laugh, tried to look strict and disapproving, but Jesus, it was funny.

I was busted, big-time. I started trying harder after that. You know, it's one thing to make a conscious decision to use language that is generally unacceptable to a lot of people, but it's another thing entirely to hear it coming out of your baby's mouth. I wanted her to have the control over language that I used to have, wanted her to have control over a lot of areas where I lacked self-control. It's like that—you don't even know it's happening, but you find yourself wanting things to be less fucked-up for your kid than they were for you. Not that all that much was fucked-up for me—but it was the close calls that worried me for Lena. I couldn't imagine her shooting-up some day, endangering her life like that. I couldn't imagine a Rob fucking her at age thirteen.

It's weird, because as happy as I was on that holiday in Hawaii (and I still can't use the word *vacation* because Carol hated it so much), all these weird fears were creeping in. Maybe I was so happy, I thought if I didn't worry, I would somehow jinx it. I had one hell-of-a nightmare toward the end of our stay there, too.

The dream started out with Juan and me and Lena walking in a meadow on Mt. Tamalpais. Juan was holding Lena and the sun was bright, high in the sky, like at noon. We came to a cliff where there were stairs carved into the mountainside, going down. We stepped onto the first stair, and suddenly it was dark, and we were in a building. I couldn't see Juan or Lena, and I realized that I was actually in an elevator that was dropping fast, out of control. As my eyes adjusted to the darkness, I saw that Rob was the elevator man. His eyes glinted evil, and he said, "How low do you want to go, Emmy?" I was terrified, but I knew I had to act nice and not let him see my fear. I had to pretend to like him so he wouldn't hurt me—so I could plan my getaway. I started singing, trying to lull him into thinking I was relaxed and happy.

Then the elevator started filling with water and I was alone, treading water, thinking maybe I could escape through a hatch at the top of the elevator when the water had risen high enough. Now I was singing to keep myself from getting freaked out. As the water enveloped me, I woke up gasping for air, and realized that it was a dream, that I must have fallen asleep in the meadow. Juan and Lena were playing by a stream in bright sunlight. Then I realized I hadn't escaped—that I was still in the dream, taking an afternoon nap in our bed beside Juan and Lena.

I woke up still again in the dream, and at just that moment, through our bay window I saw a dark planet come soaring across the sky, so large it blotted out the sun. Linda, my astrologer friend, walked in through a shimmering, blue doorway and I called to her, "Is it Saturn? Is it Saturn?" She gave me a chilling, enigmatic smile, then turned and walked back through the doorway.

And then the dark planet turned into a black hole, and started sucking everything toward it. Juan was lifted up out of bed and his body flew toward the doorway in a giant arc. I jumped out of bed, ran to the doorway, and blocked it with my body—arms and legs outstretched. But it was no use—the pull from the planet was too strong, and I was picked up and flung back out into the meadow, where I watched helplessly as Juan was pulled into the black hole.

I was crying, and Lena was splashing my face with water from the stream, stroking my hair.

I woke to find Lena staring into my eyes playfully, stroking my hair, as I often do hers. I looked around, grateful to see Juan just lying there asleep.

"Jesus," I muttered, "What a dream."

"Je-sus, Je-sus," Lena repeated.

The dream stayed with me for days, like a persistent, extra beat of the heart, a flutter in the stomach, a glimpse of the old shadow figure. I didn't want to tell Juan about it—it was just too goddamn freaky. But I talked to Margie about it one night after dinner at the resort, asked her what she thought it might mean.

"Maybe it's me, Emma," Margie said. "Maybe I'm the dark planet. I'm big, eh?"

"It's not funny, Margie. I'm being serious here."

"So am I. I think maybe you got some premonition, Emma. Some kinda psychic thing, cause I didn't want to tell you, but now I think I got to. The cancer, it came back. There's no beating some kinds of things…I'm sorry little *haole*…don't cry now…see, I'm that black planet sucking out your happiness."

"Oh God, I'm such a self-centered jerk. Don't you dare feel sorry for me. Jesus, Margie, I'm sorry—making such a huge big deal out of a dream. Of course you're not a dark planet. You're the sun, you're the scent of flowers in the wind; I love you. How bad is it? Are you going to have to lose your hair again?"

"No chemo this time. No use. It spread too much. You gotta say goodbye to me when you go back to the mainland this time. I'll say *aloha* to my father for you, eh?"

Margie's cancer was a new solar blackout, another eclipse. I knew that it wasn't what the dream was about, but it put my nameless fears on the back burner. I sat out there at the Hana Resort's *luau* watching Margie teach Lena the hula, her great body shimmering in the torchlight, Lena's tiny body moving in her shadow, and I felt like I was watching the whole drama of life undulating in that dance.

Sonny came over and slid down beside Juan and me. "So, she told you, Emma, hey? I can see it in your face," he said, in response to my quizzical look. "Did you tell Juan?"

"Yes, she did," Juan said. "We are both so sorry…if there is anything we can do…"

"How long does she have?" I asked.

"Well, the doctor, he said maybe six months, but that was two months ago, so I don't know. She gets tired a lot now, but she don't seem so sick as she did with that chemo shit they gave her last time."

"I had no idea." I fumbled for words. "I mean, I noticed she's lost some weight, but I assumed she'd gone on a diet. I feel terrible. I don't know what to do or what to say to her."

"Hey Emma, just act regular. She don't want nobody moping around all sad. She told me she's gonna live till she dies."

So I got up and joined Margie and Lena and the small cluster of tourists who were each dancing their own versions of the hula, which varied according to their skill levels, how much they'd had to drink, age, weight, and general degree of self-consciousness. It didn't matter how you looked—unless you were doing a mating dance version, which some of the honeymooners were, actually. What mattered was how much of yourself you were willing to put into the dance, how much you would give to the spirits. I felt pangs of guilt remembering how Margie had consoled me through so much of my self-inflicted bullshit, had given so much of her vitality to me freely, and how I had accepted her gifts as though they were limitless. And now this lethal cancer was silently stripping her of her life—and there she was, still dancing.

I was grateful that I was able to say goodbye to Margie, but angry that I had to. It's just absolute shit that we're designed to give out. If I were in charge of the universe, I'd set it up so that people could live in earthly bodies as long as they want and then move on to another planet or dimension or something when they're sick of being here. I was pissed off at God, at the universe, at the randomness of illnesses, and accidents, and murders, and deaths from hunger. I was just pissed off—like a helpless child. But at some point during the flight home, high over the Pacific, Lena climbed into my lap and said, "Don't be sad, Mama." And I realized then that what I really was, was sad.

•••

We had two weeks to rehearse before going out for the whole summer. That shouldn't have been any problem at all. We were a pretty tight ass band at that point, but it didn't work out like that. Stuart, our drummer, didn't show up first day of rehearsals. We all sat around waiting for him for hours, with Daryl trying to reach him by phone. It was a wasted day, work-wise, and we still hadn't heard from Stuart that night. The next day he shuffled in trying to look cool, like nothing had happened.

"Nice of you to show up," I said.

"Whatsa matter, baby?" Stuart slurred. "Why you gotta be so cold? I had my days mixed up, tha's all. You never make a mistake?"

"No man, never made a mistake in my life. Ask anybody. Let's get to work."

We could all tell he was high as a kite, rushing on heroin; it was obvious in his timing. He kept speeding up, then overcompensating by dragging. I was freaked because I didn't think I could be in a band with someone using, and I felt like a hypocrite for feeling that way. But it comes down to survival. Weak, yeah, but the tug was still there. Just like cigarettes. I made the guys who smoked sit outside for their drug—couldn't stand the smell now. When you've been addicted to a drug, you have to do this steely mental change. You can't be halfway about it, or you'll be back to using.

What it came down to was that I had to get a new drummer, immediately. There was no time to wait for Stuart to clean up. Our first gig was twelve days away. All the great Bay Area drummers were already committed to other bands, so I put in a call to Bill. Of course, he knew just the right person, a session guy from England who had married an American and wanted to move up to San Francisco anyway.

"He'll pick your stuff up right away, Emma; he's top of the line," Bill told me. "This is going to be tough on Stuart's family. Why do people do it? I don't get it. Life is hard enough without shooting yourself in the foot for good measure."

"You're asking *me*?"

"Listen sweetheart, I heard about your friend, Margie, in Hawaii. That's a bad cancer; I'm sorry."

I had Ed call Stuart—just couldn't bear to even talk to him in the state he was in. I'd been through enough of it in my life, and on a certain level, I guess I was afraid I'd let him talk me out of firing him.

Bill's friend, David Wells, was already learning the material by the time the rest of the band showed up at four the next day. He'd taken an early flight up—was definitely enthused about getting the job. Juan and I'd decided to put him up in our cabin so he'd be close by. He seemed like a sweet dude—about twenty-two, very capable, good sense of humor, and willing to work into the wee hours. Cute, too, in that angular, ultra-skinny-but-strong, good haircut, British sort of way.

His wife was another story. Jeanie joined David about three weeks into the tour, in New Orleans. I recognized her from the L.A. scene. She had been a groupie, big time, and after a few days of watching her in action with the guys in the band, it appeared she still was. Turned out that David had married her for his green card, and he didn't care who she fucked. Which was fine, but Daryl's wife was definitely not going to be happy if word got back to her about the goings on.

I was really pissed off at Daryl for fucking Jeanie, and if you think about it, I had my nerve. I mean, my habits before I met Juan would probably have made Jeanie's escapades pale by comparison. But things had changed at that point; we had achieved a sort of stability within the band, and Daryl's wife was coming out to meet us in Florida in just a few days. I suppose empathy had kicked in, too, now that I was married and could relate to "the wife." Plus, she was coming on to Juan whenever she thought I wouldn't notice, even using Lena as a ruse. Juan would be sitting backstage with Lena in his lap, and Jeanie would be leaning over him low, oohing and ahhing over the baby, with her tits falling in Juan's face. I don't think I was jealous, because Juan wasn't in the slightest bit attracted to her, but it was an insult, a disrespect for our relationship, a deliberate rudeness to me.

After the show in Miami, Daryl's wife and kids were hanging out backstage in the hospitality room, and Jeanie came barging into the dressing room—tried to talk Daryl into meeting her later down at the hotel bar. She came out with this shit right there in front of us all, and that did it for me. I blew up—told her I wanted her on the morning plane back to L.A. I told David that if he didn't like it, he could leave too. He seemed surprised that I was so pissed off. I guess my reputation had preceded me, and he had no idea how straight I'd become. All that shit they print about you here in the States is a hundred times worse in England. Their newspapers thrive on sensationalist crap.

Jeanie was history by the next day, but Daryl's marriage had gone on the rocks. I think his old lady sensed that something had happened. It's not like all the guys in the band had always been saints or anything, but Jeanie had just brought it too close to family.

Margie died September 2nd. Another fucking September death. Stephanie had called Ed and asked him to come tell me in person. I was expecting it, you know, but it still made me feel like I was drowning. Ed was cool, but I wanted to be alone to think about it. It felt synchronistic that we were in Hartford, and Carol's last name had been Hartwell, and thinking about Margie and Carol was heartbreaking—but also good for the heart. Just that they had both existed brought love raging up to the surface of my profound sadness, buoyed me, made me long to feel Carolina's little arms around my neck. She was downstairs in the hotel pool with Juan, and I roused myself to go down and tell Juan what had happened, to take the comfort they both offered. The news was a blow to Juan, too. They were going to hold the funeral for her the following week, which meant there was no way we could attend. You can't cancel a show unless you're at death's door yourself. We sent flowers and a note for Sonny to read at the ceremony on our behalf.

...

We were home for Lena's second birthday—rounded up some kids to go with the adults, hired a pony cart, and had a big party.

November, we were back on the road, touring all the way through the end of January. We would be playing Puerto Rico, with a week off in the Caribbean for the band to have a holiday, including their families or girlfriends. It went without saying that Jeanie was not invited, and David was cool about it. Daryl and his wife were trying to patch things up, so the last thing any of us needed was for Jeanie to show up. The album had topped the charts, and the shows were selling out, so I could easily afford to pick up the tab for the whole entourage, including the crew's families, too.

Linda came to the gig in Ft. Lauderdale. I had left comps and passes for her and a bunch of her friends at the door, and she swept in backstage like a Palm Beach guru with a flock of her devotees. Hey, it was Linda; she'd found her calling. Of course she had some fancy, decorated chart for Lena, explaining the sum total of her whole life scientifically, according to the stars and planets. What if Lena had been born in England, or Africa, would she be a different person? She'd still have the same genetic map—but different stars in ascendance or whatever would alter the course of her life? Right.

Well fuck it; in spite of her pomp and all the hippie hype of her astrology, I was happy to see her. Anyway, who was I to criticize hype. We all went back to the hotel, and everybody hung out at the bar while I put Lena down for the night, and then left Trish watching her. Juan and I joined Linda and a few friends for a late night supper. Linda sat next to me and leaned in close.

"How are things with you and Juan?" she asked in a conspiratorial tone.

"He beats me on a regular basis, but apart from that, we're okay. What the fuck, Linda; what's wrong now?"

"It's not that anything is wrong; that's not how it works. You look at a chart for direction, for advice. It's a warning, not a prediction. We have free will. I'm not an imbecile, Emma. I've helped a lot of people."

"Oh God, lighten up. I respect you; Jesus. Just tell me what it is. I can't read your charts, but I can read your face. What do you see? Just tell me for Christ sake…Let's get some champagne."

Linda tapped a chart with one fingertip. "See this cluster of planets that's transiting your seventh house? This transit of Saturn could mean big changes in your relationship. This aspect over here could mean separation…or worse."

"Separation from who? You mean Juan and me splitting up? You've got to be kidding."

"No, I didn't say it was definitely Juan, although it could be. Is there anybody else really important to you who could possibly be in danger at this time?"

"Jesus, Linda, actually there is. Juan's sister—she's mixed up in some heavy shit in El Salvador. It's too complicated to explain. So, why are you telling me this? What am I supposed to do?"

"Be cautious, Emma. Don't do anything until the end of this transit. Don't make any decisions of consequence during this period."

"You're freaking me out now. What period? How can my decisions affect Cata?"

"Is Cata the sister?"

"Yes."

"You should warn her not to make any changes until the cycle is over, probably not until July, or maybe August."

I was buying into her stuff again, and I don't even believe in it. It's the guru syndrome, imported from California, embraced by Florida, beloved by all who think we can direct the course of our lives by following a few tips from a fortuneteller. It's nothing less than believing in magic; but the truth is, she had me going for it.

"But how do you even know it's about her?" I said. "What if it's about me? What if I'm going to get hit by a truck, or fall off a stage, or something? It's hard to take this stuff seriously. It's just so general. Come on, admit it."

"Well, it's not you—see, you're the one experiencing the loss here, Saturn over your natal position, you can see it right here." Linda pointed to some squiggles.

"Wait a minute, I bet I know what this is about." In spite of myself, I felt relief. "My good friend, Margie, died recently."

Linda shook her head. "I don't think so, Emma. This is serious, honestly. Everyone close to you should lay low for the next six months. You better contact your sister-in-law."

"That was fun," I said, topping off Linda's glass of champagne, raising my glass and my voice. "Let's have a toast. To transits, and teachers, and treacherous treasons…while we think up some reasons…for paranoid seasons," I said triumphantly, clicking my glass with Linda's and everyone else's at the table.

"Very funny, Emma," Linda said, still looking dead serious.

"I liked it." Juan slid in beside me, putting a little distance between Linda and me. He could feel when I needed bailing. We had that with each other. Then again, my silly toast hadn't exactly been subtle.

Linda had managed to put me on a bummer. For the next few days, I couldn't shake a sense of dread. I finally snapped out of it by reminding myself that when something terrible actually had happened, Carol's death, for instance, I hadn't felt any kind of premonition or anything. I had, in fact, been totally oblivious. I did insist that we put in a call to Juan's family though. Asked Cata if she wanted to join us in Puerto Rico, or the Virgin Islands. She said she didn't want to leave her family at Christmas, but I knew that who she really didn't want to leave was Carlos.

Puerto Rico was a weird trip—all those barbed wire fences surrounding the hotel's stretch of beach, armed security guards everywhere you looked. I thought, *Jesus, if they're that paranoid, maybe we should be, too.* It made it hard to enjoy the place. Plus, the gig itself had a Las Vegas sort of feel—like there were gangsters running the show. We were happy to leave that place, even though the weather was so bad we were all crossing ourselves and muttering prayers on the flight out of there to St. Thomas.

We landed in what seemed like a hurricane, but was evidently nothing out of the ordinary for the small airline. A fleet of Mercedes taxis met us at the airport, and drove us across the island, where we boarded a ferry to St. John. It was the first time any of us had been there, but Bill had sworn by the place, so we'd booked a week at the one resort hotel on the island. Mother Nature settled down after our first night there. We woke up in the morning to a gleaming, white sand beach, emerald water, and blue sky that stretched to the ends of the earth.

Juan had taught Lena to swim in the hotel swimming pools, so she had no fear of the ocean, and anyway, the Caribbean was like a big bathtub in the sheltered cove of the resort. We played in the water together everyday. Lena even learned to snorkel. I'd soak up the sun while Juan built castles in the sand with Lena. She had Juan's thick, dark hair, but the texture was like mine, fine and curly. Her eyes were mine, too, bright blue, but ringed with Juan's super-dark lashes. And her skin was the same luscious, permanently tanned color as Juan's. Of course I thought she was the most beautiful creature on this planet, but best of all, she was smart like Juan. We doted on her shamelessly, but honestly, she was really a nice kid, too. I guess everybody thinks that about their own children, or at least they should.

Ed had arranged a big Christmas banquet for the band in a private dining room at the resort, complete with a palm tree decorated in tinsel. It was good for the band to have that time to just hang out together.

Ray and Stephanie joined us for the New Year's Eve show in New York, where we were headlining a huge venue. We ended the tour at the Oakland Coliseum, late January.

...

Rainy weather or not, we were happy to be home. Lena ran from room to room, re-discovering her favorite spots, finding her old toys, reveling in the freedom of all that space after being confined to hotel suites for so long. We had a few gigs in the Pacific Northwest in February, but we would be home until the middle of March, when we'd be going to Japan.

Every once in a while I'd hear some disturbing rumblings from dark corners—when I'd be thinking of Linda's dire warnings about this particular period of time—or remembering the Saturn dream. I told myself the disquiet probably had to do with going back to Japan, too—memories of getting Carol busted, and the fall-out that ultimately led to her death. But mostly, I was pretty fucking cheery, involved with my two-year old, digging my old man, framing pictures of them and the rest of the family and hanging their faces all over the house.

The flight to Japan with a two-year old was a harrowing experience. Forget what I said about her being a nice kid. Right at the beginning of the million-hour flight, she turned into Mr. Hyde before our eyes. First of all, she wanted to run up and down the aisles when she was supposed to be strapped in for take-off. Then she screamed bloody murder because her ears hurt. Just when we got her calmed down, the fasten seat belt sign came back on, the plane started bobbing all over the place, and Lena decided that there was no way in hell she was going to be strapped back in—and she let the whole plane know it.

Juan and I both resorted to begging her for just a glimpse of the humanity we remembered her possessing, but it was to no avail. She had the word "no" down big-time, and she wasn't afraid to use it. Talk about a humbling experience—Juan and I were hunched down in our seats, pleading with our daughter to please keep her seat belt on for a few more minutes. Under pressure, we broke every rule in the book within a few minutes. We bribed her with candy, threatened her with physical force, cajoled her till we were blue in the face. You could just see everybody thinking what a spoiled brat she was.

Then, as suddenly as the demonic possession had occurred, it was over. The seat belt light went out, and Lena picked up the crayons she had held in such disdain a moment before—started creating colorful modern art pictures that some people might mistake for scribbling. The stewardess came by, offered her a soda, and you'd have thought she was competing for best-mannered kid in the world.

"Yes, please," she said to the stewardess, flashing her a wide smile that erased the last forty minutes of her behavior.

She's like I used to be, I suddenly realized.

Trying to acclimate a toddler to such a drastic time change proved impossible. Thank God for Trish! I had a hard time, too. My sleep was restless, disturbed. The gigs were great though, with audiences who knew my lyrics and had obviously thought about them, even if they couldn't quite pronounce the words. The press was intellectual and respectful, too.

We may have been on the other side of the world, but we weren't hard to reach. Band families were always given detailed itineraries. About half way through the Japan tour, we got a phone call backstage. It was Stephanie.

"Emma, baby. How are things going?"

"What's wrong, Mom? I can hear it in your voice—something's wrong. Is Ray okay?"

"Ray's fine. It's not that. Ricky called me. His parents are freaking out."

"What are you saying, Stephanie? What do you mean they're freaking out? What's wrong? Oh God, is Cata alright?"

"Cata's disappeared."

I felt like I was back in the Saturn nightmare, but I tried to stay calm. "How long has she been gone? What about Ricky? Does he have any idea where she might be?"

"I don't know; he didn't tell me much—just that she's been gone over a week, and their parents are really worried."

Stephanie sounded like she was on the verge of tears. "Okay, don't worry, Mom. I'm sure she's fine. She probably ran off with Carlos."

"I hope so. Naturally, Ricky wants you to call him—doesn't matter what time."

Juan was beside me now. He'd heard the last part of the conversation and his face had turned grey. "Is it Cata?"

I nodded.

"Is she alright?"

"She's missing. We've got to call Ricky."

Juan was already dialing Ricky's number. "I knew Carlos was going to get her in trouble," he hissed in my direction. Then he focused on the call. "Ricky! Yes, I'm calling from Japan. Lena's fine. We're fine. What's happened to Cata?"

I went into a small room where there was an extension phone, and picked it up. "I'm here, too, Ricky."

"Okay, so tell us both, from the beginning," Juan said.

"Cata and our parents got into another big fight. They locked her in her room, but she sneaked out and went to a student demonstration—and they found out."

"How did they find out?" Juan asked.

"Uncle Fernando showed them photos of her amidst the protestors. And she didn't come back from that rally. Mama said all her clothes are still in her closet."

I spoke up. "This is not good. Women don't leave their clothes behind."

"She's alright, Emma," Ricky said.

I was trembling so hard, the phone was vibrating against my ear. "How do you know she's alright? Wasn't your cousin killed at one of those rallies?"

"Emma's right," Juan said. "Leaving her clothes behind is not a good sign."

Ricky's voice became conspiratorial. "Cata is with the *guerrillas*, in the mountains outside San Salvador. Don't ask me how I know, just take my word for it. I can't tell you…"

I interrupted him. "Just take your word for it? Jesus, Ricky!"

Juan spoke up. "Tell us what you know. These lines couldn't possibly be tapped. How *do* you know she's okay?"

"I talked to somebody a few days ago—a friend of Cata and Carlos. She's in a safe house high in the mountains; I'm not sure exactly where, but she's with Carlos and some friends. She's fine. My sources say there's no military action in that area."

"I understand what you're saying," Juan said. "But after Ramon, it worries me."

"It's a completely different situation. Ramon was at a demonstration. She's in a remote location. And, it's temporary; she'll go back home soon."

"How do you know that?" I asked Ricky. "What if your uncle finds out where she is or something? This is freaking me out."

"Emma's right." I could hear Juan doing his deep breathing—obviously, he was as stressed as me, but his voice was calm. "Cata could be in danger, even as we speak."

"No, she's in a secure place. Trust me. I wouldn't worry about it, man, or you either, Emma. It's our parents who are flipping out. They think she might have been kidnapped, or *disappeared.* Obviously, I can't tell them what I know. You better call them, Juan; but don't tell them what I told you, of course. Just assure them that it's a matter of the heart, and she'll be back."

"When?" I wanted to know. "When will she be back?"

"How long do you think Cata can get by without all her make-up and clothes and records? She'll go home soon. Tell her, *hermano*. You both need to chill out—it'll be okay. I send my love, and kisses to Carolina."

The call to his parents was decidedly less reassuring. As I listened in, *Doña* Margarita got on the phone and insisted that Juan come home immediately. She was so hysterical that even Mr. Juan Rational himself couldn't get through to her. Listening to him trying to calm his mother down, I was reminded of the way he'd tried to tell me he didn't want to be in close contact with his family. I could see now it wasn't because he didn't care about them. It was because he cared so much about them that in spite of all his intellectual insights about the "family dynamic", he was still an emotional basket case in the hands of his mother.

I couldn't believe that Carlos had led Cata down such a dangerous road, but at the same time, I understood. Juan ended the phone conversation talking to his father, assuring him that he'd help out in any way he could as soon as the tour was over.

We had to do a gig right after that phone call. It was surreal because, you know, the show must go on and all that; but Juan and I were totally blown away. On the other hand, it was the best thing we could be doing because it kept our minds off the situation, and we were absolutely, fucking powerless to do anything about it anyway. At least we had Ricky's confident reassurance that no harm had befallen Cata.

Over the next couple of weeks, we did everything we could with our limited resources to try to track her down. I called Bill—thought he might have an address on Carlos or something. He did, in fact, but who were we supposed to give it to? Not Juan's parents, that's for sure. And Ricky was in school on the East Coast, so he couldn't do anything about it. Juan called some of his old friends from *Las Sombras* to try and get some information from them about the situation in El Salvador. Dead end—they didn't know as much as Ricky did. Basically, we just had to sit on the situation until we got back home. I felt sure that by then we'd have come up with a strategy for enticing Cata to come live with us again.

•••

We got home to lovely spring weather—wild flowers blooming all over Mt. Tam. Our roomy house was splashed in sunlight, brighter even than during the summer when the fog often rolls in. We were all exhausted from the long trip and the time change, so we were lying low for a few days. It was a Friday, in the middle of a glorious afternoon, when Juan's parents called. I listened to Juan talking up a storm in Spanish, feeling impatient with myself that I hadn't learned the language.

The moment he hung up, I was in his face. "So, what's the story?"

"It's not good." He sounded grim. "My parents are convinced that a major Communist offensive will be launched this summer in Nicaragua—and it's already causing trouble in El Salvador. My uncle, General Estrada, is a powerful man, and he has warned my mother that his troops are going to sweep the mountainside—he says that he cannot protect Cata if she's with the *companeros*. Do you understand?"

"Jesus, Juan, of course I understand. We've got to get her out of there. We'll think of something, baby. Come lie down and let me rub your neck."

Juan lit a joint, took a couple of hits, then passed it to me.

"No," I said. "I want to give you a real massage, and then you can relax me."

We made love lazily that afternoon, as though we had all the time in the world to touch each other. Eventually, Trish knocked on our door, asked us if Lena could come in. Lena came bounding into the room, took a leap and landed right dead center between us. It felt like completion, the last part of the puzzle. We had brought her into this world and she belonged here with us, at the center of our lives.

Another call came through from Ricky in the evening.

I couldn't understand Juan's rapid-fire Spanish, but I felt a chill as he hung up the phone.

"I'm going to have to go home and find Cata, *reina*. There is no other solution." Juan's face was grave. "Ricky can't leave school this close to the end of the semester; he offered to, but it would mean the whole semester would have been in vain. My parents are worried sick. They can't even get messages through to her because they're perceived as the enemy. Apparently the situation is worse than we thought. I have an address for Carlos and some phone numbers he gave Bill. I think I could find her in a day or two. But I don't know how much good it will do. You know how willful Cata is."

"I'll go with you," I said. "I can convince her to come back with us. She listens to me. We could offer to put Carlos through medical school at some good university here. We could use the argument that he can serve his people better if he trains here, maybe at UCSF. Cata could go to SF State. They could get married."

Juan said nothing, so I tried again. "It'll work out, baby. We'll take Lena. Your parents will chill out about everything when they see her. Trish can come with us, too."

Juan turned around abruptly, and folded me into his arms. I could feel him trembling, fighting to regain control. Finally, he broke from the embrace and led me over to the sofa. We sat down, and he took my hands in his.

"You're not understanding the situation, Emma. You can't come with me. Don't you understand that after the last album, my parents are furious with you? They feel that you have betrayed them, 'spit on their hospitality,' as my mother put it. Haven't you felt my mother's iciness when she calls?"

"What, because of *Do You Know*? I didn't think she understood English well enough to pick up on those lyrics."

"She doesn't, but her brother, the general, was educated at Yale. She gave him a copy of the album, and he understood every word. He told her what the song was saying. I should have given it more thought before letting you put a song like that on the album. I was careless, and arrogant to think that we were invulnerable."

"But baby, you liked the song. You said it would be good for your parents to see how the world regards them. Oh fuck, so they're really pissed off at me? Shit. I didn't mean it to be about them specifically…or maybe I did, I don't know. It was about the whole scene down there—Guatemala, too. What do you think they'd do if I showed up with you, holding Lena in my arms?"

"To begin with, I don't think you could get a visa. You're too high profile for the government to intimidate you, so they would probably deny you admission into the country instead. Besides, think about what it was like when Ramon was killed. It's worse now, and even if you could get in, they would follow us everywhere. It would make it impossible to find Cata."

"I don't think that's necessarily true. The song could work for us, too—with the other side."

"You're not coming with me, Emma." Juan's jaw was clenched. "I'll leave on Tuesday, and be home within a week, or possibly two weeks, depending on how fast I can get Cata out of there. I'll be home in plenty of time for your birthday." He tried to simulate a reassuring smile. "We'll have a big party for you to celebrate your last year in your twenties. Next year you'll be old, like your husband."

I argued with him about it all weekend—kept trying to convince him that my celebrity status might be a safety net for Cata and her friends. "It should be good for something," I said.

"We could even do a free concert while we're there."

"Emma, you're dreaming. Anyway, I'll be in and out of there before you two even know I'm gone," Juan said as he jumped into the pool, Lena on his back.

Our travel agent made all the arrangements, but I drove him to the airport. It was weird to have him be going somewhere without me, but I tried to be cool about it. I didn't want to freak Lena out. We parked in short-term parking and saw him off at the gate, hugging and kissing, and finally, waving bye-bye.

Juan called around nine that night. He's gotten there okay—no lost luggage or anything, but his family was in crisis, big-time. Marta had met him at the airport, but his parents had waited at home for him.

"They're angry at me, too, Emma. They don't say it in words, but I feel it in every word my mother utters. Marta told me they believe both you and I have been a bad influence on Cata."

"Don't let them get to you, baby," I said. "You did your best to get her to tow the line. Me, now that's another story. Why should they blame you anyway—it's not fair."

"It's complicated. As the eldest, they think I should have set a better example for my little sister. Yet our values are so far apart now that it's difficult to communicate about anything. But they do want me to take Cata to California, so the situation is salvageable. My parents are as they have always been. They haven't changed." He was totally down, but I could feel him shifting gears. "So how is my baby girl? What did you do after I left?"

"We went to the zoo, ate hot dogs and ice cream—hit rush hour on the way home. Oops, hold on, someone wants to talk to you."

I gave Lena the phone and listened to her chat happily about all the animals we saw at the zoo. "I love you too. Bye *Papi*," she said, and handed me the phone.

"I'm going to go to Carlos' house tomorrow," Juan told me. "His family should be able to put me in touch with him. Carlos would have told them they could trust me. I'll probably call you late tomorrow night, because if I have to meet Carlos and Cata in the mountains, I won't have access to a phone until I return to the city."

"Don't make it too late; I'll be worried. Jesus, Juan, what are we talking about here? You shouldn't go up any fucking mountains; he should be coming to you—after all we've done for him."

"Don't worry *reina*. I'm sure Carlos will do what he can to find a convenient meeting place."

Juan called again on Wednesday night. As it turned out, he was having a harder time connecting with Carlos and Cata than he'd anticipated, and all hell had broken loose in San Salvador that day. A crowd of people were protesting something outside a cathedral, and soldiers moved in and killed a bunch of them. Not only that, but Juan said the bodies were left lying there for everybody to see—women, kids, all of them shot as they were trying to run into the church. Jesus, fucking El Salvador.

He reassured me that Cata definitely wasn't in the demonstration, or he'd have known it by now; but I could tell he was worried. With all the crazy shit going on there, it would be at least another day before he would be able to get any information. Finally, a meeting was scheduled for Saturday, there in the central marketplace of San Salvador where we'd walked around together. I was just enormously relieved that he wasn't going to have to go up to some *guerrilla* hiding place in some fucking mountain. When I talked to him on Friday night, he seemed relieved about it, too.

"I'll probably be home next week." He sounded like he was bone-weary, but trying to put on an optimistic front. "It's heavy here right now. I intend to find Cata and bring her back with me, the sooner, the better. I cannot tolerate this barbarism." He paused, and I could hear him sigh deeply. "At least twenty people were killed and more were wounded on Wednesday. There was blood running down the stairs of the *Metropolitan Cathedral*, Emma. And I can't talk to my parents about it. They say the communists are to blame—and they don't accept any responsibility for the situation." He paused again, then asked, "Will you put Lena on? I need to hear her voice."

"She's already asleep, baby."

"Give her a kiss for me then." He sounded disappointed. "I miss you and love you more than you can know, *corazon*."

Juan didn't call Saturday night, or Sunday. By Monday, I couldn't take it anymore. I picked up the phone and called El Salvador. *Doña* Margarita answered.

"Juan is not here in our house," *Doña* Margarita said. "We think he will find Catarina. Maybe this is not so easy achievement. He will call you when he returns. How is Carolina Rosa? She is a happy child?"

Well, that conversation went nowhere; so I called Ricky. No luck. I tried to take comfort in what I thought *Doña* Margarita had said. Maybe Juan met with someone who took him up in the mountains to meet with Carlos and Cata. He probably couldn't call me because there were no phones, or because of security.

This is a good thing, I told myself. *This means he was successful in contacting them, and he's probably persuaded them to wrap things up and come back with him.* But the more I thought about it, the more holes I found in my own reasoning. It wasn't like Carlos could just say 'Okay Juan, let's go," or anything. He was probably up the creek because of Cata's involvement with him. Jesus, it was hard to wait, not knowing. But then again, we had gotten Carlos out before and it had taken some time.

Cata called me Tuesday morning. Trish came and woke me up for the phone call. For a second, I thought it might be Juan. I took the call out in the hall, so as not to wake Lena. Cata's voice was hushed, as though she thought we were being listened in on. Juan hadn't shown up for his appointment with her friends on Saturday, and she was worried—wanted to know if I'd heard from him.

I heard her voice through a ringing in my head, through a sudden knot in my stomach. I fought to find some reason why this wasn't what it was, some explanation that would mean the ground had not just exploded under me, that I wasn't starting to swallow dirt—some reason to believe that the black hole had not claimed Juan.

"Emma, I can't talk long. Are you there? Tell me you've heard from him."

"No." That was all I could choke out. It closed in on me—that "no" took possession of me, threw me into a dark room with doors all around me, each one a possibility of hope, a logical explanation—each one closed, locked, padlocked, massive chains around it. "No."

"Emma, he has probably been taken by the National Guard. Don't panic; Uncle Fernando won't let them hurt him. We'll find him." She was crying, I could hear it in her voice. "I love you. Have to go. I'll call again as soon as I have information. Love you, kisses to Lena."

The dial tone was a monotonous ringing, like the buzzing sound in my head. I stared at the phone as if it were a foreign object. I didn't know what to do with it.

Trish took the phone out of my hand. She must have known from looking at me that it wasn't good news.

"Sit down, Emma. Here, let me get you a cup of coffee."

She disappeared, and I sat there in a vacuum, listening to the buzzing in my head. Then she was back, and thrusting a cup of coffee in my hand.

"I laced this with Irish Whiskey. You need something." Her voice came from a vast distance. "And I called Ray and Stephanie. Now, please tell me what's happened. Is Juan with Cata?"

I shook my head 'no', and I could see by the look on her face that she got it.

"Emma, call Ricky. He may know something. Do you want me to do it? Stephanie is on her way over."

She tried to hug me, but I shrugged her off. I went into the living room and curled up on the couch. I wanted to think, to figure out what to do, how to unlock those doors, but the ringing in my head was too loud, and it was too dark. Dark and freezing, like the distance between stars.

Suddenly, Stephanie was there. She came bursting into the room, pried apart the darkness and shattered my isolation. "Tell me what's happening, Emma. Right now! We've got to take action. Pull yourself together. Lena could wake up any minute. I have to know what's going on. Tell me now."

Lena was the word that got my attention. I turned my gaze to Stephanie.

"What did Cata say, sweetheart?" she asked gently.

"He didn't show up for his meeting. Nobody knows where he is. He's been missing for days."

"This is not good, but it's not terrible. We need more information. Have you talked to Ricky or Marta?"

"No."

"I'm going to call them. Trish, do you know where Emma's phone book is?"

She tried Ricky first—still no sign of him. But she got through to Marta, who told her that she'd heard from Cata.

I reached for the phone. "Let me talk to her."

Marta had told her parents about Cata's call. She told them what Cata had said about Juan missing the arranged meeting. Now her parents were worried that he had been kidnapped by Leftists. Police were at the house.

I was shaking. "Was somebody going to tell me about this?"

"I did not want to worry you until we had more facts. I was waiting until I talk to Cata again. She will call some time today. I wait here for her call now."

Her tone was polite and caring, but it was also distant. Juan had been right—I had offended his family with that damn song.

"We better hang up then, if she could call at any time. I wouldn't want your line to be busy. You will call me as soon as you hear anything, won't you?"

"Yes Emma, I will call you as soon as I have more information. It is difficult for *Mamá* to talk to you because she is very upset, and she forgets English when she is upset. Kisses to Carolina; she is okay?"

"Yes, she's fine. Still sleeping. Kisses to Silvia and Oscar. Call me."

I hung up the phone, and then retreated back into the darkness to have another look at those doors. One of them could be a "Leftist Kidnapping." My mind darted past all the locked doors until I found the one that wasn't chained shut. If the Left had kidnapped him, they would want a ransom. He would be okay. It would just be about money. I could handle that easily.

The door creaked open a few inches. Maybe there was some hope. Cata would find out. But when?

Trish brought me another Irish coffee, and one for Stephanie, too. If there was any mercy that morning, it was that Lena slept in for a change. She didn't get up until after eleven, and then she came and cuddled up on my lap. That did it—I started to cry, but softly, hoping she wouldn't notice.

"What's wrong, Mama, you got a tummy ache?"

I stoked her soft curls. "No baby, everything's okay,"

Trish took Lena into the playroom to watch cartoons. Stephanie and I sat there quietly, just waiting. Eventually, Trish reappeared with omelets for Stephanie and me.

"I've put Lena down for a nap," she said. "You've got to eat to keep up your strength. I want you to eat this *now*."

But neither Stephanie nor I could touch the food. "A bottle of wine might go down easier," Stephanie said.

"Will you go into town and get me a carton of Sherman's," I asked Trish.

Stephanie looked worried. "Oh honey, I'd hate to see you get addicted to cigarettes again."

I gave her a look that shut her up immediately. Smoking was the least of my worries.

Afternoon wore into evening. No news. Bill called to see what was up. Stephanie talked to him briefly. And there were the usual number of calls from friends who had no idea anything out of the ordinary was going on. I let the machine pick up those calls. Trish took Lena for a walk in Muir Woods, and then out to dinner and a Disney movie. Around seven o'clock, Stephanie and I ate a salad. It was either eat or be too drunk to talk when someone finally called with news. Trish brought Lena home around eight-thirty. Still no word.

"Mama's sick," I told Lena. "Will you watch cartoons for a while and let Trish or Grandma put you to bed tonight? Please honey."

I could see it scared her to see me looking so freaked, but I couldn't help it. She wasn't buying that I was sick, either.

"What hurts, Mama?" she asked sweetly.

"My tooth," I lied, grabbing her and squeezing her to my body.

"Okay, I'll watch TV now," she said, but I could tell she didn't believe me.

Ricky called around ten. "I don't have classes on Monday. I was with a girlfriend all weekend and I went straight from there to my classes today, and then I went out with friends. I just listened to all the messages. Have you heard from Juan? Is there any news?"

"Your parents think he's been kidnapped by Leftists. Cata was looking into it. I haven't heard from her yet. Haven't you talked to any of the family today?"

"Emma, the Left wouldn't kidnap Juan. You two are well known to them. Cata has distributed your album, and *Do You Know* is a big hit among the *guerrillas*. You are admired by them. It had to have been our uncle. He probably had him picked up just to scare the rest of us. It's a warning to the subversives in the family."

"It's my fault with that damned song...oh God. I'm worried sick."

"Don't be, Emma. I think they want to keep us worrying for a few days, and then they'll let him go. I don't think it's as serious as it seems right now. Uncle Fernando would have our mother to answer to if anything happened to Juan."

"But what about your cousin? Wasn't he killed by your uncle's men?"

"Yes, but it was an accident. He was in a group. Juan would have been alone. They would know who he was."

Ricky's reasoning cut through the chain on the door that had already been opened a crack, blew it wide open. "I've had enough of this bullshit! I'm going to go down there and find him myself."

"I think you better wait until one of us has heard from Cata before you go anywhere, just in case."

"Trish will be here. Unless I hear from Juan tonight, I'm going tomorrow."

I hung up the phone and flopped down on the sofa heavily, accepted a brandy from Stephanie. "Ray can't come because he's in the middle of a job," she said. "But I'm going with you. I'll look after Lena."

Stephanie put in a call to my travel agent—had her book us both a flight for the following night, and a seat for Lena, too. Then we went back to waiting. In the wee hours, Lena padded into the living room, tugged on my arm to wake me up.

"Mama, wake up. I had a bad dream. There's a tiger under the bed. He doesn't want you to know. I want *mi papi*. When's he coming back? I want him now. Why are you sleeping in here?"

I picked her up and carried her back to our room, curled up next to her, holding her body close to mine. We slept till past noon, and woke to the smell of pancakes. Stephanie had been in the kitchen for hours, waiting for us to wake up. She was wired from a hundred cups of coffee, and had been monitoring calls all morning. Still nothing from Juan.

In spite of the knot in my stomach, I managed to choke down a couple of pancakes, which pleased Lena to no end. She squirted syrup all over my plate with expertise, pursing her lips slightly, the same way Juan did when he was concentrating.

"We're going to El Salvador tonight, where your papa is from," I said.

"Papa is there," she said happily. "I sleep with you and *Papi* tonight, okay Mama?"

"We're going to sleep on the plane. We won't see Papa till later. You're going to see your other grandma and grandpa. Do you remember them, honey?"

"No, only Ray and Stephanie. No more Grandmas and Grandpas. I don't want more. Grandma Stephanie makes pancakes." She beamed up at Stephanie.

Cata called at seven minutes past two in the afternoon. She sounded hoarse, as though she'd been crying. "Nobody knows anything. Don't believe anything Marta tells you. She has no idea what's going on here."

"She said that Leftist *guerrillas* have kidnapped him. You don't think it's true?"

"It is a lie, but she probably believes it. Our best hope is that Uncle Fernando has him, and he'll be released in a few days. Oh Emma, I'm so sorry. It's all my fault."

"But you don't know for sure, do you? It could be a kidnapping just for the money, right? It doesn't have to be politically motivated. Anyway, I'm coming there tonight. Can we meet tomorrow? I'd like to see you as soon as possible."

"Emma, I can't. Don't you understand—they'll follow you, and if they catch me, they'll try to force me to turn my friends in. I would die first."

"So I won't even be able to see you? Couldn't we set up a secret meeting? Couldn't you just go home, for Christ sake?"

"I think you know the answer already. I'm sorry, but I can't contact you while you're in El Salvador. Maybe I can have someone get a message to you. I'll try. Let's have a password: your mother's first name. Don't trust anyone who doesn't know the password. I won't say it on the phone. Kisses to Lena. I love you."

I called Marta to let her know we were coming. I told her that I would stay at a hotel since her parents were so pissed at me, but she insisted that it would be an insult—assured me that her family would have a car for me at the airport. It was a short conversation. I said nothing about what Cata and Ricky had told me.

Shortly after I talked to Marta, *Doña* Margarita called, insisting that we stay with her, putting it on the level of refusing her hospitality—nothing less than spitting in her face again, I guess. I understood though. Now wasn't the time to play Family Feud. Anyway, I wanted to be in the heart of the information center, and wanted Lena to be with her family there. I wanted to sleep in the bed where Juan had recently slept.

The airport in El Salvador hadn't changed all that much since I was there last. The military police with their machine guns looked as menacing as ever. It was morning, and kids were walking around trying to sell newspapers, holding them up, hawking their wares. Lena was the first to notice.

"*Papi*!" She pointed to a newspaper.

There was Juan's face, unmistakable, on the front page of the newspapers. Just a small photo, but Lena had spotted it immediately. Not that she was concerned about it; she was used to seeing our pictures in print. Marta was there to meet us with Silvia and Oscar, who immediately took possession of Lena's attention.

They could speak some English, and Lena could speak some Spanish, so they teamed up easily. The kids skipped around happily while we waited for our luggage.

I pulled Marta aside. "What are the newspapers saying about Juan? Is there any new information?"

"They say he's been kidnapped by leftist insurgents, that he's being held for ransom," Marta whispered.

"How do they know? Has there been a ransom note?"

"Not yet, but the family is expecting one."

"Marta!" Stephanie's voice sounded alarmed. "Why is that military guy hovering around the kids?"

"He's one of our guards," Marta replied.

"One of them?" I said. "How many do we have? Why do we need guards?"

"Only four," Marta said matter of factly. "It is a precaution. You are an important person. My family is concerned for your safety."

"Jesus, Marta, I don't want these guys following me around. It creeps me out."

Marta ignored my protests. A limo was waiting outside, an armed guard leaning against its side. A jeep was parked in front of it, and another one right behind it. The guards escorted us to our car, then jumped into the jeeps, and we took off. I noticed that our driver was armed, too. It was Stephanie's first trip to El Salvador, and it was plain to see that she was appalled by the show of force; but she was as genial as ever with Marta. We couldn't really talk about Juan in the car because of the kids.

I had no plan of action whatsoever. I had thought I could hunt down Cata's friends while I was here, but it was obvious the family wasn't going to give me a second alone to do that. Still, I was glad I had come. It was better than sitting around at home doing nothing. As we entered the section of the city where Juan's parents lived, we passed a big, ornate church, and suddenly, I knew what to do.

It all came back to me—Juan and Cata talking about "Liberation Theologians"—Juan saying they were Communist influenced. Those priests might know something, and it would be an easy ruse to pull off—just tell the Avelars that I want to go pray. Of course, I didn't have the slightest idea how I would tell the Liberation priests from the non-Liberation priests, or whatever, but it made me feel better to have a plan.

Chapter Twenty

The Lethal Line — 1979

Emma arrived at the Avelar home early in the morning. Even under ordinary circumstances, things would have looked strange to her because she wasn't used to being up at that time of day, but the events of the past twenty-four hours had tossed her into the Twilight Zone. *Doña* Margarita actually came to the door herself and held out her arms to Lena. For a blissful second, Emma savored an "I told you so" for Juan. She'd known his mother would welcome her because of Lena, no matter what else had passed between them.

Don Gilberto appeared behind his wife, took Lena from her arms and held her up in the air—the same way Juan always did. For a moment, Emma saw Juan's eyes looking out of his father's face.

Marta stayed by Emma's side, translating, and attempting to help smooth things over within the family. Emma tried apologizing for the song, but they all assured her that it was of no importance, that she should not worry herself over such a small matter.

Two policemen were at the house, in addition to the six armed guards patrolling the property.

"The policemen will tape the call if the kidnappers phone to demand ransom," Marta explained. "And it is necessary to have personal security at all times now, Emma. Many prominent people have been kidnapped by the Communist insurgents. They are trying to destroy our way of life, to overthrow our government."

"Your safety is our responsibility," Don Gilberto added.

After what seemed an interminable breakfast, one that only the children could eat, Emma finally excused herself to take a nap. All she wanted was to take some Valium and float out of consciousness for a few hours. A maid showed her to the same room she had stayed in with Juan, and there in the closet were some of his clothes. They looked so normal, so common—just clothing hanging in a closet.

She leaned into the closet and inhaled. Gasping for breath, she took a shirt off the hanger, and held it to her skin. Juan's scent was still on it.

Still clutching the shirt, she walked into the bathroom. His toiletries were laid out neatly. She picked up his hairbrush and looked around, half expecting to see him come strolling into the room at any minute. *All his stuff is here; how can he not be here?*

Stephanie had been given a bedroom close by, and a nursery readied for Lena, which showed how well the Avelars knew their granddaughter. Lena would only sleep in a bed with Emma or Stephanie—or Juan, of course. But at the moment, Lena was running wild with Marta's kids and Emma knew that she would be well looked after, so she took the Valium and passed out.

Waking at mid-afternoon disoriented and groggy, Emma drew the curtains and looked out onto the lush, manicured grounds. All the beauty felt like an affront. She shuffled back into the bathroom, took Juan's aftershave, and splashed it all over her body. The scent exploded into the air. Big mistake. Instead of soothing her, it made her more acutely aware of Juan's absence. Stepping into the shower, she scrubbed herself with peppermint soap and lathered her hair with coconut-scented shampoo in an attempt to override the scent of the aftershave. It was too much—being surrounded by the trappings of Juan's life. All those objects, but no Juan. She got dressed, and went downstairs to find Lena and Stephanie.

"*Donde esta mi mamá y mi hija*?" Emma asked one of the maids. She was momentarily pleased with her sentence and surprised that she could feel pleased about anything. The maid showed her to the large parlor and there on the sofa, talking to Stephanie, sat Bill.

"What are you doing here?" Emma blurted, and then broke into sobs.

Stephanie immediately went to Emma's side, put her arm around her and led her over to the sofa. "Bill has heard from Cata," she whispered.

Bill explained. He'd gotten two calls from the guys in *King Snake,* who were back in England—one from Jack Riggs, and one from Alex. Evidently, the May 9th Cathedral Massacre was big news in England, and they had both tried to get hold of Emma and Juan to see if they were okay. When they couldn't get through, they had called Bill.

"But aren't you in the middle of recording?" Emma asked him.

"I took a few days off. Everybody's worried about you, sweetheart. I think you should come home. You can deal with things better from there."

"I'm not leaving here without Juan."

Bill moved closer to her on the couch and lowered his voice. "Cata called. She wants you to go home. She gave me the names of some people you can call, and some organizations, but not from here in this country. Apparently they're watching your every move and would monitor your calls. She said you can do him more good at home."

Emma had stopped crying. "What's that supposed to mean?" She tried to keep her voice down, but it spiraled out of control. "Do him more good! What the fuck is that supposed to mean? She's just trying to cover for her friends."

Bill put his finger to his lips. She got what he meant, and lowered her voice. "He's been kidnapped. They'll want a ransom. I need to be here when they set him free. I need to pay the ransom. I can't leave."

"Then I'll stay with you," Bill said. "Stephanie, would you mind letting *Doña* Margarita know that I will be accepting their hospitality after all?"

When Stephanie had left the room, Bill dropped his voice. "I'm with you on this, Emma. Whatever it takes, we'll get to the bottom of it. But sweetheart, you need to know that Cata said this whole kidnapping thing is a ruse. She's positive he wasn't kidnapped by the Left, and she said to tell you it wasn't her uncle's men who took him. It was a different right-wing faction. Do you know what she means?"

Emma felt a door slam shut in her face. It took her breath away. "What right-wing faction? Is that some kind of euphemism? How does she know it wasn't some professional criminals or something? Christ, I wish she'd meet with me."

Before Bill could say anything, Stephanie came back into the room with *Doña* Margarita and a formidable looking armed man in a military uniform—her brother, the much-discussed General Estrada, or Uncle Fernando as the family called him. Both Emma and Bill jumped to their feet at the sight of him, but he invited them to sit back down. He seemed to take command of the space around him effortlessly, shaking hands with Bill and then reaching for Emma's hand with both of his.

"Emma, at last we meet. I am your admirer; it is unfortunate that we meet under such terrible circumstances."

Emma was completely taken aback. She had expected him to be colder than *Doña* Margarita, and to have it in for her because of the song about El Salvador. His friendliness disarmed her. "Where's Juan?" she blurted.

"I've brought some chilled champagne and some of the small lobsters that our coastline is famous for. Margarita, shall we sit on the verandah?"

As the small group moved outdoors, Emma felt shell-shocked, as though she were part of a surreal film, going through motions with no will of her own. The general was directing, and they all took his cues, settling into plush cushions, partaking of the lobster and champagne, answering his mundane questions. And then abruptly, the small talk was over.

"I am aware of the rumors you have been hearing, Emma," said the general. "But I can assure you they are not true. My nephew is not in my custody. I wish he were. As Margarita well knows, I would not have Juan arrested, no matter what he did."

"I assure you he speaks the truth," Margarita said quietly.

The general smiled fondly at his sister, then continued speaking in an even tone. "Even though I disapprove of Catarina's behavior and her choice of friends, I protect her because she is my family. Regardless of what Catarina has told you, her friends are alive because of my intervention. Young people are so reckless with their lives, and she doesn't understand that my influence can extend only so far. Catarina should come home for her own safety. I believe you can convince her. Don't bother to deny that you are in contact with her."

"Jesus!" Emma jumped out of her chair so abruptly that it fell over. She heard herself shouting, but she no longer cared what *Doña* Margarita or anyone else thought. "Where's Juan? What's all this about Cata? I thought you were going to tell me where my husband is. If you don't have him, then where the hell is he? Just tell me what the fuck is going on. Is he being held for ransom?"

"It is possible," the general said calmly.

"What do you mean, it's possible? If he's not being held for ransom, and you don't have him, where the fuck is he?" Emma looked from the general to *Doña* Margarita and back again. Neither of them spoke. "What are the other possibilities?"

Silence. The meaning of the silence crumbled her anger. It drained her of the rush of adrenaline that had kept her fighting, and she broke into tears. "I just wish to God I could get a straight answer out of somebody."

Stephanie put her arm around Emma. "What Emma is trying to find out," she said, glaring at the general, "is, have the kidnappers contacted anyone? Were there any eyewitnesses to his disappearance?"

Doña Margarita turned pale at Stephanie's words. "Please, we do not use that word for my son. He is not *disappeared.* He will return."

Now even the general looked uncomfortable. He shifted his feet and cleared his throat a few times. "We will understand more about the situation when Gilberto arrives home."

"What do you know?" Stephanie turned on the general, eyes blazing. "My daughter has a right to know. Can't you see the agony you're causing her with all your oblique inferences!"

"I'm sorry, but it is the situation that is causing your daughter pain. I am trying to help her. Don Gilberto is making inquiries; we will know more soon." He turned on his heels as if to walk out, then turned back and addressed Stephanie again. "I am willing to talk to Emma, but I must ask you to give us some privacy."

When Stephanie, Marta, and Bill had left the verandah, the general patted the seat next to him. "Margarita, sit here beside me, and Emma, pull your chair close so we can talk. But you must remember that I give you confidential information. I can tell you only that we believe Juan was kidnapped by a rival political faction. We'll find out what has happened to him when we learn for certain which brigade was involved."

Emma blinked. "Are you talking about the Leftists? Is that what you mean?"

"No. You ask a disingenuous question. I'm sure you're aware of your popularity with the insurgents. But your song has not made you so popular with the government of President Romero—surely you can understand this."

"I'm sorry about the song." Emma dried her eyes, looked up, and met the general's gaze head-on. "It was stupid of me—I didn't know it would turn into such a big deal. I guess I didn't think it would have much impact here—because of the language difference and all."

"Yes, I believe that you didn't think of the consequences, but the situation is more complex than you are aware of. Gilberto and I have reason to believe that a coup will be attempted. Certain factions would like to implicate our family in treasonous activity. They have been jealous of us for many years, and now they say that we have been corrupted by Communist infiltration."

The general shifted his weight, choosing his words deliberately. "First it was Ramon Bernal protesting in the streets with known Communists, then Catarina began associating with Communists and has now joined them in the mountains…as you already know." He paused, burning Emma with his cold gaze. "But Juan's participation in the recording of that seditious song about his own country was the final insult to our president. It has brought our family's loyalty into question. This is confidential information. Do you understand? You must say nothing of this to anyone or it will put Juan's life in danger."

Emma had begun to shiver, despite the heat. *Doña* Margarita was weeping into her brother's shoulder.

"We are clear?" the general demanded of them.

"No, nothing is clear," Emma said. "What do these brigades do to people? Who are they? What about if I offer a million-dollar reward for his safe return? Do you think they would let me talk to him?"

"We will know more when Gilberto returns. Until then, I suggest that we present a brave face. Margarita, please ask the others to join us. And have more champagne brought out."

It was more than two hours before Don Gilberto returned. Emma sat through those excruciating hours in complete stillness, waiting. She saw everyone and everything through a thick haze. The sound of people breathing clanked noisily—her nerves were at screaming point by the time he arrived.

Marta had been looking after Lena and her own children, but she entrusted them to the care of a servant when her father walked in.

It was clear to Emma from looking at Don Gilberto that the news was not good.

The family gathered in the parlor. Stephanie was allowed to join them, but Bill was asked to retire to his bedroom upstairs.

When the doors to the parlor were closed, Don Gilberto asked everyone to sit down, and then took a seat beside his wife on the couch.

"Juan has been found," he said quietly. "I'm sorry."

Through the buzzing in her head, Emma was distantly aware of *Doña* Margarita screaming, Marta sobbing, and some other persistent noise that sounded like the demon wind roaring through the rafters of her old house in San Francisco. That demon had been holding its breath, gathering strength, waiting for the right moment to exhale, and now it was howling through her head, laying waste to every last shred of hope. It destroyed everyone in its path as it blew through the room.

Emma sat silently on the couch, rocking back and forth, staring off into space, watching Saturn grow large as it hurled toward her.

"Cry, honey." Stephanie was there—with both arms wrapped around her daughter. "Let yourself cry, please baby. Oh God, this can't be happening."

Emma heard her mother's voice through the howling in her head. It brought her immediate surroundings back into focus. She looked around the room, found Don Gilberto, and stared hard at him.

"Where is he?" Emma's voice was flat and calm. "I want to see my husband."

"We will go at once. Please choose appropriate clothing for his funeral. Marta will make necessary preparations for the wake, and perhaps Stephanie will assist with the children."

Emma turned to the general. "You knew, didn't you?" The roaring in her stomach was now as loud as the howling in her head. "You fucking knew, even as you were feeding us your goddamn champagne and lobster. All that bullshit about other factions, I don't believe you. You're a fucking liar!" Suddenly, she vomited all over the floor, all down the front of her clothes, and just stood there in the mess.

Stephanie took her by the hand and led her upstairs where she stripped her clothing off and put her in the shower, then helped her dress in a long, black skirt and a simple, black shirt. Bill came into the room at some point and Stephanie gave him the news.

Bill shook his head. "I can't believe it. I thought Juan had some immunity from all this insane violence because of his family. He's dead? They killed him? Should I go with Emma? What about Lena?"

Stephanie looked panicked. "Lena, our baby. Oh God. Emma is going to have to talk to her right away—before she finds out from someone else."

"I can't talk to her right now, Mom," Emma said. "I have to see to Juan's things. Tell her I'm sick or something."

"Can't do it, Em. She's going to be sensing that something is wrong. You're going to have to pull it together for your child, baby. I'm going to go get her."

Emma stood staring after her mother. *She's not really going to bring Lena to me. I'm in a foreign body—she won't recognize me. How can I tell her about her papi?*

Bill reached for her. "Emma, baby, let me help you. Tell me what to do."

She shuddered and pushed him away. "Don't touch me. I'm trying to get it together." *What did Juan used to say about focusing on breathing? Okay, inhale...deep breath...exhale. Concentrate.* She looked up at Bill. "Oh God, I don't want to scare Lena—she's only two."

Lena came bounding into the room a few steps ahead of Stephanie. "Where's Papi? Silvia said he's with angels. I don't like angels," she said with a pout. "I want my papi now. I want him to read a story."

"Not tonight, honey." Emma held out her arms. "Come sit on my lap."

But Lena was not to be dissuaded so easily. "I want *Papi*," she said more insistently. "Tell *Papi* I want him now. I don't want you. You're too sad. Papi is happy. I want him."

"Mama's not feeling well, honey."

"You're always sick. I don't want you. I want my *papi*. Where is he? Where is the heaven?"

It was too much. Emma began to sob, slowly at first, unable to stop herself. Lena softened when her mother began to cry, went and sat on her lap and stroked her face. "It's okay Mama; I didn't mean it. I want you, too; but where's *Papi*?"

Emma looked up at Stephanie, pleading silently for help. Stephanie took charge. "Bill, will you please go call Ray and tell him what's happened. Ask him to take the red-eye here tonight." When he had left the room, she took Lena from Emma's lap. "Something's happened to your daddy, sweetheart. He's not coming back to you in this lifetime. He's gone into the loving arms of the eternal."

"What's a turnal?" Lena asked.

"The word eternal means that it goes on forever. Emma, perhaps you'd like to help me explain."

When Emma didn't answer, Stephanie stumbled on with her explanation. "Papa came from the eternal, and he's returned to the eternal. He's left his body and gone on to his next reincarnation."

"Jesus Christ, Stephanie! At least tell her something she can understand." Emma put out her arms to Lena. "Come here, baby. Honey, Papa is gone. He died. I'm going to go now and dress him in his nice clothes, but he's not in his body anymore. He'll always be alive in your heart, but he won't live with us anymore. Do you understand?" Emma stroked Lena's hair, choking back her own tears. "You can still see him in your dreams. *Papi* was a dreamer—his band *Las Sombras*, *The Shadows*, was about the dream world and you can still find *Papi* there."

Lena began to cry. "Silvia said he went to angels. I hate angels! I don't want *Papi* to be at angels. I want him to read a story."

Emma soothed Lena, rocking her gently—rubbing her tiny back, and singing softly until she fell asleep out of sheer exhaustion. She laid her down in the bed gingerly, careful not to wake her.

A thought crossed her mind, simple, like a slogan that those old bi-planes write in white across a clear blue sky—stark against a neutral space, impossible to miss. *I don't want to be alive anymore.*

Dispassionately, Emma stared at the white writing in the heavens, watched as the letters dispersed and dissolved into powder, like fine granules of heroin. The sudden craving for a fix was so urgent that it jerked her back to earth. *It couldn't be that hard to score here. I wonder who would know.*

Marta knocked on the door. "Emma, our parents are waiting for you. They are anxious to leave."

Emma looked up at her, trying to focus on what she was saying. When she got it, it infuriated her. She couldn't keep the bitterness out of her voice. "I don't see what the big hurry is since my husband is already dead. I'm trying to deal with this—you think you could all give me some fucking space!"

"He should be buried within twenty-four hours. It is the custom," Marta replied. "Family will be arriving at the funeral parlor tonight…soon."

"Wait a minute. What are you talking about? Your parents intend to bury him when? Here? I need to think about it. He should be near his daughter. We're his family now. It should be up to me to say what happens to him."

"Please Emma, he is my brother. It is painful also for me. You can discuss these things with my parents. But if you do not come now, they will go without you."

"I was just telling Lena that her father is dead. It's not something you can rush through."

Stephanie spoke up. "What about this shirt, honey?" She held up a deep green cotton shirt. "And maybe this white linen suit."

"No, I want him in his rock n' roll clothes—his black leather shirt with the thunderbird painted on the back, and his black jeans. That's what he would want."

Stephanie packed Juan's things in a small canvas bag, and added some toiletries for Emma. "Go on, honey," she said. "You have the right to be there. You need to see what's happened to him.

I think they expect me to bring Lena to the funeral home tonight. What do you want me to do?"

"I don't know."

"Carolina must attend her father's wake," Marta said. "It is important for the journey of his soul that his family stays with his body until he is buried."

Emma stared at Marta in disbelief. "It's my decision, Marta, not yours. And I don't want him to be buried. I want him cremated, so I can take his ashes back to Marin County with me. I want to bury his ashes under a tree in Mill Valley or something."

Marta looked horrified. "It is impossible. Cremation is barbaric. He will lie with his ancestors. But, of course, you know so little of our customs. You do not have to go with my parents just now. They go to pray for his soul as his body is prepared for burial, but you do not need to be there. It might be too difficult for you. I think in your country you are more impersonal with your dead."

Emma turned to her mother. "What's she talking about, Stephanie?"

"Honey, I think she's trying to prepare you for watching them literally dress Juan's body."

Marta nodded. "Yes, exactly. In our family, we care for our departed. We do not feel that it is fitting for a stranger to prepare the body to leave this world. But do you think you can do it, Emma? My parents will take the responsibility for you if you don't want to come with them now."

"I'll take care of my husband. You needn't worry about that." Emma straightened her shoulders and tossed her hair out of her eyes.

Emma piled into one of the family cars with the Avelars. She sat very still, her body rigid. *None of this is real. It's a mistake. It won't be Juan. Doña* Margarita was also rigid, as aloof as she'd always been. Don Gilberto, however, was attempting to make contact.

Taking Emma's hand in his, her father-in-law placed it in his lap next to *Doña* Margarita's. "We need to function as a family in these difficult times," he said. "I have seen Juan's body. He was…tortured. I have hired the best mortician to make him presentable, so it will not be such a shock to you, but you will see the marks on his body…and the mutilation. I will avenge the people who have done this to my son, but until that time, we must act with caution. We will accept the investigator's findings for the time being, but when the time is right, I will act swiftly."

Out of nowhere, laughter filled the car. Emma didn't realize it was her own until she saw the looks of horror on the Avelars' faces, and then heard her own voice from a million light years away.

"Saturn, after all," she said, and then retreated into silence.

Juan was lying naked on a table in a barren room. Emma hoped he wasn't cold. She, herself, was freezing. It wasn't right that he was so exposed, so she wanted to get his body sponged down in a hurry, so she could dress him—but she lingered over his hands. She wiped each of his long, beautiful fingers carefully. His wedding ring was gone.

Gilberto and Margarita were working on his legs, crying non-stop.

Emma worked her way up his arms, held her breath as she cleaned the gunshot wounds in his chest. The holes went all the way through his body. She stepped back to take a better look, fighting back tears. Someone had cut his hair. It had been hacked off in haphazard, random sections, close to the scalp, so that it stuck out at odd angles. She regretted the loss of those thin braids he had always worn. It would have been nice to have the braids. They could have been put in a special drawer, saved for Lena. The cigarette burns on his torso dotted around his multiple wounds, and the absence of his genitals were too much for her to take in; her eyes passed over them, and moved back to his head.

"Why did they have to fucking cut his hair?" she muttered, as she slicked gel onto what remained of it.

"Let's put the shirt on first, Emma, then you can finish with his hair," Don Gilberto said.

Emma watched as his parents efficiently dressed Juan's body, then hung a rosary around his neck.

"Wait a minute; he wasn't Catholic."

"He was baptized Catholic, and he will be buried Catholic." Don Gilberto's voice was flat and firm. "The priest will be here soon."

"But he was a Buddhist," Emma said quietly. She didn't have the energy to go against them. Anyway, where was she going to find a Buddhist monk in El Salvador?

Juan's body was lifted into an ornate casket. Don Gilberto kissed his son's cheeks, and *Doña* Margarita kissed Juan's mouth. Then they both stepped back to allow Emma access to his body.

She couldn't kiss him. It wasn't him anymore. Juan had been stolen. What lay there in his clothing was just a sinister wax figure that had eaten Juan's soul. It was a horror movie—the big coffin with the bright red satin. Juan had hated that gaudy shade of red.

The men shut a layer of the coffin lid across the top. A window covered the upper portion of the casket, so that part of Juan's body was visible. Now she was looking at him through glass that provided another layer of separation, another level of distortion.

The coffin was taken into a chapel-like room, formal and somber, with pews and an altar. Emma followed her in-laws. There was no fight left in her. What had remained of her spirit had been hacked off, like Juan's braids, like his masculinity. Let them bury him Catholic or Buddhist or whatever—it didn't matter. He was gone.

Stephanie showed up with Lena and Bill at some point, and in the morning, Ray was there with Trish, too. The chapel room had filled up with people by daybreak, all the cousins and aunts and uncles. All the people Juan had tried to leave behind when he started his new life in Los Angeles. All the people Emma had reconnected him with.

Emma sat through the wake and the funeral rites, cloaked in a depression so heavy it obliterated her. She could barely breathe under the weight of it. At intervals throughout the ordeal, the cloak would part for Lena, but it inevitably fell back into place again, leaving her alone in darkness. Lena was the only person she owed anything to, and while she knew she should be more present with her, should try to explain what was happening to her, she couldn't. She was unable to make sense of what was going on herself. And Stephanie was there to look after Lena. Lena was safe with her grandmother. Within the privacy of the cloak, Emma was acutely aware of her craving for heroin.

A big fuss was made about the archbishop who conducted the funeral mass in a huge, echo chamber of a cathedral. Emma hoped he was saintly and would be of some comfort to the family. She was, herself, beyond comfort.

It was pouring rain when they left for the graveyard. Juan's casket was laid in a large stone, oblong box, which was then placed in his family's huge chapel-like burial place, the *mauseleo*. The building looked to Emma like something from the dark ages.

As they left the *mauseleo*, Emma paused and looked back at the wooden door. She turned to Stephanie, let her gather her close. "Mother, why couldn't they have let him be cremated?" she sobbed. "I'm positive he would rather have been scattered to the wind in Marin, than to have to spend eternity in this hideous land of his birth—this land of his murder.

"I know, honey, I know." Stephanie kissed Emma's cheeks and hair.

That night Emma held Lena close as the child slept fitfully, breathing in shallow little gasps. The air had thinned out around them both.

•••

A couple of days later, driving through the Rainbow Tunnel into Marin, Emma was appalled that everything looked the same when everything about her, everything about her family, was completely different now. She could feel the change all the way down to her molecular structure.

Stephanie dogged her every step. Emma knew why—her mother had sensed what she had locked into. She told Emma that she wasn't about to let her compound the tragedy of her life by getting strung out again. Emma didn't have the energy to oppose her.

The summer tour was canceled. Bill took care of the arrangements and helped Stephanie field the calls that came in from all over the world. Reporters wanted interviews—real reporters, not tabloid hacks. But Emma could no more handle an interview than she could accept the reality that her life had been obliterated. Friends sent flowers, and the bolder ones tried to get in to see her, but Emma had Stephanie turn them away. She didn't want their sympathy. Sympathy is something you get when your dog dies.

The press reported that Juan had been killed by kidnappers, that he was a victim of the latest spate of lawlessness instigated by Communists in El Salvador. The bitter irony of that version of events stuck in Emma's throat, choking the life out of her, yet she said nothing—just spent her days and nights drinking whiskey and tequila, smoking cigarettes, and popping Valium. For Lena's sake, she stayed away from heroin, but it didn't stop her from craving it.

She was lying out by the pool one day in early June, feeling the sun trying to burn its way through the icy scales that had spread out from her heart and covered her whole body—trying to space out everything but the sensation of the heat, when the sound of her daughter's voice broke through her solitude.

"Mama, are you asleeping?" Lena asked softly.

Emma's eyes popped open. "No, but aren't you supposed to be taking a nap or something?"

"Mama, let's go down on the bottom of the pool. We can stay there, be with *Papi*."

Emma blinked. "What?"

"I don't want to be here. I want to see *Papi*. We can get dead, too."

Emma began to shiver in the sun. The icy scales on her body cracked and fell around her. *Oh God, what did she just say to me? Our baby, our little girl! No, no, I've got to do something.* She tried to arrange her face into a smile. "No Lena, Papa wouldn't like that. You're all that's left of him. He would want you to stay alive and be happy."

"You're not happy."

"But I will be, honey. I'll be happy for you. Do you want me to swim with you like Papa always did?"

"I want you to sing," Lena replied, staring down at the cement. "I want you to sing 'Hush Little Baby'."

"Right now?"

"Yes, now."

Emma picked Lena up, placed her between her legs on the lounge chair, and sang the lullaby to her over and over again. She tried to keep desperation out of her voice. *What the fuck have I been thinking? I could lose her, too.*

Lena's little body was as warm as the sun. She sang along with her mother, rocking in Emma's arms, and the sound of her voice lured Emma out of hiding. It came to Emma with absolute clarity: even though she had completely lost interest in her own life, she cared very much about Lena's.

The next day she asked Stephanie to set up an interview with Wade, her friend from Rolling Stone. She had decided to try to set the record straight about what had really happened to Juan.

...

Sitting by the pool, Wade and Emma talked for hours. He understood about right-wing death squads, had smelled the propaganda of the "kidnappers" story a mile away. He asked Emma questions, but he also filled in a lot of spaces for her.

"It's going to get worse, Emma. If the Sandinistas take over in Nicaragua, our government is going to give those military dictatorships even more support."

"They already get away with murder," Emma replied flatly.

"Exactly," Wade said. He assured her that Rolling Stone would print the story accurately, no problem, but felt that she should also release something to a UPI reporter. "People need to know what's going on down there. The situation is heating up, and it involves us because we set these guys up. Our tax dollars helped put them in power, and helps keep them in power."

"Now you sound like Catarina," Emma said.

...

Emma's 29th birthday, June 10th, dawned gray and foggy in Mill Valley. Lena woke her mother around noon by jumping on the bed and tickling her. Stephanie followed, bearing waffles and mimosas on a brass tray. Propped on the tray was a bright picture of a sun shining down on a small mother, a larger daughter, and a still larger grandmother, all holding hands. The biggest image, however, was a gigantic coffin-shaped box, with a large stick figure inside, plainly visible through the brown scribbling. The three females had been painted with garish smiles in an obviously determined effort to cheer the scene up. Across the bottom, in laboriously printed large letters, was the message, "Happy Birthday Mama. From Carolina."

Emma put her hand to her heart, and bit her lip to keep from crying. "Oh honey, what a beautiful picture. Is that you in the middle, holding Stephanie's and my hands?"

Lena smiled. "Yeah, that's me. And that's you, right there—see your pretty dress."

"I see, honey." Emma blinked back tears. "Mama's going to be bigger next time you draw us. I'm going to take care of my little girl."

"It's okay, Mama. Grandma and I take care of you."

"No, not anymore, *corazon*. Mama's getting better. I'm not sick anymore." Emma patted her eyes, and broke into a wide smile, then turned her attention to the tray. "Oh, my favorite—waffles!"

"Lena helped make them," Stephanie said, giving Lena a proud smile.

Taking a bite, Emma proclaimed them the best waffles ever made. "This is the best birthday breakfast in the whole world, and I'm the luckiest mama...so where shall we go today? Do I get to choose cause it's my birthday?"

"It's your turn, Mama. You get to choose! Okay, Grandma?"

"Okay by me," Stephanie said.

"How about...Disneyland?" Emma said. "Would that be alright with you two?"

Juan had said he'd be home for her birthday—easily. He'd told her he'd be gone a few days, straighten things out, and be home in plenty of time to plan a party. Right. But in spite of how wretched she felt, Emma realized that she had to exhibit some joy for Lena's sake. Juan would want her to make their child happy.

Disneyland offered them VIP passes, which meant they didn't have to stand in lines. They stayed three days at the "Happiest Place on Earth," and Emma could see Lena falling for her act—believing her mama really was excited about the rides and seeing all the Disney princesses.

No alcohol in Disneyland, but the hotel where they escaped by monorail for lunch each day, and stayed at night, was a different story. Emma managed to keep herself in a comfort zone as they went on all the kiddie rides; she smiled and posed for pictures with Lena and the countless suited cartoon characters. She signed autographs and acknowledged the expressions of sympathy from fans who spotted her. The employees of the place, who were mainly more of her fans, treated Lena like a little princess.

It was when they returned home that the days became interminable again. Emma had no interest in writing songs, no interest in seeing friends or going out, and if it weren't for Lena, she probably wouldn't have bothered getting out of bed.

To fill the time, she fell into a routine of taking Lena to the beach every day. Lena loved to play in the sand and paddle around in the surf. Emma would see her talking away when no one was with her. When she would ask her about it, Lena would readily inform her that she was talking to Juan.

Bill came back into town at the beginning of July and parked himself in one of the guest rooms. "Go away, Bill," Emma told him. "I don't want to write, and I don't want to talk about anything. I just want to be left alone."

"Nonsense," Bill said. "You need me. Anyway, Stephanie invited me up for the 4th of July barbeque at their house. We're going together; didn't you know?"

It had long been a tradition of Ray and Stephanie's to host 4th of July festivities because you could see the fireworks over the bay from the big windows in their living room. Only their closest friends were there that year, plus a few of Emma's friends.

Everybody tried to be cool, but their awkwardness was tangible. There was a forced merriment during the day, but as the sun went down and the alcohol and pot took hold, people started expressing their sympathy, some of them crying and wanting to be held. Emma found herself comforting one person after another, and to her surprise, it felt better than silence.

...

During those long summer days that she sat on the beach, Emma tried to write lyrics, but scattered bits of prose came out instead.

Grief stretches out so long and so thin that at times you barely know it's there. But that thin, almost invisible line can be lethal. You can be playing on the beach with your child, go running headlong into the wind, and be decapitated by that line. You can't forget it's there or it will take you unaware.

Summer dallied that year, stretched into September, and beyond, into October. It eventually lulled Emma into occasional lapses of grief. She would be sitting on her deck chair in the sand, drink in hand, watching the idyllic moments of childhood play out in front of her, eyes on the children building castles, running and laughing in the face of it all; and her eyes would stray to the thin line of the horizon, then back to Lena, so brown now, like her father. *Snap*. Emma would run smack into that lethal line. Her head would fly off her shoulders—she'd find herself looking up at her own headless body—sand stinging her eyes...and no way to rub them.

Sometimes grief pounces on you, beheads you with a single blow, then stretches like a cat, extending its reach, growing longer and thinner, compacting its potential to strike until it is harder to spot than a snake in the grass. Emma grew to expect its assaults. Even her dreams were wary.

...

Nonetheless, she threw a big party for Lena's third birthday, October 8th. Stephanie had invited the children from the pre-ballet class she had been taking Lena to, and informed Emma, in a significant tone of voice, that the kids' parents were excited about meeting her. That forced Emma to venture out of her alcoholic haze for the day and be sociable. Christina and Marianne were there, helping out, and Bill had come up for the day, bringing along Jack Riggs, of *King Snake*.

Stephanie bustled around, busily keeping everything in order. She told Emma she was worried about fire, and insisted that Ray keep a hose right next to the barbeque, just in case. In the midst of all the activity, Emma could hear the snake rustling around. She kept a sharp eye open for thin lines.

Juan's parents called to wish Lena a happy birthday, then Marta and her kids, and finally, just before Lena's bedtime Ricky called from New Haven. Lena seemed delighted to talk to her uncle, but it also saddened her. Emma could see it in her eyes—the recognition of how similar Ricky's voice was to Juan's. Ricky was back at school, but he wasn't doing too well. He told Emma that he was having a hard time concentrating on his studies, that they seemed meaningless.

Wade talked to Ricky on the phone for a while, too, asking him for specific details on the *guerrilla* movement and Juan's level of involvement in it. It made Emma wonder if he hadn't believed her account of events.

The interview she had done with Wade had brought reporters out of the woodwork. The Sandinistas had indeed wrested power from Somoza's U.S. backed regime in Nicaragua in July, and the United States had gone into hyperdrive to try to "stop the spread of Communism" in Latin America. Judging by what she'd seen of the neighboring countries, Emma imagined Nicaragua was probably overdue for a revolution. But she didn't have a lot of backup on that one in mainstream America.

As a result of the interviews, she developed a rapport with a number of investigative journalists. They seemed to know more about what was going on in Central America than the U.S. government did. These reporters tried to bring Juan's murderers to justice, calling for the U.S. government to put pressure on Romero's regime to stop the death squads.

El Salvador made the news for another reason later in October. On the 15th, there was a coup, and General Romero was ousted. Supposedly, the new government was going to stop death squad activity and restore peace. When she heard the news, Emma wondered if it meant Cata was going to come down from the mountains and go back to living with her family.

…

On October 16th, Juan's birthday, Emma woke slowly. Even in the depths of slumber, she sensed the presence of the snake in the grass, and so she crept up into consciousness cautiously. She allowed herself a brief layover in that place between waking and dreaming—where filtered through a lens of desire, memory plays vividly on a timeless backdrop. She and Juan ran across the meadow on Mt. Tam in that place. Made love in the tall grass, crushing wild flowers beneath their bodies. But Emma had learned she couldn't stay long in that place. The longer she stayed, the harder it was to come back to waking life. The land of in-between was shaky ground, a conditional gift, full of contingencies, with ethereal but lethal boundaries.

A phone call came from Ricky in the late afternoon. He had already been depressed since Juan's death, and now on top of it, he was worried about the ramifications of the coup on his family. He asked Emma if she had heard from Cata at all, and began to cry when she said she hadn't. "I couldn't live if something happened to her too. I should have gone to find her. It's my fault they got Juan."

Emma sighed. "I thought it was my fault because of the song. But I don't think we should do this…I'll tell you whose goddamn fault it is, and that's those bastards who did it. Do you think anyone's even tried to find the killers?"

"Maybe with the new government they will. It's difficult to predict how things will go now."

Another important call came through in the early evening. A pleasant female voice asking for Emma.

Emma was surprised that someone she didn't know had her phone number. "Yes, this is Emma. Who is it?"

"I'm a friend of Cata's. I just got back from El Salvador."

"Is she okay? When did you see her? Where the fuck is she?"

"If we can meet in person, I'll be happy to tell you everything I know."

"How about tonight?"

"I'm still in D.C. but I'm planning a trip to California, perhaps next week. Cata is holding up well, but I'm afraid my line might be tapped. I'd prefer to talk in person. Your phone is probably tapped, too. Cata told me that today was your husband's birthday. I'm so sorry. It must be especially hard on these special occasions."

"Well, you're obviously American. What were you doing in El Salvador that you have a tapped phone line and would run into Cata?" Emma blurted.

"I'm a Maryknoll nun. I was working as a nurse in the rural areas when I met Cata, but can we wait until we meet to delve further into the subject? I know how anxious you must be; my prayers are with you. Shall we agree to meet next Tuesday? I'll call you when I get into town. My name is Alice, and I am to say hello to Stephanie."

"From who?" Emma asked, and then she remembered. *Stephanie*. The password Cata had given her to know whom she could trust.

Emma felt like she had been caught up in an intrigue so blatant it seemed preposterous. Yet the reality of it laid dead center in the fact that Juan was gone. Here she was on his birthday exchanging passwords with a mysterious nurse-nun who was the only person who knew the whereabouts of her dead husband's missing sister.

Sister Alice called the following Monday to say she was in San Francisco. Emma wanted to send a limo for her immediately, but Alice had prior commitments and was firm that she couldn't see her until noon the next day.

"Why don't we have lunch at my house?" Emma said. "I'll send a car for you at around 11:30, if that's okay."

"That sounds great. I'm staying with some sisters in the Mission District. Is that too far for your friend to come?"

"What friend?"

"I'm sorry, didn't you just say a friend of yours would pick me up?"

"Oh, no…a car…you know, a limo, not a friend."

"A limousine? Well, that's style alright. If you're sure, then great. It'll be my first time. Do I tip the driver, like in a cab?"

"No, I'll send my regular driver. It'll be taken care of."

In the morning, Trish prepared a Chinese chicken salad and sent Lena in to wake Emma in time to be ready at noon. Emma was already up and in the shower.

…

The woman who stepped out of the limo looked nothing like Emma had expected. In her mid-to late-twenties, dressed in jeans and a cotton hand-embroidered blouse, Alice looked like someone Emma would see at one of her own gigs, or at a Grateful Dead concert. Long, curly light-brown hair tumbled around a tanned, pretty face. Her slim body gave the impression that she might break into dance at any moment.

Lena was the first to reach her as she stepped out of the car. "Who are you?" she demanded.

"I'm Alice, and I already know who you are." Alice laughed and scooped Lena up into her arms. "I know all about you, you little beauty."

"*How* do you know?" Lena asked with a giggle.

"Your Auntie Cata told me. Your name is Lena, short for Carolina, and you like to swim and eat pizza. I have something for you from Cata."

"What, what?"

"First of all, a hundred kisses; I'll give you five right now." Alice showered Lena with kisses, which sent the child into a fit of laughter. Still holding Lena on her hip, she rummaged through her bag and pulled out a small, handmade doll. "This came from the people in the mountains who your auntie is helping. They are very poor, but they made this dolly out of old clothes especially for you. Cata said you are to think of how much she loves you when you hug the doll. Can you do that?"

"Oh yes," Lena said. "I love my Aunt Cata." Then turning her attention to Emma, she said, "Mama, look what I got. This is my new friend, Alice. I love her."

"Well, you won her over fast," Emma said. "She doesn't usually take to people quite that easily."

"Experience with children, I suppose." Alice shifted Lena to her other hip and extended her hand. "Alice O'Brien. Pleased to finally meet you, Emma."

Emma shook her hand and smiled. "I thought nuns are supposed to wear big, clunky, black and white outfits, or something. You look so normal."

"Appearances can be deceiving."

Emma laughed. "Come on in. I thought we'd have lunch out by the pool. Are you hungry now, or would you like to sit and talk for a while first?"

"As you like. I was hoping Lena would show me how well she can swim before she has to take her nap. I can't believe I'm actually here with you two. Cata told me all about you and your fabulous career. I felt like a movie star myself, riding up here in that fancy limousine. Have you been in a limousine before, Lena?"

"I've been lots of times; tell her Mama. I've been a hundred times." Squirming down from Alice's hip, Lena ran toward the house. "I'm gonna put on my bathing suit now; you'll see how I can swim. Just a minute, okay?"

Emma admired the way Alice had handled the situation with Lena—including her in the conversation, yet establishing boundaries for her inclusion so that the adults would have some time alone to talk. Trish brought some fresh fruit and a pitcher of iced mint tea out to the pool area.

"Actually, I'm having a glass of white wine," Emma said to Alice, somewhat sheepishly. "I don't suppose you drink wine, or do you? I'm sorry, but to tell the truth, I don't know anything at all about your religious trip."

Alice flashed a smile. "Don't worry about it. I don't know all that much either. A glass of wine would be super, only maybe I'll wait until lunch. Otherwise, you'll be mopping me up from the floor."

After Lena had demonstrated her swimming abilities, she told Alice all about Disneyland, then gave her a detailed account of her cousins, aunts, uncle, grandparents, Bill, Trish, and finally, of her *papi*. "He lives with angels now, so I only see him at night, when I'm asleeping."

Before she would agree to go down for a nap, Lena insisted on dancing for Alice, too. Alice seemed to love every minute of Lena's shenanigans, treating her with a respect few adults give children. Emma was grateful for the happiness it brought Lena, but she was also anxious to question Alice about Cata. It was after three o'clock before they finished lunch and Trish finally coaxed Lena to bed.

"So, tell me everything," Emma said.

"First of all, how are you?" Alice reached across the table and took Emma's hand. "Cata told me everything. Word reached her that Juan was tortured and mutilated. You have had such a heavy burden to bear."

Emma felt some of the scales fall from her body, leaving vulnerable patches exposed to the snake's fangs. "I'm fine."

"Of course you are." Alice squeezed Emma's hand. "You're more than fine; you're admirable. And I can tell what a good mother you are by how intact your daughter's spirit is—in spite of all your family has endured. Forgive me if I'm too familiar. I'm a 'stranger in a strange land' here in the midst of all this opulence. I've just returned from the mountains of El Salvador where everything is so different."

She watched Emma, waiting for a response. But when Emma said nothing, she went on. "Poverty and constant danger have created a climate of fear, where social graces are just basically omitted. If you meet someone you like, you let them know it, because you both know it may be the last time you'll see each other."

Emma was surprised by the nun's candor. "You've read Heinlein?"

"One of my favorite writers. I love Sci-Fi. Have you read Childhood's End, by Clark?"

"Yeah, but the good guy looks like the devil. Didn't that offend you?"

Alice laughed. "I'm almost impossible to offend."

"Me too," Emma said. "More wine?"

"Why not? As long as I'm being chauffeured around, I might as well take advantage of it."

"So what did Cata want you to tell me? Are there any new developments?"

"Not really, I'm sorry to say. Things are still totally grim. But I do have news about Juan's death. Cata found out that a death squad operating under ARENA murdered your husband. It turns out it definitely wasn't the National Guard. I'm sorry. This has to be a painful subject."

"So it absolutely wasn't his uncle after all?"

"It appears not…but General Estrada *is* responsible for many other deaths. Still, Cata is hopeful that the new government will bring about some positive change in the country. That is, if they can control the military and the death squads." Alice sipped her wine. "There's something else I'm supposed to tell you. Cata feels responsible for Juan's death, and begs your forgiveness. She said that she'll understand if you can't forgive her, but that she will stay in the mountains until the end of the revolution, so that Juan's death will not have been for nothing."

"Is she crazy? How could she send me a message like that? Juan's death *was* for nothing—he wasn't even political. She's a goddamn lunatic—'not for nothing'. It's just bullshit, all of it."

"I'm sorry, Emma, but I've delivered her message exactly as she requested. I agree with you about El Salvador—it *is* crazy. But Cata isn't crazy—just eaten up with guilt. It's a 'blame the victim' mentality. The ones who actually are guilty seem to feel no shame, whereas good people like Cata and Carlos feel responsible."

The conversation lasted into the night. Alice described the conditions in the mountains in such vivid terms that Emma felt part of Cata's life again.

"Carlos is one of the most highly trained medics they have behind the lines, and as you are no doubt aware, he hasn't even finished medical school," Alice said.

"Wait a minute; how do you know all this? Are you actually working with the *guerillas*? Isn't that unbelievably dangerous?"

"I minister to anybody who needs me. I don't ask the patient's political affiliation before treating the sick and the wounded. I treat the military and *campesinos* alike. We are united in Christ." Alice lowered her eyes, then looked back up into Emma's. She spoke in a soft voice. "But it's hard to ignore the brutality of the military, as you know only too well. I'm sorry, Emma. Everything I say sounds callous, considering what you've suffered."

"Would you like to see some pictures of Juan?" Emma asked.

"Yes, if you can bear it. I imagine he looked like Lena and Cata. He must have been extremely handsome."

For the first time since his death, Emma pulled out photo albums full of pictures of Juan—prints of their wedding, snapshots of their honeymoon in Hawaii, Lena's birth, the band on stage, one book after another full of a life that had been stolen, kidnapped, and murdered. Alice cried with Emma over the photos, exclaiming on the beauty of them, encouraging her to show more. Eventually they exhausted each other.

"Why don't you just stay here tonight?" Emma said. "God knows there's plenty of room. I've got four goddamn guest rooms…oops, sorry, shouldn't say that, should I? Isn't it a sin or something?"

"Not a very big one if it is. Compare your 'goddamn' to the atrocities being committed in El Salvador, and I don't think it ranks very high in the hierarchy of sin."

Emma smiled. "You're not like I thought you would be."

"Neither are you."

"Stay here tonight. Lena would be so happy to see you in the morning. Please."

…

Alice and Lena were already splashing around in the pool when Emma got up the next afternoon.

"You have a dolphin, not a daughter," Alice said, as she pulled herself up from the water. "How are you today? Did you sleep well?"

"You're the guest. Shouldn't I be asking you that?"

"She slept the best she has in ages, Mama," Lena shouted, treading water. "She sleeps in hammocks most of the time, and she gets all scrunched up."

Emma didn't want to let Alice leave. She had brought an impossible optimism into the household—a cheerfulness that, hard as she tried, Emma had been unable to create for Lena. The air felt lighter, easier to breathe. This nun, who apparently had nothing, who spent her life in depressing surroundings taking care of sick people under appalling conditions, radiated joy.

Emma smiled at Alice. All through their conversation the night before, she'd been thinking that Alice reminded her of someone. And now, seeing her standing there in bright sunlight, Emma got it: Margie.

"Why don't you hang out here for a week or two?" Emma said. "We'd love your company."

Alice pulled Lena up out of the water and began drying her off. "I wish. But I can't, of course. I'm booked to speak in a church in Sacramento tonight, and Davis tomorrow night."

"Well, come back afterward then."

"As much as I'd like to, I can't. I have a whole slew of dates to speak in churches around the country. That's why I came back—to raise awareness about what's going on in El Salvador—and to raise funds for our relief work there."

"Jesus, Alice! That's no problem. I can help you raise funds. We'll do a benefit."

Chapter Twenty-One

Emma — 1992 — Looking Back

Same old dance, same old song—there I was all the way in Cleveland, and just before I was supposed to go on stage, they told me I had a call in the production office. I picked it up, thinking it must be Lena, but it was Margarita, calling from El Salvador to let me know they'd be showing up in September in order to help plan Lena's sixteenth birthday party.

"Wait a minute," I said. "You got to plan the *Quinceanera*. This one is mine. We're going to have the party at our house, with a band and all of Lena's friends there. It's not going to be some big deal. Just come for the party. Honestly, I don't need your help."

Silence.

"Well, I would appreciate your help if you're sure you have the time," I said, lying through my teeth.

Jesus, talk about timing. Of course I couldn't get into a big discussion at that exact moment, and Margarita said she understood, but it was obvious she didn't. She still had the ability to make me feel like I was disturbing her, even though *she* had called *me*.

I had kowtowed to Margarita like crazy last year—let her do the whole fifteenth birthday, *Quinceanera* thing at their mansion in Beverly Hills. A girl's fifteenth birthday is a huge, big deal in Latin America, so I went along with the grand shebang, but I wasn't going to do it again. I shifted from foot to foot, pretending I was paying attention to her demands, anxious because I had to be on stage in five minutes. Finally, I came right out and told her I had to hang up.

It was just more of the same old shit between us, the kind of controlling stuff that had driven Juan away from his parents. But I cut them a lot of slack nowadays because they've been through so much, and because for better or worse, we're family. Anyway, they're back in El Salvador now. They moved earlier this year, after the Peace Accords were signed, so I don't have to deal with them as much anymore.

...

Back in 1981, Gilberto and Margarita were forced to flee their country. Even Margarita's bigwig brother, the general, barely escaped with his life. It was a bitter irony that as right wing as the Avelars and Estradas were they were thought of as leftist radicals by the military dictatorships that turned El Salvador into hell all through the eighties. They had to just pack up their bags and get out—leaving Cata behind in the mountains doing God knows what. With their Swiss bank accounts and embassy connections, they weren't exactly part of the stream of starving Central American refugees flooding into the States at that time though. They bought a mansion in Beverly Hills and sat out their country's civil war by the side of their pool.

I don't know how any of us got through the eighties. It was as if a gigantic shadow of greed covered the land—the shadow-creatures no longer had to crouch in dark corners—they could venture out in broad daylight under a mantle of respectability. Corporations bought up America—bought up the music business, that's for sure. Suddenly, my label was owned by a multi-national conglomerate that fired the music lovers in the company, like my long-time friends, Carl and John, and hired A&R men who referred to music as "product."

In the first presidential election of the decade, the eighties were prepackaged and sold to us as the great era of prosperity, yet in the very first year our streets began to fill up with beggars...but oh, I'm sorry, we call them "the homeless". Well, at least the package came with a president who looked and sounded like everybody's dearly beloved grandfather—the ex-governor of California himself: Ronald Reagan. An actor.

Even Mill Valley changed during that decade of decay and erosion, when our tax dollars paid for genocide in Guatemala, and mass murder in El Salvador. I'd venture down Mt. Tam to go to the store, and I'd feel out of place in my own town. Where did all the artists go? Never mind the artists—how about the teachers and carpenters, the regular people who didn't have a million dollars, but were part of the community? Mill Valley had become expensive real estate, and all the old cabins were bought up, torn down, and replaced with mansions. At least the old estates, like mine, escaped the wrecking ball. Of course, the fact that the eighties were the follow-up to the lowest point in my life didn't make them any easier to cope with. I don't know what I'd have done without Alice.

...

Alice just kind of blew into our lives that warm, windy October of '79. We looked up and there she was, like a hippie Mary Poppins stepping out of a limo. Maybe she came because we needed her, like the family in the movie Lena was always watching. I had no idea I was going to offer to do a benefit for her until I heard the words come sailing out of my mouth, so maybe she was wielding some magical powers. I got caught up in her trip without realizing I'd left the ground. She peeled off my layer of scales so subtly that I didn't feel them falling. It was the way she put things—her assumption that I was a better person than I actually was. She started telling me about Cata and Carlos, how Carlos had grown up in such poverty, and how he was so committed to helping the poor of his country, and before I knew it, I had just jumped right into a commitment.

I wasn't thinking, wasn't taking into account the fact that I didn't have a guitar player, for one thing. It wasn't like I could *replace* Juan. I not only couldn't imagine going on stage without him, I had forgotten what anything was even like before I met him.

There was just this before-death and after-death tape of my life with Juan that looped through my memory, and left precious little room for anything else.

However, Lena wasn't on a loop. She was a work in progress, and she needed me. And she was very enthused at the prospect of a concert—good memories for her, I suppose. Stephanie told her about it, probably to keep me from backing out of it. Lena could get me to do almost anything, and Stephanie knew it. My mother was obviously convinced that if she could keep me away from heroin long enough, I'd come back to the land of the living.

It pissed me off the way she interfered, but I was totally dependent on her, and I appreciated her as much as I resented her, so the whole complex dynamic became part of the Juan A.D. loop. God knows, Lena's life would have been hell without Stephanie. And then there was the core issue, which she was right about, of course. Heroin would have finished us all off; there would have been nothing to come back to when all the scales were finally shed.

When we first got back from El Salvador, I'd wake up with my heart going a mile a minute, pumping adrenaline throughout my body—like it does when you need to take action, or when you're worried something is going to happen. My mind would race, keeping time with the rush of blood, hard to access through the roar of fear in my veins, and then it would hit me in the stomach that the worst had already happened—that I could settle down into the crevices, drop back into the fissures—it didn't matter—I didn't need the adrenaline. Juan was already gone. But then I'd remember Lena telling me that we ought to just drown ourselves in the pool, like motherless puppies or something, and my heart would start thumping again—and I'd realize that I had to use the adrenaline to get myself fired into action. I had to get it together for Lena's sake, somehow. I could give a shit about my own life at that point, but Lena was worth pulling myself out of the fissures for.

Enter Mary Poppins.

Alice flipped over the benefit offer. She immediately started planning how the funds would be used, getting all excited over the prospect of medical supplies and food for the people in the mountains. It was a rush, her enthusiasm, and I fell into it, let it carry me away. One hand on her umbrella, the other clutching a bottle of champagne, and off we went, planning this event that was just a ludicrous idea in the harsh light of sobriety.

Nevertheless, there it was. Alice and I had set something in motion I couldn't back out of without feeling like a complete jerk. How could I not try to help the people who were opposing the people who had killed my husband? I didn't want to be involved, but I *was* involved, and that was just the way it was. The one out I left for myself was that maybe I would organize the benefit, but not play at it.

Bill Graham came on board immediately. He was always a good bet for producing benefits, probably because he was a Holocaust survivor and could identify with victims of injustice. Anyway, he felt sorry for me—everybody did. It would have been pathetic, except it was real. Bill Graham talked to the Dead about it, and they came onboard immediately. They were like that. Jefferson Starship committed right away, too, and then word got out that they were playing, and other musicians started calling me to offer their services.

Christ, the last thing I wanted to do that miserable fall of '79 was start talking to everybody and their brother about aid for El Salvador, but good old Stephanie kept putting the calls through to me—thinking she was acting in my best interests, which she was, of course. I insisted Alice stay with us to help organize things. Her community was excited about the prospective funds, so they released her from all other duties, and she moved into the big guest room overlooking the pool.

There was a big coup in El Salvador, October of '79, and Alice thought things might get better for the people with the new government in power. Then our president, Jimmy Carter, announced he would be providing "non-lethal" military aid to El Salvador, and we both knew what that meant: If the U.S. was going to strengthen the military down there, the people were going to get fucked. The military already had the power anyway. Unlike our country's, Alice's focus was always on humanitarian aid—and that I could understand. I kept thinking about how Juan had gotten so mad at me for comparing the poor of his country to flowers, when I'd meant it as a compliment. I finally understood why it had inflamed him.

Things got even more bizarre on the political front that November of '79. Some lunatic religious fanatic took over Iran, seized the American Embassy, and took a bunch of hostages. As events unfolded, it became apparent that the people over there hated us because we had put some corrupt dictator in power, this Shah, who was no more than a puppet for our government. But at least our dictator had given women some freedom. The new guy was forcing women to wear veils and stripping them of all their rights. He sounded worse than our own fundamentalist nut cases—the ones you see on late night TV telling you that God wants you to send them the five dollars you've got tucked away for your new winter coat. You couldn't like the new guy and the old one was bad, too; so there it was again—the same old shit. Iran sounded like Central America East.

The benefit was set for Friday, December 22nd, and it was a scramble to get all the promo done in that short a time. I couldn't get my band together—just couldn't bear to have us all in the same room rehearsing, and no Juan. Anyway, with Starship and the Dead headlining, they didn't need me to help draw, and Lauren thought they could bill a mystery guest appearance, which would be me. *If* I could do it.

As it turned out, I did go on that night, in a big jam session. The energy was so amazing that when Jerry announced they might have a special guest, glancing over at me in the wings, his eyebrows raised in a question mark, I didn't hesitate. For the first song, I did a standard with the musicians who were already up there. Then I turned around, and there were my guys: Daryl on bass, Sam on rhythm guitar, and Neil at the piano. They broke into "Way of the World," with Mickey Hart drumming, Pete Sears on the Hammond B-3, and Bobby and Jerry sharing lead guitar lines. The audience went nuts. I started crying in the middle of the song, but it didn't matter.

Alice was over on the side of the stage dancing with Lena on her hip, smiling ear to ear. I pulled them both on stage with me, and that opened the floodgate; all the families and friends of the bands backstage poured out onto the stage, and we all danced together for the final song.

Stephanie had called my band mates and asked them to show up. It broke the ice—helped shoot me back into the flow of music, safely downstream from the whirlpool of heroin.

We raised a ton of money for aid for El Salvador, although that then became a source of anxiety because it meant Alice would be going down there to administer it. Despite all her assurances that they wouldn't dare touch a member of a religious order, I was nervous. They wouldn't have dared touch a member of the oligarchy either. That had been the line when Juan went back down there.

All my energy had been focused on the concert. When it was over, I was left with the life-threatening prospect of my first Christmas without Juan. I had already bought mountains of toys for Lena, found some rare jazz records for Ray, and had Marianne help me pick out some clothes for Stephanie and Alice's gifts. I figured bonuses would do the trick for everybody else that year. Trish and Stephanie had bought a tree, and we had all decorated it the previous week. There was nothing left to do but wait for Christmas to descend like a pendulum.

I awoke on the afternoon of the 23rd to the smell of cookies. Lena was perched on a high stool in the kitchen, surrounded by Alice and Stephanie and Trish. Bright colors were splattered on her face, bits of frosting and glitter, as she looked up from her serious work of decorating a star cookie.

"Mama, I saved you some." She jumped down and grabbed a covered tray of plain cookies. "Look, you got one of each shape. I made these just for you."

I tried to put on a smile. “Yeah, baby, they’re amazing. I’ll just have some coffee first, okay?”

The four cookie makers were in high spirits, talking excitedly about how fun the concert had been, and how Santa Claus was coming soon. I hung out with them and decorated the cookies and laughed for Lena’s sake, but by sundown, I was ready to explode. Stephanie took Lena out to the Marin production of “The Nutcracker” that evening, and Trish went to be with her family, which left just Alice and me at home. Alice heated us some leftovers, but I wasn’t hungry.

“Emma, you need to eat,” Alice told me. “You need to keep your strength up. You look exhausted. Performing at a big concert like that must take a lot out of you.”

“It’s not that. I’m used to that. It’s just…I just can’t do it, Alice.”

“Do what, Emma? Tell me what’s troubling you.”

“It’s all so fake, all the pretending, all the bullshit about peace on earth, goodwill to men. I just don’t see how I’m going to get through it. The first time I made him see his family was at Christmas—did I tell you that? He didn’t want to see them and I invited them anyway. I always thought I knew better than anybody else how things should be. If he hadn’t met me, he’d probably still be alive.”

“Guilt is the heaviest burden. In my faith, we forgive—even ourselves—for our own mistakes,” Alice said gently.

“Well, that must be great for you,” I snapped. Her face turned ashen. “Oh shit, sorry Alice. I didn’t mean to jump all over you. It’s just that I can’t. I mean, I understand what you’re saying. I’m usually the one telling people not to feel guilty; but it isn’t only Juan’s death. I played a big part in my best friend’s death, too. Christ, it’s like I generate this storm of destruction around me, while I stay safe right in the fucking eye of it. You should run from me. I’m lethal for those I love.”

“Okay, Emma. I’m not going to try to talk sense into you. That’s your truth at the moment. I understand. But let’s go over to the Mission district tomorrow and dish out some food. That always makes me feel better. Skip Christmas Eve at your parent's house and come work with me instead. There's a large group of Salvadoran refugees at Compassion House. We could go buy some toys and take them over there. We should bring Lena—she'll love it. Lots of kids."

"I can't do it, Alice."

"Sure you can," she said. And by God, she dragged me out of bed at noon the next day—had Lena come in and jump on the bed, all hyped up about our adventure in refugee wonderland. Off we went in the limo to FAO Schwarz for toys and then over to a funky part of the City.

The first big surprise was Sandy. Alice was introducing me to all these people, and someone told me to wait, that they'd go get the director of the place, that she'd want to meet me, and what the hell, out walked Sandy. Crazy-dancer-who-tried-to-kill-herself-on-my-tour-because-I-broke-her-heart-Sandy. She looked as surprised to see me as I was to see her.

"Emma, it's been so long!"

"Well, yeah," I said, fumbling for words. "How are you?"

She threw back her head and laughed. "Better than the last time you saw me, that's for sure. I'm sorry about all that." She turned to the others. "Emma and I were friends during the worst year of my life, right before I came out." She turned back to me and took my arm. "Come on, let me show you around."

Before I knew it, I was swept up in the flurry of preparing dinner for what seemed like a billion people, and when the people actually swarmed into the room, they floored me. These were faces I recognized from El Salvador and Guatemala. I had to work to keep from crying into their food. I kept thinking *these are the people Cata is with. Juan would be so happy that someone is helping them.* By the time we had cleaned up after dinner, I was so exhausted that I forgot how miserable I was.

Sandy had organized a Christmas Pageant featuring the little kids, and she naturally included Lena in it. I sat there on a fold-up chair, watching my child enact the ancient story of Jesus' birth with these kids from her father's country, and it was the most beautiful performance I'd ever seen.

Then the kids began to open their presents. Lena went squealing around the room in delight because she got to help hand them out. She was never this excited about the piles of loot she always received on such occasions. Alice's eyes caught mine at some point, and if she weren't such a goddamn saint, I'd swear I saw an "I told you so" smirk on her face. I realized I was smiling through tears, and the world looked better for it.

By the end of the evening I had revised my opinion of Sandy, and that left me looking at what a jerk I'd been to her. You know, I never called to see how she was doing or anything—after she tried to kill herself, for Christ sake. Jesus, what had I been thinking?

...

Sandy became one of my best friends—a constant source of inspiration. I've tried many times to apologize to her for being such an asshole in the past, but she always insists that she was just as much to blame…which isn't true, but that's Sandy. She sees the cup as half-full, even if it's empty. As we got deeper into the eighties, and things got progressively worse, there were so many refugees that the shelter had to expand, and it still couldn't meet the needs of all the people. Nonetheless, Sandy would maintain that things always get worse before they get better—all evidence to the contrary.

...

Christmas Day of '79 was low-key at Ray and Stephanie's. I got through it with a lot of champagne and cognac, and thinking about what we might be able to organize in the Bay Area to help Compassion House. Juan's family called from the East Coast, where they were spending the holidays visiting Ricky. It looked like they weren't going to be encouraging their surviving son to come home and get murdered. I had hoped I might hear from Cata, but it didn't happen.

...

Alice left for El Salvador that January of 1980, and I turned into a nervous wreck. The big hope for some kind of peace down there had dissolved with the collapse of the new government. The civilian ministers had been unable to control the violence of the military, so the whole damn thing fell apart. The Death Squads were evidently carrying on business as usual, and there was Alice, marching right into the whole mess.

I started writing lyrics again—out of self-defense. It seemed traitorous to Juan to be writing without him, and the songs were melodramatic, but the activity settled me down a little. Lena and I started spending time at Compassion House, too. She liked it cause of all the kids, and Sandy's dance lessons. I liked it because it gave her a chance to keep up her Spanish, and it was something for me to do that felt of some use.

One day in March, Lena and I showed up at the House, and Sandy met us at the door with a conspiratorial grin on her face. "We've been waiting for you. Come into my office. There are some people who want to meet you."

Sitting in her office was a Salvadoran couple and five kids whom I presumed were their children.

"Emma, allow me to introduce you to the Carpios, Carlos's family," Sandy said.

Carlos's family! I whooped for joy and embraced them, crying, and exclaiming over each of the children. They hugged me back and spoke to me in excited Spanish that was too fast for me to understand. "What? What are they saying?" I asked Sandy.

"They bring you happy greetings from Carlos and Cata that they are safe, and are married now, and oh, they say they think of you and Lena always. Also, Cata told them— specifically—to send her love to *Stephanie.*"

Stephanie: the password again.

I jumped right on the bandwagon with my new in-laws because although there wasn't anything I could do hands-on for Cata and Carlos, there was definitely stuff I could do to help the Carpios. I rented them a house in the Mission, close to Compassion House, so they could take English lessons every day. Manuel and Yolanda had gone through hell, losing two children to the Death Squads, and one to some hideous fever—not to mention Carlos being in hiding up in the mountains. They had virtually no money or possessions. They'd used what little they had to pay someone to get them across the border. But they didn't want charity. They wanted to work—so I started asking around for them.

It wasn't easy. They had no language skills or documents, so most of the jobs available to them were menial labor, like gardening and housekeeping. Manuel had grown up in the city, owned a small store, didn't know the first thing about gardening. Yolanda was willing to clean houses, but that would have meant leaving her kids all day, which is what most of the refugees had to do. Eventually, I helped Manuel get a job with the local Spanish TV station.

In the midst of getting the Carpios settled, something happened in El Salvador that actually made the news here. Archbishop Romero, the same big honcho who had presided over Juan's funeral service, was murdered by a Death Squad gunman during Mass at a cathedral in San Salvador. The audacity of the murder was unbelievable. The murderer just walked right in and shot him in front of God and everybody. So much for Alice's assurance that members of the church were immune to the violence.

When Alice first left, she called me once a week. But after she went into the mountains to deliver supplies to the rural villages, I didn't hear from her for almost three months.

Then, in July of 1980, Lena and I got back from the beach to find Alice taking a nap in the guest bedroom.

I watched her from the doorway as she slept. Lena wanted to wake her immediately, but I insisted on letting her sleep. She was very thin, and looked a tiny bit older for the wear.

When she finally awoke at dinnertime, she was as energetic and enthusiastic as ever. She'd seen the newlyweds. Cata and Carlos were healthy and happy, living in ditches and makeshift shelters up in the mountains. She was full of stories about how the aid money had saved lives by providing medical supplies, and helped sustain people whose crops had been burned or stolen by the army. She stayed with us a couple of weeks, and then left for D.C. to speak at some church thing. We met her for dinner at the airport in S.F. before she left for Salvador again. There was no stopping her, of course.

She called in September to say that she was heading back into remote places where there was no phone service, and not to worry.

Then, at the beginning of December, it was all over the news that the bodies of four U.S. nuns had been found in some rural area of El Salvador. They had been raped and murdered. I held my breath as they named the slain churchwomen, expecting another lethal blow. But Alice wasn't one of the victims.

I felt ashamed of the relief I felt, but the shame quickly turned to outrage the next day, as Jeane Kirkpatrick, our foreign policy advisor, assured a reporter that the Salvadoran government wasn't responsible for the murder of the churchwomen. "The nuns were not just nuns. The nuns were also political activists," she said—as though it was their fault that they got murdered. Along the same line of thought that a woman is asking for rape by wearing a short skirt, or how about, just by being a woman. Oh yeah, Alice was down there doing the same kind of activism, only in her religion it was called aiding the poor. If I'd been nervous before, after that incident I was flat out terrified.

True to my natural instincts, when fear moved in, I took flight. Since my old escape via heroin was no longer an option, and Lena always freaked out when I got over-the-top wasted, there was nothing to do but go somewhere. It had to be someplace that wasn't a Juan before-death scene, someplace we'd never been together. Bill suggested Bali, so I gathered up Ray and Stephanie, Trish and Lena, and off we went for the holidays.

Bill met us there a few days after Christmas. On New Year's Day, 1981, we woke up in bed together, with Lena snuggled down between us. He had put the move on me, but it was too soon—I couldn't go through with it, although as guilty as it made me feel, I wanted to. He held me all night anyway, and when Lena came shuffling in around five a.m. like she always did, it didn't seem to faze her to find him there. She just plunked down between us and went back to sleep. It was Bill, after all.

We arrived home to find that our new president, Ronald Reagan, had resumed military aid to El Salvador and Guatemala—in spite of the news of ongoing atrocities, in spite of all the international human rights organizations' reports supporting the news stories, in spite of the murder of churchwomen—in spite of Juan. In March, Reagan gave them another 25 million, and the bloodbath began in earnest.

Alice came back to the States that June, in time for my birthday. I was on the road with my *Follow the Sun, '81* tour. She met up with us in St. Louis, full of news of carnage and bloodshed. At least Cata and Carlos were still alive. Alice stayed with the tour a week, then off she went on a speaking engagement. In New York, at the beginning of August, Alice joined us again and we held an impromptu press conference about the situation in Central America. The reporters were interested because of the four slain nuns in El Salvador. The situation in Guatemala had also finally become news.

Father Stanley Rother, the same priest Juan and I had met in Santiago, Atitlan had been murdered by one of the death squads. All the Mayas getting killed off like cattle hadn't made the news, but the murder of a priest from Oklahoma got Time Magazine's attention. The article didn't say *why* he was killed, but Alice knew.

"When the Guatemalan army, which is trained by U.S. forces, marched into town and began killing people," she explained to the reporters, "he rounded up most of the villagers and gave them sanctuary in the old mission church." Tears filled her eyes, but she carried on speaking in an even tone of voice. "He saved the lives of thousands of innocent Mayan villagers that night. But the army got even—the death squads came back at a later date and shot him as he slept in his own bed. And the violence just kept coming. The army came back for the *campesinos*—men, women, and children. It was a massacre."

"And the same kind of thing is going on in El Salvador," I chimed in." I would know—my husband was one of the victims of the so-called *civil war*. It's nothing to do with communism, like our government tries to say. It's about economic justice—about people whose children are starving!" I realized I was close to yelling, and that tears weren't far behind, so I opened the conference up to questions.

Most of the journalists paid close attention to what Alice and I had to say. I couldn't believe how they stayed on topic—I could never get them to do that in the interviews I used to do before Juan's death. Then again, considering the self-absorbed shit I used to talk about back then, it's no fucking wonder.

...

Actually, I try not to say 'fuck' out loud anymore, or I have to put a quarter in the 'swearing jar.' It's a system Lena and I came up with to try to control our use of language. We count the quarters at the end of the month and whoever has the most has to give the other person her quarters, plus a twenty-minute back rub. I think she suspects that I'm not going to go broke losing a few dollars a month, and it's not exactly torturous for me to rub her back, but I complain up a storm if I lose—which I usually do.

...

That *Follow the Sun '81* tour, I got back into the swing of performing. Bill had found me a great lead guitarist—a chick, for God sake, and it turned out to be the best thing that had happened to me since Alice. Chrissie was only twenty—couldn't even go into bars yet, but Jesus, she could play the guitar. Plus, it was great to have another female in the band.

The record company had just about had it with me before the tour—were all but threatening my life if I didn't get out there and do something. It was more of the same old thing—time limits on how long you're allowed to grieve.

The tour generated album sales, and *This Time Around* went double platinum, but that wasn't enough for the record company. Before I was even off the road, the pressure was on for another album. Herbie and some company execs came to the show in New York and started in about how the label was anxious to get a new record out by Christmas—Christmas, for Christ sake! Herbie even had the nerve to throw in a line about music being a business.

When I got home in September, Bill paid me a surprise visit. "I thought we should start writing some songs," he said.

"I have a better idea," I told him. "Let's go get some Indian food in town instead."

We talked about small things over dinner, laughing about our early recording days—agreeing that it was miraculous that anything ever got done, with me wasted most of the time. On the ride home, I glanced over at him, and noticed he had put a small gold hoop in his ear—it looked sexy, contrasted with his strong jaw line. I glanced at him again, and my stomach fluttered. Unexpectedly, I felt self-conscious. He caught my eye, and we both fell silent.

We pulled into my driveway, and Bill came around to open my door for me. He gave me his hand, but instead of just helping me out of the car, he grabbed me and backed me up against the car. Suddenly, we were kissing and tearing at each other's clothes. We would have done it right there in the driveway if it wasn't for the possibility that Lena could be watching.

Bill was breathing hard. "Let's go into the guest cabin."

"Yes," I said, over and over again. We went into the cabin, went for a swim afterward, then back into the cabin, and eventually we ended up doing it one more time in my bed. It was good; it was very good. It wasn't Juan and me, but it had its own magic.

I lay awake long after Bill had gone to sleep. I wondered if Juan could see what was going on…if there is a heaven or something, where you can still see your loved ones below…was I being unfaithful to Juan?

The next morning, instead of being romantic like I expected him to be, Bill started in on me about writing. “Alright, sweetheart, I understand you don’t *feel* creative, but that doesn’t mean we shouldn’t try. Let’s just mess around for a couple of hours and see what happens.” He laughed. “I can’t afford my lifestyle if we don’t start being productive. I might actually have to start working again. You don’t want to do that to me, do you?”

“Very funny, Bill.” I glared at him. He just kept smiling.

“Come on, Emma. I’m playing with you.” He tried to rub my shoulders, but I shrugged him off.

“What am I to you?” I yelled, but I was thinking: *What would Juan think about this...Bill sleeps with his wife, and then wakes up making stupid jokes.* “What are we doing here, Bill? Get out of my house. You shouldn’t be here—get out.”

He didn’t budge an inch. “I’m not going anywhere; not this time. I’ve always been here, sweetheart. I love you. But that doesn’t mean I’m going to sit around and watch you twiddle your thumbs. You’ve got to start writing again.”

My anger broke and I fought back tears.“ I *have* been writing, Bill, but you won’t like the lyrics. Everything I write is a big, fucking downer. Nobody’s going to want to hear it, don’t you get that?” Now I was sobbing.

Bill put his arms around me and pulled me close. When my tears subsided, he said, “That never stopped you before, baby. What have you got? Come on, show me.”

“You think you can handle it, Bill? There,” I said, and handed him a sheet of lyrics.

Not A Day Goes By

I close my eyes
And imagine you across the room
But when I look
I see only loss and gloom
And not a day goes by

When I don't think of you
And not a day goes by
When I don't want you to
Be kissing me…holding me
Passion of your body molding me
Your hair shining dark like polished slate
Reflecting desire that will not wait

No, not a day goes by
When I don't cry
And not a day goes by
That I don't try *(chorus)*
To believe we'll be together again
Because love is not supposed to end
Not a day goes by
No, no, not a day goes by

I close my eyes
And imagine there is peace on earth
But when I look
I see a gaping dearth
And not a day goes by
When a child doesn't cry
And not a day goes by
When I don't wonder why
The fields do burn, the crops they die
The people yearn to just get by
To tend their corn and beans in broad daylight
Feed their children, keep them safe at night
No, not a day goes by…(repeat chorus, first verse, chorus, and out)

He looked up after he finished reading through the song. "I didn't expect anything else. Let's start with this—I like the hook. It's good, Emma. And it's okay—I can handle it, if you can."

I went to take a shower. By the time I was dressed and ready to begin the day, Bill had come up with the perfect chords for *Not A Day Goes By*. It turned out to be the title track for my next album. I was impressed that he could put aside feelings that had to be heavy for him, considering what he'd just told me, and do the work. But, hey, it was Bill—always the professional. I cried when he played me the tune. He took me in his arms. "It's okay, I know you'll always love him…it's okay."

"I can't help it, Bill. It doesn't mean I don't have feelings for you."

"Don't worry about it. Juan was a great guy. But he's gone, sweetheart, and it's okay for you to love me now. It doesn't mean you loved him any less."

I couldn't look at him. "I'm not ready for this yet, Bill. Can we take it back a few notches?"

He pulled me to him. "Whatever you need. I've got to get back to L.A. to finish up a project, but how about if I bring my stuff up when I come back? I could stay in the guesthouse, and we could get a lot done." He breathed into my ear. "We can take things one step at a time…whatever you want."

…

Bill was back in time for Lena's fifth birthday party in October. The Avelars came up for the big bash, Marta and kids in tow. We had dropped the *Don* and *Doña* bit by that time. I just refused. Since they were living in the States, I didn't see why I had to refer to them like they were fucking royalty or something. Anyway, we were closer. The vast chasm between us had filled in with tears.

Watching Lena make a wish and blow out her candles, I wondered what she was wishing for—probably that she had her papa back, I guessed. I was wrong about that. As I was tucking her into bed that night, she said, "Mama, want to know what I wished?"

"If you want to tell me, baby, okay; but you don't have to."

"I wished you'd stop smoking. I'm scared you're gonna die—like *Pap*i. It's bad for you; I saw it on TV."

Well, that blew my mind. The perils of television—Jesus! At first I was pissed off at the mere thought of losing a huge source of comfort, but the reality of Lena's fear kept dripping away until it finally wore through my thick skull. Yeah, I gave up cigarettes again—this time for good.

After Lena's birthday, it was a countdown to Juan's birthday again. Fucking horrible occasion, a birthday, when somebody is dead. I wrote a song for him that year.

One More Innocent

It's so easy to close your eyes
Just believe what the leaders say
Or if you don't like what your country's doing
You can look the other way
In the interest of security
We set a dictator up today
Send our money to aid murderers
It's just a game that nations play

But every time we close our eyes
One more innocent dies
Every time we believe the lies
One more innocent dies *(chorus)*
We steel ourselves against their cries
And one more innocent, one more innocent
One more innocent dies
They say Communism's moving in
Nobody knows where it will spread
So they kill teachers, nuns, and intellectuals
To stop a country going Red
See the hungry eyes of little children
Hear them crying to be fed

It's true we have the food to send them
But we send them bombs instead
(Repeat Chorus)

Bill was enthused about the lyrics and immediately started working on the music. "The chorus is really good, sweetheart."

"Yeah, thanks, but do you think it's too heavy? Why do I think the company isn't going to like it?"

"It's perfect. It expresses what you're feeling. What else would they expect you to be writing about after what you've been through? I'll make the music up-tempo. It'll work."

We spent that October of '81 writing, and started recording in Sausalito in November. Bill had become a permanent fixture in my bed, although technically he was still staying in the guesthouse. One day Lena skipped into the room after school to wake us up, climbed into bed between us, and said, "Bill, are you my new papa? My friend, Sunshine, got a new papa. His name is Tom, and he took her fishing. I wanna go fishing."

"Do you want me to be your papa?" Bill sat up and gathered her onto his lap. "I'll take you fishing either way. Ask your mama, buttercup."

I glared at Bill. "Maybe, we'll see," I told Lena.

"Please Mama. I want Bill to be my papa. I love Bill."

"I know you do, sweetie, but what about Juan? He's your real papa."

"Sunshine's got two papas. I wanna have two. *Papi's* dead. He won't be mad. You said he wants me to be happy."

Out of the mouths of babes.

Lena went into the kitchen for a snack, and I turned to Bill. "Well, that was brave—*Ask your mama, buttercup*!"

"You know the score, Emma. I'd like to marry you, and I would definitely be into adopting Lena."

"Did you just propose to me?"

"What would you say if I did?"

"I'd say it's too soon. But you might as well move your stuff into the house. I believe Lena just gave us her royal permission to live together."

Bill chuckled. "Yeah, I guess I might as well move in—I ain't got nothin else going," he said, with an exaggerated hillbilly accent.

I punched him in the arm. "You know that's not what I meant."

"Sweetheart, I'll take you any which way…it's your call. But I would like to take Lena fishing. Why don't we go back to Bali for the holidays?"

A fish was caught in Bali. When we got home, its corpse was mounted on a plaque and hung in Lena's bedroom. Bill says Lena caught it, but she gives him credit for helping her. She's fair-minded, like Juan was. If it'd been me, I'd have bragged that I brought it in single-handedly.

Still, I didn't like the looks of the damn thing. I tried complaining about it to Bill. "It's revolting—a big dead fish hanging on the wall."

"That's what you think, Emma. You want everything in her room to be pink and frilly cause she's a girl?"

I laughed. "Fuck you, Bill."

Bill put his arms around my waist. "Listen sweetheart, that fish represents something Lena and I brought in together. You and I have brought a lot into the world—countless songs, and albums…but there's something else we could bring in together—something way more important." He kissed the back of my neck and ran his hands down the front of my body, coming to rest on my stomach.

"Oh…oh…" When it dawned on me, what he was getting at, I was stunned. It had never occurred to me to have another child. "Jesus, Bill, that's heavy…really? That's what you want?"

"Just think about it, Em."

I turned around to face him. "It's too soon. You know I love you…but I'm not over Juan." Tears welled up; I couldn't help it. "I don't think I'm ever going to be over Juan. I can't imagine it."

"I can live with that, sweetheart. I can live with Juan being part of the family. I see him every time I look at Lena…and it doesn't make me love her less."

"I know. Let's just see what happens. I need time, baby."

We finished the album in February '82. A spring tour was booked to promote it. I wanted to go be with Bill in L.A. for a while, but Lena was in school. He had to do an album, but promised that he would try to book the next one in Sausalito or San Francisco. It would take him over a year to move his entire base of operations to Northern California, but in the meantime, I was out on the road a lot anyway. I wasn't tempted by other men, either. I had no desire to fuck up a good thing. Besides, the situation in Central America had grown progressively worse, and I was too busy to get into trouble. If I wasn't doing interviews, I was speaking at benefits and peace rallies.

The first time I told my story, I could barely get the words out. I felt naked, like I was exposing myself in public. Which is pretty ironic, considering how much I really did expose myself back in my wasted days—without giving it a second thought. I was exposing myself in a much more intimate way, telling the story of my husband's murder, telling about the poverty and the Death Squads. But I felt like I had to do it for Juan, and for Cata. For myself, too.

The press went easy on me with *Not A day Goes By*. The reviews were less cynical than I'd thought they'd be. I suppose it was because they pitied me, or maybe they actually liked the record—I'll never know.

One day in '82, I was having lunch with my reporter friend, Wade, in North Beach. It was one of those beautiful winter days in San Francisco when the air is crisp and the sun is shining, and I mentioned to him how the quality of reporters had changed so much in the years since Juan died.

He actually chuckled. "You're kidding, right?"

I just stared at him.

"You're the one who's changed, Emma. The good reporters were always there—you just weren't meeting them."

"Oh come on, that's not fair."

"Look, if it comes to reporting a sexy singer's opinion on the status of the student protest movement at Berkeley, or describing her giving an actor head under the table in a nightclub, which do you honestly think people are going to want to read about?"

"You never wrote shit like that."

"But you did shit like that all the time. It made good press."

"I can't believe you would defend the paparazzi. Christ, not you, too."

Wade reached over and took my hand. "Listen Emma, for me it's always been about the music. You write good songs. This album is more than good, and people respect you for what you're doing…and oh, by the way," he said with a sly smile, "the magazine wants to do an article on you for our political section. What do you think?"

I thought about that conversation a lot because it surprised me. It had honestly never occurred to me before that it was my behavior attracting those hack types. I had always functioned under the assumption that things just happen—and you go with the flow; do your own thing, *man.*

Wow, an interview in the political section! It made sense because I *had* become political by that time—had, in fact, been beheaded and tossed into the political arena. One thing leads to another, and before you know it, your bodiless head is rolling around in blood, screaming things like, *You can't separate social injustice from environmental destruction, or corporate collusion with military dictatorships from Death Squads…from death…from Juan's death.*

But speaking of attracting certain types, between the album and the interview in Rolling Stone, I attracted a whole new circle of friends—people who astonished me, like Alice did. Our government may have been hell-bent on keeping the military dictators in power in Central America, but the people I met were putting their lives on the line to help the ordinary people of those countries.

In October of ’83, a couple of days after Lena’s seventh birthday, Alice brought a doctor to the house. She was grinning ear to ear. “Emma, Bill, this is Charlie. He’s been living behind the lines in El Salvador. I thought you might have a thing or two to talk about.”

“Really? You were behind the lines where? Which zone? Did you ever meet Carlos Carpio, or Cata Avelar?”

“Yes, both of them. They send you their love, and said to tell you how much they miss you and Lena.”

“You’re kidding! You talked to them—I don’t believe it! So, they’re okay?”

“The conditions are bad, but they’re fine. Cata is going to make a great doctor. She’s been assisting Carlos and me in surgery; she’s a wonder at removing shrapnel.”

Wow, how had that gone by me all this time? “What? Cata’s going to be a doctor, too? I thought she was a fierce female warrior or something.”

“She’s one of our best medics—trained on the job. She doesn’t fight unless she has to. Not all of the FMLN are fighters, you know.”

“Well, maybe you’re not, but Cata was always so kick-ass. You’re telling me she’s non-violent now?”

“When it’s your job to patch people up, you lose the taste for inflicting those wounds—fast. Carlos doesn’t fight either. He’s too valuable to the people as a doctor. But if you have to, you bear arms. It’s a fact of war.”

“Nobody tells me a damn thing.” I glared at Alice.

“It was going to be a surprise. Cata wanted to tell you herself,” Alice said.

“Did it never occur to you that I wouldn’t worry so much if I knew she wasn’t fighting?”

Charlie smiled, looked from me to Alice and back. “Don’t worry about Cata. She’s healthy, and she has uncommonly good sense. Bombs are indiscriminate anyway. It doesn't matter much what you're doing—luck of the draw. I think Cata is lucky." He focused in on me. "She's lucky to have someone like you who cares about her, that's for sure."

Bill shot Charlie a piercing glance, but it was obvious he was joking. "You're not coming on to my old lady, are you?"

"Can you blame me?" Charlie laughed.

His "old lady"—Bill had just casually dropped the term into his sentence. I mulled it over for a few minutes, weighing how it felt. I sensed that Bill knew what I was thinking about. Even though he went on with the general conversation, he was waiting for my reaction. When I finally looked up at him, I was smiling. It was a small moment between us, but it sealed the deal.

We sat around talking to Alice and Charlie for hours, drinking wine and exchanging stories. Life in the mountains sounded brutal. Charlie, Carlos, and Cata had been the only doctors for the guerrillas and peasants in the dangerous Guazapa zone. They'd been treating patients with no medicine, not even aspirin. And they'd been performing surgeries without anesthetics. Everybody was constantly sick with diarrhea from the lack of good water, and they had to stay on the move to avoid being killed, but apart from that, everything was fine. Jesus!

The night wore on as we talked. After discussing diarrhea, no subject was off limits. I asked Charlie what the women were doing about birth control, and he glanced at Alice.

She shrugged. "It's fine. Tell her. I don't agree with the pope on the issue of birth control, anyway. Things are bad enough for those women, without having to be pregnant and worrying about a baby."

"Oh God, right. I didn't think that one through, Alice. I'm glad it's not an issue for you. Then does that mean that all those Catholic women don't use birth control?"

Charlie spoke up. "Basically, it's up to the individual. We try to accommodate the women in every way we can." He got up and started collecting his things. "It's late; we should probably get going."

Bill got up too. "No, you don't have to go. Why don't you spend the night? We have plenty of room. Alice, you could take your usual bedroom, and we can put Charlie in the guesthouse."

I knew that Alice was celibate, but I thought I sensed some sparks between her and Charlie, so I piped up. "Unless you want to stay together, that is."

Alice turned bright red. "Good grief, Emma. What a thing to say!"

"Just checking—you might have changed your mind about the celibacy thing." She seemed so flustered that it made me curious. "Actually Alice, I've never asked you before, have you *ever* had sex? Is it okay to ask?"

"Well, you're nothing if not candid! Yes, I have in fact, but it's really bad mannered of you to ask."

"You have?" I was dumbfounded. Somehow, I'd thought she'd say no. I guess I saw her as the Virgin Mary or something. "Isn't it against your religion?"

"Oh Emma, it was a long time ago—before I joined my order. I was engaged to a guy when I was in college. He graduated a year before me, and then he got drafted. He died on his second day in Vietnam."

Jesus, I hadn't lost my touch for putting people on the spot, or for making an ass of myself. I went to her room later that night and apologized.

"Don't worry. It was a long time ago. But you know how it is—you don't get over it. He was my first and only lover. What about you? Was Juan your first love?"

That made me laugh. "First of all, there's a big difference between love and lover on the planet I grew up on." I flopped down on her bed and stretched out. "I had a lover at age thirteen, but I sure as hell didn't love him."

Alice stared at me in bewilderment, her mouth open. "You were having sex at thirteen?"

“Jesus, Alice, we’re not all nuns. Yeah, I was thirteen. He was a friend of Ray’s.”

“Your father, Ray?”

“Yeah, but he never knew about it. You know how teenagers are about wanting to have something separate from their parents. It made me feel grown-up. I never told Ray or Stephanie.”

“Emma, you were molested. Is this man still around?”

“Yeah, maybe you’re right, at first…okay, maybe so.” Suddenly, I felt queasy. “But I wasn’t molested on an on-going basis. Jesus—don’t try to turn it into something it wasn’t. I was into it…sort of.”

“You were too young to have consensual sex. It was molestation. It’s not something to be ashamed of.”

“I’m not ashamed. What? Are you trying to make me out to be a victim? I hate that victim shit. I’ve always done what I want. Fuck that. I’m sorry I told you.”

She wasn’t about to let it rest. “Will Lena be old enough to have sex at age thirteen—and with a man old enough to be her father? Would it be okay with you?”

“I’m going to bed, Alice.” I stormed out of the room.

That conversation haunted me because Alice had come right out with a truth that I’d never looked full in the face. It was the demon that lurked in shadows, and she had taken it on without a second thought. Of course, she wasn’t the one who felt the shame of it.

Anyway, Rob was dead. He’d died drunk driving—took two other people with him. Of course, I couldn’t get too judgmental about that, considering all the times I’d arrived somewhere so wasted that I had no clue how I’d driven there.

Alice’s take on the Rob episode gnawed at me, clawed at me—left me furious with Ray and Stephanie for not protecting me better, furious with myself for allowing it to happen, and furious at Rob.

So there I was, Fall Tour of ’83—this furious, heartbroken person, out on the road performing my ass off, calling home twice a day to talk to Lena and Bill, missing them both like crazy, and I had this dream that woke me up.

I was in a room by myself. Lights began to shimmer—there was something menacing about it. Electricity filled the air, and I knew that some evil thing had entered the room. I was frozen with terror, couldn't move, couldn't speak. The crushing evil was all around me…and then I felt it enter my body: the demon. I knew I had been *possessed.*

I couldn't bear having the hideous creature inside me. I struggled to regain control of my limbs, and with great effort, managed to move one of my arms. I thrust my hand inside my body, right through my skin, into my heart, and pulled the thing out.

I had the demon by the leg or arm, and suddenly, I was in a crowd of people, angrily dragging the thing across the floor as I shoved my way through the dense crowd. I was jerking it along roughly, furiously, when I happened to glance down at it…and saw that it was a kid. I saw childish, naked genitals, and realized that it was just a little girl. I immediately felt remorse. Here I'd been—dragging a little girl through the dirt.

I leaned over and gently picked her up, started carrying her in my outstretched arms, crying, saying over and over again, "Please, let me through. Can't you see how fragile I am?"

I woke up sobbing—fumbled around for the lamp switch in the unfamiliar hotel room, my hands sweaty and shaky. My first thought was that I needed a drink, but I didn't pour myself one. I went over the dream in my mind, and a cold shiver shot down my spine, in spite of the heated room. I fought an impulse to curl up under the covers like a child—got up and began pacing the room instead. I turned on the TV and tried to watch it, but I was too freaked out. Then I had it—I'd call Linda.

It was the wee hours for her, but she answered her phone. "Emma, what's wrong? Are you okay?"

"Yeah, I'm okay…well, actually, I'm not. I'm freaked."

"Are you high?"

"No, no, nothing like that. I had a nightmare, and I thought you might know what it meant."

"You're kidding. No, you're not kidding, are you. Okay, fine, tell me, but I'm still half-asleep."

"I'm sorry about the time change; please don't be mad at me. I'm desperate."

"It's okay, Emma. I'm listening."

I told her the dream as clearly as I could. She uttered a knowing "uh huh" every now and then, and when I had finished, she pronounced, "It's you, Emma. That's obvious. You're trying to heal a part of yourself that was wounded as a child—flushing out your demons, literally. It's a good dream. Think about it. I gotta go back to sleep. Call me tomorrow."

I sat up for hours examining the dream, trying to look at it as "good," as Linda had told me to do. Was Rob the demon that tormented me for most of my adult life? That wouldn't make sense, because the demon turned out to be a little girl—presumably, me.

I sat with the dream for days, and then, out of the blue, I had an ah-ha moment. Rob didn't have the power to haunt me—only I could do that. It was me—haunting me. Jesus! It was my attitude toward the child I'd been that was screwing with me.

Sandy likes to say it's what you repress that damages you. She'd know. She did a hundred years of therapy after her suicide attempt. I called her while I was still on the road—got the name of her therapist. Wherever that dream was going to take me, I was willing to go. I'd had it with being afraid of dark corners.

In January of '84, I started therapy. It wasn't something I'd ever imagined doing, but once I got into it, I wondered why I hadn't started years ago. I guess I thought that if I got too happy, I'd lose my creativity, or some such bullshit.

Believe it or not, that demon dream was the beginning of a healing process…and it didn't lead to loss of creativity or anything else.

I hadn't repressed the memory of Rapist Rob, but I'd spent all my adult life trying to deny the impact he had on me. I was always looking for an older, wiser version of myself who could face the demons and banish the ghosts. Then Juan came along and did it for me. And then Juan was stolen from me.

Without Lena, I'd have been totally screwed. I loved her enough to resist the temptation of drugs, but I couldn't control their pull. It was only through forgiving Rob that the ties alcohol and drugs had on me were snipped, and I was freed from even the temptation. Yeah, I said *forgiving.*

Right after I started therapy, I allowed the enormity of what Rob had done to fully hit me, and as a result, I fell into a lockstep with him again. All the hatred I had harbored for years turned into a Technicolor bitterness starring Rob—featuring a matinee and multiple screenings each night. I relived the rape over and over again, saw it clearly—how he not only raped me, but robbed me of my childhood. He had controlled my life from his lair in my unconscious for years, and now that he was forced out into the open, he had taken up residence in plain daylight. I hated him with a bloody vengeance that kept him alive.

So I took my problem to Alice—after all, she had forced the issue to begin with. I told her I needed to see her—it was an emergency.

Alice came to dinner. I had to share her with Lena until bedtime. When we were finally alone, I poured us each a cognac, and we sat down together.

"Are you going to tell me what the emergency is now?" Alice smiled. "Somehow I don't sense that it's a national disaster."

"Maybe not to you, but I've been freaking out. Didn't you tell me that the truth sets you free? So how come the whole fucking Rob thing's got me tied up in knots all over again?"

Alice didn't skip a beat. "You've got to forgive him, Emma."

I'm sure my jaw must have dropped to the floor. "You're kidding, right? I'm supposed to forgive him? Unreal, Alice, just fucking unreal."

Alice shook her head. “No, it’s not for him. It’s for your own peace of mind. I don’t want to sound preachy, but it’s true. We can’t always control what happens to us, but we can control our responses.” She took my hand and tried to get me to meet her eyes. “His hold on you is your own bitterness—let it go, and the ties that bind will be severed.”

I avoided her gaze. “Easy for you to say.”

“No, it isn’t actually. If I thought it would help you, I’d hate him right along with you…but I know it would only allow him into my life, too.”

“How can I forgive such a bastard?” I was holding back tears.

“Take back your power, Emma. As long as you hate him, he’s still calling the shots. If you forgive him, he loses all power over you. Cut him loose.”

“But how?” I looked up at her and tears rolled down my face. I hated crying—I felt humiliated that the bastard could reduce me to tears. “How the fuck do you summon up any kind of positive feelings for a child molester?” Alice hugged me and held me until I quit sobbing. I pulled away from her and rubbed my eyes. “ It’s okay; I’m okay now.”

“Listen Emma,” Alice said calmly. “It isn’t a matter of feelings; forgiveness is a choice. Feelings are unreliable—dependent on your hormones, or how much you’ve slept, or how hungry you are. You, your will, your higher self, has to be in control, and you can *decide* to forgive, regardless of how you *feel*.”

I dried the last of my tears. “I’m sick of being angry all the time. Look at how much the refugees have been through, and they don’t walk around permanently pissed off.”

Alice nodded. “It’s humbling, isn’t it. After Allen was killed in Vietnam, my grief and anger almost destroyed me. In many ways, my work in El Salvador saved my life.”

“I know—thinking about someone other than yourself, right?”

“That’s definitely a big part of it. But there’s another element that is spiritual in nature, and it involves free will.”

“You think it’s a choice—that you can *choose* to get past it?”

"We write the book of our own lives. The things that are out of our control are still part of our own personal history—we choose the way we want to remember it. And you can change the narrative any time."

"Christ, Alice, you are a saint. And you're a fucking poet, too. Why don't you write me some lyrics."

"Maybe you should write a letter to Rob."

That floored me for a minute. "He's dead, Alice. You know that."

"It's not for him; you know that."

So, I did. I sat down and wrote a long letter to Rob. I listed all the shit he did to me—the rape and the prolonged molestation—how it had affected my life. It felt disgustingly uncomfortable to even write the word "molestation", much less in a letter to a dead man. So much of who I am has been based on never seeing things in those terms, but then again, that aspect of who I am is not exactly the best part of me. I took Alice's advice—listed every way in which Rob had abused me, and followed up each sentence with: *It's not alright that this happened—it will never be alright, but I choose to forgive you.* I don't know if I could have done it if he was still alive.

I burnt the letter. I was done with Rob. It was finally over. In secret, I even said the little prayer like she told me to, asking God to forgive Rob…just in case there was something in it.

With Rob gone, a whole new space opened up inside me…made more room for Bill. We had an agreement, Bill and I. He'd asked me to marry him a number of times, and I'd always replied that I wasn't ready. Finally, he told me he was going to quit asking, but that I had a standing invitation. He said, "Just let me know when you're ready."

I was on tour in New York, June of '84, and Bill had flown out to be with me on my birthday. I had a show that night, so we went out for lunch. We sat outdoors at one of our favorite Italian restaurants, enjoying the sun and drinking champagne.

Bill reached into his pocket, pulled out a small box, and placed it in front of me. "Happy Birthday, darling."

Inside was an antique diamond ring. "It was my grandmother's," Bill said. "Wear it on any finger you like."

I took the ring out and handed it to Bill. "Let's try the third finger on my left hand. See if it fits."

Bill paused. "Does this mean what I think it means?"

•••

We were married that September, at Ray and Stephanie's house. We had imagined a small, intimate wedding—just close friends and family…no way! Family and close friends, plus band, did not equal small…but it was intimate. It was a group of people aware of the bullets we'd each dodged, grateful to be alive and celebrating a new beginning. Bill and I exchanged the vows we had each written, there in the living room of the beautiful home I grew up in.

During our first holiday season as a married couple, I tried to think of a perfect Christmas present for Bill. What could I give a man who had been there for me during absolutely every crisis of my life—who had not only celebrated all my accomplishments, but helped me achieve them. The chain of hit records and songs he produced and wrote had made him a wealthy man—he didn't need anything. It had to be something only I could give him.

I quit taking my birth control pills…in secret.

April of '85, I knew. I hoped Bill hadn't noticed how queasy I'd become in the mornings. I waited till I saw my OB and it was confirmed before I said anything.

I was back home for a few weeks between tours and I tried to set up a perfect moment. "Let's have dinner at El Paseo tonight, just the two of us, okay Love?"

Bill ordered a fabulous bottle of wine and we both sipped a glass before dinner. When our food arrived, Bill tried to pour me another glass, and I refused it. He eyed me suspiciously. "What's the matter, Em? You seem distant."

Just wanting to have some fun, I scowled at him. "I have a secret."

Bill turned white. "A secret? What are you talking about?"

I broke into a smile and shoved a handful of birth control packets over the table. "My little secret. Merry Christmas, darling."

Bill's right eyebrow went up in that confused expression of his. He sorted the packets, counted them, then looked up at me. "Merry Christmas?"

"Yep, stopped those last Christmas, and the little one should be here around this Christmas."

Bill's eyes filled with tears. "Are you sure?"

I was sure alright. What I wasn't sure about was whether I could love another child as much as I loved Lena. I kept that fear to myself. By thirty-five, I had finally gained enough common sense to know that I shouldn't shoot my mouth off about everything that went through my head. Anyway, I didn't want to hurt Bill.

My fears were in vain. When Will was born, December 23, 1985, I looked into his eyes and instantly loved him as much as I'd ever loved anyone. His energy was so different from Lena's, yet as irresistible to me as she'd always been. We named him William, after Bill, who was named after his father and grandfather; only, we called him Will—Willy, when he was a baby.

Shortly after Will was born, I allowed Bill to legally adopt Lena. She wanted Bill's last name, same as her brother, but I drew the line there. We settled for Rothman-Avelar as her surname. My name got dumped, but it wasn't unexpected. I didn't catch fish with her, and anyway, she'd always been a daddy's girl. We gave Will the hyphenated name: Allison-Rothman.

During my pregnancy, a new fear had taken up residence in the back of my mind. Bill was approaching his forties, the decade in which he'd lost both his parents to cancer. All the talk of genetic predisposition to diseases made me nervous. But it's always the things you don't see coming that get you.

Stephanie died in 1989—of breast cancer, which is rampant in Marin County. Nobody can explain why in the most affluent county in the United States, where women live in a pristine environment, are highly educated and accomplished, we have a plague-like situation—the highest rate of breast cancer in the nation.

It was a gruesome five months—chemo, radiation, Stephanie growing thinner and weaker each day, and suffering horribly.

A few days before she left, went into The Great Eternal, as she called it, I had some time alone with her at home, where she chose to die, in the living room turned into a hospital room, where she could see the bay and the Golden Gate Bridge—the view she loved so much. I sent Ray to bed—he was exhausted—wearing himself thin, obviously thinking that if he suffered along with her, he could ease her pain. She was worried about him.

"Make him go take a nap, Em. Please. Anyway, I want to talk to you alone."

"Okay Stephanie, I'll get him to rest if I have to slip him a sleeping pill."

When I had brought her a cup of tea and settled down beside her, Stephanie said, "I failed you, Em. I'm sorry, darling. You've been the light of my life and I know I let you down. I should have been more of a mother."

I tried to reassure her. "What are you talking about, Mom? That's nonsense—you don't know what you're saying."

She shook her head and looked into my eyes solemnly. "Tell me honey, I need to know. You were angry at me all through your teen years and most of your twenties, too."

"I was a brat—a spoiled brat; it wasn't you, Mom."

"No, I failed you." Tears started pouring down over her sunken cheekbones, but her voice was even and clear. "Tell me honey—was it Rob?"

I couldn't believe my ears. "Mom, please don't do this to yourself."

"Em, that night we came home and Rob had been here, when you were about thirteen…you were different. My gut told me that something had happened; but you denied it, and I chose to believe you. But I've always felt that something happened—please tell me."

"Oh Mom, I wanted to spare you that."

Now Stephanie gave in to loud, gulping sobs. "I knew it, I knew it…and I did nothing." Her head thrashed on the pillow. "My gut told me, but I ignored it. Honey, it's not an excuse—there's no excuse…but I was afraid Ray would kill him if he had done anything to you. Ray loved him, and he was never worthy of Ray's love. I always knew that." She rose up onto her arms, and I adjusted the pillows for her so she could sit up a bit. "Honey, Ray honestly believed that even though Rob might flirt with you, he would never harm you. They were friends since their school days, you know."

"It wasn't your fault—I should have told you."

"No, you were a kid—I should have listened to my deeper self. And I shouldn't have let you go to New York alone either—I knew better on that one too, Em."

"Oh Mom, it's water under the bridge. You were a great mother."

"No, I should have been more of a mother and less of a buddy. You wouldn't have gone through all that suffering with heroin if I'd been more on top of things." Stephanie's sobs subsided and she regained control. Her voice was weak, but she continued. "It's only that my own mother was so strict, and I wanted you to have the freedom I didn't have till she died."

"No, don't apologize for anything; you were perfect."

Stephanie was quiet for a few minutes, obviously thinking about something painful. Her wasted-away face was forlorn as she lay there with her eyes closed. Eventually, she took a deep breath and looked up at me. "I've always felt guilty about my mother, Em. She loved me, but she was so old fashioned; and I was different from the beginning. I hated her New England staidness—

I always felt like she was suffocating me. I wasn't allowed to do any of the things that modern girls were doing…and you couldn't oppose her. She locked me in a closet for five days once—when I was eighteen—because she heard I was talking to a local boy…just *talking*! She'd bring me one plate of food a day, and a pitcher of water—that's all; and I had to use a bucket as a toilet…it was so degrading. And then she got sick—when I was nineteen; remember, I told you? It was lung cancer, and she died so horribly—drowning in her own blood." Stephanie shuddered.

"Sh, sh, Mama. It wasn't your fault."

"Instead of helping my father, I ran off to New York; and I didn't grieve for her. You understand I was still angry at her about the closet incident. I never went home again. I met Ray in Greenwich Village, and we moved here, and my father didn't fly, so I never saw him again. Aunt Mildred took care of him in his last days."

I stroked her hair and tried to soothe her. "Mom, don't. It was a long time ago. Don't do this to yourself. We're all imperfect, and I'm sure your mother understood."

Suddenly, she clutched my arm and pulled me down to her face. "Please don't tell Ray about Rob," she whispered. "I'm afraid he'll commit suicide. Honestly, Em, he won't be able to handle it." Her whisper then gave way to a tone I'd never heard my mother use. "If Rob were alive, I'd kill him myself," she said.

I cried for days after that conversation. It was true that I had wasted precious years being mad at Stephanie, and now I felt closer to her than ever and she was leaving me. She knew how much I loved her though; I'm sure she did.

Her death was one more blow to the heart, but at least it wasn't sudden. We had time to talk things out—to say our goodbyes. Per her request, my mother was cremated in the antique blue velvet dress I had given her years ago. She was beautiful even in death. I miss her horribly and always will; and I'll regret till the day I die that I took her love for granted for so many years…that I blamed her for Rob. I was lucky to have such a mother.

It's weird how life plays out. Stephanie gave me so much rope because her mom kept her on such a tight leash, and now I watch both my kids like a hawk. I'm all over Lena's every move, and she'll probably grow up and have children and raise them like I was raised. Isn't that what they say—everything skips a generation? I know it's hypocritical, as wild as I was, to keep Lena under lock and key, but I'd keep her in a rocking chair if I could. Nobody has come near her the way Rob did me, and they won't until she's an adult—until she's capable of real consent. She says I'm stricter than her friends' straight parents. You better believe it. I know what's out there.

...

1992: I wanted to go to the signing of the Salvadoran Peace Accords in Mexico in January, but I was on tour. Both Cata and Carlos were there—as delegates from their country! Not only did Cata call me from Mexico, but she asked if the offer for Carlos to attend medical school up here was still good.

"What about you?" I asked. "Your friend, Charlie Clements told me you'd make a great doctor."

"He flatters me. But yes, Emma, I would like to go back to college, too, if my parents will help me. They are no longer so angry with me. I have no money left, but I could work part-time."

"Just come," I said. "We'll find a way."

I wasn't rolling in dough the way I had been in the seventies, but I wasn't hurting either. I had put most of Juan's money into a trust for Lena, and with the rest of it I'd formed a foundation to aid groups working in El Salvador and Guatemala, as well as places like Compassion House that helped the refugees. I figured Juan would want to help the Mayas of Guatemala, considering how flashed out he was by them—and the fact that their government was trying to wipe them off the planet. I did a benefit once a year to help keep the foundation afloat, and donated twenty percent of my royalties to it. Not that I was competing with Alice for sainthood or anything—it was a huge tax break for me, and I'd rather put my money where it could do some good than have my tax dollars aid those bastards who killed my husband.

I could still sell records, but I was way out of mainstream pop, to say the least. Back in 1982, I went triple platinum with *Not A Day Goes By,* and *Love Letters*, in '84, sold two and a half million copies. But the big record of '84 was Michael Jackson's "*Thriller*."He floored us all with his Moondance, and alerted the corporations to just how much money there was to be made in the music business. Here I was with records that were nothing short of political agitation, trying to get people to pressure our government to stop supporting the violence in Central America—set against a backdrop of the Iran-Contra affair, with Reagan comparing the murderous Contras to our founding fathers—and my fans bought my records anyway.

But after *Love Letters*, sales slowed down, as the taste of the nation changed. It was the multi-national conglomerates buying up the record companies in the eighties that really changed the music business, though. To say they commercialized it would be the understatement of the century. Bands like the *Grateful Dead*, and artists like Bob Dylan and Van Morrison just kept on keeping on. They rode out that decade doing what they do, and they're going stronger than ever now.

There was a big push by my record company in the mid-eighties to get me to go "modern." They wanted me to wear clothes I hated, choreograph my free-form dancing into a routine, use drum machines and synthesizers on all my songs, and record "outside", more commercial, material. Couldn't do it. I took some time off while I was pregnant with Will, and after he was born, I didn't tour for over a year. When my contract expired in '86, I switched to a smaller, independent label that actually liked my music. I started touring again in '87—smaller venues, but the shows sold out, and still do. Now, my records fall into the "alternative rock" category, which has a way more appealing ring to me than "mainstream" anyway.

•••

They were waiting for me at the airport when I got back from the Winter '92 Tour in March: Cata and Carlos—both of them—alive! Carlos's hair was long now, and he wore a goatee and a thin moustache. A million tiny fissures outlined his eyes and creased his forehead, but he was still hot. Cata looked a lot older, too, but the lines in her face were kind and intelligent. Christ, she was younger than me, but life in the mountains had left its mark.

Still, she was as gorgeous as ever, with her dancing eyes and shiny, thick, black hair. We all piled into the limo, where I sat next to Cata. We embraced, and then we both started crying. Squirming her way in between us, Lena hugged us both, muttering soothing words. She had honed in on that middle ground just like she had always done with Juan and me. Balancing Will on his knee, Bill opened a bottle of Dom Perignon to celebrate our reunion, and poured a little bit for Lena, too.

Cata squeezed Lena's shoulder. "I can't believe my little Lena is all grown up now. And Will, he's so handsome, but he won't give his Auntie Cata a kiss."

Bill laughed. "Give him time."

"I don't kiss girls," Will said.

I patted my knee. "Except your mama. Come, sit on my lap. I've missed my boy."

Bill had moved Carlos and Cata into the guesthouse, which was perfect because we had years to catch up on, especially Cata and me. Juan had always been at the center of our relationship, and was no less so now because he was gone. Although the core had become an epicenter, the point from which pain radiated, we both took comfort in our shared experience of life in that zone. Cata had matured into an enormously capable person, and smart as hell, like Juan. Once in a while I'd see traces of that petulant teenager in the way she related to Carlos, but not often.

Bill and I, and Cata and Carlos were sitting out on the rocks at Muir Beach one gorgeous spring day a couple of months after they came back, talking about everything, ruminating about the past decade—wondering what had become of all the people who'd gone to Woodstock—musing on the phenomena of designer jeans and the peace symbol as a marketing tool. Cata, of course, steered the conversation toward Central America, stating adamantly that the revolution in El Salvador would have been successful if those people, the counter-culture of America, had been in charge.

"I don't know about that," I said. "I wish I could agree with you, but you don't understand. Americans get totally freaked out at the mere mention of Communism. After the Cuban Missile Crisis, everybody was paranoid that the Communists were going to get a foothold in the Americas…and then God knows what might happen!"

Cata laughed. She knew when I was being ironic.

Carlos frowned. "But the revolutionaries weren't Communists. Cata and I considered ourselves Socialists in the British tradition, but most of the *guerillas* didn't even know what Communism was—they only knew they couldn't feed their families, and that they had lived under terror and oppression for too long."

Bill nodded. "I hear you."

Cata chimed in. "Why should our tiny nation have been considered such a threat? The whole 'domino theory' was absurd, an elaborate ruse. An excuse to protect American business interests."

"Watch it now; you're preaching to the choir here," Bill said good-naturedly. "You should go into politics, Cata."

A big wave suddenly splashed us all with water. I shook myself off and lay back on the warm rock. "All this talk about Communism…Juan used to say that Liberation Theologians were Communist-influenced, but I haven't met any who are. Alice isn't, of course—and none of her friends are. They say their work is based on the bible—that their religion commands them to help the poor."

Cata smiled—and it was Juan's wry smile. She said, "Juan liked to play the devil's advocate. No matter what I used to say, he would take the opposing viewpoint. I think he did this to teach me to think more clearly. Perhaps he did this with you as well."

I squeezed my eyes shut to keep from breaking into tears. Every once in a while, Cata's resemblance to Juan knocked me off my feet. I gave myself a moment, then sat back up and confronted Juan's smile. "Hey, I helped him think more clearly about just as many things…but you're right—he taught me a lot." We were all quiet for a minute, and then I looked over at Bill and got pulled back to the present. "Juan didn't teach me everything," I added.

Bill slid over and put his arm around me. I could tell he was about to deliberately steer the conversation back into safer waters. "You know, it's clear to us that if we hadn't supported the military dictatorships, your country could have moved into a socialist-type government, and then progressed into a real democracy."

Carlos sighed. "Well, we tried. We never wanted a war. But now it is…so much water under the bridge—is that not the expression?"

"We're going to need a bridge to get out of here if we don't get going," Bill said, referring to the waves crashing around us as the tide came in.

We had to wade through waist-deep water, drenching our clothes in the process, as we scrambled down from the rocks. We all flopped in the warm sand, quiet in that way you can only be with people you've been to hell and back with.

The *Journey Thru—92* summer tour turned into a party, with Lena, Bill and Will, Trish, Ray, Cata, Carlos, and Ricky all there for most of the gigs. I watched as guys started flirting with my little girl, and watched as one of us always scared them off. Except the new lighting guy's kid—a cute sixteen year-old who was not put off by all the grown-ups' posturing. By the end of the first week on the road, it was obvious that he and Lena had a crush on each other.

We were sitting around a hotel room on the afternoon of a show, and Lena said, "Hey Mama, call off your watchdogs. I need some space. I want to hang out with Adam at the gig tonight." I guess I must have tensed up, because Lena laughed. "You don't have to worry. I'm not going to have sex with him, or do Ecstasy, or anything. But I'm almost sixteen. I'm old enough to have a boyfriend. You probably had a boyfriend at a much younger age, didn't you! Come on, admit it," she teased, tickling me, trying to get me to laugh.

She was right, of course. Lena had more sense than I ever did, at any age, but I had kept her so sheltered that she didn't have street smarts. I just had to ask; "You know you absolutely have to use condoms because of AIDS, if you do decide to do it…right?"

"Jesus, Mother."

I realized it was ridiculous to keep harping at her about the same thing, but the risks of having sex with someone were so enormous now. In the sixties, we might get the clap. You'd get a shot—no problem. In the nineties, you get AIDS—you die.

"Just so you know," I said one more time.

Lena lay back on the pillows and sighed in exasperation. "Okay Mama, if you need to do this again, we will. First, let me assure you once again that I am not ready to have sex yet, and second, that when I am, I'll go to Planned Parenthood and get condoms, which I will always use. Because I know that you couldn't stand to lose me, and also because I have no desire whatsoever to contract AIDS. Okay? Got it?"

After the show that night, I didn't see Lena. I rushed up to Bill and asked him if he'd seen her.

"Darling, you're trying too hard to control her. She's fine."

"I'm not trying to control her. Jesus, Bill, whose side are you on?"

"She's hanging out in the lighting booth with Adam, if you must know; and don't even think about going to find her."

He was right. I had to give Lena some space to make her own mistakes. Anyway, Adam didn't turn out to be a mistake. He was a sweet kid, perfect for Lena—went to Urban High in the City, good student, smoked a little pot but not a druggie, played guitar, was crazy about her. When school started, they continued to see each other on weekends, and he became part of our scene.

•••

We were only back from tour a few weeks when Gilberto and Margarita showed up. Cata and Carlos moved into the main house so the Avelars could have the guest cottage. While I still found Margarita prickly, and Cata tiptoed lightly around her, Lena adored her. Margarita's face softened whenever she looked at Lena. You could hear her armor clanking to the floor when Lena entered a room. There was a tenderness in their relationship, as though Juan was there between them. It always softened my attitude toward Margarita, seeing the way she related to my daughter.

Fifteen may be a girl's coming of age in Latin culture, but "sweet little sixteen" was the big one in my books. Lena's upcoming birthday was going to be a huge event. Everybody I'd ever known was coming to the party, plus Ray and his jazz band buddies, and all of Lena's friends from school. Linda was coming from Florida, Sonny from Hawaii, a million people from L.A. and Herbie from New York—Christina, too. Then there would be the Salvadoran contingent—Marta and her family, a dozen cousins, even old Uncle Fernando, the general. I smiled to think of him off his turf, talking to Sandy and Charlie and the whole group of principled individuals who knew what he had been, what he had done. Eventually, even he'd had to eat humble pie during the civil war, but unlike most of his victims, he'd survived it.

Jesus, it was bizarre that Lena could be so old. I had moved out of my parents' house when I was sixteen! I wanted to tell her so much. I wanted to hold her to me and never let her go, and at the same time, I wanted to give her my blessings to fly away. I tried to compromise, but it was scary. It wasn't the same world I had grown up in. For one thing, I wanted her to have a college education, no matter what she might choose as a career. I wanted to prepare her for the proverbial slings and arrows, but I also wanted her to find her own defenses.

Meanwhile, Bill and I had started writing for the next album. We had hired a local band to play at the party—one that specialized in cover tunes, so the kids could make requests. But I knew that at some point in the evening, I would be persuaded to sing. My band was ready to go. With all our old material, we could have played for days, but I wanted something new for Lena, something written just for her on the occasion of her sixteenth birthday. These milestones have a way of spinning your head off your body, leaving you dismembered, with a broken heart and a head full of heartache—of dredging up a loss as though it just happened.

A few days before the party, I caught the song as it came swimming by me:

A Light Rain of Grace

What could I have done
If only I'd known
Would have stayed by your side
Never left you alone
But then how could I know
When the dark angels flew
When they spread their great wings
They were coming for you
My tears blacked out the sky
They fell down in the rain
Till in the smile of a child
The bright angels came
And the sun always shines
In the light of her face
And I find in her eyes
A light rain of grace

(musical interlude)

2nd Verse

We've come so far
Still there's so far to go
Just an infant race
There's so much we don't know
All the thousands of years
Are no more than a day
In the fine sands of time
They soon slip away
As we sift through the sand
Still trying to find our place
Trying to make sense
Of what we are as a race
With my feet on the earth
I look up into space
And I find myself praying
For a light rain of grace
And I find myself praying...
For a light rain of grace

Jeannette Sears

Acknowledgments

A huge thank-you is due to my amazing friends Jan Zimmerman and Ann McNamee for reading each chapter as I wrote it. I am eternally grateful for their encouragement and feedback. A big thank-you is also due my good friend Linda Rouda, who provided all the astrological information, even to the point of doing charts for the main characters.

Thank you to Deborah Grabien for her careful editing, support, and advice, and to Alexandra Fischer for applying her incredible talent to the cover art.

I have to thank my family. My husband Pete Sears, of course, and our son, Dylan, his wife Danielle, and their children Ophelia and Westley Sears, as well as our daughter Natalie, her husband Jeff Sullivan, and their children Silas and Ellora. My deepest gratitude is due each of them for being the magical, creative, caring people they are. And thanks to my beloved adopted Iraqi daughter Farah Al Mousawi, and my good friend Ellen Kutten for help with formatting.

Thanks also to Jo-Lynne Worley and Joanie Shoemaker for their efforts on my behalf. And to Vaschelle Andre for the cover photo.

For inspiration, encouragement, and love, thank you Vivian Snyder, Ariana & Matt Ticciati, Tess Nottebohm, Nancy Baysinger, Louise Kutten, Ray Telles, Mary McCue, and Carolyn Leavitt.

Lastly, I am grateful to Janis Joplin because I had the great privilege to know her and to stand on her stage, crying in awe while she sang our hearts out.

Jeannette Sears
Marin County, California 2017

Jeannette Sears

About the Author

Photo by Vaschelle André

Jeannette Sears is a rock lyricist who with her husband of 42 years, Pete Sears wrote many of *Jefferson Starship's* popular and critically acclaimed songs, including *Stranger, Save Your Love, Awakening, Be My Lady*, and the title track *Winds of Change*. These songs are featured on the Gold and Platinum albums *Freedom At Point Zero, Modern Times, Winds of Change*, and *Nuclear Furniture*. A number of their songs were turned into some of the first MTV music videos and received heavy rotation.

Jeannette and Pete were active in the environmental and peace and justice movements of the 1960s and 1970s, and are still active today. They are quoted in the definitive book about Greenpeace by Rex Wyler. In the 1980s, their involvement deepened and they created a concept album, *Watchfire*, by Pete Sears and Friends — including Jerry Garcia, Micky Hart, David Grisman, Babatundi Olatungi, Mimi Farina & Holly Near. Jeannette wrote the lyrics to all but one of the songs, *Let The Dove Fly Free* which she co-wrote with Mimi Farina. All the lyrics reflect Pete's and Jeannette's concerns about the future of the planet and the effects of the United States' disastrous foreign policy in Guatemala and in El Salvador (effects that are still manifesting today with the so-called "immigration crisis"). *Watchfire* received critical acclaim and lyrics were quoted in many environmental magazines, which also used the songs to help promote fund-raisers for their NGOs. One of the songs, *Guatemala*, was turned into a powerful music video, partially funded by Jerry Garcia and the Rex Foundation, and directed by Emmy award winner Ray Telles. The video was shown on Canadian MTV but pulled by American MTV at the last minute because of the "violent" content. The objectionable footage showed scenes of a kidnapping by a death squad in Guatemala. The video was picked up by numerous organizations, including Amnesty International, and used to raise awareness about human rights abuses in Central America. Amnesty is still using it.

Many of the themes of some of Jeannette's best songs can be found in this, her first novel *A light Rain of Grace*: forgiveness, social justice (with an emphasis on Central America), family and community values, and of course—love. Jeannette is uniquely equipped to tell this story, having spent many years in the company of rock stars, including Janis Joplin and Grace Slick.

Her other works include short stories in two anthologies: *Tales From The House Band,* Volumes 1 & 2. The story in Volume 1 is titled *Family Values* and Volume 2 features *The Gift*.

Jeannette lives with her husband Pete in the San Francisco Bay Area.

A Light Rain of Grace

Jeannette Sears

Made in the USA
San Bernardino, CA
23 January 2019